FIELD
OF
BLOOD

Also by Denise Mina
in Large Print:

Deception

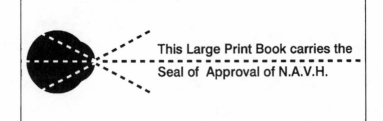

This Large Print Book carries the
Seal of Approval of N.A.V.H.

FIELD OF BLOOD

DENISE MINA

 WHEELER PUBLISHING

Published in 2005 by arrangement with Little, Brown and
Company, Inc.

Wheeler Large Print Hardcover.

The text of this Large Print edition is unabridged.
Other aspects of the book may vary from the original edition.

Set in 16 pt. Plantin by Ramona Watson.

Printed in the United States on permanent paper.

Library of Congress Cataloging-in-Publication Data

Mina, Denise.
    Field of blood / by Denise Mina.
        p. cm. — (Wheeler Publishing large print hardcover)
    ISBN 1-59722-116-3 (lg. print : hc : alk. paper)
    1. Children — Crimes against — Fiction. 2. Glasgow
(Scotland) — Fiction. 3. Women journalists — Fiction.
4. Large type books. I. Title. II. Wheeler large print
hardcover series.
PR6063.I457F54 2005b
    823′.914—dc22   2005021097

For Fergus.
Fight on, baby.

National Association for Visually Handicapped
serving the partially seeing

As the Founder/CEO of NAVH, the only national health agency solely devoted to those who, although not totally blind, have an eye disease which could lead to serious visual impairment, I am pleased to recognize Thorndike Press* as one of the leading publishers in the large print field.

Founded in 1954 in San Francisco to prepare large print textbooks for partially seeing children, NAVH became the pioneer and standard setting agency in the preparation of large type.

Today, those publishers who meet our standards carry the prestigious "Seal of Approval" indicating high quality large print. We are delighted that Thorndike Press is one of the publishers whose titles meet these standards. We are also pleased to recognize the significant contribution Thorndike Press is making in this important and growing field.

Lorraine H. Marchi, L.H.D.
Founder/CEO
NAVH

* Thorndike Press encompasses the following imprints: Thorndike, Wheeler, Walker and Large Print Press.

Judas . . . purchased a field with the reward of iniquity. . . .
And it was known unto all the dwellers
  at Jerusalem . . .
that [the] field is called . . . the field of
  blood.

ACTS 1: 16–19 (*King James Version*)

ONE

SMALL WONDERS

1981

I

They were still traveling, into the dark. They had been traveling for a long time, and in Brian's mind every inch of every step took him away from his mother, and She was all he wanted in the world.

He couldn't cry. They hurt him when he cried. He thought of Her, the softness of her breast, her fingers with the rings, how the world was warmer when she was there, and he struggled for breath, his bottom lip bumping noisily against his teeth. James, the boy sitting by his side, slapped him hard on the ear.

Surprised at the sharpness of the pain, Brian squealed and his mouth fell open. Callum, the boy on his other side, laughed at him.

"Don't be a crybaby," said James.

"Yeah," said Callum. "Don't fucking cry."

They laughed together, leaving him out. Brian didn't cry. Brian thought about his tummy insides hurting and his sore foot, but he didn't cry. It was only when he thought about her that he cried; just when he remembered not being here, then he cried. Tears raced down his cheeks, but he breathed in, managing to keep quiet.

"You're a big baby," said James loudly.

"Aye," said Callum, showing his teeth, his eyes shiny. "You're a fucking big cunt baby."

The boys got excited, saying "cunt baby" over and over. Brian didn't like that word. He didn't know what it meant, but the sounds were jaggy. Certain he was going to sob and be hit, he covered his face with his spread-out hands and held his breath until his ears popped.

He couldn't hear the boys now. With them out of his thoughts he could re-member her hands washing him, scooping soothing warm water that smelled of soft-ness over him, picking him up to carry him, even though he was bigger, feeding him with bread dipped in hot mince gravy, with chips, with sweets from the ice-cream van. She tucked him into bed and left the hall light on and the door open and came to look at him throughout the night so he wouldn't ever be alone. She was with him, always around a corner, in another room.

They were leaving the light. There were no houses outside, just dark and mud. The door opened and James pushed Brian into the black void, toppling him over so he tumbled out and down, landing on his side. He tried to stand up but his ankle wouldn't work. Inside his Welly boot his foot was big, the rough cloth lining pressing against his skin. He fell over onto his shoulder and into the dark, outside the yellow fan of light at the door.

It was darker than he had ever seen, black like gravy, like smoke from toast, like bitter medicine for a cold. The ground was frozen into hard lumps. He heard wind and moving things, running things coming towards him, creeping things. A surge of panic gripped his chest as he used his good foot and both hands to drag himself back into the smudge of light from the van.

He saw the boys' shoes and felt sudden relief that he was not alone. They put their arms through his on either side and lifted him, trying to balance him on his feet, but he toppled to one side, grabbing at the frozen earth, struggling to keep his face near the light at least. The boys lifted him again, and again he fell.

Brian couldn't walk, his big foot wouldn't work, so the boys, huffing and puffing, dragged him backwards, over the edge of the world and down a steep hill. It was windy and dark, so dark at the bottom that Brian clung to James, holding tight onto the sleeve of his anorak, afraid that they would leave him. He couldn't stop himself and he began to cry, sounding loud because there was no telly and no wireless, nothing to cover his noise like there had been in the stranger's house. James moved around in front of him, standing with his feet apart and raising his hands. Callum pulled at James and said, No, no, over here, by the track.

They dragged him farther down the hill until there wasn't a hill anymore, and then they left him to stand alone. He fell forwards, banging his front teeth on metal; one of them broke and hot water came all over his chin. His crying seemed very loud now, and he sputtered through the warm liquid, breathing it in and coughing through his sobs. James stood in front of him again, planting his feet and reaching down, putting his hands on Brian's neck.

Brian felt himself lifted up until he was looking into James's wild animal eyes.

Brian heard his own noise stop, heard small animals scamper for cover on the far bank, heard the brittle wind ruffle his hair. And then he saw black.

II

James strangled him and then Callum hit his head with rocks. The baby's head was all mess. They looked at it, afraid and not wanting to, but drawn to the sight. They hadn't expected the baby just to stop moving or to do a smelly diarrhea, he hadn't told them that would happen. They hadn't expected him to stop being annoying so suddenly, hadn't expected him to completely stop being anything. The baby's foot was facing all wrong. His eyes were open, popping out as if he couldn't stop looking. Callum wanted to cry, but James punched his arm.

"We . . . ," said Callum, staring at the messy baby, looking sick. "We . . ." He forgot the rest of it. He ran up the steep hill and disappeared over the bank.

James was left alone. It had blood all over its chin and down its front like a bib.

The blood was warm when he had his hands in it, when he had his hands around the baby's neck. He imagined the baby standing up with its messy head and black chin, swelling up to the Incredible Hulk and beating him up in slow motion.

He tilted his head and looked at it. He smiled at it. He poked it with his foot, and it couldn't even try to get away from him. He didn't feel scared being here with the broken baby. He felt other things, but he didn't know what they were called. He crouched down.

He could do anything to it. Anything he wanted.

TWO

THE REAL PADDY MEEHAN

I

If there was any other angle to the Brian Wilcox story, none of the staff of the *Scottish Daily News* could find it. They had interviewed the missing child's family and neighbors, retraced all possible routes, commissioned aerial photographs of the area. They had written features about children who had run away in the past, printed countless column inches on the future of missing children, and the little bastard still hadn't turned up.

Paddy Meehan was standing at the Press Bar when she overheard Dr. Pete telling a crowd of drunks that he'd strangle the three-year-old himself if it would bring an end to the story. The men around him laughed and slowed and laughed again in a ragged wave. Dr. Pete sat still among them,

15

looking even more desiccated than usual, his features organized into a smile around his heartbroken eyes. She watched his reflection in the mirror behind the bar. His bushy eyebrows billowed out from a face scarred by a decade-long hangover. He lifted his glass to his mouth, eyes shut, feeling for the rim with the gray tip of his tongue. Rumor had it that he was a bigamist.

Paddy didn't like the men or want to keep their company, but she did want to have a place among them, to be a journalist instead of a gofer. She would have felt like an interloper in the bar if she hadn't been on *News* business, here to get the picture editor's tankard filled. In front of her, McGrade, the bar manager, was flushing the leads to the taps, taking an age to draw the beer through spluttering pipes. Pints of syrupy white froth were lined up along the bar.

The Press Bar was painted a pragmatic tobacco / spilled beer yellow, furnished with small chairs and mean little tables covered with ashtrays and beer mats. Screwed tight to the walls were archive pictures of news sellers and pressmen holding up significant copies of the *Chicago Tribune* and *New York Times*: VE-day, Pearl

Harbor, Kennedy's death. The photos were from another time, another place, and largely irrelevant to Glasgow, but they represented a plea for loyalty to the bar's principal clientele and the justification for its special license. It was one of the few pubs in Glasgow that didn't shut at two thirty in the afternoon, but the bar was too far from the city center to attract passing customers, too close to the city to be anyone's local, and relied on the *News* for all its trade. An adjoining wall divided the two establishments, and the absence of an internal entrance was often bemoaned, especially in the winter.

It was the only occupied table in the bar. The men sipped their elevenses under a slick of blue smoke. They were the early shift, men of indiscriminate age, all drunks and renegades who couldn't be sacked because of their length of service. They did the bare minimum of work and did it quickly before hurrying off to the pub or the house or the desk where the next party was being held.

Today the head of the union, Father Richards, was penned protectively in at the center of the crowd, looking tired, being cheered along by them. Richards was rarely among the drunks. He was a good

17

father to the chapel and had negotiated longer breaks and the right to smoke anywhere in the building, even in the print room. Beer fat around the middle, he had the prison pallor of a man who worked indoors all day every day. Usually he wore aviator glasses with a thick steel frame, but they were missing today, replaced by a long diagonal cut under his eye, perfectly tracing the line of the absent lens. Someone had punched him in the specs.

The laughter died down and the boys sat back. Paddy could feel them casting their attention around the room, looking for something, anything, to ridicule. She was usually immune because of her age and miserable position, but when drink was thrown into the mix they could turn on anyone. She braced herself, twisting her cheap diamond-chip engagement ring around her finger, willing the barman to finish with the beer pipes and serve her. Three seconds shrieked by. She could feel a preemptive blush starting on her neck. Her ring finger was getting sore.

One of the drinkers at the table broke the silence. "Fuck the Pope."

The men laughed, watching a fragile Richards reach unsmiling for his drink. As his pint glass docked at his mouth a broad grin burst on his face and he poured the golden beer in, letting little rivulets tumble down his jowls. The men whooped.

Out of a reflexive sense of loyalty, Paddy disapproved of Richards's saying nothing. Only ten years ago job adverts routinely carried codicils saying Catholics need not apply. Housing and schools were segregated, and Catholics wouldn't feel safe to walk along certain streets in Glasgow. But here was Richards, sitting at a table of Protestants, siding with them against his own.

"I don't care about the Pope," shouted Richards. "I don't care. He's no friend of the workingman."

Dr. Pete waited until the audience had calmed down. "We have nothing to lose but our rosaries."

They laughed again.

Richards shrugged, showing he didn't mind. Not one bit. Meant nothing to him. He took another drink and, sensing her disapproval, glanced at Paddy's feet, drawing the gaze of the men to her, giving them her scent.

"You," he said. "You a Pape or a Marxist?"

"Leave her alone," said Dr. Pete.

But Richards pressed the point. "Pape or Marxist?"

They knew from her name that she was Catholic. She even looked bog Irish, with black hair and skin the color of a paper moon. She didn't want to talk about it, but Richards pressed her.

"Are you religious, Meehan?"

The men were looking at their drinks, uncomfortable but not prepared to stand between them. It was between two Papes, it wasn't their business. Paddy felt she'd better speak or they'd smell the fear.

"How does my conscience come to be your business?" Her voice was higher than she meant it to be.

"Will you attend mass tomorrow? Do you go to communion, confession? Do you drop your mite in the collection every Sunday and develop crushes on the parish priest?" Richards's voice grew as he spoke. He was a little drunk and mistook speaking a lot for speaking well. "Are you saving yourself for your husband? Do you pray each night to bear children who'll uphold the faith of our fathers?" He took a breath and opened his mouth to speak again, but Paddy interrupted.

"And what about you, Father Richards? D'you attend weekly meetings and demos? D'you contribute a portion of your wage to the revolutionary fund and develop crushes on all the young Marxist girls?" She couldn't quite remember the shape of what he had said next, so she just got straight to the point. "Your job is basically interceding between the management on behalf of the shop floor. You go about enforcing rules and distributing money to the needy. You're just a priest in a polo neck."

Without really taking on board the content of what she had said, the men laughed at Richards for being slagged off by a woman, and a young woman at that, thumping him on the arm, egging him to retort. Richards smiled into his drink while Dr. Pete sat very still, looking at Paddy as if he had just noticed she existed. Behind the bar McGrade snorted affably, taking the picture editor's tankard out of Paddy's hand and filling it three-quarters full with 80 Shilling, topping it up with two shots of whisky.

"The shape of your beliefs is exactly the same as it was when you were practicing," Paddy continued. "The only difference is that you've replaced the basic text. Classic failed-Catholic mistake. You're probably more religious than I am."

The door behind her opened suddenly, banging off the wall, and a gust of cold air blasted into the room, curling the gray

21

smoke. Terry Hewitt's black hair was shaved tight like an American soldier's, cut right into the wood so that pale pink scars on his scalp showed through. It made him seem a little bit dangerous. He was plump with disproportionately short legs, but there was an air about him, an aura of dirty-bad man, that made Paddy's mouth water when she dared to look at him. She imagined him going home every night to a comfortable house with parents who read novels and encouraged his ambition. He'd never have to worry about losing his monthly Transcard or wear cheap shoes that let in the rain.

"Hoi, Hewitt!" shouted Dr. Pete, waving his hand in front of his face. "Shut that door. This good woman's trying to coax Richards back to the chapel."

The men laughed as Paddy carried the pint to the door, calling after her to stay, Woman, save us all.

She turned back to them. "You know, one day all your livers are going to explode simultaneously and it'll look like Jonestown in here."

The men screamed with delight as Paddy backed out of the door. She was pleased. Being a lowly copyboy was a pre-carious position: a bad choice here or a vulnerable moment there could mark her out for a lifetime of bullying.

It was just as the door was swinging shut behind her that she heard Terry Hewitt ask, "Who is that fat lassie?"

II

She sat on the top deck, chewing through her third consecutive boiled egg as she looked down on the bustle in the street. It was a disgusting diet, and she wasn't even sure it was working.

Outside, pedestrians were wrapped up warm, closing their faces against a needle-sharp wind that found its way through scarves and tights and buttonholes. The wind buffeted the high side of the double-decker bus on open stretches of road, making passengers grab at the back of the seat in front, smiling sheepishly around when their alarm passed.

Richards had annoyed her. She kept re-running the conversation in her head, thinking of better, faster retorts, reshaping her speech so that it better reflected his. She had made the point well, she thought, even though Terry Hewitt's remark had ruined the effect entirely.

Classic failed-Pape mistake.

The phrase rolled around her mind, catching its tail, rolling and repeating in the lug-bugga-lug rhythm of the bus. She knew all about replacing the central text. At least Richards's substitution had made him more useful to the world. She couldn't tell any one of the people she loved about the black hole at the heart of her faith. She couldn't tell Sean, her fiancé, or her favorite sister, Mary Ann, and her parents must never know, it would break their hearts.

Downstairs the bus swung on the sharp turn into Rutherglen Main Street, hurrying to catch the green light. Paddy was on her way to the rosary at Sean's dead grandmother's house, ready to perjure herself once more.

Granny Annie had died aged eighty-four. She wasn't a warm woman, or even an especially pleasant one. When Sean cried for her Paddy knew he was really grieving for his father, who had died of a heart attack four years before. Despite his broad shoulders and deep voice, he was a boy at eighteen, still eating lunchtime sandwiches made by his mum and wearing the underpants she left out for him at night.

The old woman's death was a big event

in Rutherglen. Some nights the rosary was so busy that a portion of the mourners had to keep their coats on and stand in the street, praying towards the house. As they chanted the prayers for the repose of Annie's soul, the young kept their voices low while the older ones sent up their sighs in Irish accents, copying the priests who had taught them.

Annie Ogilvy had been brought to Eastfield in a handcart in the dying years of the last century. Paddy's family, the Meehans, arrived from Donegal in the same year and had stayed close to the Ogilvys ever since: religious duties and odd immigrant habits bound the two families together, and the limited job opportunities for Catholics meant that most of the men were workmates in the mines or foundries.

Annie grew up in Glasgow but always affected an Irish accent, as was the fashion among immigrant girls in her day. Over the years her accent got thicker, shifting a few miles every year, from a Dublinesque soft brogue to a strangulated Ulster gargle. In her old age her children took her on an Irish coach tour and found that no one there could understand her either. All her tastes and songs and cooking, although distantly related to things in Ireland, were reproduced nowhere. Annie yearned her whole life for a fond remembered home that never was.

The presence of the corpse in the house gave Paddy the creeps, and she stayed well away from it. When they settled down for prayers she sat on the front room floor, facing the settee, each night staring at a different configuration of puffy legs in support stockings, mottled blue papery skin chopped into links by pop-sock rims.

The bus was approaching the end of the Main Street. Paddy finished her egg and stood up, making her way downstairs. It was an open-backed bus and the cold, windy night battled hard with the warmth from the heated cabin. Paddy put a foot on either side of the pole, resting her hip against it, letting her weight swing her out of the open back of the bus into the windy void. Crosswinds whipped her short hair, making it even messier. She could already see the crowd gathering in front of the small council house across the road.

She wasn't through the garden gate before someone caught her arm. Matt Sinclair was short and fifty and wore glasses with dark lenses.

"There's my wee girlfriend there," he said, eyes like dead televisions. He shifted his fag into the other hand and took Paddy's hand, pumping it hard. "I was just talking about you." He turned and addressed another small, smoking man behind him. "Desi, here's wee Paddy Meehan that I was telling ye about."

"Oh ho," said Desi. "You'll be interested to meet me, then: I know the real Paddy Meehan."

"I am the real Paddy Meehan," said Paddy quietly, moving towards the house, wanting to get inside and see Sean before the prayers started.

"That's right. I used to live in the high flats at the Gorbals, and Paddy Meehan's wife, Betty, she lived on my landing." He nodded adamantly, as if she had forcefully expressed disbelief. "Aye, and I knew his pal, Griffiths."

"Who's that?" asked Matt.

"Griffiths was the mad guy with the gun, the shooter."

"And was he a spy as well?"

Desi blushed around the eyes, suddenly angry. "For Godsake. Meehan was never a spy. He was nothing but a bloody hood from the Gorbals."

Matt kept his lips tight and his voice low, looking around the crowd. "Here, mind your language. We're at a rosary."

27

"Sorry." Desi looked at Paddy. "Sorry, dear. But he wasn't a Soviet spy. He's from the Gorbals."

"Spies don't have to be toffs, do they?" asked Paddy, trying to be respectful even though she was correcting him.

"Aye, they need an education. They need to speak different languages."

"Anyway," Matt said, looking at her as he spoke, "the *Daily Record* said they framed him for the Ross murder to discredit him, because he was a spy."

Desi blushed again and spluttered indignantly, "They were repeating what Meehan said, and no one believes him anyway." He raised his voice angrily. "What would a common thief have to tell the Soviets?"

Paddy knew. "Well, he knew the layout of most British prisons, didn't he? That's how they helped their spies escape, because he told them how."

Matt looked interested. "So he was a spy?"

Paddy shrugged again. "He might have sold secrets to the Soviets, but I think the Ross investigation was just incompetent. I don't think one had anything to do with the other."

Abandoning reasoned argument, Desi raised his voice. "The man's a known liar."

"Aye." Matt looked at Paddy blankly, wishing, she sensed, that he had never introduced her to his volatile friend. "Well, he's back living in Glasgow, I hear."

She nodded.

"Living up in the Carlton. Drinks in the town."

She nodded again.

Calmer, Desi tried to reclaim his place in the conversation. "How did ye end up named after him, well?" He looked at Matt to deliver the punch line. "Do your parents hate ye?"

Matt Sinclair tried to laugh, but the phlegm in his lungs gurgled and made him cough. "Desi, man," he said solemnly when he had recovered, "you're awful funny."

"I was six years old when the other Paddy Meehan was arrested," Paddy said. "And everyone calls my mum Trisha."

Now reconciled, Matt and Desi nodded in unison.

"So," said Desi, "you got stuck with Paddy?"

"Aye."

"How d'ye no call yourself Pat?"

"I don't like that name," she said quickly. Building on the success of a joke about the Irish homosexual Pat MaGroin, some of the older boys at school had nick-named her Pat MaHind, a name she hated and feared for its unspecified sexual con-notation and her uncontrollable blushing when they shouted it after her.

"What about Packy?"

"Hmm," she said, hoping they weren't going to say anything about black people. "I think that word means something else now."

"That's right," explained Matt knowledge-ably. "A Paki means a Indian now."

Desi nodded, interested in this useful in-formation.

"It's rude to call someone that," said Paddy.

"Big Mo that runs the laundry," ex-plained Matt, "he's a Paki."

"Not really," said Paddy, feeling uncom-fortable. "I asked him, and he's from Bombay, so he's Indian."

"That's right." Matt nodded and looked at Desi to see if that had cleared things up any.

"But Indians and Pakistanis're not really the same thing," Paddy said, sounding un-sure when she wasn't. "Because didn't the Indians and the Pakistanis have a big war? I think it's like saying an Ulsterman is the same as a Republican."

The men nodded, but she could tell that they had stopped listening.

Desi cleared his throat. "Oh aye," he said, not grasping her angle at all. "Everything's more complicated when darkies are involved, eh?"

Paddy cringed. "I don't think that's very nice," she said.

The men looked blank as she let herself be washed into the house on a wave of mourners. She felt their eyes on her back, judging her, thinking her a snooty wee cow.

THREE

A TYRANNY OF EGGS

Paddy had spent her lunch hour wandering around the Sunday-shuttered town, nibbling boiled eggs wrapped in tinfoil, carefully avoiding newsagents with sweets counters. She hung her duffel coat on the hook by the door, carrying her yellow canvas bag over to the copyboy bench, setting it underneath. She'd had the bag for two years and liked it. She had inked the names of bands on it, not bands she necessarily liked to listen to but ones she wanted to be associated with: guy bands like Stiff Little Fingers, the Exploited, and Squeeze.

From their bench in the corner Paddy could see down the entire hundred-foot-long, open-plan newsroom and notice when anyone raised a hand or called them for an errand. She slid her bottom along the buttery oak, pulling up next to Dub.

"Right?"

"I hate weekend shifts." Dub glanced up from the music paper he was reading. "Quiet."

Paddy scanned the room for raised hands or open faces. No one wanted anything. She found her thumbnail running along a gouge she had made in the wood. She liked to run her nail along the soft grain, imagining herself in the future as a grown-up journalist in a fancy suit and real shoes, on her way out to a hard story or an evening at the Press Club, brushing past and seeing the little indentations, remembering where she came from.

Murray Farquarson, known as the Beast Master, shouted out from his office. "Meehan? Is she in?"

"She's in," shouted Dub, nudging her to go.

Paddy stood up and sighed, affecting reluctance like they all did when called to do any work. She muttered under her breath, "For Godsake, I'm just bloody back," dragging her feet over to Farquarson's door, secretly pleased that he had asked for her.

Farquarson called for Paddy by name whenever he needed a discreet job done. He trusted her because she had no allegiances; none of the journalists had groomed her for an acolyte because they'd assumed she wouldn't stay. They wouldn't have known what to talk to her about even if they had wanted to recruit her: she didn't like sport or know any of Hugh McDermid's poetry. The journalists had a lot of odd ideas about women; she was always having to stay late and lift heavy boxes to show that she could. The only other women on the newsroom floor were Nancy Rilani and Kat Beesley, a genuine news reporter who had been to university and worked on a paper in England before coming home. Nancy was a heavy-breasted woman of Italian descent who wrote the agony column and most of the weekly women's page. She never spoke to Paddy or Heather Allen, the part-time student, wouldn't even look at them, and gave the impression that she would trade any other woman to any man for peace and favors. Kat was proud. She always wore trousers, kept her hair very short, and sat with her legs open. She stared at Paddy's tits whenever she bothered to talk to her. Paddy didn't quite know what the story was with her.

She peered into the dark office and found Farquarson sitting at his desk, looking through cuttings about Brian

Wilcox. He was a skinny, agitated man, all angles. He lived on a diet of sugar and tea and whisky. He didn't look up when he heard her at the door.

"JT's in this office somewhere. Get him in here pronto. Best guess is the canteen."

"Right ye are, Boss."

Something big had happened in the Wilcox case or he wouldn't be asking for the chief news reporter.

"And I want clippings about missing kids dying in accidents — railway lines, wells, quarries, that stuff. See what Helen's got." He pointed an accusing finger at her. "Say the clippings are for a freelancer, and don't tell anyone about this."

"Okay."

Paddy walked briskly through the newsroom, out into the stairwell, and up the two flights to the canteen.

Gina and David Wilcox's three-year-old son had been missing for almost four days. In the *Daily News* photo Baby Brian had a shock of white hair and a stiff, coaxed smile on his face. He had been sent out to play in the front garden at twelve o'clock and was alone for fourteen minutes while his mother spoke to the doctor on the phone about a personal matter. When Gina hung up and looked out the front door her child was gone. The child's parents were divorced, a rare occurrence in the west of Scotland. It was mentioned in most of the coverage, as if it wouldn't be hard to misplace a tiny child in the decadent chaos of two separate houses. The story was all over the papers — the child was pretty and it was a welcome break from tales of galloping unemployment, the Yorkshire Ripper, or Lady Diana Spencer's simper.

The self-service canteen on the top floor was bright, the long, wide window overlooking a dirt-floor car park across the road. It was just midday, and the queue for hot food was already fifteen men long. They were printmen in blue overalls with inky fingers, hollering casual conversations at one another, shouting because the presses they worked on all day were so loud. Paddy didn't like going down there because they had pictures of naked women on the walls and the Linotype operators stared at her tits. JT wasn't in the queue. Through habit and affiliation the tidy rows of tables and chairs were segregated into blue-collar print workers' and journalists' areas. JT wasn't sitting in either.

She ran down three flights of stairs. Staff weren't allowed to use the lifts, nor were they usually allowed to enter or leave the building through the black marble reception area, but she was on urgent *News* business. The immaculately groomed Two Alisons who manned the front desk and switchboard stopped talking to watch her scuttle to the front door, pulling her cardigan around herself as she ducked out of the building. Outside, a queue of *Daily News* delivery vans were backed up, rear doors rolled up, showing bare metal floors strewn with sacking and tape. Paddy passed them, hurrying the four steps along the road to the door of the Press Bar.

The pub was lunchtime busy. Men were shouting to one another with an air of forced levity, anxiously squeezing in as much drinking as they could. Paddy pushed past Terry Hewitt, blushing to think what he had called her, and found JT standing at the far end of the pub, wearing a blue shirt under a brown suede safari jacket. He was nursing a half of bitter. Paddy had watched him: she knew he didn't much like to drink, but he had to sometimes or the drunks on the paper would hate him even more. He was laughing joylessly at one of Dr. Pete's jokes, his eagerness to fit in setting him apart. He looked relieved when Paddy told him he had to come right away, and he put down his drink with indecent haste, not even attempting to finish it or to grab one last precious mouthful. Paddy saw Dr. Pete watching the fresh young drink thoughtlessly abandoned on the table. He narrowed his eyes and shifted his gaze back to JT, his face shriveling with disgust. Oblivious, JT followed Paddy outside.

"What's it about?"

"I don't know." Paddy didn't want to mention the accidental death clippings in case anyone overheard. "Might be the Wilcox boy."

"Right," said JT, lowering his voice. "Don't tell anyone."

He dodged past her, sprinting into the lobby and up the stairs. Paddy chased close behind and got to Farquarson's office just as JT shut the door. Through the slats on the venetian blinds she could see Farquarson explaining something, looking angry and irritated at JT, who was nodding excitedly, tapping the desk with his finger, suggesting a plan. The boy hadn't been found dead; if he had they wouldn't be excited, they'd be moving slower. Something else had happened.

Farquarson spotted Paddy standing outside the door and snapped his fingers at her, telling her to go and get the clippings.

She watched for another moment, yearning for a taste of the glory, not knowing that JT and Farquarson were discussing a development in the Baby Brian case that would tear her cozy life apart forever.

FOUR

THE OFFICE FOR THE DEAD

It was four-thirty and the last slice of sun was perched on the horizon, the failing yellow light oozing through the dirty windows on the upper deck. In the back three rows teenage boys kicked at one another while diffident girls smoked and smirked and pretended not to watch.

Paddy sat alone, surreptitiously eating from a plastic tub. The three cold boiled eggs had been sitting in her bag in the hot office all day, and the texture was alternately rubbery and clay dry. All she had to chase away the aftertaste was a sour quartered grapefruit. She'd have the black coffee when they got back from the chapel. The diet had been scientifically worked out in America: three boiled eggs, grapefruit, and black coffee three times a day would build up into a chemical reaction that actually burned off fat at a rate of six pounds a week, guaranteed. She projected forwards to her goal weight. In just one month she could tell Terry Hewitt to go and take a flying fuck to himself. She imagined herself with an unspecified but better haircut, standing in the Press Bar, dressed in that size ten green pencil skirt she had optimistically bought from Chelsea Girl.

"Actually, Terry, I'm not fat anymore."

It wasn't very witty. It had the essence of what she wanted to say but didn't sound very real.

"D'you know, Terry, on balance, I'd say you're fatter than me now."

Better, but still not very good. If the journalists heard her say that, they'd know she cared about her weight and she'd never hear the end of it.

"Terry, you've got a face like two buckets banging together."

That worked. Paddy smirked to herself. She'd wear the green miniskirt, pointy-toed winklepickers, and a tight black crewneck pullover. An unforgiving outfit. She'd need to be really slim to wear that. She only ever wore black pencil skirts with woolly tights and sweaters baggy enough to cover her lumps and bumps.

Paddy knew she was fat before Terry Hewitt commented on it — she wouldn't have attempted the disgusting Mayo Clinic Diet otherwise — but it hurt that her weight was the only thing he had noticed about her. The *Scottish Daily News* was a fresh audience, and without seventy-odd relatives preceding her she felt she could be anyone. She didn't want to be the clever fat girl again in this new incarnation.

Finishing the last piece of grapefruit, she put the soft plastic lid back on the tub, dropping it into her bag, and cautioned herself: there'd be a lot of food when they got back from the chapel, mounds of cheese sandwiches, hot salty sausage rolls, rough-cut gammon on soft plain bread spread with chips of hard butter. She'd better avoid physical proximity to them if she was to stick to her diet. Nor should she approach the iced rings or moist coconut snowballs or jammy biscuits or butterfly cakes or the arctic roll. She was salivating wildly as a talon hand clutched her shoulder.

"You're wee Paddy Meehan, eh?" The voice sounded like a man's but for a single strain in the timbre.

Paddy turned around to face a woman with a face like a dried chamois. "Oh, hello, Mrs. Breslin. Are ye going to Granny Annie's laying-in?"

"Aye."

Mrs. Breslin had worked with Paddy's mother in the Rutherglen Cooperative when they were both first out of school. She had seven children of her own, five boys and two girls, all of whom were considered a little bit scary by the other young people of the area. The Breslin kids were rumored to be responsible for the fire that burned down the Salvation Army Hall's shed.

Mrs. Breslin lit a cigarette from the stub of her last one. "God rest her soul, wee Granny Annie."

"Aye," said Paddy. "She was a lovely woman, right enough."

They avoided each other's eye. Granny Annie wasn't lovely, but she was dead and it would be wrong to say otherwise. Mrs. Breslin nodded and said Aye, right enough, so she was, God rest her.

"I hear you're a journalist now?"

"Not a journalist," said Paddy, pleased at the mistake. "I run messages at the *Daily News*. I'm hoping to become a journalist, though, one day."

"Well, lucky you. I've got four out of school now, and not one of them can get work. How did you get that? Did someone put in a word for ye?"

"No, I just phoned up and asked if they

were taking on. I'd done articles for the school paper and that. I gave them some things I'd written."

Mrs. Breslin sat forward, her smoke-stinking breath smothering Paddy as effectively as a cushion. "Are they taking on now? Could you put in a word for my Donal?"

Donal carried a knife and had been giving himself tattoos since he was twelve.

"They're not taking on anymore."

Mrs. Breslin narrowed her eyes and turned her head away a fraction. "Fine," she said spitefully. "Help me up. We're there."

Mrs. Breslin was fatter than Paddy remembered. Her shoulders and face were deceptively slim, but her buttocks were fantastically large: the shoulders of her pale green raincoat were halfway down to the elbows to accommodate her shape. Paddy watched down the narrow stairwell as Mrs. Breslin slammed from side to side while the bus took a corner, and wondered if she herself would be that fat after seven children, or as oblivious to the truth of what her kids were like.

The bus stopped in the middle of the street, blocking the traffic. Paddy helped Mrs. Breslin down the steep step to the road, leading her across the still traffic, snaking through the smoking cars.

Every Catholic in the neighborhood was wearing black and converging outside Granny Annie's tiny council house. They climbed out of cars, walked around corners, came down the Main Street. Smoke and icy breath rose like steam from cattle as the frosty black tarmac glittered silver around them.

Fifty yards up the side street Mrs. Breslin saw someone she was more annoyed at than Paddy and went over to spoil their day.

Looking out for Sean's flattop, Paddy waved to cousins across the road and accidentally caught the distant eye of Mrs. McCarthy, an overemotional neighbor who cried with joy whenever she saw Paddy. Mrs. McCarthy had done an unrequested month-long novena before Paddy's interview at the *Daily News* and subsequently felt she had a claim on her, having effectively snagged her the job. Mrs. McCarthy mouthed "Thank God," and Paddy nodded stiffly, grateful for the hand reaching for hers. Sean Ogilvy, tall and dark with ninety-degree shoulders, dipped at the knee and gathered Paddy's hand into his.

"Bloody hell. I met stinky Mrs. Breslin on the bus, and then Mrs. McCarthy saw me. I got caught by bloody Matt the Rat last night and had to have the whole Paddy Meehan conversation again."

"You used to love talking about that Paddy Meehan case."

"Well, I'm bored of it now." She avoided his eye and looked around the crowd, seeing that a lot of her own extended family were there. "I'm sick of knowing everyone and everyone knowing me."

"Why aren't you interested in Paddy Meehan anymore? I thought you were going to try and interview him."

"Ye grow out of things, though, ye know?" she said uncomfortably. "I don't care about that anymore."

"Please yourself." He pulled off one of Paddy's woolly red gloves, tucking it into her duffel coat pocket, and slid his hot hand around her bare skin, making the peace. "I thought you'd be interested to meet him, after knowing so much about the whole story and following it for so long."

"He's just a fat old man now." She tutted and looked away. "He drinks in the town. All the wasters at work know him. I can't be annoyed with it."

"Well, well, well," Sean said, squeezing her hand playfully. "Don't get shirty with me about it."

They smiled at the silly turn of phrase and stood pressing their shoulders together, looking at the crowd but thinking about each other. Paddy's breath felt warmer when Sean was with her. She felt thinner and taller and funny suddenly because he loved her and they were promised to each other.

The undertakers were bringing the coffin out of the house. A respectful hush descended on the mourners. Those having conversations too urgent to abandon lowered their voices. The chief undertaker took his place at the head of the procession and the hearse began its glide down the quiet street, gathering the crowd in its wake. They formed in the natural order of family, then friends, followed by neighbors and pals from chapel, until a hundred and fifty people were behind the car. Sean's mother and brothers were up front, but he held back, squeezing Paddy's hand tight. She saw him blinking hard, and the tip of his nose darkened as he struggled for breath. At eighteen, Sean was as tall as a man and his voice was deep, but sometimes under all the bluster she saw the sweet boy she met at school, before his growth spurt made him six foot one, before working for Shug gave him those shoulders.

The hearse took a right, turning into the Main Street, and the line of mourners braced themselves, standing taller, pulling the small children into the center. The chat got louder, as if they were trying to swell the numbers. It was a tense time for a Catholic procession: Pastor Jack Glass was giving speeches all over the city about the whore of Rome, and the troubles over in Ireland were ferocious. A Republican woman MP had been shot in her home in front of her child, and prisoners in the Maze were starting a second hunger strike to demand political status. A demonstration in support of the men had been organized, and everyone knew there was going to be trouble. Whenever feelings ran high in the six counties, Glasgow teetered on the edge of the violence. As the nearest foreign city to Belfast, just over a hundred miles away across the Irish Sea, Glasgow was the traditional place of exile for Unionists who had lost their position but were too contentious to kill off. They drank in Dennistoun pubs and held raffles for the cause back home. Rogue Republicans got the better deal and were exiled to America.

The procession made its way down one side of the Main Street, and the cars on the other side slowed to show their respect. A couple of drivers sped up, crossing back and forth between the lanes. One man drove past hanging out of his window, shouting belligerent abuse about the Pope. Protestant pedestrians watched in silence from the pavement, some waving to friends who were walking, some uncomfortable or mocking because they didn't understand the custom.

The hearse stopped in front of St. Columbkill's modern yellow-brick chapel, and Annie's coffin was carried carefully across the low-walled courtyard, up the stairs, and through the huge yellow-timbered doors. They were committing her to the safety of the chapel for the night, to guard against the devil stealing her soul before the funeral mass and burial in the morning. Paddy spotted a crowd of four girls she had been at primary school with, standing on the steps, hands clasped piously in front, eyes cast down respectfully. Her two brothers, Marty and Gerald, were queuing behind them. Behind them again she saw an old neighbor who was in her Granny Meehan's knitting bee.

"For Godsake, this is like a bloody dream sequence," she said quietly. "Everyone I've ever known is here."

Sean nodded. "Yeah, it's nice." He took a breath and pulled himself up tall. "Wherever we go in this life, we'll always belong here." He squeezed her hand. "These are our people."

She knew he was right, that there was no escape. If she traveled a thousand miles and never came back, if she sold their gold, she would still belong to them. Sean tugged her hand gently, leading her up the stairs to the Office for the Dead.

FIVE

SALT FISH AND BLACK TEA
1963

I

It was afternoon and the date was December the fourth, that much Paddy Meehan did know. He couldn't be certain where he was in the world, hadn't been told where they were flying to, but he had seen the date on a German-language newspaper folded under the arm of a man climbing up the embarkation steps in front of them. Rolf had seen him looking at it and shifted to the side, blocking his view but doing it playfully, smiling back at him.

The plane was busy. Forty boys of all ages in red-and-beige uniforms played a call-and-answer game in Russian across the seats. Rolf stopped at a row of three seats, checking the numbers several times against their ticket before stepping back to let them in. Meehan shrugged out of his stiff gray overcoat, hurrying to get the window seat, but the young lieutenant shouldered him out of the way and ducked in, laughing as he took the seat for himself. Even the upholstery was luxurious. Meehan and the lieutenant put their hands on the back of the seat in front, working their fingernails into the thick blue-and-orange pile, giggling at the delicious depth of it. They were all excited to be on an airplane. Rolf smiled at their games as he carefully folded his coat and placed it on the rack above his head. He sat down in the aisle seat, straightening his hair, his jacket, his small moustache.

The deafening engines revved up to a whine and they taxied to the runway, finally taking off, prompting squeals and cheers of the children.

Once they were in the air and the plane had righted itself from an anxious upward angle, Rolf took a hip flask and three red plastic tumblers from his briefcase. The flask was much dented and loved, an oval curve of peeling silver plate with the brass showing underneath. He poured a stiff, stiff vodka into each tumbler and handed them down the line, first to the lieutenant,

then to Meehan, and finally one for himself. Meehan handed around cigarettes as
his contribution to the party and they all lit
up, flicking open the little ashtrays in the
arms, letting the sweet smell of a hundred
smoky journeys waft out into the cabin.

"Up yours," said Meehan jovially, lifting
his tumbler in a toast.

Rolf and the lieutenant raised their
drinks in response and echoed "Up yours"
innocently, as if they didn't understand.
The three men smiled and drank together.

"So, pals, where are we going to now?"
asked Meehan.

Rolf frowned at him. "To Scotland Yard
with you, my friend."

The young lieutenant laughed, slapping
his thigh for emphasis. He was still excited.

"We're going to Russia, eh?" said
Meehan. "The kids are all chatting away in
Russkie. You're taking me to Russia."

Rolf raised an eyebrow and shifted in his
seat, reaching down, as he often did, to
pull the cheeks of his arse apart. It was an
odd habit for such a well-groomed man.
Meehan wondered if he had hemorrhoids.

"Yes," said Rolf, "perhaps we will go to
Russia. After we have been to Scotland
Yard."

"You, *springe aus dem fenster,*" said

Meehan, pointing the orange tip of his cigarette at the window.

Rolf nodded politely, acknowledging the joke without going to the trouble of laughing. Meehan was still struggling with his German accent despite studying hard for the last nine months. He had nothing else to fill his time with between meals and interrogations.

"Springe aus dem fenster," he repeated quietly to himself for practice.

He thought about the Gorbals and the Tapp Inn, where he knew every single rogue that came through the doors, or was likely to. He wondered what they would think of him sitting in an airplane from East Germany, chatting in the lingo on his way to Russia. They hadn't told him why he was being moved; for all he knew he might be on his way to a bullet in the head, and he still couldn't help but smile.

They drank the vodka down, and very quickly Meehan fell asleep, head lolling forwards on his buckled neck, drooling onto the blue serge suit they had given him to wear.

The landing jerked him awake and he sat up, puzzled and annoyed. He was pleased when he found himself on a plane.

"And so we have landed," said Rolf unnecessarily.

It was dark outside the window, but occasional lights rolled by on the horizon. The scout troop had slept and were waking up whiny, bickering, looking around the cabin, stretching and yawning. Their miserable, puffy faces reminded Meehan of his own kids, out in Canada, waiting for him with Betty. They had been there for nine months, waiting to start again on a new continent with the money he'd promised to bring back. He'd promised them a home and a small business, a shop maybe, a new beginning where he wasn't in and out of pokey all the time. He was smarter than the average crim. He'd escaped from Nottingham jail and managed to get himself over to East Germany, but this was a different order of game and his plan was full of holes. They had no reason to give him money for his information. He was an ant, a nothing. They could easily kill him: the British government wouldn't complain if a small-time safe blower went missing, and he knew he'd be leaving East Germany with his life if he was lucky. He was dreading Canada and Betty's reproaches, the disappointed, saddened eyes of his children, who knew, long before children should ever know, that their father was fallible.

The plane stopped moving, and Meehan leaned forward to see if he could spot a name on the terminus building, but they were parked nose-first and the view from the window yielded no clues. The uniformed children clambered out of their seats, reaching over and under the chairs for luggage, squabbling and pushing one another in their hurry to get into the aisle.

"We must wait until the others are disembarked," said Rolf, explaining why he was still sitting down.

At last the plane emptied and Rolf stood up, unfolding his coat and throwing Meehan and the lieutenant theirs. They gathered their things together, and Rolf watched the male steward by the door for a signal.

"Yes," he said. "Now we go."

On the steps Meehan noticed that it was colder and windier than the place they had left, but it was night here and day when they departed, so it wasn't really a useful comparison. A windowless van was waiting at the bottom of the stairs. Three men in long overcoats and fur hats stood by it, looking up at them expectantly. Rolf saluted them and introduced Paddy as Comrade Meehan. None of the men saluted or took his outstretched hand. Everywhere he had been in the East they spoke to him as an equal but treated him as a prisoner. At least at home the screws hated you honestly.

Inside the van the rows of seats were bolted to the floor and the cabin was cut off from the driver by a wooden partition. With the van doors shut firmly behind them, they drove a couple of hundred yards, and then they stopped. The noises were different here, they sounded internal; a water drip echoed loudly, a distant whirr, like an outboard motor, bounced between walls, amplifying. The six men waited inside the van, nodding pleasantly at one another, smoking, and checking their watches. A sharp knock on the side of the van caused the driver to shout something, and the man nearest the back opened the doors. They were parked in a hangar. While their luggage from the plane was being handed in, Meehan spotted a fire hydrant on a wall, sitting above a bucket of sand, and he saw that the instructions were in Cyrillic script. He was in Russia.

He had been pacing the small gray cell for ten minutes when a surly female guard of about forty brought in a tray. She had blond hair and very blue eyes but didn't look at him as she laid the tray on the bed and turned away quickly, locking him in again. The meal consisted of greasy gray salt fish still in the tin, dry black bread, and lemon tea. The fish was inedible, but he ate all the bread and drank the bitter tea. The moment he pushed the tray away along the bed, the same female guard opened the door and gestured for him to follow her out.

The corridor was low and plain with pipes along the top of the wall. Including his own cell, there were only three doors off the corridor. The guard led him to one end, paused at a big gray steel door, and knocked. Metal slid against metal and bolts were pulled into place. The window slid open and a male guard looked them over, checking carefully behind them before opening the door and letting them through. They followed a staircase down one flight, their footsteps sounding tense and shrill, jittering against the concrete. One floor down they stopped at a door, knocked, and waited. A smaller, oblong window opened, also metal, and a handsome guard in a smart pale blue uniform looked out at them. He shut the window abruptly and pulled the heavy metal door open.

When they stepped out of the stairwell they found themselves in what appeared to be a rococo palace. The high-ceilinged hallway was duck blue, trimmed with gilt detailing and white plaster tracery. The floor was a rich mahogany parquet that deepened the noise of their footsteps, making them purposeful and dignified. The woman guard led Paddy across the hallway to a fifteen-foot-high double door flanked by uniformed military guards. She paused outside, pulling her tunic straight, touching her hair.

On her signal the two guards reached across and opened both doors at once, like the start of a Hollywood dance sequence. It was a ballroom. The ceiling was painted with gods and women and fat babies, all set in trompe l'oeil gold frames. Three long windows at the far end of the room would have led out into a garden or a balcony, but they were blocked out with blackout blinds, disguised behind dirty net curtains.

Facing Meehan in the middle of the room sat a long table with seven people at it, all dressed in mufti, their erect posture and cardboard haircuts making it obvious they were military. To his left-hand side sat three typists at a separate table, two of them young and pretty, the third old and dried up. Rolf and the lieutenant, made small by their surroundings, were perched on seats against the other wall. The young lieutenant was not doing the interpreting this time; he had been replaced by a stocky woman in a belted dress with thin black hair scratched up into a bun the size of a small chocolate. A man with a gray complexion and bushy black eyebrows sat in the middle of the center table. His head and body were square, like a cube balanced on a larger cube. He had an air of amused authority about him, like a judge with so much power he didn't need to be intimidating. He drawled loudly in Russian, his deep voice booming around the large room, and the interpreter turned to Meehan.

"You are invited to sit," she said, pointing to a dirty canvas-and-metal chair.

Meehan sat down. He felt very exposed. He was in the center of the room, everyone was looking at him, and his chair didn't have any arms.

The square man nodded at him and spoke for a long moment. The woman said: "You claim that you have come to give us information on British prisons. You want to help us to free imprisoned comrades in the West. Why would you do this?"

"I'm a communist myself," said Meehan. "I've had sympathies that way for many years. Since I worked in the Glasgow shipyards."

She told the important man what he had said, and he spoke again, holding Meehan's eye.

"Yet you are not a registered member of the party in your country," relayed the woman.

"Aye, well," shrugged Meehan, thinking that, actually, that probably did seem strange. "I'm not much of a joiner."

When he heard this the man smiled and spoke again, but his smile was forced.

"If you are motivated by political sympathies," said the woman, "why have you asked us to give you money for this information?"

"I need a new start in Canada. I have a wife and children."

The woman translated. The square man nodded and spoke again.

"He says . . ." The woman paused, wondering how to say it. "What are we to think of a communist who will not join the party and wants money for doing his duty?"

Meehan smiled weakly. He glanced at

Rolf, but neither he nor the lieutenant would look at him. They were going to kill him. The square man spoke again.

"Do not feel threatened," the interpreter ordered briskly. "We are friendly to you."

But Meehan felt sick. He thought of Betty and their disappointed children. He wanted to cry or pray, he didn't know which. The square man leaned forward, looking furious now, and it took Paddy a minute to work out that he was speaking in English.

"Is ver' good," said the man, slurring as he worked his tongue around unfamiliar open English vowel sounds. "Glasgow Rangers — is ver' good."

Paddy Connolly Meehan nodded. Whether it was the fear or a loyalty reflex, he felt himself getting hot and said, "Glasgow Celtic better."

The panel looked puzzled for a moment until the square man laughed, and then they joined in nervously, glancing from side to side, almost believing at one point that they found it funny.

Over the following few weeks they asked him repeatedly about British prison security, made him draw maps of the layouts of all the prisons he had been in and tell them about weaknesses in the window bars and acceptable methods of bribing guards. They presented him with a problem: how to get a two-way radio in to a prisoner who was under constant surveillance. Meehan suggested two identical transistor radios, one with the two-way facility and one without. If they delivered the special one to any other prisoner who wouldn't be searched thoroughly and had the normal one delivered to the subject, a switch could be effected a few days later by anyone with a pass card. They made him go through the plan over and over again and apply it in detail to the layout of several different prisons.

Three weeks later Rolf and the lieutenant accompanied him back to wherever the hell they had been in the first place. They were in the air before Meehan felt he could relax. He had heard a lot of people come and go from the adjacent cells during the three weeks, heard women keening softly in the night and sobbing men being led away shouting in Russian dialects he didn't understand, final, desperate words laden with regret — a woman's name, perhaps, or a place. Meehan knew they wouldn't be sending him on a plane if they intended to kill him. They would just have popped him there and then.

Rolf took out his old hip flask and gave them a vodka each. They sparked up Meehan's cigarettes again and drank a toast to Scotland Yard. The young lieutenant looked to Rolf for permission and then he told Meehan that President Kennedy had been assassinated in Dallas a month ago.

II

It was a blindly sunny day and they were standing where half of East Germany wanted to be, on the right side of the Wall at Checkpoint Charlie. Rolf had come too far over, Paddy could tell by the agitated faces of the East German guards. They wanted to challenge him but couldn't because of his rank. The British consul, a small man with a brown trilby and an ill-fitting camel overcoat, was waiting by a large official car with little flags on the bonnet. He stayed ten feet away, avoiding coming over to them, waiting instead for Paddy to come to him, as if communism were contagious.

In the car on the way there, Rolf had given Meehan a check, cashable only in an East German bank. It wasn't much money in the East, and outside it worthless. All

Meehan had for seventeen months of interrogation was an unusable check, two packets of cigarettes, and a bar of chocolate. Two packets of fags and a bar of chocolate and handed back into the hands of the British authorities, who would question him endlessly before returning him straight to prison to finish his sentence. The communists were sending him back as a carrier pigeon. They had put information his way so consistently he was sure it was wrong. Each of his many East German cellmates carefully passed on the same unsolicited information about guard-changing times and security measures.

They couldn't drag it out any longer: the guards were getting pissed off and edging towards them. The time had come to part. Meehan put out his hand and Rolf shook it politely.

"You are a clever man, Comrade Meehan."

Two packets of fags and a bar of chocolate. Meehan saw a turn in his eye. He would never have suspected it before and would lie to himself about it for the rest of his life; but for that small moment, he knew for certain that Rolf despised him. He thought Meehan was a cheap turncoat prick.

SIX

SHOVELING FOOD IN
1981

I

They could hear the burble of the gathering before they turned the corner to Granny Annie's. All the lights were on, the front door sat open in welcome, and the shadows pressing up against the front window showed how busy it was.

As Paddy came through the front door she dipped her finger into the holy water font hanging on the wall, but Annie had been in hospital for a fortnight and dead a week, and the little sponge at the bottom had dried out. The contact left a sour stain on Paddy's fingertips. She only kept up the habit because it pleased her mother so much when she witnessed it.

Someone's auntie was doling out the entrance drinks from a table just inside the door, assisted by Paddy's Gran Meehan, a small woman who had taken an abstinence pledge at the chapel twenty years ago and had neither enjoyed a drink since nor allowed a drink to be enjoyed in her company. The auntie pressed a glass with a smear of whisky into Sean's hand and an inch of sweet sherry into Paddy's. Afraid the sherry would interfere with the chemical reaction of the eggs and grapefruit, Paddy sipped, trying to mitigate the damage by not really enjoying it.

Annie had been a strict adherent to pre–Vatican II old-style Voodoo Catholicism, and it showed everywhere in the house. Holy pictures were hanging on every wall above the grab rails, and novenas were neatly tucked into the corners of toothy school photos of her grandchildren. A romantic plaster statue of Saint Sebastian, shot through with arrows and wilting in ecstasy, sat under a grimy glass dome on a windowsill, and a chipped Child of Prague was on the mantel, tipped at an angle by the silver ten-pence coin placed underneath it, a fetish that would invite prosperity into the house. Apart from superstition, sanctimoniousness, and a general distrust of Protestants, Annie's only real weakness was the Saturday-afternoon wrestling on the television. She had a signed photo of Big Daddy on the wall below the Sacred Heart.

Paddy wasn't even in the living room proper before the first industrial-sized baking tray of gammon rolls came past her nose. She managed to resist, saying No thanks, she'd just eaten as the bearer pressed her for the second time. A delicate white hand darted out over her shoulder, taking a roll and giggling a thank you. She turned to see her sister Mary Ann biting into the soft bread, her teeth sliding through the salt butter and sweet gammon. She giggled her appreciation, groaned, and took another bite, eclipsing her mouth with the rest of the roll, ashamed that she was savoring food so publicly, but then she laughed again because she liked it. Mary Ann was shy and inarticulate but had made an eloquent language of laughter that required a practiced ear. Unobservant people thought her a dolt. Her laughter was contagious: sometimes, as the swell and ebb rolled back and forth between them, Paddy thought that laughing with her sister was the purest form of communication possible.

Mary Ann took another bite, grinning as

she chewed, and nodded to the door. Paddy turned to see Trisha and Con Meehan coming through the crowd, holding hands like teenage lovers. Trisha still French-combed her hair up into a high crowned bouffant for formal occasions. Behind her thick glasses her eyes were a beautiful shade of gray, so pale they looked silver in a certain light. Of all the children only Marty had inherited them; everyone else had Connor's brown eyes. Con had a neat little David Niven moustache on his florid face and the same stocky build as Paddy. He was wearing an inappropriately jaunty dog-tooth jacket.

"Dad," said Paddy, as Mary Ann laughed incredulously, "why in the name of mercy are you wearing that?"

"Your mother gave it to me."

"He looks very swish," said Trisha, brushing an imaginary speck from his lapel.

A man next to them who had been at school with Sean's dad leaned over to Con. "Are you selling nylons?"

The gathered company laughed at the weak joke and Con joined in, not uncomfortable with his position in the pecking order. Mary Ann laughed hard into Paddy's hair. Their father was a meek man, a gentle little soul, always in the audience laughing at a bigger man's jokes. They both loved it about him.

"Well," Trisha bristled, small-mouthed and angry as ever, "you're hardly a fashion plate yourself."

And Con laughed away at that one as well.

II

An hour of small talk with a hundred relatives later and the singers were organizing their turns in the corner of the room. Paddy watched them conspire and wondered why they bothered: each always sang the same song anyway, choosing the one that best suited their voice. Trays of delicious food swayed above the heads and through the room.

Mary Ann was being silently chatted up by John O'Hara, the quietest boy in the parish. They sat close on the settee, ostensibly ignoring each other, backs stiff, each intensely conscious of the other. Mary Ann gave out occasional irrelevant laughing hiccups when tension caused John O'Hara to twitch his arm against her elbow. When Paddy couldn't stand the silence a moment more, she said she needed the loo, pulled her sleeve from Mary Ann's frantic pinch, and wandered off through the crowd.

Sean was in the kitchen doorway, nodding as a red-faced old union official ranted about the recession. The government wouldn't dare, the old man said, pointing adamantly at Sean's shoulder; they'd be provoking a national strike, and the shipyards were central to the Scottish economy. It would be a catastrophe, he said, a disaster. You don't remember before the war, you don't remember what the Tories are really like underneath the consensus. Sean shook his head instead to see if that would mollify the old man. And you young ones, the man warmed to his subject, you don't care, you don't see what's happening. It's you who'll pay. He pointed at them each in turn. It's your generation who'll end up on the rubbish heap. Paddy and Sean nodded in unison, wishing the old man would be quiet and go away. Having delivered his message and spotted a friend across the room, he did both.

"Well," said Sean, "that's me told."

He smiled down at her, and over his shoulder she saw her oldest sister, Caroline, coming through the crowd carrying her baby son on her hip. She looked exhausted. Baby Connor bared his four new nipping teeth at Paddy, raised a hand, and shrieked a greeting. A clear bubble formed at his nostril.

Caroline slipped the baby into Paddy's arms. "God, take him off me before I hurt one or both of us."

"Where's John, then?"

"He's out in the hall somewhere," said Caroline. "I'll go and find him."

She left the room quickly, stepping lighter now she was alone.

Sean smiled to see Paddy with the fat baby. "Suits you."

"God, that John's so lazy. I don't know why she ever married him," said Paddy, pretending to talk about her sister's marriage but actually sending him a message about theirs. "Hold him while I wipe his nose."

Sean took Baby Connor in his arms, burring his lips against the baby's face to make him smile, answering Paddy's worries with unspoken promises. She took a paper napkin and wiped the bubble away, making Baby Con cry.

Sean leaned over. "D'you fancy *Raging Bull* at the pictures tomorrow? It's supposed to be quite good."

Paddy didn't particularly want to see a

boxing movie, but she said she would. She felt mean for giving him trouble for John's crimes. "Bet your gran'd be pleased at the size of the crowd."

Sean nodded and nuzzled his face into her hair, pressing the baby's fat, powdery cheek against hers. "Everyone here'll be at our engagement party in May. As soon as our name comes up on the council list and we get a house, we can start working on getting one of these as well."

Paddy smiled up at him, scrunching her eyes together so that he couldn't see what she was thinking.

The baby weighed heavy on her hip, and she used the excuse to go and find Caroline and give him back. She managed to lose Sean to the back bedroom, where his uncles were singing rebel songs and drinking whisky.

She spent the rest of the night standing in the kitchen next to the oven, smiling at whoever talked to her, pretending to laugh along with the crowd. She forgot about Terry Hewitt and the spite that should have fueled her and gorged herself on slices of fruitcake and arctic roll, swallowing before she'd finished chewing, shoving food into her mouth to quell the panic.

III

Five miles across town from Granny Annie's in Rutherglen, in the front room of her small gray house in Townhead, Gina Wilcox sat in her immaculately clean living room. She had forgotten to put the heating on, and her breath hung before her like a soul leaving her body. She stared, dead-eyed, at the flickering television, waiting for word, vigilant and terrified for her baby.

SEVEN

FEARS ARE GROWING

I

Paddy was shielding her eyes against the sleet, standing at the side of Granny Annie's open grave, watching a silken cord slither down the crumbling black soil wall, when she remembered that she had left the six boiled eggs she needed for her diet sitting in a saucepan at the side of the cooker. She'd be fat all day without hope of reprieve. She almost cursed out loud. Sean felt her stiffen next to him and mistook her agitation for empathy. He put his arm around her shoulders and drew her near, tucking her head protectively under his chin, unaware that he was digging his fingers into the fat on her arm, reminding her that not only was she fat and shallow, she was fat and shallow and had horrible thick arms too.

II

She pushed open the doors and entered the newsroom, hanging her wet duffel coat on a hook by the door. Dub was already sitting on the copyboy bench. Keck, the head copyboy, was standing in front of the bench, uncertainly pivoting back and forth on one foot as Dub looked up at him distastefully.

"No," corrected Dub with mock patience, "you're not being funny. A joke or a quip are prerequisites to being funny. What you're being is fucking obnoxious."

Keck pulled the skin tight on his face, affecting nonchalance, and wandered off to the sports desk.

"What was that about?"

Paddy picked up a copy of the *News* and ran her eye over the front page. The Brian Wilcox story had JT's byline: two young boys were being questioned about his disappearance.

"That guy's a prick," said Dub softly, watching the room for calls. When he didn't see any he settled down to read again, folding one gangly leg over the other. He was wearing red-and-green checked trousers and a brown suede-fronted cardigan. One Monday morning

Paddy had seen traces of eyeliner between his blond lashes. Dub knew the names of all the local bands, the ones Paddy only heard of after they split up or left for London.

She went back to reading the paper. The boys had been taken in and questioned overnight. Two witnesses had come forward claiming they had seen the boys leading the baby away from his mother's front garden. Paddy reread the article. She could tell JT had left something out. The *Daily News* lawyers often censored important bits of information from copy, and she could sense it here. The boys were there and the baby was there, and then suddenly he was dead: the story read as if the causal paragraph was missing. A boxed insert to the story had been added at the eleventh hour, just before the edition was published. It said that the two boys had been moved to a secret location after a mob had formed outside the police station. Meehan had been mobbed outside Ayr High Court when he was arrested in 1969, and she'd done a pilgrimage there one Saturday while she was still at school to see the wide courtyard where the crowd had gathered. It had scared Meehan half to death, and he was a hardened criminal. She couldn't imagine how a child would cope with it.

She nudged Dub. "What's the deal with this Wilcox story? What aren't they saying?"

Dub shrugged.

"Are they looking for the men behind it all, or have they found them?"

"They're just looking for the baby's body as far as I know." He went back to his reading.

Dub never listened to office gossip. She didn't know why he'd applied for the job at the paper; he was hardly even interested in news.

She slapped the underside of his music paper. "Someone must have said something."

"They're looking for the baby," he repeated indignantly. "What can I tell you?"

Sudden movement across the room made them look up. A crowd of men were gathered around a telephone on the news desk, rapt, watching a standing man receive news that made him smile and nod and give the audience a thumbs-up.

"I don't know how you can read that crap." Paddy nodded at his music paper. "It's written by pretentious idiots."

"This is crap? You read true crime books, and they're not even writing."

"Don't be stupid. If it's written, it's writing."

"They're penny dreadfuls, they're printed on butcher's paper. It's not real writing."

She kicked his ankle. "Dub, *Macbeth*'s a true crime story. The New Testament's a true crime story."

He'd lost the point but wouldn't concede. "I'd never trust the taste of a woman wearing monkey boots."

Paddy smiled down at her feet. The ankle boots were only made from laminated cardboard, but they were cheap and black and they matched everything.

Across the room, Keck whinnied a subservient laugh at something said on the sports desk. He had been trying for four years to move into sports journalism, but he never wrote anything. His strategy was to hang around the sports desk and laugh at their jokes. Terry Hewitt, the barrel-bodied cheeky bastard who'd called her a fat lassie in the Press Bar, had been moved up from the bench the previous year, but promotion depended on getting a number of published articles before the editors would even consider it.

Paddy flicked through the inside pages of the paper, looking for any interesting crime stories she could follow up on. Dub let her get comfortable, waiting until her guard was down, and then he kicked her back. Luckily he was wearing inch-and-a-half-deep soft crepe soles.

"Hmm, yes, very sore. Is Heather in?"

"She's in the building somewhere."

The cavernous newsroom was divided into three sections, one for sports, one for news, and another for features. A large table sat at the center of each section, heavy gray steel Atex typewriters and blank workspaces laid out for the editors. Each desk had a different character: features considered itself intellectual, news was pompous and self-important, and sports was the good-time gal of the floor, the desk where they always had nice cakes and a laugh and seemed to be perpetually chewing chalky indigestion tablets that they left on the table.

Paddy found Heather sitting on the edge of one of the spare desks, in the distant cold corner of the office where the specialist reporters and freelancers worked on their copy. She was flipping through an envelope of clippings about the Great Depression that an economics correspondent was using. Heather only worked part-time; the rest of her week was spent studying at the polytechnic up the hill, where she was editor of the student paper. If Paddy was ashamed of her ambition, Heather was deliciously bombastic about hers: she had convinced Farquarson to let her research an article for the student paper about journalists, and out of it had wangled a union card and a monthly column about student life. Paddy felt lumpen and graceless next to Heather. She was the sort of woman who could tell one type of flower from another and wore her long hair loose. She didn't suck up to the drunks or the bullies and had the definite air of someone passing through on their way to a national paper. Even Terry Hewitt seemed a bit intimidated by her.

Heather's box pleat slipped from her knee, navy-blue tights patterned with bows and dots perfectly outlining her elegant calf. It was obvious from twenty feet away that she was flirting with the economics man, touching his arm, listening as he drew parallels between this recession and that one. He was short and had the shoulders of a twelve-year-old boy.

"God." Heather slid a hand under her mane of wavy blond hair and flicked it over her shoulder. "That's amazing." She glanced, saw Paddy, and grinned at her.

"Hiya."

"Hiya, Paddy. Coming for a smoke with me?"

Paddy shrugged. She didn't smoke, but Heather never remembered. Dropping the papers on the little man's desk, Heather stood up and followed Paddy over to a corner, where they pulled themselves up on the sill, sitting knee to knee. Heather flipped open a ten-pack of Embassy Regal, took out one of the stubby cigarettes, and lit it.

"So, listen, what time are you finishing today?"

"Four o'clock," said Paddy. "Why?"

"I've been invited out in the calls car with George McVie. D'you want to come?"

Paddy felt a trill of envy on the back of her neck. The calls car had a police-frequency radio in it and drove around at night picking up incidents and dramas all over the city. A good quarter of the paper's news pages could be filled with stories from the calls car. Every journalist had done the shift at some point. There were wild tales of leaps from multistory blocks of flats, of parties where the drink was of the bathtub variety, of domestic altercations that turned into street riots. Despite all the naked-city action, no one wanted to work the car: the working culture at the *Daily News* forbade enthusiasm, and it was much harder graft than sitting around the office at night taking occasional calls. Secretly, though, Paddy couldn't wait for a shift. Her favorite part of the car harvest was the smaller stories, bittersweet snapshots of Glasgow street life that never made the paper: a woman with a hatchet in her skull, still in shock, making polite conversation with an ambulance driver; a man masturbating in a bin shed, killed when a pigeon coop collapsed and crushed him; a violent fight between a couple that ended in the man's being battered to death with a frozen side of pork.

"How did you get invited to that?" she asked, trying to mask her mean-spiritedness. "Did Farquarson ask you to go?"

"McVie said I could tag along for a couple of hours. I'm thinking of writing a piece about the calls car shift for the poly paper."

It was all Paddy could do not to roll her eyes. Heather wrote the same two pieces over and over: she wrote about being a student journalist for the *Daily News*, and about being a journalism student for the poly paper.

"Yeah, all right, then." She tried to act casual. "I'd like to come."

But Heather could tell she was pleased. "Don't get too excited, though. I might drop out if the article doesn't pan. I've to meet him in the car outside here at eight."

She pushed herself off the windowsill and walked off, trailing smoke through the newsroom. She had left a long blond hair on the sill. Paddy picked it up and wound it around a finger, watching after Heather as she sidled through the tables, her tight little bottom drawing the eyes of the men she passed.

Paddy slid clumsily off the windowsill, lifting her legs high to avoid ripping the back of her black woolly tights on the metal ledge. The tights were going baggy at the knee already and they'd come straight from the wash that morning.

III

Farquarson's office door shut for the two o'clock editorial meeting and everyone in the newsroom relaxed into an unofficial break or started making personal phone calls. One of the news desk boys took the call.

"Brian Wilcox is finally dead," he announced, hanging up the phone.

Someone in the room said "hurray" faintly, and the other journalists laughed.

Keck nudged Paddy. "You have to pretend to laugh," he said quietly. "It's what we do when these things happen."

Paddy tried. She pulled the sides of her mouth wide, but she couldn't smile convincingly.

"You don't have to," Dub muttered across Keck's face. "It's not essential to lose your humanity, it's just useful."

Sulking, Keck responded to a hail, leaving them alone on the bench. The journalist who had taken the call about Brian ripped the sheet off his pad with a flourish and stood up, striding to the door of Farquarson's office, rapping on the window and opening the door.

"They found Brian Wilcox's body," he said. Paddy could hear Farquarson shout a loud, sincere curse. No one wanted a brand-new headline in the middle of an editorial meeting. "They strangled him and left him at the side of a railway line near Steps station."

Paddy nodded at Dub. Steps was miles away, far too far for the boys to walk from Townhead. "An adult took them there."

Dub shook his head. "You don't know that."

"Bet ye any money."

"Any money it is, then."

Through the open door, Paddy heard Farquarson cursing and ordering this schedule to be moved, that to be dropped, the police statement for page one, telling someone to get JT down to Steps with a photographer. "Check that those kids are still being held, and tell one of the boys to get me a large whisky from the Press Bar."

A features subeditor stuck his head around the door and looked at Paddy. "Did ye hear that?"

Nodding, Paddy stood up and headed for the stairs.

Down in the bar, McGrade was quietly filling up the back shelves with tiny tinkling bottles of mixers. Two journalists were warming up the table for the lunchtime rush. McGrade gave her a large Grouse when he heard it was for Farquarson and wrote it down in the big blue book he kept under the counter.

When she got back upstairs everyone in the newsroom was either out or on the phone. Farquarson was sitting alone at his desk with his head in his hands. She slid the drink between his elbows and he glanced up gratefully.

"Let me know when you've finished,

Boss. McGrade'll want his glass back."

"Thanks, Meehan."

"Um . . . Boss? Me and Heather Allen are going out in the calls car with George McVie, if that's all right? Just for a couple of hours, for work experience."

Farquarson smiled wryly into his drink. "McVie's awful nice, isn't he? Check with the Father of the Chapel first, make sure it's okay with the union. And Meehan? Calls car is a hard shift, night shift is hard. George may be . . . lonely. Keep your hand on your ha'penny when you're with him."

She nodded.

Father Richards was in the canteen eating a Scotch pie crowned with beans and smoking simultaneously. The cut under his eye was healing, but he was still having to manage without his glasses. His face looked raw without them.

"Ah, here she is," he said when he saw Paddy standing at the side of his table. "Chair to the Union of Catholic Mothers."

Paddy ignored it. She explained that McVie had invited Heather Allen, who in turn had invited her. Richards dropped the fork to his plate with a loud clatter and took a lascivious draw on his John Player Special.

She held up her hand. "Stop. I don't need you telling me. I'm well warned about him by Farquarson. I just want to check the union isn't bothered about it."

"Why would the union bother about McVie trying to ride two birds at once?" said Richards, and he laughed until his face was pink.

Paddy crossed her arms and waited patiently until he had finished. "Can I go, then?"

"Aye," said Richards. "Please yourselves. If ye were my daughter, I'd say no."

To cover her excitement Paddy pointed at his eye. "I hope ye got that sore eye from the last woman ye laughed at."

He drew lugubriously on his cigarette and ran his gaze all over her. "You're the last woman I laughed at. Would you like to hit me?"

The words were innocuous, but she felt uneasy, as if he were propositioning her somehow.

"No," she said, threatening him in the only way she knew how. "But I'd like to take your job."

EIGHT

AND PEOPLE ARE ARSEHOLES

I

George McVie was not allowed to drive the calls car. He wasn't even allowed to sit in the front seat next to Billy, because during one of their arguments he'd gone for the wheel and almost killed them both. Neither he nor Billy spoke to the other in the conventional sense. McVie grunted when he wanted to follow up a radio call; sometimes he shouted when he wanted Billy to call back to the office for a photographer; other than that they said nothing. They had been working nights together for five months and were ready to kill each other.

Billy, with his shoulder-length wet-look perm, was already in the car, tuning the radio and putting his fags on the dashboard, making sure he had change for the burger van. McVie, dressed in a crumpled raincoat and cheap acrylic pullover, stood by the car under a heavy gray sky.

"What d'you mean, she's not coming?" He glowered across the roof of the car at Paddy with exhausted baggy eyes.

"She isn't coming out in the calls car tonight, but I asked Farquarson and Father Richards, and they both said it would be fine if I come."

She tried to smile, but he wasn't buying it. He looked from her to the building, to the newsroom window and Farquarson's office, as if expecting to see his boss there, standing at the window, laughing down at him while fucking Heather Allen himself.

"Farquarson said for me to come," she repeated.

McVie looked at her again, just to be sure that Paddy was indeed as dumpy and not-Heather as he had originally thought. He tutted bitterly, leaning across the roof of the car to her. "Right, you, I've got a lot to do tonight. Don't talk over the radio calls and stay in the car when we get anywhere. I'm not babysitting you all fucking night. Just fucking shut up and we'll get on fine."

Paddy stood back, exaggerating her astonishment. *"Listen you to me.* There is absolutely no call for that sort of rudeness. I've been perfectly polite to you, haven't I?"

McVie glared at her.

"Haven't I?" She was determined to make him say it. "Have I been polite to you?"

McVie shrugged grudgingly.

"You're pig ignorant." She opened the car door and got in.

She had never met Billy before, but he introduced himself, shaking her hand over his shoulder as he smiled at her in the rearview mirror, relishing the sound of someone else fighting with McVie.

They sat there for a moment while McVie fumed, slapping the roof of the car a couple of times. Each time Billy cheerfully waggled his eyebrows at Paddy in the mirror. Finally McVie yanked open the back door and climbed in next to Paddy, angrily pulling the tails of his mackintosh out from under his seat.

"What in the name of fuck does 'pig ignorant' mean?"

"You," Paddy shouted back, sticking her finger in his face, "don't know how to behave around people."

Billy muttered amen to that and turned

the key, starting the engine. The radio crackled into life, drowning out all hope of a continued dialogue, even a bawled one. They sat for a few minutes listening to long pauses and requests for police cars to go back to the station. Livid at being ganged up on, McVie kicked the back of the seat, and Billy pulled the car out into the street.

Paddy sat back and watched the dark city slip past the window, enjoying the rare sensation of being in a car. They passed by a rough pub in the Salt Market. Two drunk men were wrestling outside, one in a gray leather bomber jacket squeezing the throat of a man in a crombie overcoat, holding him tight in the crook of his elbow, his opponent frantically reaching back, grabbing air, feeling for his attacker's face. Both men were too old for a dignified street fight, their bellies and stiff legs restricting their movements, turning it into a jerky, adamant dance. Behind them three other men leaned against the pub's outside wall, watching the fight, detached, as if it were an audition. If Paddy had been standing at a bus stop the sight would have scared the life out of her, but she felt secure in the smart car and able to observe it, imagining herself as a journalist. She had dreamed of this since she was at school, ever since Paddy Meehan got his royal pardon because of the work of a campaigning journalist.

II

It was the first of their nightly rounds. Billy stopped the car in a broad street on the north side lined by industrial warehouses, and McVie got out, slamming the door behind him. His hand was on the door to the police station before he realized that Paddy was at his back.

"Bint, stay in the car."

"Farquarson told me to go with you, so that's what I'm doing."

McVie sighed, shutting his eyes and pausing dramatically, as if being pleasant to Paddy was the hardest call of his life. He reached up and pulled open one of the double doors, leaving it to close in her face.

Inside she found herself in a waiting room with dirty plastic chairs arranged around the walls, some slightly soot-stained where a visitor had used a cigarette lighter on the underside and back. Cheerful posters on the walls carried warnings about pickpockets and burglaries and gas leaks. Two tired young men were slumped disconsolately on the chairs, waiting and waiting and waiting.

Seated behind a high desk was a middle-aged policeman, his pink skin blistered with acne. He dabbed at his neck with a tissue, touching a weeping spot just below his ear, while he wrote in a large black book tilted towards him on the desk.

"God," Paddy said to McVie when she caught up with him at the desk, "you're an awful curmudgeon."

"Who's a curmudgeon?" The duty officer looked up from his ledger.

"Him," said Paddy, thumbing at McVie. "He's a torn-faced misery."

The officer smiled pleasantly and dabbed again, flinching slightly as the tissue touched open skin.

"What's going on?" McVie nodded at the big black book on the high desk.

"Nothing. A couple of suicides. One a schoolgirl found in her school uniform in the Clyde. She'd failed her mock O Grades. The other . . ." He looked down the ledger, guiding his eye with his finger. "A guy hanged himself at Townhead."

Paddy expected McVie to go for the suicidal schoolgirl. It was the obvious

94

choice: an emotive and tragic story with spin-off articles about the pressure of exams, a grieving family who would almost certainly give a quote about how it was someone else's fault, and a good excuse to print a picture of a girl in school uniform. McVie flipped open his pad. "Whereabouts in Townhead?"

The desk sergeant was surprised too and had to find the entry in the ledger with his finger again. "Kennedy Street, just an hour ago. Street suicide, hung himself off a lamppost."

"What's the name?"

The officer looked at the ledger again. "Eddie McIntyre, but he doesn't live there. He did it outside a girlfriend's house." He ran his finger along the entry. "Her name's Patsy Taylor."

McVie wrote down the names and addresses. "Right, Donny, give me it straight. Are they here?"

The officer flinched, checking behind McVie, reassuring himself that the waiting men couldn't hear. "I'm not answering on the record." He hardly moved his lips. "What we don't want is a repeat of last night."

McVie nodded. "They going to charge them?"

Donny shrugged and nodded at the same time, dabbing the clear yellow liquid pooling on his neck.

"What's the charge?"

Donny kept his lips tight. "Murder."

McVie leaned into him. "What are the families like?"

"Hmm, aye, well, one — okay. Other one — Wild West," he said, as if the sin of breaching a professional confidence could be tempered by using broken language.

McVie stepped back from the desk and smiled warmly at the sergeant. "Donny, you're a pal." He turned, heading for the car and forgetting to hate Paddy for the moment. "Let's go."

Paddy had her suspicions but waited until they were sitting in the backseat again. "Who is in there?"

McVie looked out of the window. "Never mind."

She caught Billy's eye in the mirror.

"The Baby Brian Boys," Billy said, starting the engine.

It made them sound like a sinister jazz band. She knew immediately that the name would stick forever.

The street was dark, filled with deep, sharp shadows. As they pulled away Paddy looked up at the tiny cell windows, imagining a child up there in a cell alone with no one to stand up for him. It would have been a terrifying prospect for an adult.

She tried to make it sound casual. "Are they looking for the men behind it?"

"No." McVie seemed sure. "If they were looking for a grown-up, they'd be charging them with conspiracy to commit murder, not murder."

"How's that different?"

"It means they weren't the brains behind it, they're not as culpable. In sentencing terms it's a difference of about ten years."

Paddy looked out the window and thought of Paddy Meehan being mobbed outside Ayr High Court. Someone had run out of the crowd and kicked him so hard on the shin that they drew blood. She wondered if the person who did that had felt ashamed when they heard that he was innocent.

They passed the brightly lit bus station. Billy was driving along a broad back road to Townhead, around the back of the bus station, skirting the shut and empty town.

"Why're we going to this story, anyway?" Paddy asked. "The schoolgirl was a better story."

Neither of them answered her.

Billy crossed at the lights and pulled into

the housing scheme. Townhead was on a subtle hill between the city center and the motorway. They were good houses, built with quality materials on a small scale after the city planners had learned the lessons of the slum clearances. Its housing stock ran from individual houses with tiny gardens to low blocks of flats to four giant high-rises. The surrounding area was carefully landscaped into steep little green hills with trees on them, giving a false perspective, like a grand estate on a minigolf scale. Respectful residents looked after the area jealously: houses could go empty for weeks without having the windows smashed.

Billy stopped outside the entrance to Patsy Taylor's block of flats. The stairs were open to the elements. Each flat had a front room window that curled around the corner of the building, a veranda at the side, and a porthole window next to the front door.

"D'you want to see what this shitty city's about?" asked McVie vindictively. "Then come with me."

The walls of the open-mouthed entrance were a green and cream, but the steps were cold gray concrete. The flat they were looking for was one flight up, the door flanked by tripod plant-pot holders holding withered somethings. A fake

98

mother-of-pearl nameplate was fastened to the door frame. McVie looked disappointed.

"Well, at least it's not Sawney Bean again," he muttered, referring to a famous Scottish cannibal who had lived in a cave, eaten travelers from England, and interbred with all fifty of his daughters. Bean was fictional, a clumsy piece of anti-Scottish propaganda from the eighteenth century that backfired: the Scots loved Sawney from the moment he was launched onto the international bogeyman scene, taking him to their hearts and private kinky nightmares, extrapolating from his wild and lawless life to develop a national personality.

McVie took a deep breath and knocked on the door, an authoritative, firm three times. A stocky balding man with a ring of cropped white hair opened the door. He was sucking a freshly emptied pipe and wearing an itchy woollen dressing gown over his day clothes.

"What can I do for you, my friend?"

"Good evening, Mr. Taylor. My name is George McVie and I'm the chief reporter for the *Scottish Daily News*. I understand there has been an incident here this evening. I wonder if I could have ten minutes of your time to ask you about it?"

Paddy was astonished at McVie's skill

and grace. Mr. Taylor was charmed too, and flattered that the *Daily News* would send out its chief reporter for his story, a fact that McVie had anticipated when he told the lie.

Mr. Taylor invited them into his formal front room and packed his pipe from a yellowing rubber pouch while his silent wife made tea and grandly offered around custard cream biscuits. The electric fire wasn't on, but the red light spun slowly under a dusty coal mountain range, regular as a siren.

Mr. Taylor had taken the large armchair for himself and put McVie next to him on the settee. Paddy was relegated to the far end by the door, farthest away from the core of the conversation. Listening over the ticking of the clock, Paddy thought she heard someone down the hall sobbing low and regular, like a boiler ticking down to cool.

Under McVie's surprisingly gentle prompting Mr. Taylor told how his wife was washing the dishes at the back of eight when she heard a commotion in the street. They both looked out the window and saw a body hanging from the streetlight opposite their house. Mrs. Taylor called the police and ambulance services from the neighbor's telephone, but the man was dead. They found a letter pinned to his chest, addressed to Patsy, Mr. Taylor's daughter. When the police came to the door Patsy admitted that she had received another letter at work that morning. The hanging boy was Eddie, a lad from her work who was angry because she didn't want to go out with him. Mr. Taylor kept his eyes on his cup of tea as he explained the background, and Paddy felt strongly that he was lying.

"Could I see the letter, please?" she asked suddenly. "To check the spelling of Eddie's name. I'll get into terrible trouble with the lawyers if we spell it wrong."

Both men had forgotten she was there. They sat up and looked at her in surprise.

"That's your bit of the job, is it?" said Mr. Taylor.

Paddy nodded and pulled a notebook out of her bag. It was pristine, a navy-blue hardboard cover with a matching elastic band around the middle. She'd only stolen it from the stationery cupboard that afternoon.

Mr. Taylor hesitated for a moment. "There's a lot of language in it."

"That doesn't bother me." Paddy smiled bravely. "I've heard it all in this job. I just ignore it."

He reached under his cushion to pull out a pale yellow envelope, handing it to Paddy. "You're surely not a journalist?"

She glanced at McVie. If he was the chief news reporter, she could be a journalist. "Aye," she said, "I am."

McVie drew his attention away, asking him to repeat the story again because it was vital that they get the times right.

Paddy slid the folded sheet out of the envelope and opened it. She moved her pencil across her pad as if she were copying out the name while she read the letter quickly. The sheet of paper was from a small girl's writing set, a little sister's maybe. It had a faint picture of a black horse on the face of it, galloping through a misty field. It was obvious that Eddie and Patsy had been more than passing acquaintances. He referred to previous outings, and to her father calling him a bigot. But Eddie was an angry man. He told Patsy she was a bitch and he'd kill himself if she didn't meet him tonight. Paddy folded the letter carefully and slipped it between the pages of her notebook, putting the empty envelope on the table in full view.

McVie noticed and stood up, gesturing to Paddy to get up too. "Thank you for your time. It's very much appreciated."

Mr. Taylor glanced at the envelope, and Paddy knew immediately that he saw it was empty. He knew he had made a stupid mistake. He lurched forwards in front of McVie, grabbing the notebook with one hand and Paddy's wrist with the other, trying to yank them apart.

"Mr. Taylor, let go of her at once," said McVie, as indignant as the Pope in a go-go bar. "She's just a girl."

"Ye devils!" Mr. Taylor pulled the notebook away from her and found the letter inside. "Dirty, lying devils. Out!"

He chased them into the hall, pushing them out the front door and slamming it behind them. McVie looked at Paddy, panting and exhilarated.

"It was the father who split them up, then?"

She nodded.

"Thought so." He nearly smiled but caught himself. "You didn't fuck that up too much at all, bint."

"Thank you," said Paddy, accepting the compliment in the spirit in which it was intended. "You ignorant shit."

As they left the mouth of the close and headed down the path, Billy reversed slowly back, letting the car roll to the end of the path. Paddy didn't want to get back into the car with Billy and all the animosity and unpleasantness.

"It's a pretty poor thing to do." She slowed her step to a stroll. "Kill yourself to upset someone."

"Aye, well." McVie slowed down alongside her. "That won't make the page. We won't publish an article saying 'Moody wee bastard kills himself.' It's the details that tell the real story. The truth is a slippery bastard, that's what you learn in this game. That, and never trust the management." He looked up at the streetlight where Eddie had hanged himself, carefully considering whether he had any more important information to pass on to the next generation. "And that people are arseholes."

McVie's mood had mellowed, even to the extent of talking to Billy. "Well," he said as he got back into the car, "there actually was a story in it."

Billy shrugged. "D'you want to go anyway?"

"Aye, why not."

"Go where?" asked Paddy.

Neither of them answered her.

Billy didn't get faster than five miles an hour, crawling along slowly for a couple of streets. At the heart of the housing project they cruised past a dark swing park with mini-chutes and barred baby swings glistening with frost. Billy took a sharp corner a little too fast and drove along for a hundred yards before parking.

It took Paddy a minute to work out where they were. Following McVie's gaze she looked up the gentle incline of the road and recognized the green ribbon fencing before anything else.

There was no one outside the Wilcoxes' house, but the lights were on in the living room. The only thing that picked it out from the other houses on the modest terrace were the yellow ribbons tied randomly to the railings, the dirty bows soggy from exposure to the elements. One of them was a big perky bow from a bouquet of flowers and remained obscenely cheerful, hanging at an angle near the gate.

"Gina Wilcox's house," said Paddy.

Billy smiled in the mirror. "We're here looking for a story to save his career." He glanced at McVie. "He wants to get off night shift, but he's annoyed too many people. Careers'll be made over those boys. Could be bigger than the Ripper."

"Aye, you'd know," said McVie. "You're a fucking taxi driver. Right, bint, you want to be a reporter. What do you see in there?"

Paddy looked at him half amused, expecting him to laugh at the paper-thin ruse, but McVie didn't laugh back. He genuinely expected her to tell him everything she could glean from the scene without questioning his right to use it. Flustered, she looked back at the house.

"Um . . . I dunno." Maybe there was some unspoken rule about giving up information and no one had told her about it. Paddy could see into the empty living room. The curtains in the window were unlined, the ornaments small and cheap. "Nothing much."

The settee and armchair were brown and old, antimacassars pinned over balding arms and backs. It was an elderly person's suite, perhaps donated to a poor new house by a kind relative or bought second-hand. At the center of the wall above the gas-fire mantel was a wooden clock in the shape of Africa with two red dots on the lower coastline. Someone in the Wilcox family had emigrated to South Africa. A lot of working-class families went, drawn by tales of ex–bus drivers with swimming pools, of plumbers with private airplanes.

"I can't see anything at all. Are the two boys from around here?"

"No, Barnhill," said McVie.

Paddy knew the area. She had been to a funeral there once. "That's a couple of miles north. So they came here, got the baby, went to Steps, left him there, and went all the way home alone? What ages are they?"

"Ten? Eleven?"

Paddy shook her head. "Why were they here in the first place if they live in Barnhill? Do they know someone here?"

McVie shook his head. "No. The police think they came to use the swing park after seeing it from the road, maybe from a bus into town; came to have a go, saw Baby Brian, and . . . well, you know. Pop."

They had passed the swing park and Paddy noticed that it was for babies and under-fives. The chutes had a gradient as gentle as the horizon. There was even a sandpit and rubber matting around the ridey horses for tiny tots to take tumbles on. Paddy looked around. Across the road, over a grass verge and broad dual carriageway, was the high back wall of the bus station. The swing park wasn't even visible from the road: it was tucked in tight into the center of the estate. She was sure those boys had been brought here by someone who knew the area. An adult had brought them here.

"Well," Paddy said, sitting back. "Can't see anything."

Billy pulled the car from the curb and Paddy watched the housing scheme pull past the window. Little drops of not-quite rain started to smear the windscreen. She hid her mouth under her hand, trying not to smile. She could read the scheme. She could see patterns that McVie and Billy were blind to.

III

They were on the Jamaica Street bridge when they heard it over the radio. A christening in Govan had turned into a gang fight — one dead so far. McVie kicked the back of the seat and Billy swung the car around, cutting in front of a bus on the other side of the road and getting honked for his cheek. The snow came on heavily. Flakes as big as rose petals tumbled gracefully out of an ink-black sky. Pedestrians evaporated off the streets and traffic slowed to a cautious crawl. In the ten minutes it took for them to get to the address, the snow grew thick, sticking to soot-blackened walls in patches.

The gangs had dispersed by the time

they arrived in Govan. The tall street was bare of cars, a deep valley between two long red tenement rows, the crisp sheet of snow covering the ground punctuated by regular warm pools of orange from the streetlights. A few stray policemen were still standing in the tumbling snow, teasing out names and addresses from shivering witnesses desperate to get back into their houses and out of the weather, wishing they hadn't bothered to come for a look at the dead boy.

Billy pulled the car over to the pavement. Invited, Paddy followed McVie out of the car. Big soft snowflakes stuck to her hair and face and lay on her shoulders and chest, dampening her duffel coat. She looked down at the pavement and saw fresh scarlet speckles melting into the snow on the curb.

McVie walked over to one of the policemen. "Alistair, what's happening?"

The policeman pointed around the corner and explained that an eighteen-year-old boy had been chased into an innocent family's house by five members of an opposing gang. The boy had tried to escape by jumping out of the window, but his foot got caught and tipped him upside down. He landed on his head, dying instantly.

As the policeman spoke, Paddy stood five feet away looking at the deep dots of blood melting through the white snow to the black pavement beneath, tracing the path of the body to the ambulance tire tracks in the road.

"C'mon." McVie flicked his finger and Paddy followed him to the alley running between two blocks of flats.

The snow had barely reached the ground in the dark, narrow lane. It was lit by overspill from the kitchen windows above. McVie stalled in front of her, inadvertently sucking in a disgusted gasp through his teeth. Looking around his legs, Paddy saw a jammy, lumpy mess arranged in a halo around a central point of contact. A clump of long brown hairs was soaking up the blood. He must have had very dry hair, she thought. She stared at it, unmoved, surprised at her cold reaction. She felt nothing, just hot excitement at being there, bearing witness to events that would have happened anyway.

McVie looked up at an open kitchen window on the third floor, tracing the boy's trajectory from the window to the ground. The window was still sitting wide, and inside a hub of people were gathered. A uniformed policeman squinted down at them and, seeing McVie, waved happily. McVie was busy scribbling something in his pad, so Paddy waved back in his stead.

She found herself standing in the cold, dark alley next to a stranger's blood. Her feet were going numb and she was hungry. She looked down at the blood of a dead man her own age. This was exactly what she wanted to do for the rest of her life. Exactly.

McVie flipped his notepad shut and nodded her towards the car. "Right, then. That's tonight finished. We'll drop you home."

"I'm not going home. The shift's not finished yet."

"Look, that snow's gonnae shit down and we'll get stranded." He pushed her out of the alley, but she knew he meant it nicely. "Everyone stays home when the weather's like this. They don't even fight with each other. The calls will all be stranded motorists. We'll go back to the office and get the rest of the night's stories over the phone."

Paddy didn't know whether to believe him or not. She chapped on Billy's window, and when he wound it down she asked if they would be going back to the office. Billy looked up at the sky. "Yeah," he said. "We'll end up stuck in snow other-wise."

Snow muffled the noise of the night city. The few people they passed in the street were making their way out of the weather, stepping carefully, as if tiptoeing through oil. Billy concentrated hard on the road, while McVie and Paddy listened to the radio calls getting fewer and farther between. The city was putting itself to bed. They passed through the Gorbals and the blazing lights of the damp Hutchie E housing scheme, past the edge of Glasgow Green and Shawfield Stadium dog track, and on through Rutherglen. By the time they arrived at Eastfield the snowdrifts were half a foot deep.

The snow had cleaned up the Eastfield Star beautifully. All the roofs on the cottages matched, and the unmanaged gardens looked tidy. With a blanket of snow the overall design of the scheme was clear and coherent. Even the broken cars and tattered fencing looked clean and pretty. Lights blazed bright and warm from every home. Flocks of wily pigeons gathered on the snow-free roofs of uninsulated houses. Paddy felt proud to come from such a solid working-class background. She wished McVie had some friends at work he could tell about it. Maybe word would get around and people would respect her for it. Maybe Billy would tell someone.

She got out and leaned back through the door, telling Billy and McVie to come back to her house if they got stuck: they would be more than welcome to spend the night there, please don't hesitate.

"Fuck off," said McVie, pulling her door shut. "We're not coming back to your scabby wee house."

She watched the car roll away until it was swallowed by a white curtain. It was only when her back was turned and her face was hidden in her duffel hood that she burst into a smile. She was a journalist. She had to run around the block twice to burn the buzz off before she went home.

NINE

ON THE LIGHT TABLE

I

Paddy smiled to herself and leaned her head on the window of the early-morning train, looking up at the passing tenements, dark and full of sleep, households warmly savoring the last delicious half hour before the alarm. She was thrilled by her night in the calls car. She could do that job, she knew it.

Beyond the cold windowpane, frosting and cleared by her breath, the thin blanket of snow had blunted the edges of the landscape, softening bare trees and jagged buildings, rounding the coal carriages in the sidings, sitting inch-thick on the overhead cables. The sun rose abruptly, turning the sky a brilliant crystal blue. Paddy could see her whole future in the same color.

A large portion of the staff at the *Daily News* had inexplicably been made late by the melting inch of snow. The building was half shut, the car park almost empty, and even the clattering of the print machines was subdued.

Through the open printworks door Paddy could see that only two of the three presses were working. The side door was still locked and chained, and she had to make her way through the main reception. Inside, a single Alison was sitting at the desk wearing her furry-collared coat.

"D'ye get in all right?" asked Paddy.

Alison shrugged, reluctant to chat. "S'pose," she said, picking her ear with a manicured fingernail.

On the way up the stairs Paddy picked up a copy of the paper and was delighted to find the street suicide story about Eddie and Patsy in its own boxed paragraph on page five. McVie had managed to edit it into a noble story about thwarted love, a death with meaning.

The newsroom was half dead. They were so short staffed that even Dr. Pete had been drafted onto the news desk. He sat dumbly with his jacket off, staring at a typewriter as if it had just insulted him. Before Paddy had time to hang her coat up inside the door he raised a hand to call her over. As she walked across the floor he typed three consecutive letters and sat back, staring at the machine suspiciously.

"Go and ask a news sub if I have to do this."

Paddy looked around the newsroom but could see only one sub, and he was on the phone. The lights were on in the pictures office. Sometimes subs and journalists hid in there to make a private phone call or have a quiet smoke.

There was no answer when she knocked at the door. The light seeping underneath seemed unusually sharp. She opened the door and a hyper-white light erupted through it. The light table, three feet square of buzzing brightness used to view negatives, had been left on at the back of the room. Next to it sat Kevin Hatcher, the perpetually drunk pictures editor. He was sitting in a desk chair at a strange angle, his head hanging to the side, his hands loose in his lap. He looked like a posed corpse.

"Kevin? Kevin? Are you okay?"

He blinked his bloody eyes to signal that, yes, he was fine, and blinked again. The harsh light seemed to be drying his eyes out. She stepped across to the white panel and found two large-format pictures sitting on the burning surface, the photographic paper arching away from the heat. She lifted the pictures, stacked them on the tips of her fingernails to avoid burning her fingertips, and turned off the light table.

It took a moment for her eyes to adjust. She was blinking down at the top picture as it came into focus. It wasn't printable quality. It had been taken through the tiny window of a moving police van. A third of the frame was a flash-bleached hand slapping at the outside. Inside, a policeman was sitting on a bench, slightly off his seat, next to a small blond boy clutching the edge of the seat, his knuckles white, his head down defensively so that the whirl of his crown was visible. The second picture was taken one window farther down. A dark-haired boy sat on the other side of the policeman, eyes shut tight and lips pulled back in a terrified grimace. The scalding picture fell from her hand, zigzagging to the floor.

Paddy knew this boy. It was Callum Ogilvy, a cousin of Sean's.

She bent over to look at the picture on the floor. She hadn't seen Callum since his father died and Sean had taken her to his funeral a year and a half ago, but his face was the same shape, his teeth still gray and dun, set in long gums.

The boy was related to Sean through both their dead fathers, who were cousins or brothers, she couldn't remember. Callum's family lived in Barnhill, on the opposite side of the city from Sean, and his mother suffered from an unnamed mental illness no one liked to talk about. Paddy had only met her at the father's funeral, and she'd looked like a colorless hippie, with frizzy graying hair and leathery skin. The Ogilvy children were very subdued, that much Paddy did remember, but their dad had just died, so it hadn't seemed that strange. She remembered Callum trying desperately to get attention from the older cousins, guessing Sean's favorite footballer and showing off by jumping fearlessly off a wall. Sean had tolerated the boys politely enough, but he didn't like them. He had never been back to see the family.

"Kevin?" She picked up both pictures and held them in front of his face. "Kevin, what are these pictures of?"

Kevin looked at them. "Bibi Bri."

"Baby Brian?"

He nodded, shutting his eyes at the effort.

Paddy dropped the pictures to the floor and walked out of the room.

III

Ignoring calls from journalists, Paddy marched straight through the newsroom and out the double doors, running up the canteen stairs two at a time, ignoring the twinges in her lungs and her aching knees. She was surprised to find herself breathless as she pushed open the double doors.

Terry Hewitt sat alone at a table, about to take a bite of a sandwich. The sharp smell of eggs wafted across the room. Through the window behind him she saw snow dropping lazily from black clouds. She had never spoken to him directly before.

"Have you seen Heather Allen?"

Terry lowered his sandwich, looked surprised, and shook his head, his face composing itself into a smug smile as he inhaled to speak. Paddy didn't wait. She pushed back through the doors and walked away.

The ladies' toilet on the editorial floor was Heather's private office. It was a particularly nice toilet, and because no woman was ever promoted to editorial it was private, used so little it only needed a clean once a fortnight. Paddy opened the door to the smell of smoke and Anaïs Anaïs perfume.

"Heather?" she whispered in case anyone in editorial heard them.

Heather's hushed voice came from inside one of the far cubicles. "Paddy?"

"Heather, it's Paddy."

After some rustling of material and a flush, the door opened and Heather peered out. "What's wrong?"

Paddy took a deep breath and held it in. She sat down on a hand towels bin, drinking in deep, calming breaths.

"What's going on?"

Paddy shook her head, aware that she was half enjoying the drama.

Heather patted her arm. "Let's have a ciggie, that'll calm you down."

She took one for herself and gave one to Paddy, bending over to light her up with a book of matches from Maestro's, an intimidatingly trendy nightclub Paddy had never been to. For the first time in her life Paddy inhaled smoke.

"God." She grimaced, rolling her tongue around her mouth. "God, that's . . . I feel sick." She lifted her hand to the sink.

"No!" Heather took the cigarette back

from her fingers. She pinched the hot tip into the sink and tapped the loose tobacco out of the end, twisting the empty paper into a little point. She filed the amputated cigarette back in the packet. "Is it a long story?"

Paddy shrugged and nodded.

"Just hang on, then . . ." Holding her cigarette above her head, Heather trotted into a cubicle and dragged out a blue sanitary towel bin, trailing the smell of flowers rotting in ammonia across the floor. She sat down on the soft plastic bin, making its sides bulge. "Okay. I'm ready."

Paddy smiled at the sight of her sitting on the stinking bin just to get eye level. "You need to promise you won't repeat this to anyone."

Heather crossed her heart and frowned. "You're very serious."

"I was up in Kevin Hatcher's office and I saw some photos of the Baby Brian Boys. I know one of them."

Heather gasped. "You lucky bitch."

"He's Sean's wee cousin."

Heather sat back. "You bloody lucky cow." She grabbed Paddy's sleeve. "Look, you could do a piece about the family, about the background. God . . . I bet you could even get it syndicated."

"No, I can't." Paddy shook her head.

"Sean'd never talk to me again, and my family'd disown me. They don't approve of talking to outsiders about family business."

"But, Paddy, if you get a syndicated story out of it you'll be published all over the country. It could be your calling card. You could make brilliant contacts in other papers."

"I can't use the story."

Heather tipped her head to one side and narrowed her eyes, pretending it was against the smoke, but Paddy could tell that she was envious of her. She relished the novelty of it.

"I can't, Heather. Sean'll be gutted when he hears about this. They just left those kids up there with that crazy mother. I mean, they'll feel terrible. You would, wouldn't you? Anyone would feel terrible. And he's got five brothers and sisters. One of them's wilder looking than the next. I met the wee guy at his dad's funeral. He'd fallen into a machine at the St. Rollox works in Springburn, drunk. He was all chewed up."

"You should use the story, Paddy. It's unprofessional not to."

"No, I just can't."

Heather looked faintly disgusted, but Paddy knew she couldn't do it. The Ogilvys were a good family, they did voluntary work, they cared for their neighbors and were meticulous in their devotions. She wished she had never seen the picture and didn't have to be the one to tell Sean. She felt suddenly queasy as she remembered the amount of arctic roll she had eaten at Granny Annie's laying-in.

"He was going on about our engagement party the other night."

Heather exhaled slowly, shifting her weight on the bin. A corner of the soft plastic buckled slowly beneath her, and Paddy realized that mention of the engagement was one inadvertent triumph too many. Heather avoided her eye and took a draw on her cigarette, tipping her head back. Her blond hair slid off her face.

"I broke my diet really badly. That's what made me think of the engagement. I can't stick to it at all." She smirked at herself. "I think I'm actually getting fatter."

Heather went back to her cigarette.

"The egg diet?" said Paddy. "You know it? I haven't done a poo for a week."

Heather half smiled at the floor, so Paddy tried harder, telling her about Terry Hewitt asking who the fat lassie was in the Press Bar.

"Terry Hewitt's a knob," said Heather spitefully, "a complete fucking nob. He fancies himself so much. Did you see him in the newsroom earlier, trying on Farquarson's coat while he was down here on editorial?"

"No."

"He stood on a chair so everyone could see him. It was pathetic."

A fleck of Heather's spittle hit Paddy on the top lip. She resisted the urge to wipe it away.

"Give us that half cigarette," she said, "and I'll try again."

Paddy tried to smoke it, pulling silly faces and making herself the fool for Heather, trying to get them back on an even keel. Heather smiled politely and let her make an arse of herself. Eventually she stood up.

"You should use the story."

"I can't," said Paddy, ashamed of her soft heart.

"Fine."

Heather stood up and ran the end of her cigarette under the tap. She threw the smelly stub of it into the sanitary bin, checked her hair and lipstick in the mirror, and said "See you later" as if she hoped they'd never meet again.

Paddy watched the door swing behind her. Now she had no one.

TEN

THE EASTFIELD STAR

I

The snowflakes were just as heavy as the day before but dissolved where they landed on the wet ground. Paddy tightened her scarf around her head, keeping her hood up, and trudged up the steep hill to the Eastfield Star.

The Meehan family home was on a tiny council estate at the southeastern tip of Glasgow's sprawl. The estate had been built for a small community of forty or so miners working the now defunct Cambuslang coal seam. From a central roundabout of houses, the five legs radiated out with six houses on each, some containing four flats, some free-standing with five bedrooms to accommodate large, extended families. Built in the cottage style, the houses had low-fronted gable ends, sloping roofs, and small windows.

The Meehans lived in Quarry Place, the first prong to the left on the Star. The two-story house was low and built so close to the soil that every room was slightly damp. Paddy's mother, Trisha, had to bleach the skirting in the hall cupboard every three months to get the mold off it. Gray, eyeless silverfish had colonized the bathroom carpet, making a five-second pause necessary between flicking on the light and entering the room, giving them a head start in their slither off to dark places. Theirs wasn't a large house: Paddy shared a bedroom with Mary Ann, the boys got separate rooms after their sister Caroline's wedding, and their parents had a room.

Each of the Eastfield houses had a decent amount of land around it, a few feet of front garden and a hundred-foot strip at the back. Mr. Anderson on the roundabout grew onions and potatoes and rhubarb and other sour things that children wouldn't steal to eat, but the rest of the gardens were just scrub land, bald brown grass in the winter and thicker grass through the summer. Wooden fences hung to the side, and grass grew freely between the paving stones.

They were only two or three miles from the center of Glasgow, close to wide-open fields and farms, but the families who lived on the Star were city people, workers in heavy industry, and didn't know how to tend gardens. Most found the persistent encroachment of nature bewildering and a little frightening. A tree had somehow grown at the bottom of the Meehans' garden. It had started growing before they arrived, and they'd mistaken it for a bush until it really took off. No one knew what kind of tree it was, but it got bigger and branchier every year.

Hunched against the falling snow, Paddy walked carefully up the quiet road to her family house, passing the garage, swinging open the garden gate, and stumbling over the brick the Beatties from next door kept the garage keys under. The freestanding garage was built on the Meehan side of the fence, but the Beatties had somehow annexed it over the years, using it to store unused furniture and boxes full of toys and mementos. Con Meehan had never agreed to let them have it but pretended he had to avoid an argument. Con's horror of confrontation had shaped his life more than his choice of wife, more than the city or times he lived in, more than his job at the British Rail engineering works. It was why he had been passed over for promotion all his life, why he never got on in the unions despite being an articulate and politically sincere man, and why he had never once, not even in his heart, questioned the teachings of the church.

Paddy took out her keys and opened the door to the home smell of wet coats and warm mince. She dipped her finger into the holy water font inside the door and crossed herself before sitting on the bottom stair, unlacing her boots, and peeling off her thick tights. She hung them over the banister and tripped through to the living room.

Con was lying on his side on the settee, watching the news, his hands tucked between his knees, still bleary after a pre-tea nap. "Hello, hello. How's you?"

"Aye, Dad." Paddy paused and touched his hair with her fingertips. Demonstrations of affection made her father uncomfortable, but she couldn't always stop herself. "Good day."

"Good girl." He pointed at Mrs. Thatcher on the telly. "This balloon's up to no good."

"She's a creep."

Paddy paused to watch for a moment as the local news came on. The top item was a report about Baby Brian's body being found. The footage showed a short green bank of land with a tiny square white tent erected on it and a lot of uniformed policemen standing around looking serious.

Paddy opened the door to the small kitchen. Her mum turned and smiled politely. "Thank God you're home safe," she said formally, indicating company.

Sean was sitting at the table eating an enormous plate of black minced beef and nylon-orange turnip. Amazed at himself, he pointed at the plate with his knife. "This is my second tea tonight."

"He's been waiting for nearly an hour," said Trisha indignantly. Trisha believed that women should wait for men and never the other way around, which was part of the reason Caroline had settled for such a lazy husband. Paddy sat down at the table as her mother spooned white cauliflower soup speckled with black pepper into a bowl and set it down in front of her. "If this weather keeps up, all the works'll be off and I'll be tripping over the lot of you for the next couple of days."

Paddy commiserated but knew her mother's lifelong dream was to have five housebound children with voracious appetites. "I'll be going into work anyway."

Sean reached for a slice of buttered

bread from the plate in the middle of the table, stretching his legs as he did so, wrapping his ankles around Paddy's. She felt a pang of guilt when she saw the grapefruit in a red net bag sitting on the windowsill. She decided just this once to enjoy her food. She could start again tomorrow.

Trisha assembled a dinner of mince, mashed potatoes, and turnip and put the plate by Paddy's elbow as she finished off her soup. "Take a bit of bread." She nodded at the plate of buttered half slices on the table. "Ye need to build up your strength after being out in that."

"I'm hardly going to fade away, am I?" said Paddy, glancing at Sean.

Trisha looked at Sean. "Oof, you're not going to start all that rubbish about being fat again, are you?"

"Mum," said Paddy, talking to Sean again, "I am fat. I just am."

"Paddy," said Trisha firmly, "that's puppy fat. It'll disappear in a couple of years and you'll be as slim as the rest of them." She turned away quickly, as if she didn't believe it either.

Sean dipped his bread in the gravy on his plate and looked confused when he noticed Paddy scowling at him. He could have stood up for her at least, she thought.

Inside the back door Trisha was cleaning the dishes and putting the kitchen to bed for the night. None of the Meehan family smoked, so Paddy and Sean had to stand on the back garden step for Sean to have a cigarette.

They were wrapped up well in scarves and woolly hats, standing shoulder to shoulder under the sheltering lip above the kitchen door, watching the blizzard through half-closed eyes. It was starting to lie. A delicate net of white flakes covered the black ground. Giant flakes hurtled sideways and up, floating into Paddy's mouth and nose, getting stuck on the underside of her eyelashes, and melting into her eyes. Sean lit his cigarette inside his jacket, pinching the filter between his thumb and forefinger, keeping the cigarette safely cupped in the cage of his hand.

"Sean, I need to tell you something."

Sean stared at her, the tenderness in his eyes rapidly cooling into fear. "What?"

She considered backing out.

"What?" he insisted.

She took a deep breath. "I saw a photo of the wee boys who killed Brian Wilcox. I think one of them's Callum Ogilvy."

He stared at her and blinked. "Get tae hell."

"It was him. I looked and looked at it. It had his wee teeth and his hair. It's him."

"But the Ogilvys live in Barnhill. Those boys were from Townhead."

"No, the baby was from Townhead."

Puzzled and anxious, Sean searched her face for signs that she was making some sort of bizarre joke. He looked away and took a deep draw on his cigarette.

"A mob formed outside the station where they were being held, so they moved them. I saw a photo taken through the window of a police van."

He wiped his face with a big hand, rubbing it hard across his eyes, trying to wake himself up. "How good a picture could it have been?"

"It was good enough." She tried to take his hand, watching him calculate the possibilities.

"That's stupid." He pulled his hand away. "We'd have heard. They'd have phoned us, wouldn't they?"

"I don't know. Would they?"

His voice dropped to a hoarse whisper. "Did they kill that baby?"

Paddy felt she'd said enough. "I don't

know exactly, I just know they're in custody."

"So it might be nothing?"

She lied to make it easy on herself. "Might be nothing at all." She pressed his hand again.

Satisfied that he had made her back down, he flicked the ash from his cigarette into the pristine white snow. "Who did you give me a dizzy for last night?"

She was surprised at his hurt tone and touched his elbow. "Ah, no, Sean, I didn't blow you out, I didn't. I couldn't go to the pictures because of work. I got a chance to do something."

"So, you just stayed at work alone, did you?"

"Actually, I went out in the calls car." She thought back over Mr. Taylor's living room and the moment in the alley when she waved to the policeman in the bright kitchen window.

"Yeah, see?" said Sean, suddenly caustic. "I wouldn't actually know what a calls car is because I don't work there."

"It's just a car that drives around and goes to the police stations and the hospitals to pick up stories. It's got a radio in it." He didn't seem very interested, so she tried be more specific. "We went to a gang fight where this guy had jumped out of a window and before that to a house where this guy killed himself to upset his girl-friend. Can ye imagine that?" He didn't answer. "The story was in the paper today, just a few lines, but being there . . . it was . . ." She wanted to say fascinating, that it was exhilarating, that she could do that every night for the rest of her life, but she curbed it. "Interesting."

"That's disgusting." He took a sulky draw on his cigarette.

He sounded so mean she didn't know what to say. She looked away down the snowy garden. It was like this between them more and more now. They were all right with other people there. Then they'd hold hands and feel close and wish they were alone, but as soon as they were, they'd bicker.

"It was an interesting night." She leaned out beyond the shelter, into the slowing blizzard. "I wasn't supposed to go, but I asked and they said it was all right."

"You're so ambitious," Sean said reprovingly.

"No I'm not," Paddy snapped back.

"Yes you are."

"I'm not *that* ambitious."

He took a last drag on his cigarette before throwing it away. "You're the most ambitious person I know. You'd cut me in half for a leg up."

"Piss off."

He twitched a bitter little smile. "You know it's true."

"I might be ambitious, but I'm not ruthless. That's a different thing."

"Oh, now you are ambitious?"

"I'm not ruthless." Paddy petulantly kicked snow off the step. "I've never done anything for you to say that about me."

They stood on the step looking out, each silently continuing the argument.

"Why can't you be content to rub along like the rest of us?" He sounded so reasonable.

"I'm just interested in my job. Is that wrong?"

She understood why it made him angry: Sean wanted them to stay in the same place near the same people for the rest of their lives, and her ambitions threatened that. Sometimes she wondered if he was going out with her, a dumpy girl half as attractive as himself, because he could count on her to be grateful and stay.

"And you're competitive," he said, as if confessing his own flaws reluctantly.

"I am not."

"Ye are, everyone knows you are. You're competitive, and to be honest," he added, dropping his voice to a confidential mutter, "it frightens me."

"For Godsake, Sean —"

"If it was a choice between me and your job, which would you choose?"

"Bloody hell, will ye drop it?"

He threw his cigarette into the garden, to the spot where he always threw his cigarettes. Underneath the snow Paddy knew there were roll-up dog ends from last year's long hot summer, when they had both just left school and clung to each other. She'd just started at the *Daily News* and didn't know if she would be able to hack it. Over that was another layer of ash and filters from the rainy autumn, when Sean had started work and had a bit of money for real fags. And over them were the Christmas cigarette ends, when they sat on the step in the dark with a blanket over their knees and cuddled together; where Sean proposed after lunch on Boxing Day. All that closeness had evaporated since they'd got engaged, and Paddy couldn't understand where it had gone.

Sean kept his eyes on the lonely thin tree at the end of the garden. "I worry that you're gonnae leave me."

"Oh, I'm not gonnae leave ye, Sean." Paddy fumbled for his hand, callused and swollen from hard work, and lifted it to her mouth. She kissed the well of his palm as hard as she could. "Seanie, you're my sweetheart."

He cupped his free hand around her cheek and they looked at each other sadly.

"You are," she said adamantly, not sure whom she was trying to convince. "You're my dear, dear Sean and I'll never leave you." But even as she said it, she was wishing it were true. Her throat was aching. "Come upstairs with me and we'll have a winch, eh?"

He looked at his feet. She kissed his hand again.

"Sean, I shouldn't have said that about the boy. I don't know what I saw. Come up with me."

She tugged his sleeve encouragingly, opening the back door, afraid to let go of Sean in case he disappeared off into the snow forever. She held on tight and pulled him through the door, leading him into the warm.

III

The bedroom door was blocked by a large wardrobe, so that the room had to be entered sideways. Beyond it were two single beds with a narrow aisle in between. At the foot of each bed sat a set of drawers where the girls displayed their most prized possessions. Paddy had a jar of clear green Country Born hair gel for spiking her hair next to all the crap Sean had bought her: a bottle of Yardley perfume; a ridiculous neck ruffle to attach to her clothes for an instant New Romantic look; a little model of two teddy bears wrestling each other, wearing capes cut out of J-cloths and silver electrical wire belts Sean had made during an idle morning at work. Mary Ann kept her eye shadows on top of her chest of drawers, set out in little troops of blues and greens and pinks. She had a lone black one that Paddy bought her for her birthday, and she sat it at the front, next to the chewy blue eyeliner pencil she always used.

Paddy had a poster of the Undertones above her bed. It was the first picture she had ever seen that mirrored her own life: a lot of cheaply dressed, ill-nourished people squashed into a small living room with a picture of the Sacred Heart on the wall. Mary Ann preferred pictures of dewy-eyed heartthrobs: Terry Hall and sad-eyed Patrick Duffy looked down on her side of the room.

With six adults smashing around the place, there was very little privacy in the Meehan household. To make it worse, Paddy and Mary Ann's bedroom door was first at the top of the stairs, so anyone coming up could hear what was going on. Invariably, when Paddy and Sean got into heavy winching, someone would come up and interrupt them, but tonight everyone was out and Trisha and Con were downstairs watching a never-to-be-repeated program about the miraculous visions of Saint Bernadette. They were as close to alone as they had ever been.

"I'm the Man" dropped down the record player spindle as Paddy sat down next to Sean on the bed. She didn't want to lose him. She wanted to make a great, reckless, beautiful gesture to bind them together so that he couldn't slip out of her life while her attention was elsewhere.

They sat on her bed and kissed softly. She put her hand on his chest, pressing lightly, urging him to lie back.

"No, Paddy," he murmured. "Your folks might come in."

She smiled as she kissed him and pressed again, catching him off balance, toppling him back a little.

"No," he said sharply, slapping her

hand away, bouncing back to vertical.

He started kissing her again, not expecting her to mind being so bluntly corrected. But she did mind. Hiding her annoyance, Paddy let her hand rest on his thigh until he was comfortable with it, kissing him gently, rubbing her nose on his cheek and very slowly stroking up his thigh. He flinched, so she slowly moved her hand back to his knee, keeping it there until he was comfortable before moving it again. She reached the seam of his crotch.

"Don't," he said, letting her continue. "Don't."

He was very hard, she could feel it through his trousers, and she liked that she could do that to him. Groaning, Sean yanked her hand away and crab-walked his legs around the edge of the bed away from her. He was panting. She reached out for his arm but he slapped her away.

"No."

He was bent over and she didn't really know why. She didn't understand the geography of men's genitals. She'd seen a cross section in a biology textbook. The teacher refused to teach the module on religious grounds because it contained information about contraception. She told them which page of the textbook it was on, as if they needed to be told, and gave them an hour to read through it in silence. Paddy knew that everything was arranged differently when men weren't naked, cut in half and perfectly side-on.

"You shouldn't do that," he whispered.

"Why?"

"I might not be able to stop myself."

"Do you have to stop yourself?" He didn't answer. "Maybe I can't stop myself either."

He smirked and went back to nursing himself. "We agreed to wait. What if your mum came in?"

Paddy reached out to him, sliding her hand over his thigh. "I don't want to wait," she blurted.

Sean looked at her and snorted a laugh, bending over his lap again.

"I don't want to wait, Sean."

He was shocked. He sat up, staying on the other end of the bed, and looked at her. "Well, I do. I want it to be special when we get married. I want to know it's the first time for both of us."

Shame, as pernicious and sticky as napalm, rippled through her. She should want to wait. She shouldn't want to touch him, shouldn't want any of it, because she was a girl. Her virginity would never be hers to give, only his to take.

Sensing her resentment, Sean reached across to her forearm, pulling her over the bed towards him. He held her tightly by her shoulders in a restraint position, pinning her arms to her sides. "You mean so much to me, Paddy. You mean the world to me. Do you know that?"

"I know."

"And you're a little sexpot," he said, trying to be kind about the transgression. "What are you?"

"I'm a sexpot," she said miserably.

He heard the fury in her voice, saw her pinched face, and knew it wasn't okay. Slipping his hand around the back of her neck, he pressed her face into his chest so he didn't have to look at her anymore.

"No," he said firmly. "You're a *little* sexpot."

ELEVEN

TWO LADY WRESTLERS

I

She was covered in a gentle sweat of sheer terror. They would never, ever forgive her. Sean, her dad, everyone — they'd think Paddy had sold the story. They'd never believe it wasn't her.

Paddy stared out the train window at the dark morning, a copy of the *Daily News* limp in her lap. She looked at the paper again. TWO ARRESTED FOR BABY BRIAN. The headlines were huge, an old layout trick to cover up a lack of printable copy, but it was the insert at the bottom of the article that pained her. It was a first-person account of life in Child A's family, about the shame and shock and grief of the extended Irish Catholic family who had abandoned the boy. The piece was overwritten, punched out in short, conversational sentences. To an unfamiliar reader the bad grammar would have seemed like a heavy-handed, hokey touch, but Paddy recognized them as habitual conversational mistakes of Heather's, left in by the subs to make it sound like the authentic voice of a greenhorn Catholic, the sort that might have evil monsters for kin. She read through the rest of the paper to keep her eyes busy. Caspar Weinberger, Reagan's new defense secretary, was saying he would use a neutron bomb in Western Europe if necessary for American security. Paddy looked out the window at the white world and wondered whether Caspar might do her a favor and press the button before home time.

II

Dub couldn't believe it when Paddy offered to dish out the new edition to all the departments. No one ever volunteered to do anything, and handing out the papers was a boring, messy job that stained hands black and ruined clothes. Paddy couldn't sit still any longer. She carried twice as many papers as usual, getting her heart rate up as she carried them up and down the stairs, trying to tire herself out.

She was tired but wired, still bristling with nervous energy, when she came back into the newsroom and saw Heather sitting on the edge of a desk, dressed smartly in a white blouse and red skirt.

Paddy stopped in the doorway, astonished at her gall. She had at least expected Heather to stay out of the office today. She watched her smile along with some news guys, coyly rolling an elastic band between two fingers, and realized that she had come into the office to capitalize on her coup. She didn't give a shit what Paddy thought of her.

Aware that a small, square body was standing in the doorway, being jostled by people coming in and out, Heather looked up and blushed when she saw who it was, raising a hand in greeting until she saw Paddy's face. She tried to smile, showing all her marvelous teeth, but Paddy didn't flinch. Heather muttered an excuse and slid off the desk, standing up and walking towards the back stairs.

Paddy found her shrill voice filling the entire newsroom. "You." Heather froze. Paddy thumbed over her shoulder. "Out."

Heather stood still for a moment. A hush fell over the mesmerized men. They looked from Heather to Paddy and back again.

Someone tittered. Sensing that she had the support of the audience, Heather crossed her arms and shifted her weight to one leg.

"Do you want to talk here?" Paddy was shouting. "Will I tell them what you did?"

Heather shifted her weight nervously to the other leg. There were few crimes that could not be forgiven in the *News*. Stealing a colleague's wallet from their jacket was bad, sleeping with their wife wasn't good either, but using someone else's story was unforgivable. Everyone appreciated the threat of losing a good story.

Heather uncrossed her arms, dropping them awkwardly to her sides, where they twitched and hung still. She turned and walked reluctantly over to Paddy, who held the door open and followed her out onto the landing and pointed her across the lift lobby and into the ladies' loo. Back in the newsroom a huge falsetto whoop was followed by a gale of derisory laughter.

Heather began her defense before the toilet door had even banged shut. "I knew you weren't going to use the story. You told me you couldn't. I didn't see any harm since you weren't going to." She lit a cigarette and offered the packet to Paddy.

Paddy didn't take one. She looked at the

packet and felt her lip tremble. "My whole family'll think I did it."

It was the one soft moment when Heather could have sympathized and made it all right, but she was frightened and ashamed and missed her cue. "Look, things can't just be nicey-nice all the time. I'm not in this business to get popular. I'm sorry, but that's just the game we're in." She crossed her arms over her chest again, not defensive but elegant this time, her cigarette hand resting on her upper arm. A clean thread of smoke rose high above the cubicle doors, making her taller.

There were so many reasons why what she had done was wrong that the words in Paddy's mind became entangled. She opened her mouth to speak but stammered loudly and stopped, shocked at herself. Heather's eyes widened triumphantly.

"Never mind," she said, placing the cigarette between her lips.

Paddy slapped Heather so hard that she snapped the cigarette in half. The amputated tip bounced once on the floor and continued smoking. They stood for a moment staring at it, both shocked, a red blush flowering Heather's cheek. Paddy was nervous but excited. She shouldn't have done that. She was a bully. It was wrong.

She reached roughly around the back of Heather's head, grabbing the thick blond hair at the nape. Roots popped from Heather's scalp as she tugged, dragging her forwards into a toilet cubicle, shoving her head into the bowl, and yanking the handle. Paddy watched the water swirl around her head, catching her thick hair, sucking the tail of it down through the U-bend. Heather spluttered and tried to stand up, using all the strength in her back. She was very strong, but Paddy used her weight, leaned against her neck, and kept her down. The toilet water saturated Heather's blouse: Paddy could see the adjusting clips on her bra strap. Farquarson might sack her for attacking another member of staff. It would placate Sean if she did get sacked. It might even convince her family that it wasn't her who wrote the article. The recession couldn't last too long; she'd get another job somewhere.

She lifted her hand away and stepped back, watching Heather bounce up from the bowl gasping, throwing her head back, her hair tracing a great wet circle through the air. She turned to Paddy, astonished, her mouth hanging open, panting for air. Paddy saw the fright in her eyes. She couldn't look at her anymore. She turned and left the toilet.

Out in the lobby Paddy's hot face throbbed. She was ashamed and a little shocked by what she had done. It was ignoble and undignified and thuggish and she wouldn't have thought herself capable. She loitered on the landing, listening to the rumble from the newsroom, disentangling long blond hairs from the fingers of her right hand as she waited for her blushes to subside.

III

They were laughing at her. Paddy saw them sniggering and glancing over at her as they repeated the story, trailing their hands down from their heads to their shoulders to describe Heather's wet hair. Some guys on the features desk called her over and asked her to go to the stationery cupboard and bring a couple of lady wrestlers.

Everyone who came back from the Press Bar at lunchtime seemed to know what had happened. Paddy guessed that instinctively they would be on her side because Heather was attractive and not yet having sex with all of them, but she didn't care. All she could think about was how embarrassed her mum and dad would be. They'd try to believe her when she insisted the story wasn't her fault, but they'd be wrong. It was her fault. She knew that professional journalists made difficult choices, tricked information out of people, and broke confidences for stories. She'd been prepared to steal the letter from Mr. Taylor. A good journalist had to be prepared to take off-the-record asides and turn them into stories. She should have known. She was a naive idiot.

She was in the canteen, queuing for teas and practicing her apology to Sean, when Keck approached her looking serious and angry, vicariously annoyed on behalf of the management as he told her that he was to get the teas for the news boys because Farquarson wanted to see her.

"He's in his office," he said, sliding in front of her in the line, keeping his back to her as if she had already been sacked.

She walked downstairs slowly, loitering on the final landing to catch her breath. She was determined not to cry if he sacked her. The side lights were on in his office and the door was closed, an arrangement that usually denoted some kind of drama. She knocked on the door and he answered immediately. She opened the door a little and slid in.

Papers littered the floor around the desk. Farquarson was trying to break into a catering box of macaroons he had stolen from the canteen, chiseling into the thick plastic around the box with a penknife. He lost his temper and pulled at the plastic, stretching it until it ripped suddenly and the bars spilled in a messy pile on the floor. Farquarson bent down, picked up three and started to unwrap one. He nodded Paddy towards the pile. "Get stuck in."

Paddy picked up a bar and thanked him. She opened the wrapper and took a bite, hoping that eating together might establish a bond between them. Macaroon bars were almost too sweet even for her. Made with potato saturated with icing sugar, they made her teeth ache and the skin on her gums wither. Farquarson slid into his seat.

"Meehan," he said through a mouthful of sticky white paste, "a Mr. Taylor phoned this morning to complain. He said he'd been harassed by two journalists from the *Daily News*." He paused to chew. "D'you know anything about the unions in this business? D'you know that *The Scotsman* has just had a weeklong work-to-rule because a journalist winked at a print machine? Richards gave you permission to go out in the car, not to misrepresent yourself as a journalist at the *Daily News* or to steal letters from grieving members of the public. I've calmed Mr. Taylor down and McVie'll keep it quiet, but I don't want you telling anyone you're a journalist again. We could have a walkout on our hands, understand?"

Paddy nodded.

"You'll have to get used to tiptoeing around the unions. It's part of the job." He took another large bite. "Now, are you going to tell me what happened in the ladies'?"

"I had an argument with Heather."

"I thought she had an argument with the lavvy."

It was a stupid joke. Paddy didn't know if it was benign. She looked at her feet and kicked the table leg.

He cleared his throat. "I don't want to know why you did that —"

"She's a shit." She sounded so vicious she surprised herself.

Farquarson looked up, eyebrows raised. "Meehan, I'm not going to umpire."

"But she is a shit."

"Listen, she's been convinced not to make a formal complaint, and I'd drop it if I were you. She's flavor of the month with editorial because she's just brought us a very important story."

"It's not her story," snapped Paddy. "It's my story. Callum Ogilvy's my fiancé's cousin. I saw a picture of him and was upset and I confided in Heather. My family'll disown me when they see today's paper."

Farquarson was very still. "The boy's a relative of yours?"

"I'd never have used that story." Suddenly angry, reckless of the sack and a life at the sink, she slapped the table, hurting her hand. "And what has being Irish Catholic got to do with anything? Why does it say that in the story? If they'd been a Jewish family, would you have put that in the second paragraph?"

"I'm sorry."

"It's not right."

"I can't do anything about it now," he said flatly, "but I understand why you were so angry."

They were quiet for a moment and tried not to look at each other. Farquarson took another bite of macaroon, snapping the bar between his teeth as gently as possible. He chewed quietly until Paddy broke the silence.

"Did the baby die in an accident? Were the boys just playing with him?"

"No, it was murder. They killed him."

"How do they know?"

"Do you really want to know the details?"

She nodded.

Reluctantly, Farquarson rolled his head back and then just told her. "They strangled him and smashed his head in with stones."

"Jesus."

"It was brutal. They stuck things up him. Sticks. Up his backside." Farquarson looked down at the sweet in his hand, suddenly disgusted, and laid it down on the table.

"Could they have the wrong boys?"

"No. Their shoes matched the marks on the ground where the body was found, and his blood was on their clothes."

Paddy was shaking her head before he had even finished the sentence. "Well, blood could get on them any number of ways. It could have been put there. Someone could have put it on them."

Farquarson wasn't entertaining the possibility of a mistake. "He ran for it, the Ogilvy boy. When they went to his school, before they'd even mentioned the baby, he tried to run away."

"That doesn't mean he's guilty," she

said, thinking of Paddy Meehan's arrest and James Griffiths's wild run. "He could have run for any number of reasons. He might just have been frightened."

Farquarson sat back, suddenly tired of tolerating the bolshie copyboy. "Right." He pointed to the pile of macaroon bars. "Take one for your journey and tell me this: Are any of the early-shift boys in yet?"

"A couple," said Paddy, wondering what possible use he could have for them. They never seemed to do any work. "Which ones were you after?"

"Doesn't matter," said Farquarson. "They're all interchangeable."

TWELVE

NO GOOD REASON TO RUN

1969

I

Paddy Meehan heard the mob from half a mile away, chanting in a low, slow bray, getting faster and faster, until he began to sweat with panic, adding to the stench of piss and worry inside the police van. It was nine thirty on a weekday morning, but three hundred people had found the time to gather outside the court to see the bastard charged with old Rachel Ross's murder.

He kept thinking that the van was in the middle of them, that the noise was as loud as it could get, but then another second would pass, the van would move another few feet, and the crowd outside would get louder. When they finally rolled to a stop

the sound was deafening. The two uniformed policemen glanced at each other
nervously, one holding the door handle,
the other holding Meehan's arm. They
turned to the plainclothes CID men sitting
near the back of the van, looking to them
for the signal to go.

"Right, boys," one of them shouted at
the uniforms. "You two stay in front, we'll
follow up and watch his back. On three.
One, two . . ." The blanket went over
Meehan's head, and in the darkness his
face convulsed with terror. "Three."

The rear doors to the van flew open and
the two officers on either side pulled
Meehan into the road. He could see the
pavement below him, the glint from the
coppers' shiny shoes, and the first step up
to the court. Stumbling in darkness, he
heard men's voices and women screaming,
children shouting that he should hang, that
he was a bastard, a murderer. The CID
men grabbed the back of his jacket, reckless of skin, shoving and pushing, hurrying
him up the stairs. The policemen were
frightened. Tightening their lock on his elbows, they lifted him off his feet. In the
sudden darkness beneath the gray blanket,
he heard the fast slap of feet running on
road and encouraging cries from far away.

The policemen jerked sideways as a brown shoe scraped his shin. The assailant was pulled off, and the policemen dragged Meehan up the final steps and bundled him through the doors.

Every time Meehan had ever been in court before, he had waited patiently in the holding cells, but not this time. When they pulled the blanket off him he found himself in a witness room annexed to the court. He couldn't let them see how shaken he was, so Meehan grabbed the nearest CID man by the lapels and screamed out all the terror and panic. "Do your fucking job! Do your fucking job!" They pulled him off, wrestling the grasp of his fingers from the fabric. He was wildeyed and panting. "Find Griffiths. Check my fucking alibi. I gave you his address. What's wrong with you?"

Meehan fell back into a chair and looked down. His trouser leg was soaked with blood from the brown shoe.

This was all wrong. He was a safecracker, a professional for Godsake, a peterman. He learned his trade with Gentle Johnny Ramensky; he had references. He wouldn't get involved in a tie-up. And anyway, he had a solid alibi. He was in Stranraer with James Griffiths on the night of Rachel Ross's murder, and they'd been seen. They had picked up two Kilmarnock girls and driven them home. All they had to do was talk to Griffiths or the girls and he would be free.

II

At the same time that Paddy Meehan's van set out for Ayr High Court, five officers of the Glasgow Criminal Investigation Department were pulling up in a Ford Anglia outside the address Meehan had given them for his alibi, James Griffiths.

Holyrood Crescent was a graceful curve of town houses facing onto private central gardens. Griffiths had a couple of outstanding warrants for car theft, but the officers weren't interested in them. They wanted to know if he would corroborate Meehan's story about the night of Rachel Ross's death.

It was midmorning on a gorgeous summer's day, and the generous trees in the central gardens of Holyrood Crescent were lush and full, rippling in the warm wind. The house had been built as a single dwelling, chopped up into apartments for let to commercial travelers and decent families who were down on their luck but wanted to keep a good address. Detectives had done a reconnaissance of the property earlier that morning. They questioned the caretaker about Griffiths's habits. He would just be getting up now, the man said, and he promised to leave the front door to the house unlocked.

Now the officers were led by their superior up the three flights, following the red stair carpet worn threadbare in the middle. Griffiths's room was on the attic floor, in the old servants' quarters, where the stairs were narrow and listing.

It was a small landing with a single four-paneled door. The first officer to reach the top of the stairs banged on it sharply, shouting, "James Griffiths, open up. It's the CID."

A chair scratched against the floor inside. They glanced at one another.

"Come on, Griffiths, open up or we'll open up for you."

A floorboard squeaked. Griffiths was messing about in there, taunting five officers. The detective inspector pointed to a detective constable and then at the door, motioning for the other officers to back down the steps and give him room. When everyone had finished noisily rearranging themselves around the tiny hall, the DC shouted at the door, "Step back, Griffiths, we're coming in."

He ran at the door, shoulder first, aiming for the lock but hitting and breaking one of the panels, pushing it in so that it flapped open into the bright room, then snapped shut. They saw him for less than a second, and not one of them believed it. Griffiths was sitting on a wooden chair facing the door, a blank expression in his hooded eyes. He wore bandoliers of bullets across his chest, and resting in his lap was a single-barreled shotgun. The DC had had his head bowed against possible splinters from the wood and had seen nothing. He backed up and ran at it again. This time the door panel cracked and snapped off, dropping inside the door.

Framed in the splintered opening, James Griffith rose from the chair, lifting the nose of his shotgun. The first blast hit the DC in the shoulder, spinning him round, the meat and blood of his arm splattering over the landing walls. The second shot hit the ceiling, a plaster-and-horsehair cloud exploding in the air. Policemen tumbled over one another to get down the first narrow flight. They reassembled on the floor below and carried the DC down the rickety stairs in an ungainly blood-smeared scramble as Griffiths fired random shots out of windows and at walls.

Downstairs they ran out into the street and found a passerby lying in the road, shocked and speechless, bleeding from the leg. The DI shouted into the radio that Griffiths had at least one gun, someone thought they saw a rifle as well, send someone with a gun right now, get the army, anyone, because the bugger was firing into the street. They could still hear shooting in the house.

Griffiths fired a last shot from his rifle into the hallway before running out the back door. In the walled garden wooden bedsteads were propped up with veneer peeling off them; broken chairs and a settee were piled up on rotting linoleum. The door to the lane was blocked by a tallboy. Climbing on top of it, Griffiths dropped the shotgun and the rifle over the crumbling brick wall and hoisted himself over, dropping down the far side. He picked up his guns and ran down the back lane.

He felt higher than he ever had in his life, like stealing cars times ten. He was a lifelong criminal and knew the score. The police wouldn't let him live after this. He wouldn't have to face the consequences. It would be like before, when he robbed or got chased, but he wouldn't ever go to jail again.

Ecstatic that this was his final day he ran faster, stumbling on the uneven ground, acutely sensitive to the wind pushing his hair off his face, the warm, damp breeze on his skin. His shirt flapped loose around his body, feet landed on damp turf, and his own, lonely heart thumped hard in his chest. The high walls dropped away and he was in a bright residential street. The sudden sun frightened him, so he raised his rifle and fired three times. He could see figures running, melting into the brightness, and then, as if the fact of other people had been a mistake, he was alone again.

He breathed, felt the sun prickle at the sweat on his brow, heard his breath suck in, push out. His hand was sweating on the steel of the gun barrel. Streets away a car stopped too quickly. He wanted to be alone, but when he was alone he got confused. He needed an audience to be brave in front of. He was too excited to drive, too heated up. He needed a drink.

It was a small pub with an unassuming exterior, painted black, with red trim on the high windows. Inside, two old men sat at separate tables. One was reading a paper, keeping up the pretense that a quarter gill of whisky at half ten in the morning was a casual enjoyment. The other old man stared straight ahead, dead-eyed, dreading the last of his glass.

The day gleamed through the windows, but the sunlight didn't temper the gloom. The pub was peaceful, a contemplative pocket of calm reflection. Behind the bar was the charge hand, a well-built ex-boxer named Connelly, who was looking down his flattened nose at the glass he was drying when Griffiths kicked the swing door open into the stale and dusty room. Connelly looked up, smiling at Griffiths's bandoliers, thinking he was in fancy dress.

"I'll kill the first man that moves," shouted Griffiths. The two old men froze, the newspaper reader holding his glass still to his mouth. "I've shot four policemen this morning."

Griffiths stood up on the foot rail and grabbed a chubby bottle of brandy from behind the bar, uncorking it and drinking from the neck. It tasted peppery and exciting. Griffiths saw himself standing there, taking what he wanted, and felt like giggling. Instead he swung his shotgun vertical, fired into the ceiling, and a burst of plaster hit the floor. The man with the newspaper twitched forward to put his glass down and Griffiths spun around and fired the rifle. The dead man slumped forward, a ribbon of red fluttering from his neck to the black floor.

"You bastard," whispered Connelly, dropping the dishtowel to the floor. "You complete bloody bastard." He reached for the brandy bottle and yanked it away from Griffiths's greedy little mouth, dropping it so it bounced and rolled to the wall, glug-glugging its contents to the floor. "Look at him." He pointed at the old man facedown on the table, the flow from the hole in his neck pulsing in time to the noise from the brandy bottle. "Look at Wullie. Look what you've done to that wee man, you bastard."

Unable to contain his anger anymore, Connelly ran out from behind the bar, and Griffiths could see that he didn't care how many guns he had.

"Out! Get out of my fucking pub!" Connelly took hold of Griffiths's shirt and pulled him towards the door. Griffiths scrambled for purchase, holding his rifle and shotgun tight to his body. Connelly let go and Griffiths backed out hurriedly through the door, instantly swallowed by the white summer light. Connelly shouted after him, "And fucking stay out, an' all!"

He just had time to take a deep breath and convince himself not to chase the guy into the street when three shots ripped through the open door, one of them tearing the sleeve off his shirt. Connelly contracted, bending his knees and stiffening his thick neck, and sprang through the wall of light, screaming to the full capacity of both his lungs.

"Arsehole!"

But Griffiths had run off, lifting the two unwieldy guns up high to shoulder height as he legged it around the corner. He was out of sight, but Connelly knew exactly where he had gone: everyone in the street was frozen still, staring at the first right corner. Cars had stopped in the middle of the street so that drivers could stare.

Around the corner, a long-distance lorry driver who had parked to consult a map of Glasgow heard a series of bangs. He looked up to see what appeared to be a small, hatless Mexican bandit running towards him, followed by an angry muscleman a hundred yards behind. The cab door opened next to him and a shotgun barrel was pointed at his face.

The man fell out of the lorry and Griffiths swung himself up into the cab, started the engine, and sped off, leaving Connelly standing by the side of the road, so angry that he kicked a wall and broke three small bones in his toes.

Griffiths managed two miles. His last ever turn was into the center of a Springburn cul-de-sac. He stopped the engine and pulled on the hand brake. A packet of Woodbine cigarettes was sitting under a yellowed newspaper on the dashboard. He sat back in the seat and lit one with a match, watching the entrance to the cul-de-sac in the nearside mirror. He couldn't back out; he was convinced that the police were right behind him. He waited, smoking his cigarette and watching. They didn't come.

Sure that they were waiting around the corner, he slowly opened the driver's-side door and dropped the yellow newspaper onto the ground, expecting a police bullet to hit it. Nothing happened. The paper fell into the road with a soft thud. The summer wind flicked through the crispy pages. Griffiths reasoned that he must be in a blind spot. He stepped out tentatively, holding his guns across his chest. His footing slipped as he stepped down from the high cab and he landed heavily on his heel, feeling slightly foolish for the very last time.

Resting his guns on his hips, he stepped away from the cab. He pointed the guns at a streetlight, at an already broken tenement window, at the entrance to the road. He was scaring the locals, the coppers, making the law wait for him for once, standing like the cowboys did in the movies.

There was no one there. The unarmed police had kept too much of a distance and had lost him. The street Griffiths was in was derelict; the tenements were damp and rat infested. James Griffiths's last living moments in the soft summer air were pissed away, like his life, posing for an audience that wasn't watching.

Over and beyond the surrounding tene-ments he could hear children laughing and screaming, enjoying the summer holidays. A magpie flew over his head, a beautiful flash of turquoise on its broad, black wing, and Griffiths suddenly felt profoundly sad to be leaving. It had been a poor excuse for a life. A surge of self-pity prompted him to run, and he bolted for the farthest tenement, running through the close mouth and up the stairs. It was a rotten building: patches of plaster the size of a child were missing from the burgundy walls, the windows on the landings were all smashed. He ran all the way up to the top floor and kicked open a door.

It was an abandoned room and kitchen; dirty gray net curtains flapped at the broken window. The walls were lumpy and stained brown by galloping damp. Through the window he could see a swing park, sliced in half by the shadow cast by the building. This is where it was going to end, in a dirty flat with a bad smell and a broken window. He stood and caught his breath, tears itching at his eyes. They might not shoot him. They might talk to him and convince him to give himself up and send him back to pokey forever. Or else he might escape and be forced to go somewhere else and start all over again. Waiting, always waiting, for it to go wrong again.

Griffiths pulled up a stool next to the window and, raising his telescopic rifle, started to shoot at the children in the light.

The last thing James Griffiths saw was a gun barrel sliding through the letter box towards him and a tiny puff of smoke and flame. As the bullet flew towards him, his brain sent out a signal to smile. The impulse didn't have time to reach the muscles of his face before the bullet pierced his heart.

III

Meehan was in the van, being driven back to his remand cell in Barlinnie Prison. His shin had stopped bleeding but it still throbbed, drawing his mind back to the mob outside the court. He thought of James Griffiths fondly, hoping he wouldn't be too annoyed that he had given the police his home address, that he would understand how desperate he had felt. Griffiths hated the police; he wouldn't like them knowing where he stayed, but it was just a rented gaff. He could move. Meehan would offer him the deposit for a new place.

The detective chief inspector waited until the van was on the main road to Glasgow and an officer was on either side of Meehan, ready to grab him if he went nuts. He told him that Griffiths was dead, that he had committed suicide after a long shootout with many dead. When they searched Griffiths's dead body they found paper in his car coat pocket that matched a sample taken from Abraham Ross's safe.

The officers on either side of Meehan watched for a reaction, ready to jump up and give him a doing if he lashed out. Meehan had to be told three times that his friend was dead. Completely. Not sick, not winged. Dead. He sat back, pressing his head against the wall of the van. The plant of the paper from the safe would convict him, Meehan knew it. It was the Secret Service. They were setting him up because of Russia.

He waited until they got back to Barlinnie and he was put in a holding cell, one of a row of cupboard rooms at the drop-off yard with their names chalked onto the door. Naked and ready for the search, Meehan turned his back to the Judas window and sobbed with panic.

IV

That same sunny morning lingered in Rutherglen while small girls and boys gathered excitedly in the courtyard of St. Columbkill's RC Chapel. The class had been given lessons on confession for weeks beforehand. Despite having the theological basis explained to them over and over, in detail and by analogy, only the already very damaged children could properly grasp the concept of sin. All the confession meant to young Paddy Meehan was washing her soul so that she could make her first communion and wear a big white dress with flowers embroidered on the hem and a blue velvet cape. Paddy got her photo taken in Mary Ann's cape when it had been her turn. Even the three Protestant Beattie girls next door got their photo taken in the cape and veil, though they asked the Meehans not to show their mum, because she was in the Orange Lodge and marched against Popery in the summer when the weather was nice.

The boys from her class knelt in front of her in the warm, dusky chapel. They giggled and nudged one another in the pew, growing increasingly bold until spindly Miss Stenhouse walked silently out of the dark side chapel and glared at them, picking one out for a silent finger-point. The boys slid apart in the pew, only seven and still biddable with a look.

The confessional was dark and fusty, like the inside of a cupboard. Behind the trellis window she could see the brand-new parish priest, an old man with hair up his nose whom no one was allowed to laugh at because he was a priest. He was staring at his knees. He waited for a moment before prompting her to begin.

Paddy said her lines, repeating them singsong-style, hearing the rest of the class chant along with her in her head.

"Forgive me, father, for I have sinned. This is my first confession and I have committed the sin of being disrespectful to my mother and father. I stole sweets from my sister and I lied about it and my brother Martin got the blame —"

"And did you own up then?"

Paddy looked up.

"When your brother was blamed for your theft, did you own up then?"

Paddy hadn't been told about the priest speaking. It was throwing her off. "No."

He exhaled a whistle through his hairy nose and shook his head. "Well, that's very bad. You must try to be honest."

Paddy thought she was honest, but a priest was saying she wasn't, and priests knew everything. She was afraid to tell him more.

"Are you sorry for what you did?"

"Yes, Father." Martin always blamed her when he did things. He always did.

"And what other sins have you committed?"

Paddy took a deep breath. She'd peed up

a close once and hit a dog on the nose for snarling. She couldn't tell him those things, they were even worse than blaming Martin. She took a breath and abandoned herself to the terrible sin of not making a good confession. "I can't think of any others."

He nodded heavily. "Very well." He muttered absolution, gave her a penance of five Hail Marys and two Our Fathers, and dismissed her.

Kneeling in the front row of the chapel, Paddy looked at the child next to her. The girl was counting off three fingers as her lips moved through the prayers. Paddy owed God seven fingers. It seemed to her infinitely, grotesquely unjust. Ostentatiously holding up three fingers, Paddy looked around at the moving lips and closed eyes of the other children and smiled sweetly to herself as she began to mutter quickly: One potato, two potato, three potato, four . . .

After the confession, just before tea, Paddy stood in the front room of their house, swaying to a song on the wireless. Her two brothers were fighting on the settee, while Rory, their ginger dog, tried to join in, his hard pinkie sticking out under his tummy.

The news came on the wireless, and the very first story made them all listen. The north of Glasgow had come to a standstill when a man went around shooting at people. The boys stopped wrestling and listened. Rory's pinkie retracted. The man had killed two policemen and injured four passersby. The police had shot him dead, and Paddy Meehan had been charged with murder.

The boys sat up and looked at their little sister, mouths dropping open, eyes wide with wonder.

Outside St. Columbkill's girls were showing off their white dresses, the boys just pleased to be together and outside. Paddy knew she would die. Her mother had dressed her carefully in Mary Ann's white dress. She had white gloves, made of a material so fine that the seams on the fingers were visible from the outside. On her feet she wore lace-trimmed ankle socks and white sandals that she would grow into. Her soul was too dirty for communion: some splinter of her was a murderer.

She once saw her father, Con, pick up a frying pan of smoking oil and run a tap into it. The water exploded, carrying particles of scalding oil through the air. Con still had red speckles on his neck. This is how it would be when she took communion in her mouth, Paddy knew it: cold water into hot oil.

Mass was conducted by her hairy-nosed confessor. He spoke throughout in the priestly four-step, a punctuation-free method of delivery that bleached all interest and meaning from his words:

> And now we see
> That God so loved
> The world that he
> Gave his only begotten
> Son for our sins

Suddenly Miss Stenhouse was in the aisle, conducting the children with her fingers, bringing a boy and a girl out of each side to walk up to the altar rail and kneel down. Paddy followed the finger, clip-clopping up to the rail in her white sandals, and knelt on the velvet cushion.

Father Brogan approached, flanked by the altar boys. She was glad he would be there. She hoped he'd get scars on his neck. An altar boy held a silver plate under her chin.

"Body of Christ."

She amen'd, shut her eyes tight, squeezing

a panicked tear from her left eye, and opened her mouth to receive the Holy Eucharist. It melted quickly in her hot mouth. The priest moved off but Paddy stayed on her knees, eyes shut. Miss Stenhouse had to tap her on the shoulder to get her to move.

She crossed herself and went back to kneel in her pew. She grinned at the girl next to her. They giggled high and fast for no particular reason, pushing a prayer book back and forth along the seat while the priest gave the adults communion.

Outside, Paddy had her photo taken many times. Mary Ann got a shot of her cape and then their mother took them to the Cross Café for a double nugget ice cream.

And Jesus didn't do anything. Paddy watched for him at school and at mass. She waited for their dog to die or her parents to fall ill. She waited for weeks.

It was after tea on a particularly bad-tempered day. Paddy and her sisters were hanging listlessly around their living room, climbing over furniture, being mean to one another because they were trapped indoors, frustrated by heavy rain. Their mother was busy in the kitchen and the radiogram was tuned to a local station, turned up loud to drown out the noise of the bickering children. It was the first item on the Scottish news. Paddy Meehan had been convicted of murdering Rachel Ross. He had been sent to live in a prison for the rest of his life.

Mary Ann looked at Paddy. "What have you done?"

Caroline nodded. "You killed a lady."

Paddy tipped her head back and screamed at the ceiling.

When Con Meehan arrived home after work, he sat down in the big chair and pulled his sobbing youngest daughter onto his knee, holding the newspaper open and making sure she was nice and comfy so he could read to her. He read the description of the court, the who-said-what, the technical things she couldn't possibly understand, rolling through it in a boring voice to calm her. Mr. Paddy Meehan had given a speech in the court, he said. He had stood up and talked to them after they found him guilty. "I am innocent of this crime, and so is Jim Griffiths. You have made a terrible mistake," he had said.

Paddy sniffed and wiped her nose dry with the back of her hand. "Is it right, Daddy? Did they make a mistake?"

Con shrugged. "Might be, Sunshine. We all make mistakes. And Mr. Meehan is a Catholic as well."

"Are the people who put him in prison Orange men?"

"They might be."

She thought about it for a moment. "But he didn't do anything wrong."

Con paused. "The prisons are full of innocent men. Mr. Meehan'll have to stay there until they admit it."

Paddy considered it briefly and began to scream again.

"Oof, for petesake." Con stood up, letting her slide messily off his knee to the floor. "Trisha," he shouted, climbing over her and heading for the kitchen. "Trisha, come and do something with her."

While he was out of the room Mary Ann snuck over to Paddy, who was screaming on the floor. She stroked her hair clumsily. "Don't cry, Baddy," she said guiltily, using Paddy's baby name. "Don't, Baddy-baby, don't cry."

But Paddy couldn't stop crying. She cried so much that she threw up her macaroni and cheese.

V

The ongoing drama of Meehan's imprisonment unfolded slowly as Paddy grew up.

179

She read and reread every article and interview, watched the *Panorama* documentary twice, and visited the sites of the case: the high courts in Edinburgh and Ayr and the bungalow in Blackburn Place where Rachel Ross was murdered. She read Chapman Pincher's account of Meehan's trip to East Germany and planned to travel behind the Iron Curtain herself one day to see if she could find corroborating evidence that he had ever been there. The British government said he was a fantasist and had been in an English prison the whole time.

Paddy didn't stop believing in Jesus, but she didn't trust him. Unable to conceive of a world without a central story, she substituted Meehan's, forming it in her mind, replaying his passion and sentence, tracing the buildup to his conviction, trying to shoehorn sense into the mess of his life. Meehan became a noble hero to her, maligned and defamed in a thousand different ways. She drew huge life lessons from the myth and emulated qualities she projected onto him: stoic loyalty, righteousness, dignity, and perseverance. He was released because of the work of a campaigning journalist, so she became a journalist. She gave talks about the case at school and changed her status from pleasant fat girl to intellectual heavyweight.

It was always the myth that fascinated her, never the real Meehan. The real Meehan was morally awkward, compromised by a life of petty burglary, a sour temper, and a bad complexion. Now he was back living in Glasgow, hanging around bars in the city center, spilling his story to anyone who would listen. Several journalists had offered to introduce her, but she didn't want to meet him. She had to face the uncomfortable truth that Meehan wasn't a nice man and he wasn't trying to help anyone but himself.

THIRTEEN

GROCERY VAUGHAN
1981

Every light in the Wilcox house was on and all the curtains sat open, spilling light out into the dark street. Paddy stood on the opposite pavement, her breath crystallizing into speech bubbles, wondering why she had come. She wasn't a journalist, she didn't have a legitimate reason for being there. She was just a stupid fat girl who was afraid to go home and face her mother.

The house was a gray rectangle with a big window on the ground floor and a brown front door. In front sat a little rug of muddy garden, tufts of grass left in the corners where Brian's shoes hadn't worn it away. Surrounding the garden was a fence of three metal ribbons, painted green and chipped. Wee Brian could just have climbed through the bars and wandered off to the busy motorway access road nearby. Anyone might have picked him up.

Paddy had been to the swing park, and it confirmed everything she thought she'd noticed a couple of nights ago. It was tucked well into the middle of the housing scheme, and Callum couldn't have found it accidentally. Even if he had he wouldn't have wanted to play there: it was a kiddie swing park with few attractions for older boys.

She thought of home, and a ball of acid flowered in her stomach. She sagged against the streetlight. If she'd had any money she would have gone to the pictures for the night.

Across the road she saw a flicker in the window. Gina Wilcox was standing in the corner of her living room. She was looking at her hands, and Paddy saw that she was holding a cloth, kneading it. She looked like an ordinary slim young woman cleaning her house, but even from a hundred yards across the road Paddy could see that the woman's eyes were as red as a summer sunset.

Gina stood still, pulling at the cloth for a moment. Her hair was brown and dank, and as she reached up and flattened her hair Paddy saw why. She must have been working cleaning products into it all day, cleaning, cleaning, trying to wipe away the knowledge that her baby wasn't coming back.

An old-fashioned navy blue grocery van with purple and white writing on the side traveled slowly down the hill behind her. It passed by, pulling up at the curb a hundred yards away. The hand-painted declaration on the side of the van announced that it was a mobile grocer's owned and operated by Henry Naismith, Esquire. The door on the back of the van was covered in colorful stickers from fruit importers and biscuit companies. Stuck over the top, wind scorched and peeling in one corner, was a band sticker declaring FRIEND OF BILLY GRAHAM.

In the quiet of the evening she could hear the gentle ratchet sound of the hand brake being pulled tight and then a tinny music-box rendition of the first three bars of "Dixie" sounded from a little horn on the roof. Someone was moving around inside the van, jostling it, and a light inside flickered uncertainly. The door opened and Paddy could see a man unfolding a step to the street. Inside, the light found its note and brightened as the man stood up. He was slim with sharp sideburns and a graying Elvis-style mini-quiff. Approaching customers chased him back up the steps. Inside the van he pulled down a wooden shelf to form a counter between himself and the outside world.

An orderly queue gathered around the steps, a crowd of five women and a man. The women nodded to one another and passed pleasantries, ignoring the man, who pretended to count the change in his hand. Paddy knew that van steps were a woman's arena as much as a pub was a man's. Friendships were made in the queue, gossip exchanged, and reciprocal child care organized.

She stayed well back and waited as they bought bread and glass bottles of fizzy juice; some asked for soap powder; others just after the wooden penny sweet tray the man proffered like a Tiffany's display. She waited until the crowd thinned before approaching.

The van smelled of soap and sweets. The man serving wore a grubby white grocer's coat with yellow action streaks around the pockets. Across his neck was a red slash scar from a long time ago, the soft skin puckered around the shiny stripe.

He smiled expectantly at her. "What can I do ye for?"

"Packet of Refreshers, please."

He reached over to his right, so sure of his stock that he didn't need to look at the shelves, and put the glittery packet of fizzy sweets on the counter.

"Okay, li'le lady. Anything else catch your eye? A loaf? A bottle of ginger?" He pointed to the glass rows of fizzy drink and winked at her.

She grinned at his fake American accent. "Listen, can I ask ye this: those boys who were arrested for . . ." She didn't know how to phrase it. "For hurting Baby Brian. Did they know anyone on this scheme?"

He pulled her change from his money belt and narrowed his lips. "Those filthy wee buggers. I say give them to the women's prison, they'd know what to do with them."

It didn't sound like a very good plan to Paddy. She frowned, and he saw it.

"No," he corrected himself, "you're right, you're right. We need to forgive."

"Aye, right enough," she said awkwardly, moving the conversation on. "Anyway, were they visiting someone here?"

"I heard they were at the swing park."

"Yeah, that's what I heard. I was just wondering, because it's kind of out of the way. Could they have been visiting someone?"

The van man shrugged. "I dunno. If they'd been at a house someone would know about it. Everyone here sees everything. Why are you asking?"

"Dunno." She picked the change up off the counter. "Just wondering about it. Seems funny, know what I mean?"

He looked suspicious. "You don't live here, do you? What are you doing here?"

"I'm a journalist at the *Daily News*," she said proudly, and immediately remembered Farquarson's warning. "My name's Heather Allen."

"Right?" He looked her up and down. "A journalist, is it? I tell ye what, could it be the ice-cream van? Maybe they were passing and heard the van coming. It stops outside the wee boy's garden."

"Really?" She was glad he hadn't pressed her about her career.

He shooed her out onto the pavement and lifted his fold-down counter, following her down the step to show her. "There." He was peering past Gina Wilcox's house. "See the wee lane?"

Paddy couldn't see it at first. She had to strain her eyes through the soupy dark to see the triple railings along the far side of Gina's garden. There was a lane down the side of it.

"That lane leads straight to the main road. The ice-cream van stops just there." He indicated the curb across the road from Gina's house. "Stops there at the back of twelve every day and then at half four again." He looked at her. "That's when the wee man went missing, eh?"

Paddy nodded. "Aye, back of twelve, right enough. Don't know if those boys'd have money for a van, though."

"Aye, well, Hughie keeps a penny tray for the poorer weans." She wondered how he knew so much about it, and he saw the questioning look. "We fell out about it," he explained. "The penny tray was my idea in the first place. His rounds are earlier than mine, so he takes all the custom. He's a snipey bastard."

She pointed at his quiff. "Were you a Teddy boy, then?"

"I *am* a Teddy boy," he said indignantly. "Ye don't stop being what ye are because it's out of fashion."

She looked at his feet and only then noticed his drainpipe trousers and crepe soles. "God, you're very loyal to your style."

"And why not? Tell me this: Who's as good as Elvis now? Who can sing like Carl Perkins these days? None of them."

Paddy smiled at his abrupt energy. "So, I suppose."

"What's your favorite Frankie Vaughan song?"

She shrugged. "Don't know any."

He was disappointed. It had been a test question, she could tell. "Ye don't know any Frankie Vaughan? Not know 'Mr. Moonlight'? Young folk today, I don't know. Do you know what he did for this city?"

"Aye, I know, that I know." The crooner Frankie Vaughan had been so appalled at the levels of violence when he played Glasgow in the fifties that he met the gang leaders and appealed to them to hand in their weapons. He became a totem for peace but was mostly now remembered by those who had caused the trouble in the first place.

"You young ones, yees don't know music at all. I bet you're one of they punkers."

Paddy laughed. "Punk was a hundred years ago."

"Drug music, that's what it is. Frankie should come back here and set them right." He did a little tap dance move, raising a hand, extending a foot, and they laughed together in the soft dark. Paddy wished she didn't ever have to go home.

The van man waved her off and closed up his back door, driving off up the street and leaving her alone.

She wandered up the road, chewing through the frothy Refreshers, and looked into the alley. Beyond the houses and the small back gardens she could see the yellow lights of the main road and the bus stop from Barnhill. The boys could easily have got off there and wandered through to the van. She hadn't read the scheme properly at all. She was wasting her time.

FOURTEEN

MARY ANN IS LAUGHING

I

As Paddy walked to the train station she felt all her future hopes fade. She was too naive to make it as a journalist. She should have known Heather would use the story. Any good journalist would have, anyone who wasn't destined to spend the rest of their career writing obituaries or fashion tips about hemlines and tweed. She'd never make it. She'd have to marry Sean and raise a hundred pyromaniac kids like Mrs. Breslin.

The platform for the low-level train was crammed with people. Paddy joined the end of the crowd of commuters gathered on the stairs. Standing in the dull subterranean light, resting her hip against the damp railing, she tried not to speculate about her mother's or Sean's reaction to her when she got home. All around her on the stairs people were reading papers with headlines about the Baby Brian Boys. It would be particularly hard, she thought, to be a child in trouble with no one to defend you but Callum Ogilvy's mother.

Paddy couldn't recall her name but she remembered her well. After the funeral mass for Callum's father the mourners had gone back to the Ogilvy house. It was dark and dank and poor. Wallpaper had been pulled off in the hall and living room and left on the floor.

By way of a drink, Sean's Auntie Maggie had dished out whisky from a bottle she had brought herself. There weren't any glasses in the house; they had to use chipped mugs and pastel plastic children's beakers. Paddy's beaker hadn't been washed out properly, and a crescent of dried milk floated to the surface, clouding the whisky.

Callum's mother had long, straggly hair that hung from a center parting over her face, slicing away cheekbones and jaw, leaving her as nothing but a pair of dead, wet eyes and bloodless lips. Sometimes her face would slacken, her mouth would fall open, and she would weep, exhausted. She helped herself to other people's cups from the table, getting drunk quickly, disgracing herself. Sean said that she'd been like that before the father died, she'd been like that for a long time, and everybody already knew about it. The mourners had stayed on just as long as was polite and all left at the same time, lifting from the dirty Barnhill house as suddenly as a startled flock of birds.

Paddy had a grudging respect for irresponsible mothers. It wasn't much of a job. Every mother she knew was anxious and fretful and never any fun at all. She tried hard to be respectful of Trisha, tried to appreciate and thank her for all she did, but couldn't stop herself sniggering along when Marty and Gerald made fun of her. All the mothers she knew worked unlauded all their lives, aging before anyone else in the family, until the only thing that differentiated them from old, old men was a perm and a set of earrings.

The train arrived and the commuters pressed forward, carrying Paddy along on the flow of bodies. She wished she could turn back and run up to Albion Street and hide in the office. She was one of the last people to squeeze through the carriage doors before they shut.

As the train pulled away from the platform she imagined herself, wearing smart clothes and a miraculous half-foot taller, swaggering into glamorous rooms with a pan-scope stretched body, asking pertinent questions and writing important articles. All the fantasies felt hollow this evening. She had an ominous sense that a shadow had marked her, that everything was fated to go wrong from here on in. Luck could curdle, she knew. The train pulled out of the dark station, dragging her homeward, delivering her to her people.

II

It was raining hard by the time the train reached Rutherglen, washing away the pretty remains of the snow. Paddy followed the crowd up the steep stairs to the covered bridge.

A crowd of drunks were gathered outside the Tower Bar, a backstreet pub with an entrance next to the public toilets. A recent patron of possibly both establishments was trying to zip up his bomber jacket, attempting again and again to dock the pin in the eye, swaying with the effort of concentration. Another man, the father of a boy she had been at Trinity with, was carefully watching the action, hugging a carryout of two beer cans. Paddy was glad she had her duffel coat hood up — he might have recognized her and tried to speak to her. Eventually the man carrying the party tins lost patience, cut across the straggling crowd coming from the train, and headed up the narrow alley to the Main Street, hurriedly followed by the drunk dresser, yanking his jacket straight.

Rutherglen Main Street's pavements were broad, a reminder of the market past of the town, when its royal charter set it up as a rival to the nearby village of Glasgow. Little of the original town remained. The long winding tail of West Main Street, lined with drovers' cottages and pubs built when Mary of Guise was on the throne, had been knocked down and tarmac'd to make a large new road to other parts of the Southside. In the course of one development, Rutherglen had gone from an ancient market town to an intersection.

Men and women from Castlemilk, the new housing scheme just up the road, would come down to find Republican and Unionist pubs, or pubs that sold drink in the big quarter-gill measures instead of the English eighth. Rolling down the hill to Rutherglen was always less problematic than rolling back up again; after lunchtime and evening closing the Main Street was littered with drunks sleeping on benches, collapsed on pavements, or wide awake and causing grief in shops.

Paddy passed bus stops where waiting workers spilled out onto the road, peering up the street through the rain, watching anxiously for the right number. She passed Granny Annie's dark house and headed up to Gallowflat Street.

Sean lived in a ground-floor tenement flat. Like Paddy, he was the youngest of a large family, but all his siblings had married and left home, and he was the last one left. His mother was a widow and had swapped her council house for the three-bedroom flat she found easier to keep. When she wasn't at home fussing around her precious Sean, she poured all her extra energy into fund-raising for the White Fathers' African missions and other charities. Natural disasters were her favorites.

Through the living room window, Paddy could hear the *Nationwide* theme coming from the Ogilvys' television. The kitchen window was steamed opaque and propped open with a can of beans; the smell of cabbage and pissy boiled washing powder seeped through the narrow opening. Paddy stopped outside the close, resting one foot on the stair, and took a breath. This was best, coming here first. Sean might even come home with her and show her mum that the Ogilvys weren't angry. She thought of Sean's face and felt a great burst of love. She'd never wanted to see him more. She walked up the close and took a breath before pressing the bell.

Mimi Ogilvy opened the door and let out a muted *eek* when she saw Paddy. She had always pretended to like her prospective daughter-in-law because she was a Meehan, but she had confided in Sean that she didn't approve of Paddy having a job with career prospects. It made her seem fast.

"Oh, hiya, Mrs. Ogilvy," said Paddy, wishing that this was going a bit better. "No need to scream, ha. It's just me."

Mrs. Ogilvy fell back into the hall, lifting her pinny in front of her mouth. She called to Sean, keeping her eyes on Paddy. He didn't come immediately, and the two women were left staring at each other, Paddy sporting a nervous smile, Mrs. Ogilvy's shock coagulating into malevolence.

Sean ambled out of the kitchen, chewing a slice of white bread folded in half. He stiffened when he saw it was her.

197

Paddy waved at him. "Hiya," she said feebly.

He stepped in front of his mother and pulled the door half shut, filling the space with his body. Mrs. Ogilvy sniffed a demand for attention behind him. "Get back inside, Ma," he said.

Mimi whispered something that Paddy couldn't hear and backed off. A door slammed behind him.

"Not the Ogilvys' favorite girl, then?"

"Go home, Paddy." He had never spoken so coldly to her before, and it threw her.

"I didn't do it, Sean." She spoke quickly, afraid he would slam the door in her face. "I confided in a girl at work when I saw the picture of Callum, and she sold the story. I only told her because I was upset."

Sean looked past her.

She felt a rising sense of fright. "I swear, Seanie, I promise that's what happened —"

"My ma's gutted. I read it at my work. I was eating my lunch and somebody showed it to me. It wasn't nice."

"You read the paper?" She was surprised, because he never admitted to reading the *Daily News*. It was a point of pride with him, because it was more of a broadsheet than a tabloid.

"Someone else bought it," he explained.

"Sean, would I do that? Would I, Sean?" She was using his name too much, her voice high and wavering. She knew her face was contracted against her will, her mouth stretching wide with fear.

"I don't know what you'd do anymore. I see the article in the paper, it's your paper, what am I supposed to think?"

"But if I'd written it, would I say we were Catholic? Would I mention that?"

He almost smiled. "What're ye saying? You'd betray me and my family but ye wouldn't say a bad word about the church?"

Paddy found she couldn't keep up the supplicant's role anymore. "Well, piss off, then, if you don't believe me."

She heard Mrs. Ogilvy tutting at the swear word behind him. The sneaky old bitch hadn't left the hall at all. Sean stepped back and shut the front door in her face.

Paddy didn't move. She waited for three minutes. Finally he opened again.

"Go away," he said quietly, and shut it again.

III

Paddy walked the two miles home in the rain, more dejected by the step, certain it

199

would be bad in the house. She thought of Meehan's seven-year protest in solitary confinement, of the keening men and women in the political prisons of Moscow and East Berlin, of Griffiths's wasted life and lonely last moments, and knew that other people faced worse than her, but it was cold comfort tonight. She was sure they wouldn't believe she was innocent. They'd have to punish her, and they'd need to let other people know they'd done it. Her parents rarely needed to discipline their children. They only did it when they were forced to, usually by the intractable opinions of their friends, but when they did it had a vicious, nasty edge to it that hinted at aspects of their personalities she didn't want to think about.

She took a deep breath as she fitted her key in the lock. The sound of the door scraping along the carpet protector was the only noise in the house, and the throbbing silence buzzed in her ears. She wanted to call a hello but was worried that it might sound nonchalant. When she hung up her coat in the hall cupboard she noticed that a lot of coats were missing. She took off her shoes and put on her slippers, all the time hoping for a call or a greeting of any kind.

It was eight o'clock but the living room was eerily tidy, no empty cups of tea or folded newspapers on the arms of the chairs. Paddy stopped in the kitchen doorway. Trisha was busy attending to something in the sink and kept her back to the room. Paddy saw Trisha's face reflected in the window, noticed the tension on her neck and the tightness of her jaw. She didn't look up.

"Hello, Mum." She could see herself, nervous, reflected over Trisha's left shoulder.

Trisha stood up straight, keeping her gaze down. She moved over to the cooker, lifted a warmed bowl out of the oven, and carelessly ladled carrot soup into it from a pot. She slammed it onto the kitchen table, flicking her finger at Paddy before turning back to the cooker. Paddy sat down and started to eat.

"That's lovely soup," she said, as she had been saying every teatime since she was twelve.

Without a word, Trisha bent down and opened the oven, took out a plate from a stack of five, and filled it with boiled potatoes from a pot, a portion of wet peas, and lamb stew. She dropped the plate to the table. The potatoes had been boiled too long and were dry and cracked, yellow inside and powdery white on the outside.

Paddy put her spoon down carefully in the soup. "I didn't do it, Mum."

Trisha took a glass from the draining board and ran the cold tap, touching the water to test the temperature.

Paddy started to cry. "Please don't, Mum, don't shun me, please?"

Trisha filled the glass and tipped a drop of orange squash into it, just enough to cloud the water. She put the glass onto the table.

"Mum, I saw the picture of Callum Ogilvy at work and told a girl, and she said I should write the story and I said no." Paddy's nose was blocked and oily tears dripped into the thick orange soup, taking a minute to sit on the surface before dispersing. She struggled to catch her breath. "Then this morning I was on the way to work and I saw the story in the paper. It wasn't me, Mum, I swear it wasn't me."

Trisha stood and looked at the floor, so angry she almost broke the habit of a lifetime and asked why. She turned and left the room. Paddy heard her out in the hall, opening the coat cupboard, tinkling metal hangers. Trisha shucked off her slippers one at a time, stamped on some outdoor ones, and then she was gone, the front door slamming shut behind her.

Paddy ate her soup. Marty had been shunned once when he split up with Martine Holland, a very holy girlfriend. Paddy came home one day and found the girl crying in the living room with Trisha listening and Con running back and forth with cups of tea and wee bits of toast. She never found out exactly what Marty had done, but the family had conferences about him when he was out of the house. He had done a terrible, venal thing to the girl. It was up to them as a family to teach him the difference between right and wrong, to guide him with love and patience onto the right path. They would ignore him, behave as if he weren't there, and they would do it for a full three days. Paddy remembered sitting at the table in the kitchen when Marty came in that evening. They all fell silent. He started to make himself a sandwich, dropped the knife, and walked out of the kitchen, leaving the bread half buttered on the plate. When Trisha gave them permission to start talking to him again, Paddy saw him tearful with relief. He didn't get back with Martine, and it was a year before he went out with a girl. He never brought them home now and had never recovered his place in the family. What Paddy remembered most about the shunning was the cozy sanctimosity of being on the inside.

Paddy ate her stew and the powdery potatoes. Then she had some ice cream, and then went back for some more even though she was very full. She sat in front of the television for a while, until Gerald came in at half nine. He called hello through the house but dropped his voice when he saw the back of Paddy's head in the good armchair. He took off his coat in silence. She turned on him as he came through the living room heading for the kitchen.

"You shit, Gerald," she said. "You don't even know what happened."

He kept his eyes down and nodded at her sorrowfully, implying that she had brought this on herself.

"Are you not speaking to me? It wasn't even me."

Gerald shrugged again, averting his eyes.

"You fucking arsehole," she said, standing up.

"I'm gonnae tell Mum you said that."

"I'm gonnae tell Mum you spoke to me," she said, storming off upstairs.

IV

Paddy had been lying in bed for three hours, listening as each member of the family came home, found she was in bed, and relaxed. She heard the television go on, listened to the formless sound of chat in the kitchen, heard them moving into the living room when they realized she wasn't coming down. Marty spoke especially loudly, laughing heartily a couple of times, and she couldn't but feel he was getting his own back. Her dad, she noticed, said hardly a word. He would be terribly hurt. She wondered if Trisha would whisper to him when they went to bed, as they heard her do sometimes, and tell him that Paddy had said it wasn't her. Con had never been the same with Marty after his shunning. He contradicted him in everything and never joked with him anymore.

Someone shut the living room door and the noises downstairs became muted and indistinguishable. They were having a conference about her behavior and the article. She could only imagine how bad it sounded.

She comforted herself by following Sean around his bedtime routine: setting out his clothes for the morning on a chair, brushing his teeth, getting into bed, pushing the pillows onto the floor so that he could lie flat on his stomach. She smelled his hair and touched the mole on his high cheekbone. He wrapped his arms around her and told her it would be okay and not to worry. A week on Saturday was Valentine's Day. They always went to the pictures together on Valentine's and shared a chicken supper on the way home. She ran through their past three Valentine's dates: the rainy one; the one when she was on an herb diet and could only smell the deep-fried meat and lick a chip; and the last one, when he proposed for the first time and she said no.

Her dark room was cold, and the wind outside shook the lone tree far away at the bottom of the garden. She heard the radiator tick, tick as the heating was turned off and the metal contracted.

She waited until she was bursting for a pee so that she wouldn't have to go twice before she fell asleep. At the head of the stairs she turned on the light, pausing outside the bathroom door, giving the silverfish a head start. Downstairs, the lonely voice of a news reader murmured. The family was listening to her move.

Paddy used the loo and washed her hands and face. She was drying them on the hand towel when she heard the living room door open and a soft footfall on the stairs. She froze, watching him through the mottled glass. Marty stopped outside, running a hand through his curly black hair, head dipped as if he was going to whisper to her through the door. She listened carefully. He didn't speak, but his cheeks bunched as if he was smiling. He straightened his arm, reached out to the door frame, and snapped off the light.

She watched him from the dark, his splintered shape dropping down the stairs and disappearing, leaving her with imaginary silverfish swarming over her feet.

One by one her family came up to bed, taking turns in the bathroom, whispering good nights on the landing as they passed each other, pretending that they thought she was asleep, when they all knew she was hiding.

Mary Ann sidled into the room on tiptoes and picked up her wash bag from her chest of drawers and her nightie from under her pillow, leaving the door open so that the bright light from the hall lit her way. When she came back she shut the door carefully behind her, clambered under the covers, and rolled over onto her side, turning her back on Paddy.

Paddy had been brave and angry all night, but she couldn't keep it up anymore. She tried to disguise her breathing by biting the blankets. She knew Marty deserved his shunning but never thought they would do it to her. Everyone at work thought she was a fat joke, and everyone at home hated her. She found herself descending to that level of self-pity God had reserved for teenagers when she felt a slap on her shoulder. She rolled over a little.

Mary Ann's eyes looked like little currants in the dark. She was hanging off her own bed, slapping Paddy on the arm, silently laughing a desperate request for a smile. Paddy couldn't. She shook her head and pulled the covers up to her mouth, trying not to cry.

"I didn't do it," said Paddy, her voice less than a murmur.

Mary Ann reached across and pulled Paddy's wet hand away from her face, squeezing it tight. She held it until her wee sister fell asleep, and then she got out of bed and tucked Paddy's chubby arm under the covers. She sat on the side of Paddy's bed, smiling until her teeth dried and her lips stuck to them, until her feet went numb with the cold.

FIFTEEN

URBAN HEROES OUT OF PUB BORES

I

Sneaking down an hour earlier than usual for breakfast, hoping to miss everyone, Paddy paused on the stairs, listening for noises, for the high tink of spoons hitting crockery or a thunk of teacups meeting the table. The house was silent. She crept down and was in the kitchen doorway before she realized that the entire family had also risen early, hoping to miss her, and were sitting in an awkward silence around the table.

She couldn't back out. They tensed collectively as she approached, looking for a chair. The only free place was next to her father. He stared manically at the back of the Sugarpuffs packet while Paddy pulled over the foldaway step stool and sat down.

She poured herself a cup of tea from the pot.

Con cleared his throat several times. Gerald glanced around the table from place to place, silently urging someone to do something, while Trisha banged plates around in the sink. Marty was the only one who seemed half content. He looked around happily, humming the chorus of "Vienna" to himself.

Trisha began the exodus. She abruptly abandoned her cleaning and left the room. Gerald finished up quickly and ran upstairs. Con left without finishing his porridge. Marty took his time, helping himself to a luxurious extra half slice of toast while Paddy and Mary Ann watched him. Eventually his affected calm ran out and he left too.

Paddy looked across the wreckage of the table to her sister. Mary Ann raised her eyebrows in surprise. "Oo," she said, and then laughed until her face turned puce.

II

It was a disgusting cover page. The main story was a picture of Baby Brian under the mawkish headline AGONY OF OUR BRIAN, four words that managed to imply not only that the child had suffered terribly but that he had, shortly beforehand, become the property of the *Scottish Daily News*. It had been written during a late editorial meeting as a compromise, a blind guess at what the public wanted to hear by senior editors so jaded they couldn't recall the taste or flavor of genuine sentiment. A pall of sticky shame hung over the newsroom, implicating everyone, pricking journalists' tempers so that they picked on the juniors, shouted at copyboys, and complained about everything. Two hours into the shift, half the staff was pissed and the other half was downstairs in the Press Bar working at it.

Heather appeared at the newsroom door. Paddy could tell that she had dressed carefully to give herself confidence: her hair was very big, extra back-combed, and she was wearing a red double-breasted blazer, like a junior executive.

Keck, to the left of Paddy on the bench, nudged her. "Check out that tart," he said. "She's gagging for it."

Dub sighed heavily on Paddy's other side, muttered that Keck was a crippled-dick wanker, and went back to his reading.

A light hush fell over the newsroom.

Paddy looked up and realized that half of the news desk and all of the sports desk were watching her, amused and waiting for a reaction.

A sports boy stood up and held his nose, announcing loudly into his fist, "And in the red corner . . ." Everyone laughed. Heather smiled graciously, dipping her head down and taking it all in good part. Paddy, raw and guileless, stared at her feet miserably until Keck nudged her.

"Smile. Act like you don't care."

"To hell with them," said Paddy, too loud, alienating anyone who had taken her side. "I'm not in the least bit bothered what those stupid old bastards think."

III

She usually left the building for her lunch, preferring to wander around the town rather than sit in the canteen, fending off suggestive conversations that were kindly meant but creeped her out. Today she was angry and fit for any one of them. She took her lunch alone, sitting at a small table tucked at the side of the busy canteen, sipping milky coffee and eating a squashed-fly slice in three inches of custard for a wee treat. She covered the tabletop with copies of the *Daily News*, the *Record*, and the *Evening Times*, reading and rereading the Baby Brian stories, carefully teasing out the facts from among the treacle.

The coverage was the same from paper to paper, with some phrases consistent from story to story, so she knew they had been lifted directly from the police's press statement. The two arrested boys were playing truant from school that day and had walked to Townhead from their homes in Barnhill. Every single story mentioned the fact that the children were alone, that there were no adults with them at any point. They were so adamant about the detail that Paddy guessed that all the journalists must have pressed the question at the police briefing. The boys had taken Brian from his garden to Queen Street station, less than half a mile downhill into the town. They took the train to Steps, a country station eight minutes away. When they arrived at Steps they walked up the long ramp to the quiet country road, crossed it, led the child through a break in the fence, down to the tracks, and killed him there.

Paddy found it hard to understand why the boys had gone all the way to Steps.

The whole of Barnhill was rich in abandoned yards and empty tracts of land that wee wild kids from the area played on and knew better than anyone else. She remembered looking out at the landscape through the beaded window of the bus, on the way back to the Southside with the Ogilvy mourners. They had passed St. Rollox, a dying train coach engineering works with innumerable crumbling outbuildings. She had seen fields of blackened, twisted metal, abandoned railway lines, and another yard of what looked like rows of ingredients set out in good order: huge containers of sun-yellow sand, stacks of timber, and coils of wire as tall as a man. Small boys would know a hundred hiding places for a guilty secret.

Aware of a shadow at the side of the table, she looked up and found the chief reporter, JT, hovering near her. He smiled modestly, self-consciously, as if thinking of himself as seen by her and, oddly, supposing himself admired. He couldn't have thought himself attractive: he had a round face that fell into his neck and a nose covered in prominent blackheads. Paddy was suddenly conscious of a thin rim of custard at one side of her mouth.

"Mind if I sit?"

She gathered up all the newspapers, arranging them into a tidy pile, and JT sat down, putting a mug of tea on the table together with a plate of chips zigzagged with ketchup, a bacon roll perched on top.

"Thanks so much." He smiled again, taking off his suede jacket and throwing it onto the windowsill with what he imagined was panache. "How are you, Patricia? Are you all right?"

He couldn't have heard anyone say her name. He must have seen it written down. She smiled but didn't answer.

"When I first came here copyboys wouldn't have been allowed to eat in the canteen with journalists." A smile twitched at one corner of his mouth. "I was a copyboy once, at the *Lanarkshire Gazette*. Can ye *believe* that?"

He left a space for her to respond, so she did.

"Can I believe that a man as important as you was ever a copyboy, or that Lanarkshire had its own gazette?"

He ignored her, continuing with the conversation he wanted them to be having. "In those days a copyboy sitting in the canteen would have been as welcome as a fart in a space suit." He smiled and looked away, leaving a pause for her laughter. She didn't

215

fill it. The crack was a Billy Connolly joke, circa 1975. JT was trying to sound like him, all drawly delivery and camp surprise. Since Connolly's rise to stardom a lot of dull Glaswegian men had started monkeying his delivery without having the material. He had made an urban hero of the pub bore.

It seemed it was Paddy's turn to speak again. " 'S that right?"

"Aye, aye, that's right." He looked suddenly sad. "Patricia, are you all right?"

She nodded.

He dropped the Connollyesque bonhomie and spoke in a careful, tiptoey tone, the sort of voice an adult would use to lie to a child. "Really? Can you be feeling all right? Well, why are you sitting here?" He gestured to the throbbing mass of the canteen. *"Alone."*

She was sitting by herself because the other option was listening to ugly old men making snide jokes about her tits for forty minutes. "I got sent on first lunch."

"Are you sure you're all right?"

"Uh huh."

JT dropped his voice to a whisper. "The past few days must have been awful for you."

Paddy looked at him for a minute, letting her eyes have the run of his unctuous face. If George McVie had been sitting there doing the act he did on Mr. Taylor, she'd have opened up a little at least before re-membering to be cautious. She had ad-mired JT, but only by reputation and results. Close up he was a weasel. She sud-denly understood why the other journalists hated him so blatantly.

He leaned over the table, waiting for an answer.

"Yeah, well, you know . . ."

He looked at her empty cup. "D'you want another coffee? I'm going to have one. Have one, on me." He stood up and turned back, waving over at Kathy serving behind the now quiet counter. He raised an imperious finger. "Two coffees over here." He turned back to Paddy, smiling and muttering con-fidingly, "Let's see if we get them."

Behind him, Kathy whispered to her boss, Scary Mary, who looked angrily over at JT and shouted, "Self-service." She held up a small card from next to the till and shook it at him. "Self-service!"

JT didn't hear her. "So, Patricia —"

"Look, everyone calls me Paddy."

"I see. Well, *Paddy,* I heard that you're related to one of the boys who did this . . ." He tapped the word "evil" on the stack of papers and shook his head. "Dreadful, *dreadful.*"

Paddy hummed in agreement.

JT tipped his head to the side. "Are you close to him?"

"No," she said, hoping he'd be disappointed. "He's my fiancé's wee cousin. I've only met him once, and that was at his father's funeral."

"I see, I see. Can you get me in to him?" She was too shocked to be indignant. "No."

"What's your fiancé called?" She had the presence of mind to lie. "Michael Connelly." She could almost hear his brain making the scratchy sound of graphite on paper.

He nodded. "What would make someone do that to a child?" He left the question hanging in the air.

"Well, the boys are only ten or eleven years old themselves."

JT shook his head. "These were hardly children. Sure, we all did stupid things when we were kids, but did you ever lure a toddler away and kill him for fun?"

Paddy looked at him, dead-eyed. He had adopted without question the lazy, pat explanation.

"No," said JT, oblivious to the waves of hate coming from his audience of one. "That's right. Neither did I."

"They're children," said Paddy.

JT shook his head. "These boys aren't children. The age of legal responsibility is eight in Scotland. They'll be tried as adults."

"They don't stop being children just because it doesn't suit us anymore. They're ten and eleven. They are children."

"If they're children, why were they so sneaky about it? They hid on the train to Steps. No one saw them."

Surprised, she half laughed. "No one saw them?" she echoed.

He was disconcerted. "The police are still appealing for witnesses. It was in the evening. It's quiet then."

"How does anyone know they took the train, if they weren't seen?"

"They had tickets on them."

"I bet they don't find any witnesses that can put them on that train."

"Oh, they definitely will. They'll find a witness whether anyone saw them or not. They always do in missing-kid cases. Women, always women, see kids everywhere. I don't know if it's for attention or what, but some woman'll say she's seen everything." He looked at her, his breath drawn, on the verge of drawing a conclusion about the stupidity of women. He stopped himself.

Scary Mary was at the side of the table,

holding the sign from the till, waiting for JT to look up. "Self-service canteen," she said again, furiously shaking the small card in his face. "The clue's in the fucking name." She sucked her teeth noisily and moved off.

A silence fell over their end of the room, everyone smirking, enjoying JT's humiliation. JT glared at Paddy.

"I think those boys are innocent," she said unreasonably.

JT coughed indignantly. "Of course they're not, ya mug. They had the child's blood all over them. Of course it was them." He looked her up and down, then, sensing that he had lost her, softened his approach. "How are your family coping?"

Paddy picked up her coffee cup and held it to her mouth. " 'S hard," she said, taking a sip to cover her mouth. "Michael's very upset."

"You know," he said, dropping his voice, "even as an employee of the *News*, we could pay you for information."

She drank the dregs of her coffee, narrowing her eyes.

"We could go as far as three hundred for your story and name."

With three hundred quid Paddy could move out of her parents' house. With three hundred quid she could enroll for night classes, do exams, get into university, and come back and eat them all.

JT's eyes brightened when she lowered the cup from her mouth. She lifted it again, drinking down to the very last frothy dribble. JT tilted his head to the side, as if she had been talking and he was waiting for her to continue.

"D'you know what?" She carefully sat the cup in the saucer.

"What's that?" JT tilted his head the other way, all plastic sympathy.

"I'm late. I'd better get back or I'll get my arse felt."

She gathered her papers and worked her way out of the seat, standing on tiptoes to get past the back of his chair. JT was the best they had, but Paddy knew she could do better than that. She could take his job in a few years.

IV

The clippings library was a corridor-shaped room blocked off by a counter four feet inside the door.

The librarians were strict enforcers of demarcation and guarded their tasks and spaces as ferociously as blood-sodden borderlands. No one who was not a librarian was permitted behind the counter. They were not allowed to lean their hands over the counter or even to shout down into the library space. Paddy suspected that they were so defensive because their job was easy and involved nothing more than cutting out paper with blunt scissors and filing.

Beyond the counter, running along a fifty-foot wall, was a gray metal filing system containing clippings from all the past editions of the *Daily News*. The clippings were arranged alphabetically by subject and stored in cylindrical drums like metal Rolodexes. Against the other long wall was a large, dark wooden table. All three of the librarians were sitting at it doing the cuttings, subject by subject, of every article in the paper that day. Part of the copyboys' responsibilities was to bring a bale of each new edition down to them.

Helen, the head librarian, dressed smartly in twin sets, tweed skirts, and shoes with a token heel. She wore her brown hair pinned up at the back, lacquered solid so that the individual hairs were hardly discernible to the naked eye. Although Helen Stutter was graceful and well dressed, Paddy thought she was a torn-faced bitch obsessed with the hierarchy of the paper who treated anyone beneath the level of editor with bald contempt. The management loved her and genuinely couldn't understand why no one else did. Paddy dearly hoped that Helen was still working there if she ever got promoted.

Helen glanced over the top of her reading glasses towards the counter, seeing that someone was there but that it was no one important. She ignored Paddy, casually twisting the red plastic beads on her glasses chain. Paddy drummed her fingers, not loudly or for attention, just because she was tense and about to tell a lie.

Helen looked up again, sucked in her cheeks, and raised an eyebrow before dropping her eyes to the paper.

"I'm here for Mr. Farquarson. I need a set of clippings for him."

Helen looked up for a third time and chewed her cheek for a moment before pushing the chair back violently and coming to the counter. She pulled out one of the small gray forms and put it on the countertop, staring Paddy out as she reached underneath for a pen. Paddy didn't want a form that could be referred to later if she got into trouble.

"Search word 'Townhead,'" she said quickly. "Full-time search."

Helen sucked her front teeth, sighed, and put the form away grudgingly, as if Paddy had insisted that she get it out in the first place. She turned and walked over to the gray steel wall and thumb-punched some letters into the keypad. The heavy drum wound itself up and turned. It ground to a stop and Helen glanced back at Paddy for one last cheeky prevarication before opening the postbox flap, reaching in, flicking through a number of files, and pulling out a brown envelope. As she ambled back to the counter Paddy could see that the envelope was full.

Helen leaned into Paddy's face. "Straight back," she said, slapping the envelope on the counter.

Paddy picked it up and left, stopping on the stairs to tuck it into the waistband of her skirt on her way to the newsroom toilets, hoping Heather was hiding in a different toilet altogether.

V

She pulled out the chunk of clippings, unfolding the papers on her knees. There were a lot of them. She put half back and balanced the envelope on the toilet-paper holder. The cuttings on her knee were pristine and crisp, folded around one another like dead leaves. Paddy took the time to prise them apart gently, carefully flattening the legs and arms.

Flicking through them randomly, she saw stories about accidental deaths, about the library being knocked down to make room for the motorway, about a street robbery and a scout troop winning a prize for raising money. There were optimistic proclamations from city councillors about the new housing scheme and reports of a bit of gang trouble in the sixties.

She folded the clippings back together, swapping them for the second batch still in the envelope.

A building in the Rotten Row collapsed while occupied, sliding down the steep hill like a knob of butter in a hot pan. Two injured but no one killed.

The rubbish buildup was averted during the bin-men strike because the maternity hospital had an incinerator.

A three-year-old local boy, Thomas Dempsie of Kennedy Road, had been abducted from outside his home and found murdered. The child's father, Alfred Dempsie, had been charged with his murder but pleaded not guilty at the trial.

In a clipping dated five years later, Alfred was reported to have hanged himself in Barlinnie Prison. The paper had republished a grainy picture of his wife at young Thomas's funeral. Tracy Dempsie had dark hair pulled up tight in a high ponytail. She looked as lost and dazed as Gina Wilcox.

Paddy made some notes on the back of a receipt and returned the clippings to the envelope as tidily as she could, following the original creases. She checked the date at the top. Brian had gone missing eight years ago to the day of Thomas's disappearance. Thomas was the same age as Baby Brian and from the same area. No one seemed to have noticed the parallel between the cases. They could have been completely different for any number of reasons, but it seemed strange that she had never even heard of Thomas Dempsie before.

Downstairs in the library, Helen was sitting at the desk, glancing through a late edition. Paddy stood there for a full minute, and although Helen tightened her forehead she refused to look at her. Finally Paddy put the envelope on the counter and shoved it forward so that it was hanging over the far edge.

"Don't leave them there." Helen stood up casually, coming over as slowly as she could. "If they went missing you'd be made to pay for them. I doubt you make enough in three months to pay for these."

Paddy smiled innocently. "Follow-up: Dempsie, Thomas, and 'murder.' "

Helen looked over her glasses and sighed heavily. Paddy really hoped she was still there if she ever got a promotion. She'd remember what she was like and pull her up about it.

She had been sitting on the bench for ten minutes before it occurred to her that no one was laughing at her anymore. Someone in features called her over using her name, not just calling her boy. Someone else picked her over Keck from the bench, something that never happened because Keck could find everything and knew where everyone was at all times. A sports desk journalist even looked her in the eye and asked if she, Meehan, would get him a coffee. It was worrying.

Paddy was starting to wonder if she was getting the sack and everyone knew but her when Keck stopped picking his fingernails with an unraveled paper clip and leaned over. "Seen your pal Heather this afternoon?"

Paddy shook her head, reluctant to get into it.

"Aye, ye won't see her tomorrow either." He pointed into the middle of the room. "Farquarson told the morning boys, and they got Father Richards down here and told him her card wasn't right and she was to get out and not come back. She was crying and everything." He sat back.

Paddy looked around the room at the serious men at the news desk, at the mess of clippings piled up on the features and sports desks, where they were all gathered around one end of the table smoking Capstans and eating a box of cream cakes, and she wondered how these graceless, ruined men had come to be her only allies.

SIXTEEN

MICROBE SAFARI

I

The Drygate flats looked like lost American tourists. Painted and peeling Miami pink, they were topped with jaunty little Frank Lloyd Wright hats and banded with balconies. The designer had overlooked the setting: a brutally windy Glaswegian hillside facing the Great Eastern Hotel, a soot-blackened doss-house for lost men.

Thomas Dempsie's mother had been transferred by the council shortly after her husband was convicted of murdering Thomas. It was less than half a mile away from the old house, just down the hill from Townhead. Paddy guessed that she would have been moved by the council for her own safety. The *News* had published her new address when Alfred killed himself in prison.

Paddy waited for five minutes in the lobby, watching the red digital display above the steel doors tell her that the lift was moving exclusively between floors four and seven, before accepting that she would have to walk. She didn't like running or hills or walking up stairs. She didn't like the feeling of pockets of fat jigging on her stomach or hips. She didn't believe thin people ever got sweaty or out of breath and felt she was drawing attention to her size when she did.

Everything in the urine-stained stairwell that could be broken was broken: rubber had been torn off the handrail, leaving a filthy black substance that stuck to the skin; tiles on the floor had been lifted, leaving bald, tacky splats of adhesive. Several landings were littered with glue-filled plastic bags, the discarded tins often lying nearby, some still giving off a detectable tang. Paddy had to stop a couple of times to get her breath on the way to the eighth floor, and each time she stopped she could hear people's lives clattering and murmuring through the walls around her, smell the evening meals being prepared and the moldy rubbish blocking chutes. She reached the eighth floor and paused in front of the gray fire door, taking another breath and reminding herself why she was there and what she wanted to ask about. She had a job to do, she was a reporter. Thrilled by the game, she pulled the open door and stepped out onto the windy balcony.

The row of front doors were painted a uniform pillar-box red. Between each was a living room window for the neighbors to peer into and a smaller, mottled bathroom window. As she stood waiting in front of 8F for an answer to her knock, Paddy noted that the net curtains in both were gray and tired. An empty bottle lay on the blurred bathroom sill, next to a pool of what looked like dried toothpaste. She felt her lip curl in disgust but checked herself. She shouldn't be small-minded about how other people lived, it was none of her business. She stared hard at the door and could see that the wind on the landing had brought hairs and dust and grit to it when the paint was still wet, giving it a textured microbe-safari finish. The door opened cautiously and a strange woman looked out at her.

"Oh." Paddy let out a little startled exclamation, surprised by the woman's odd appearance. "Hello?"

Tracy Dempsie had gone to great lengths to disguise any natural advantage she had ever had. Her hair was dyed aubergine and pulled up in a tight ponytail that dragged her face back into an unflattering mask. Her black mascara and eyeliner were thick and migrating under her eyes. Her pupils were so dilated that the blue iris was little more than a halo. Tracy blinked slowly, cutting out the scary world for a delicious moment, knowing that all the sharp edges would be waiting for her if the prescriptions ever ran out.

"Hello, Mrs. Dempsie? I'm Heather Allen," said Paddy, half hoping it would all go sour and Tracy would phone the paper and complain about her, compounding her dismissal. "I'm a journalist with the *Daily News*."

Reluctantly, Tracy opened the door, and the wind shoved Paddy into the hall. The decor was as garish as Mrs. Dempsie herself. The swirling carpet looked like an abstract representation of an argument between red and yellow. The walls were covered in jagged yellow plaster. Tracy shuffled back, walking off to the living room. Paddy paused in the hall and then guessed that she had been invited to follow.

A black-and-white portable television was on in the corner, showing a nature program about otters, their little silvery pelts slipping in and out of water. Around the set, lost in the same loud carpet as the hall, were cigarette packets and dirty plates. A saucer at the side of the settee had a bit of toast and three dog ends stubbed out on it. Two wire clotheshorses were arranged around the burning fire with sheets draped over them, sending wave after wave of wet heat into the living room.

Tracy saw her looking at it. "That's the high flats. No lines for washing. Ye can't leave a washing out on a line 'cause someone'll nick it."

"You used to have a house, didn't ye?"

"Aye, Townhead. Up the hill, know?" Tracy lifted her hand slowly and lowered it again, indicating over there, where the badness was. "Council moved us here after Alfred got the jail. Then your mob published this address." She frowned bitterly, looking at Paddy as if it had been her decision.

"They have to do that, by law," said Paddy, "to identify ye. In case people think it's someone else of the same name."

"Well, everyone knew where we'd got moved to. We lost the Kennedy Street house for nothing, know?"

They were standing facing each other,

Paddy still wearing her duffel coat and scarf, her underclothes damp after the exertion of the stairs. Tracy blinked again, oblivious to her guest's discomfort, and her eyes fell on the television.

"We got moved?" said Paddy. "Who's 'we'?"

"Me and the wean."

"I didn't know ye had other kids."

"I had a boy before. I was married before I met Alfred. I can't manage much, so he's with his dad now." Tracy nodded heavily. "Ye can sit down if ye like."

They looked at the settee together. Tracy had left some damp clothes sitting on one end of it, and they were smelling faintly sour.

"Thanks."

Paddy took off her coat and sat it on her knee, taking care to stay away from the source of the smell. Tracy sat next to her, her knee lazily pressing into Paddy's thigh. She didn't seem to notice. She kept her eyes on the telly and lifted a silver packet of Lambert and Butler off the coffee table.

"Smoke?"

Paddy could see exactly where she sucked her fags: her two front teeth had a dirty little sunrise impressed on them.

"No thanks," said Paddy, taking the

empty notepad out of her bag and leaning back so Tracy couldn't see the paper. She flicked elaborately through to the middle, as if the pages were choked with vital information from other cases.

Tracy took a cigarette out of the packet with a slack hand, lit it with a match, and took three consecutive draws, tilting her head back to expand her lungs.

"So, ye said on the phone ye wanted to see me about Thomas?"

"That's right." Paddy positioned her pen. "Because of the Baby Brian case —"

"Tragic."

"It was."

"Those wee bastards should be hanged." Tracy touched her mouth in self-reproach. " 'Scuse me, but I blame the mothers. Where were they? Who lets their boy do that to another woman's wean?"

"Well, because of it we're doing a series about past stories, and your son Thomas was one of the names that came up. Would you be all right talking about it?"

Tracy shut her eyes tight, squeezing the lids together. "It's not easy, know? Because first I loss my baby and then I loss my man. Alfred was innocent." Tracy shifted uncomfortably in her chair. "He always said that. He was at the pitch-and-toss that night. That's how he didn't have an alibi."

The pitch-and-toss were illegal gambling schools, impromptu affairs run by gangsters in pubs and sheds and open-air waste grounds all over the city. Men could bet away their family's weekly wage on the turn of a few coins.

"Surely someone would come forward?"

"No one remembered him at the pitch-and-toss. Gamblers don't notice ye if ye don't have a big stake." Her eyes deadened. "He wasn't a man you'd remember, Alfred."

The misery was vivid in Tracy's eyes, and suddenly Paddy didn't feel like a junior scoop, she felt like a fat girl cheering herself up by quizzing a bereaved woman about her private business.

Tracy nursed her fag, letting it dawdle on her lips. "You wouldn't notice him. He was a good dad, though, a really good dad. Loved his weans, handed his money in, know?" Her eyes were brimming, threatening to flood her face with mascara.

Paddy dropped her notebook into her lap. "I feel terrible coming here bringing this all up for you again."

"Never mind." Tracy flicked her cigarette ash into a dirty saucer on the floor. "I don't mind. It's always with me anyway. Every day."

Paddy looked at the television. A voice-over was explaining breeding cycles while two otters swam around each other.

"If Alfred didn't kill your son, who do you think did?"

Tracy squashed her fag out in the saucer. "D'you know what happened to Thomas?"

"No."

"They strangled him and left him on the railway to get run over. He was in bits when I got him back." Her chin contracted into a circle of white and red dimples and her bottom lip began to twitch. To stop herself crying she picked up her packet again, flicking open the lid and pulling out another fag, lifting her box of matches. "No man could do that to his own wean." The head flew off the match as she struck it and landed on the carpet, melting a little crater in the man-made fabric. Tracy stamped on it with her foot, screwing the flame into the ground. "Bloody things. Made in Poland, for petesake. As if we cannae make matches here."

"I didn't know that about Thomas. The old papers never said that."

"They're shutting all the works and we're buying this rubbish from the bloody Poles. Half this landing has been laid off. And why would Alfred leave Thomas in

Barnhill? He was never up that way. He didn't even know anyone there."

Paddy's face felt suddenly cold. Barnhill was where Callum Ogilvy lived.

"Whereabouts in Barnhill?"

"The tracks. Before the station." Tracy stared at the television. "He was there all night before he was found. First morning train went over him."

"I didn't know, I'm sorry," mumbled Paddy. Thomas's death was all too real now, and she wished she hadn't come here. She wished something nice had happened to Tracy. "Did you not marry again?"

"No. Been married twice, that was enough. I was pregnant at fifteen, married at sixteen. He was just a boy himself. Never there. In and out of Barlinnie. A wild man." She churned out a grin. "Always go for the bad ones, don't ye?"

Paddy didn't, but she nodded to be agreeable.

"He got a big shock when Thomas was killed, cleaned up his act. Tried to be a father to his own boy. Had him to stay when the neighbors were attacking the house up the road. He stays with him still."

Paddy nodded encouragingly. "At least he tries."

"Oh, he tries. He does that," Tracy conceded, dropping her voice to a whisper.

"Brian was taken on the same day as Thomas. Did you notice?"

"Of course I did. Eight-year anniversary." Tracy took a draw on her cigarette and watched the otters slither over each other, sedating herself with the television. "Stays with ye, the death of a child. Never seems by, like it's always happened this morning."

II

As Paddy stepped out onto the windy veranda she saw a swath of green light on the balcony floor, thinning between the shutting lift doors. Driven by her dread of the grim stairs, she ran for it, catching the doors with just an inch to go, frantically pressing the button on the wall.

There were two boys in the lift, both about thirteen, guarding either side of the doorway. Paddy stepped in and heard the door shut behind her before she had the wit to change her mind. With a dawning sense of danger, she turned around.

They were poor boys, she could see that, both wearing cheap parkas with flattened orange linings and thin fur edging on their hoods, both in school trousers that were too short for them, with tide marks where hems had been let down.

The lights through the tiny lift window showed them passing the seventh floor, a big industrial stamped number on the far wall flicking past and registering on Paddy's eye. After glancing at each other, the boys turned to look at her.

One of them had his hood up, covering all but his nose and mouth. The other's hair was cut so short that telltale patches of ringworm were visible on his scalp. Each of them flicked his eyes at the other again, signaling something sneaky and malign.

The most expensive thing she owned in the world was her monthly travel Transcard in her bag. Paddy pulled her bag strap over her head and held on to the base of it in case the boys tried to grab it.

They passed the fifth floor, the lift gathering momentum, the cable above their heads creaking.

The boys looked at each other again, smirking, putting their hands behind their backs and pushing themselves off the wall as if getting ready to pounce. It occurred to Paddy suddenly that one of the boys might be Tracy Dempsie's other son. Either of them looked poor enough.

"I know your mum," said Paddy, looking at the wall.

A little disconcerted, the boys glanced at each other again. "Eh?"

She looked at the ringwormed boy, who had spoken. "Is your mum called Tracy?"

He shook his head.

"Mine's is dead," said the hood, with such relish she doubted it was true.

Paddy put her hand in her pocket, feeling past the bits of tissue to her house keys, slipping them through her fingers to make a face-ripping fist. She tried speaking again, thinking that any local connection would protect her a little. "Do you know Tracy Dempsie on eight?"

The boys laughed. "She's a fucking ugly hooker," said the hood.

Paddy felt suddenly protective of Tracy, as if being insulted by small boys was compounding all the insults life had dealt her. "Hooker? Where'd ye get that word? Off the telly?"

The lift bounced to a stop on the ground floor. The boys stood still, staring at her feet as the doors slid open. The hood tipped his head back, his mouth falling open, eager to see what she would do.

Paddy held on to her bag with one hand and kept the other in her pocket. She worked hard not to turn her shoulder or give way to them, just to walk straight through the middle. She lifted her foot but faltered before taking the first step, prompting a giggle from one of the boys. As she stepped out into the foyer a cold sweat formed over the back of her neck. They could have cut her or raped her or mugged her and there would have been nothing she could do to defend herself. She was out of her depth.

She scuttled out of the lobby and the building, hurrying out of the shadow of the block and across a patch of grass, passing a garden party of old alkie men standing around a burning brazier, too late or too drunk for the Great Eastern Hotel's seven o'clock check-in time.

III

Distracted by the memory of Tracy's hollow eyes, Paddy walked up the steep hill to the blackened cathedral and cut around the back of the Townhead scheme to the old Dempsie house. She was walking fast, hurrying away from the fright of the boys and the unfamiliar air of regret in Tracy's house.

242

She felt sure she had stumbled on something significant. Someone had killed Thomas Dempsie and left him in Barnhill. If the same person had killed Baby Brian on Thomas's anniversary, they couldn't leave him in Barnhill; they would have to leave him somewhere else if they didn't want to draw attention to the similarities. That might be the reason they took him to Steps, to cover up the fact that it was a repeat murder. But it wasn't a repeat: Callum Ogilvy and his friend had killed Baby Brian. They had his blood on them and their footprints were found there, and they were toddlers themselves when Thomas died. That could be good for her, though: if Farquarson thought Thomas Dempsie's case was highly relevant, a better journalist would get to take it over. For her to get to write it up it needed to seem only quite interesting. Still, she shouldn't even be considering it. Her mum would put her out of the house if her name appeared on any article that mentioned Baby Brian.

A plyboard wall ran along one side of Kennedy Street, blocking entry to one of the many bomb sites still pockmarking the city from the Second World War. On the other side, a snake of houses followed the

243

spur of land around. They were mirror images of Gina Wilcox's house, from the concrete steps leading up to the narrow door to the three-banded green fence. A nearby household had taken offense at the Irish Republican implications of the fence color and had repainted theirs a royal blue. Apart from one house using its small garden to store bald tires, the neighborhood was well tended, the front rooms cozy and peaceful when seen from the cold street.

Around the shoulder of the crescent she saw a middle-aged man in a navy overcoat walking down the road towards her, his hands jammed into his pockets. Paddy walked towards him and saw him flinch warily, hurrying to get past her.

"Excuse me?"

The man sped up.

"Can I speak to you, sir?"

He stopped and turned, looking her over. "Are you the police?"

"No," she said. "Why would you think that?"

"Ye said 'sir.' You're not the police?" he repeated, seeming annoyed that she had misrepresented herself.

"No. I'm Heather Allen, *Daily News*. I'm here about Thomas Dempsie?"

"Oh, aye, the wee fella that was murdered?"

"Yeah. Do you know which house was his?"

"There." He pointed to the house with the tires in the garden. "The family moved away after. The mother lives in the high flats down at Drygate. It was his dad that killed him, ye know."

Paddy nodded. "So they say."

"Then he hanged himself in Barlinnie."

"Aye, I heard that too."

Together they looked at the house. Beyond the tires and the muddy grass, limp white curtains formed an arch in the window.

The man nodded. "Ye don't know what goes on indoors, sure ye don't. At least he was sorry enough to kill himself."

"Aye. Didn't they think he was taken from the garden?"

"At the start they did. He just went missing, but of course then it turns out that the daddy had him all along."

"I see."

The man shifted his weight uncertainly. "Is that it? Can I go?"

"Oh." Paddy realized suddenly that the man, ages with her father, had been waiting to be dismissed. "Thank you, that's all I wanted to know."

He nodded, backing off before turning and carrying on his way. She watched him go, amazed at the power gleaned from introducing herself as a journalist.

Kennedy Street should have had an open vista over the new motorway to Edinburgh, but the view was blocked by a makeshift barrier. Bits of plyboard had been pulled off, and Paddy crossed over to look through it. The ground was muddy and uneven. A stubborn ground-floor tenement wall stood alone with melancholy cherry wallpaper around the impression of a fireplace.

She had never met anyone like Tracy Dempsie before. Everyone she knew who had suffered terrible tragedy in their lives offered it up to Jesus. She thought of Mrs. Lafferty, a woman in their parish whose only child had been run over and killed, whose husband had died agonizingly of lung cancer, and who had herself developed Parkinson's, so that she had to have communion brought to her seat during mass. But Mrs. Lafferty was all high kicks and yahoo. She flirted with the young priests and sold raffle tickets. The possibility that suffering could defeat people disturbed Paddy. The only other person she had ever heard of like Tracy was old Paddy Meehan. The unfortunate were supposed to rise above adversity. They should become fat, bitter men in cheap coats boring people in dirty East End pubs.

It took her a moment to register the sound. Coming around the corner towards her was a hurried, scuffed run. For no real reason she thought of the boys in the lift and felt a stab of fright in her stomach, thinking she'd be pushed through the hole in the wall. Without looking to the source, she scurried across the road towards the nearest working streetlight and calmed herself. There was nothing to be afraid of. Tracy had creeped her out, that was all.

She slowed her pace to a walk and turned to see the person behind. He smiled at her with disarming warmth. He was tall, taller than Sean, with thick brown hair and a creamy complexion. He stood thirty feet away, hands in his pockets.

"Sorry, did I frighten you? I was running because I saw ye and I thought you were my pal."

Paddy smiled back. "No."

"It's a girl I'm trying to meet. By accident." He nodded and looked sheepishly back up the street. "You live here?"

"No," she said, thinking he was sweet. "I'm working."

"What d'ye work at?"

"Journalist. For the *Daily News*."

"Ye a journalist?"

"Aye."

Impressed, he looked her up and down, his eyes lingering on her monkey boots and gelled hair. "Don't they pay ye?"

"Listen, these are Gloria Vanderbilt monkey boots."

He smiled at that and looked at her with renewed interest. He held his hand out. "Kevin McConnell," he said, leaning forward to take her hand.

It could be a Catholic name, she wasn't sure.

"Heather Allen."

His hand enveloped hers, the skin powder soft. As he stepped forwards the light caught a gold stud in his ear. Paddy had only ever seen male pop stars with earrings, and Glasgow was not a city that calmly accepted blurred gender boundaries: she'd once heard of a guy being beaten up for using an umbrella. Looking at him with renewed admiration, she noticed that his eyes were small and neat and his lips were glistening.

"You need to be careful coming up here, visiting people in a scheme ye don't know."

"I was only here for a minute." She

started strolling slowly down the road, hoping he'd follow.

"A minute's long enough," he said, falling into step. "There's gangs up here, ye have to be careful."

"Are you in a gang?"

"Nut. Are you writing about the gangs? Is that what you're doing up here?"

He veered towards her slightly, keeping the space between them narrow, as if he could feel the frisson between them too. "I'll see ye out safely, then."

She kept him talking, asking if he was working (he wasn't), where he went dancing (he didn't), and what sort of music he liked. The Floyd, Joe Jackson, and the Exploited sometimes, but only sometimes. Ye have to be in the right mood, eh? Paddy knew what he meant: she never happened to be in the right mood for the Exploited.

By the time they reached Cathedral Street she was reluctant to leave his company. He was a big, handsome man, like Sean, but not annoyed at her or talking about his family or angry about her job. He walked her down to the bus station, waving her off across the dual carriageway, giving her a coy look and saying that maybe he'd see her again.

As Paddy walked down through the town

to the train station it occurred to her that maybe the world was full of men she might choose; that maybe Sean was just one of the nice men instead of the one nice man.

Reluctant to go home to her family, she took her time wandering down through the town. The closer she got to the station the smaller she felt. She wasn't Heather Allen. She wasn't a journalist at all. She was just a fat lassie playing a stupid game because she was too afraid to go home.

IV

Trisha was alone in the house when Paddy got in, and the atmosphere was worse. She dished up a bowl of broth and a plate of mince with peas and spuds and left Paddy alone to eat it, going off to sit in the living room to watch the news. Paddy could see her through the serving hatch, sitting in the armchair, her neat brown hair shot through with wild gray. She was pretending to listen to a news report about the Maze Prison hunger strikers, as if the world outside Rutherglen Main Street didn't terrify her.

Paddy would have gone to the movies, but she didn't have any money. She considered using her Transcard and taking the two-hour circular route around the city on the 89 just to worry Trisha but knew it would be a petty revenge. And the bus might be cold.

She finished eating and got up, putting her plates in the sink, meaning to wash them later as a penance, but her mother got out of the chair and silently came into the kitchen, slipping between Paddy and the sink, running the hot water and beginning to wash the plates and cutlery briskly. Paddy skulked away into the living room.

She couldn't be bothered watching the news. She twisted the channel dial to ITV and sat down before the picture had resolved itself. It was a quiz show. A saccharine host was asking a portly woman from Southampton questions about her tiny bespectacled husband, trapped in a soundproof booth and smiling like a baby sitting in warm shit.

Sean would be eating his tea right now. His mum would be smiling and chatting away to him, telling him the news of the day and who had died in the parish and whose grandchild had said a clever thing. Paddy could phone and tell him she missed him. She could try to say sorry again.

She waited until her mum had walked

through the living room and climbed the stairs to the toilet, then nipped out and dialed Sean's number.

Mimi Ogilvy could hardly speak when she asked for him.

"Please, Mrs. Ogilvy, I've got something important to tell him."

She hadn't finished the sentence before Mimi hung up.

V

Mary Ann came up to bed earlier than she normally would and silently went about her business, going to the bathroom with her wash bag and coming back dressed for bed, sorting out her clothes for the morning and putting her dirty underwear in the laundry bag at the side of the wardrobe, all the time letting off incontinent little laughs as she pottered around the room.

She turned off the light by the door, but instead of getting into bed she climbed over her own bed and sat on Paddy's, pulling out a pack of cards from behind her back and a packet of cheese-and-onion crisps. She tugged Paddy out of bed and over to the window, made her sit down, and pulled the curtain over their heads. Lit by moonlight, Mary Ann opened the packet of crisps for them to share and dealt them a rummy hand of seven cards each. Down at the bottom of the garden the lone tree waved softly in the breeze, silver moonlight glinting off the few leaves.

They played for almost an hour, laughing silently when the crisps made a crunchy noise in their mouths, keeping score in Paddy's notepad. Mary Ann mimed out the additions every time they moved on to a new hand, scratching her head and making a puzzled face, writing down ridiculously wrong numbers in her favor. Paddy let her go through her play each time, enjoying it more and more. They kept the real score on the back page.

They stayed there long after their eyes had begun to sting with sleep, playing together, their faces next to the windowpane, damp and cold, their overheated feet in the bedroom, smothering comradely giggles. The silent games would become a ritual, a nightly statement of loyalty that bound them to each other for decades ahead.

SEVENTEEN

THE CALLOUS CARS

I

The features writer was struggling to whip up a credible moral panic piece about Joe Dolce's novelty single signaling the final demise of the English language when the phone rang, giving him an excuse to turn away from the page.

"Nope," he said, running his eye over the sheet in the typewriter. "Heather Allen doesn't work here anymore."

The man on the phone seemed surprised. He had met her yesterday, he said, in Townhead, and she told him she worked at the *Daily News*.

"Yeah, well, she's left now, pal."

"Would you have another number I can reach her on?" His voice was gruff but his accent careful and affected.

"Nope."

The man sighed into the phone, sending a ruffle of wind into the journalist's ear. "It's just . . . it's really important."

The features writer's attention span was broken anyway, and the guy sounded genuinely desperate. "Well, I know she works at the polytechnic newspaper. Ye could phone them."

"Thank you," said the man. "That's brilliant."

II

He phoned the polytechnic several times, always refusing to leave a message, always asking just for Heather Allen, when would she be in, is she still not there? I'll ring back, he said. It's her I want.

It was late afternoon before Heather came into the *Poly Times* office. She was in a furious mood. She hadn't told anyone about her dismissal from the *News*. Even her parents didn't know. A latent sense of decency had stopped her from telling them about the syndicated piece. She'd known at the time that she would feel rotten for doing it, had weighed up the pros and cons, and decided that in the long term the benefits would outweigh the guilt. But she'd been wrong. She hated herself for betraying Paddy, and she'd lost her job. She felt enough of a shit without having to deal with her father's disapproval.

The *Poly Times* was a two-bit operation. Their office was a small room on the first floor of the students union block, furnished with a single table, three chairs, and a phone. Two walls of shelving held four years of back copies and all the financial records and minutes of all the committee meetings there had ever been. Lots of people applied to work on the paper, but they only printed twice a year and there just wasn't that much to do. They managed to freeze out most of the interested parties by being cliquey, intimidating, and unfriendly, which left them with a core staff of about six. One of Heather's duties as the editor was trawling through the unsolicited articles students submitted to see if any of them were printable.

Despite posters up all over campus declaring the upcoming deadline, there weren't very many submissions in the red wire basket. The office wasn't empty, though: a couple of committee members, both greasy headbangers, both supernaturally ugly, were standing by the telex machine trying unsuccessfully to send something off.

Heather ignored them, hoping they'd feel uncomfortable and leave.

She claimed the entire worktable by putting her bag on one side and the red wire basket on the other, using one chair to drape her coat on and another to sit in. One of the metal boys called over to her that a guy had been phoning for her all morning.

"Someone from the *Daily News*?" she said hopefully.

The boy shrugged. "He didn't say where he was from."

On reflection, Heather realized that the call couldn't have been from the *News*. If they had wanted her back, someone would have phoned her at home last night. Anyway, they wouldn't reverse the decision. No one went against the union. She settled back into her black mood and began pulling submissions out of envelopes and folders, piling them up.

She was halfway through reading a second-year's travelogue about interrailing around Italy when the phone rang.

"Heather Allen?"

"Yeah."

"I met you last night, do you remember?"

She didn't. "I meet a lot of people."

"I know I can trust you." The caller paused, wanting a reaction.

"Really?" She was still only half listening, balancing the receiver on her shoulder and flicking through the submissions, looking to see if there were any other travel pieces in case she needed to choose between the two.

"Do you want to know about Baby Brian?"

Heather dropped the travelogue and took the receiver in her hand. He must have heard she was the source of the syndicated piece. She covered her mouth with one hand to stop the sound carrying to the headbangers in the corner.

"Can you tell me something about that?"

"Not on the phone. Can you meet me?"

"You name the place and I'll be there."

The man explained that he was very nervous, and made her promise to come alone to the Pancake Place at one a.m. He asked her not to tell anyone where they were meeting and said she shouldn't even write it down, in case she was followed without knowing it.

Heather tore the scribbled address off the corner of the foolscap sheet and dropped it in the bin. "I'll see you tonight," she said, and waited for him to confirm before she hung up.

The boys were watching her without looking; she could feel them. She left her things on the table and went out to the lobby to buy a gritty coffee from the machine. She dropped the coins in and looked out the window, over the rooftops of low buildings towards the city chambers, smiling to herself as the machine spluttered and whirred her coffee into the plastic cup. She would skip the *Daily News* and take her story straight to a national paper. With a good story about Baby Brian and the syndicated piece about the family on her CV she would be able to walk into any job she wanted after graduation. She could go straight to London.

III

Paddy hung around the newsroom and canteen, killing time until McVie came in. The night shift gradually filtered into the newsroom, replacing the manic fussiness of the day. The skeleton staff took up their positions at their desks, setting up for the night, laying out their magazines and books for reading, one guy on the features desk tuning in a small tranny to a Radio Four program about the silent age of cinema.

McVie saw her when he came in to check the board for messages. He nodded an acknowledgment but looked annoyed when she came over to speak to him.

"Not again," he said. "I got in enough fucking trouble last time. That wee bastard phoned in and complained about us. I didn't know you weren't a journalist."

"I'm a copyboy."

"Well, just stay away from me," he said.

"I just want to ask you something about Baby Brian."

"Yeah." He pointed at her nose accusingly. "And that's another fucking thing. You're related to that bastarding child and you never told me."

Paddy raised a finger and did it back. "I didn't know it then, did I, ye big arse."

The use of a bad word seemed to placate McVie somehow, as though he suddenly, completely understood the degree of her vehemence.

"Okay," he said. "Have you got anything ye can tell me about it?"

"Nut. I don't know anything about him."

"How can you not know anything about him? He's a relative."

"Are you close to your family?" It was a

lucky guess. "D'you know what, though?" she added. "That guy JT, he tried to question me about it, and he wasn't a patch on your technique."

McVie nodded. "Yeah, but he'd swap his balls for a story. Gives him the edge. I heard he once went to collect the picture of a rape and murder victim from her mother. On his way out the door he told her that her daughter had been asking for it." He nodded in sympathy with the shock on Paddy's face. "That way the woman wouldn't talk to anyone else from the press. Made it an exclusive. He's an arsehole. What do you want anyway?"

"I wanted to ask you something about Baby Brian. What time did the boys catch the train to Steps?"

"They said it was between nine and half ten at night. Why?"

"Where were they from lunchtime until then?" She lowered her voice. "And JT said no one saw them on the train. I don't think wee guys with nothing would catch a commuter train to Steps."

McVie looked unconvinced. "They found their tickets on them."

"But Barnhill's full of waste ground and abandoned factories, and these are poor kids. Why would they spend money on a train? Could the police get it that wrong?"

It startled Paddy because she didn't know what it was: the skin near his eyes and mouth folded over and a bizarre noise gargled up from his throat. McVie was laughing, but his face wasn't used to it. "Can the police get it wrong?" he repeated, making the noise again. "Your name's Paddy Meehan, for fucksake."

"I know it happened then, but could it still happen now?"

McVie stopped doing the scary thing with his face and let it retract back to suicidal. "Most of them wouldn't fit a kid up. Although . . ." His eyes dropped to the side and he looked skeptical. "*Most* of them wouldn't. If they were convinced they're really guilty but it's hard to prove, they might plant evidence. They see a lot of villains walk; you can kind of understand it."

A night editor came over to the table with a coffee and a cigarette, settling into a seat near them.

McVie leaned into her. "I know Paddy Meehan, by the way. He's an arsehole."

Paddy shrugged awkwardly. "Well, that's something, coming from you. D'you know anything about a guy called Alfred Dempsie?"

"Nope."

"He killed his son."

"Good for him. I heard the morning boys chased Heather Allen because of what she did to you. Don't mistake that for popularity."

"I won't."

"They'd hunt you for sport just as easy."

"Hunt me for sport? What are ye talking about? I'm going to report you to Father Richards for using creative language."

McVie was trying not to smile, she could see it. He checked his watch. "Right, piss off, bint. I've got things to do before I go out."

She stood up. "Well, thanks anyway, ya big swine."

He watched her tug her pencil skirt down by the hem. "Get fatter every time I see ye."

She couldn't let him see she cared. "That's right," she said, dying inside. "I get fatter, and you get a day older in a job ye hate."

IV

Paddy walked slowly down to Queen Street, aiming to get there after nine. It was a quiet Friday night in the black city; the heavy rain had lasted for most of the evening, and even now the air felt damp and threatening. Outside a hotel on George's Square she passed a crowd of women in cheap dresses and wedge shoes, alert and frightened as a herd of deer; nearby, their drunk men shouted at one another. She tried not to look at them directly, and in her mind's eye the women became a soup of fat arms in cap sleeves, of ringed fingers patting perms as sleek as swimming caps, and raw heels persevering in razor-edged shoes.

Queen Street station was a cavernous Victorian shed with a fanned glass roof spanning five platforms. Only the pub and the Wimpy bar remained open. Reading the railway timetable plastered to the wall, she saw that the trains left for Steps every half hour and it would have taken the boys seventeen minutes at most to get there. The ticket office was off to one side of the station, and Paddy noticed that the barriers were not guarded at night like they were in the rush hour. It would have been easy for the boys to sneak onto the train without paying.

The ticket office was empty and the man serving at the ticket window was reading a newspaper.

"Hello," she said. "Can ye tell me how much a half return is to Steps?"

The man frowned at her. "You're not a half."

"I know. I don't want to buy one, I just want to know how much it costs."

He still looked skeptical. Paddy was bored with the Heather Allen lie, so she told another one. "My nephew needs to go there to visit his auntie on his own this Monday coming, and my sister has to give him the money for his fare." It sounded elaborate enough to be true.

The attendant watched her as he typed it into the ticket machine. It cost sixty pence, twice as much as the bus.

Back out on the concourse she read the boards and realized that the next train to Steps was due to pull out. She took out her Transcard, but no one asked to see it as she climbed onto the quiet train. The train doors slid shut and the carriage jolted forward. There didn't seem to be a conductor on board.

The train passed through a long, dark tunnel, emerging on the other side between two steep banks of earth, hewn away to make room for the railway lines. The jagged banks were so steep that after a hundred years of perseverance the grass still hadn't managed to grow on them. The carriages were quiet, and she could easily see small boys managing the whole journey without being spotted.

The first stop was Springburn station, eight minutes out of Queen Street. The platform was built in a deep valley with stairs up to the street. It was quiet for the moment but obviously well used: the platform was broad and had a chocolate machine and even a telephone kiosk on it. On the far side of the station, beyond the double railway tracks, a white picket fence marked off the surrounding land. It was dark behind the fence, in the wild wastes where thin trees and malnourished bushes struggled. The wilderness went on for so long that Paddy's eye got lost in it. The train started up again, shaking her awake.

The journey on to Steps took the train along a short track before forking off away from the low-level Barnhill station. She could see it through the bushes on her left-hand side, a poor, lone platform with broken lights and a single bench next to stairs up to the road. It was around here that Thomas Dempsie's tiny body had been left. She found the thought of him being left somewhere so dark almost more upsetting than his death.

She looked back at Barnhill station, disappearing behind her. It was ridiculous. The boys wouldn't have passed their home to take the baby somewhere else. Even if they had jumped on the wrong train they would have got off at Springburn and walked the few hundred yards.

The train rumbled on to Steps, passing the Robroyston high flats, forty-story paragons of architectural crime built on the top of barren hills with nothing around them to give them human scale. Beyond that it passed through dark, empty lands of bush and scrub bordering a marsh for five whole minutes. In the cold moonlight Paddy could see fields and hedges, a strange landscape halfway between abandoned industrial site and countryside.

The approach to Steps was heralded by a strip of houses on a hill. They were big and had gardens she could see into when the train slowed. It didn't seem like the sort of place that would draw wee boys from a ghetto, and it definitely didn't look like a better place to hide a guilty secret than the industrial wilderness they'd come from.

The Steps station platform was clean and neat, if a little exposed. On one side a huge wild field stretched off until it reached a school building; the other side faced the backs of houses. There was no ticket office or guard there to witness the boys' arrival. Enameled signs informed travelers that they would have to buy their tickets from the conductor on the train. No one else got off the train. Paddy didn't like to admit it, but JT might have been right: the boys could have made it all the way there without being seen. But that didn't explain how they had hidden the baby for the eight hours before they got on the train.

She loitered alone on the platform, looking down the long, straight tracks back to Springburn and onwards to Cumbernauld. The station exit was a gentle ramp up to the road. Paddy walked up it and let herself through the gate to the little humpback bridge over the tracks.

The break in the bushes across the empty road wouldn't have been obvious without the small pile of flowers and cards and soft toys on the pavement in front of it. It was a dark lane, overhung with bushes and trees. Paddy glanced behind her, making sure she wasn't being followed, and stepped over a bunch of withered carnations into the velvet dark.

The lane ran between the railway line and the far ends of long gardens belonging to big houses, evergreen bushes preserving their privacy. A craggy, leafless bush clung to a high wall of chicken wire on the railway side. The ground beneath her feet was uneven and frozen, and she walked slowly, trying to find the faint tread line in the grass.

It didn't take long to reach the blue-and-white police tape blocking the path. Beyond it she could see the hole in the chicken-wire fencing, low down, just high enough for small boys to get through. She ducked under the tape and climbed through, catching her tights on a loose wire and ripping a bullet-sized hole in the right knee.

She was standing in an area of disturbed grass. She crouched down on her haunches and ran her flat hand over it. The thin light from the distant train platform showed the pale silver undersides of the blades, uniformly flattened by the wind or a sheet, she thought, not broken by feet. Paddy felt as calm as she had in the alleyway with McVie, and reminded herself to keep an open mind about what had happened here. Anything was possible; the police weren't always right. They'd questioned and eliminated the Yorkshire Ripper nine times before he was arrested.

She stood up, walking along the rail track for twenty feet, heading away from the station until the grass became upright and undisturbed. No big feet had been milling around here gathering evidence. Dew from the blades clung to her tights, soaking into the wool, making the ankles sag.

It only caught her eye because it was a perfect square. Across the twin rail track was a geometrical patch of shadow beside a small bush. She recognized the signs from paddling pools left upended in her own family's garden for seasons at a time: the little square of grass had been starved of wind and frost for a few days. It was where the tent had been placed, where Brian had been killed and found again. Beyond it, in a diagonal slash across the lip of the hill, a dirt path had recently been formed by a hundred journeys to and fro.

The darkness was a blanket over her mouth and ears, muffling the noise of distant traffic and the world beyond the tracks, thickening the air so that she couldn't draw breath. A crisp packet fluttered against the fence, and to Paddy's alert ears the cellophane crackle sounded like a stunted cry. She backed up to the fence, holding tight, letting the wire dig into her fingers while she blinked away Brian's imagined final moments. A bright screaming train flew towards her, filling her ears, and Paddy closed her eyes to the grit and wind, glad of the heart-stopping intrusion.

The train passed and Paddy stood in the dank dark, looking down the railway line towards the bright station. It didn't feel safe, but she scampered over to the far bank, slipping slightly on an oily wooden tie, the momentary lack of balance sending a shiver of nerves up the back of her neck.

Next to the flattened square of grass, the bush had branches cut from it: recent ones severed with a sharp knife, older ones twisted until the branches came off in a stringy mess of bark and sap. She remembered what Farquarson had said about sticks being put in the baby's bottom. The sharp cuts suggested someone gathering evidence.

Paddy stepped beyond the flat grass where the tent had been and climbed up the frozen mud embankment, helping herself up by clinging onto stray roots and stones. She found herself in a large field, plowed into furrows. The unlocked gate was only fifty yards away. She could hear the sound of cars speeding past on a road nearby. A hundred tire tracks from the police cars scarred the mud in front of her. She stood up straight.

The boys hadn't stumbled on the baby after playing in a swing park for toddlers. They hadn't managed to hide for eight hours or come here invisibly on an expensive train or trampled down an unfamiliar dark alley to a hole in the fence they didn't know was there. Someone else had been here with them. All three of them had been driven to this spot by someone. It was obvious to her, and should have been obvious to anyone else who looked. But no one was looking. As it stood, the Baby Brian murder was a good story, a clean story about other people, far away.

Paddy stood in the bitter field, her hair flattened against her head, listening to the brutal February wind and all the callous cars rushing home to warmth and kindness. The story suited everyone and wouldn't be questioned until the evidence was overwhelming. It was Paddy fucking Meehan all over again. No matter how much evidence he had produced or how many people saw him on the night of Rachel Ross's murder, the police were determined it was him.

EIGHTEEN

KILLY GIRLS AND COUNTRY BOYS

1969

I

Meehan would spend the remaining twenty-five years of his life poring over the details of the night he didn't kill Rachel Ross. He told the story so often that it changed meaning: the names of the girls became pleas for understanding; the timing, where the cars were parked, when the lights went on and off at the hotel, all became a hollow mantra to be chanted when a new journalist or lawyer took a passing interest in his case.

At the time, the night seemed like nothing but another disappointing recce, like a thousand other nights in the life of a professional criminal.

They had been sitting in the hotel car park for three hours, watching people arrive and leave the bar, slumping down when a man came past walking his dog, watching and waiting for the lights to go off so they could scan the office next door, which issued automobile tax decals. James Griffiths was slumped in his stiff car coat and kept coming back to the same thing.

"I'll steal one for ya," he said, his thick Rochdale accent putting the inflection at the end of the sentence, turning it into a question. "Happilee, happilee, happilee." He stubbed his Senior Service out in the ashtray. Until James helped himself to the turquoise Triumph 2000 from outside the Royal Stewart Hotel in Gretna, the four-year-old car's ashtray had never been used. Now it was overflowing with snapped stubs and flaky ash.

Meehan sighed. "I'm not taking them on holiday to East Germany in a nicked motor, for Godsake. We wouldn't get far. The Secret Service are watching me all the time."

"You won't get done," said Griffiths casually. "I never get done. Been getting away with it for years."

"You never get done?" Meehan stared at him.

"Never," said Griffiths, only faintly un-comfortable at the blatant lie.

"What were you doing in my cell on the Isle of Wight, then? Visiting?"

"Yeah." Griffiths grinned, but Meehan didn't reciprocate.

The first time they met was on the Isle of Wight, when Griffiths was doing a three-year stretch for car theft. Griffiths was a halfwit sometimes. He did and said whatever came into his mind at the time; that's why he got the strap so often inside. Paddy had seen him without his shirt on often enough: his back looked like Euston station.

Meehan needed the car to get the family to a holiday in East Germany. He didn't really want a holiday. What he really wanted was to show his kids that he could speak German and Russian, that he was re-ceiving a payment from a foreign govern-ment, that he wasn't just another Glasgow thug. Before they got much older he was going to give them good memories of their father. He had spent the previous winter sitting next to his own father's hospital bed while he was eaten away by cancer, and during the long nights he couldn't recall a single happy time with him. Not one. There wasn't a moment spent together as a family that wouldn't have been better had his father been out. Meehan wanted to be more than that to his kids, and he couldn't take them away in a stolen car. They'd be picked up before Carlisle, he was sure, stopped at the side of the motorway and sent home fatherless. He could already see their hurt and humiliated eyes looking up at him from the backseat of a panda car.

"I dunno what you're worried about," said Griffiths. "I've been picking so many cars up here I've been rolling them over a cliff up into the water 'cause I got nowhere to sell 'em. And good ones, too, Jags and that. Not rubbish. I'll steal one for ya."

He was apologizing, Meehan knew that. They'd spent a lot of time together over the years, and he knew Griffiths's shorthand for sorry. He was apologizing because the tax decal job he'd brought Meehan to scope in Stranraer wasn't going to happen. As the hotel lights gradually went out and the patrons left in ones and twos, followed by the staff, it became clear that the spotlight on the roof of the tax building would stay on. Even if it went off, the hotel kept dogs, big bastards by the sound of them. So they sat at the dark edge of the car park, smoking and watching, Meehan going quiet to hide his dejection, Griffiths getting chatty to cover his embarrassment.

Between the tax office and the hotel they could see Loch Ryan, and beyond the hills, to the molten black sea. Big red ferryboats for Belfast and the Isle of Man bobbed on the gentle lift and sway of the water. A few lorries were already parked there, drivers sleeping in the cabs, waiting for the first crossing.

"Fuck it," said Meehan, stubbing out his fag in the ashtray. "This is pointless. Let's get back to Glasgow and get a breakfast at the meat market."

The meat dealers' café opened at four in the morning. Their fry-ups had rashers as thick as gammon steaks, and they sold mugs of cheap whisky. Griffiths took a puff on his cigarette, shaking his head as he exhaled a string of smoke. They had shared a cell for two months and could read each other's breathing. Griffiths was vexed. He shook his head at Paddy, smiling a little, and relented.

"Okay, okay." He turned the key in the ignition, leaving the lights off as he reversed out of the dark corner. "Let's get some brekkie."

Fifty miles north of Stranraer, in the small, wealthy suburb of Ayr, Rachel and Abraham Ross were in the bedroom of their bungalow, getting ready for bed. Rachel, in a sky-blue nightie and pink chenille dressing gown, sat on the side of her twin bed and watched her husband winding his watch. A single, convulsive cough shook her. She fought it off and waved a dismissive hand.

"It's nothing."

"Sure?" said Abraham, putting his watch on the bedside table.

Rachel patted his bed. "I'm fine, I'm fine," she said. "Dr. Eardly said it would come and go for a little while after the operation, didn't he? I'm fine."

She smiled reassuringly for her husband, showing a little of her bare pink gums. They had spent the past month lying in their respective beds, listening to the texture of Rachel's bronchial cough. It had left them both exhausted. The cough was so violent that it had cracked one of her ribs and caused her to have an operation. Abraham had fallen asleep in his office in the Alhambra Bingo Hall yesterday and seen Rachel cough up a river into their bedroom. She had always been the stronger, five years older than him and barren too, but in both their minds the stronger.

She pulled back the covers on her bed and took off her dressing gown, folding it carefully in half, laying it along the bottom of her bed.

"Good night, dear." She kissed her own hand and touched his cheek with her fingertips to save her bending down.

"Good night, my dear."

He waited until she was well tucked in, then pulled the string above his head to turn off the light. A cozy blue settled on the room, broken only by the puddle of yellow light from the hall. In unison they took off their spectacles, folded them and set them, side by side, on the nightstand. Rachel was propped up on pillows, having been told to sleep sitting up as much as possible to let the fluid settle at the bottom of her lungs, where it would take up less surface area. She folded her hands in front of her over the coverlet.

"Busy night?"

"Aye, a good night."

"Good takings?"

"Six thousand, give or take."

"Same as last Friday?"

"Aye, that's right," he said, and she could hear him smiling. "About the same."

She smiled too, reaching across for his bed but finding only air and patting that instead. "Well done."

They settled back, listening to each other's breathing, Rachel rasping a little sometimes but mostly even, Abraham taking long, deep breaths to set an example. They slept little now but liked to be in bed listening to each other, without the necessity of speech or the need always to be doing things. They lay for forty minutes together in the soft blue gloom. Once, Rachel reached out and patted the air again, moved by some tender memory.

A sudden loud snap just outside the bedroom door made Rachel turn her head sharply.

They both watched as a black shadow fell across the pool of light from the hall, and suddenly the door was thrown open, smashing off the bedroom wall. Two figures, maybe three, came running in. One held a blanket high and flew at Abraham, covering the old man's head with it. The other stepped on Abraham's bed and swung himself across the room, making for Rachel.

He grabbed both Rachel's wrists, wrenching her off the bed and onto the floor on the far side, kneeling on her operation scar, making her cry out with the pain. He let his weight settle on her chest. Retracting his arm at the elbow he shot his fist forward and punched her on the jaw. He could see her in the light from the hall, her toothless mouth, her thinning hair and wiry neck. He punched her again, on the cheek, on the neck, on the jaw again.

Abraham heard his wife from under the blanket and used all of his one-hundred-and-ten-pound frame to wrestle the man who was holding him. He heard the man's short breaths, sensed his surprise. He had strong fingers from doing the count every night and found the man's arm, sticking his fingers into the soft armpit, squeezing hard. The man shouted.

"Get this cunt off me, Pat!"

He was from Glasgow, Southside, Gorbals possibly, where Rachel and Abraham both grew up.

Suddenly Rachel breathed normally again and Abraham stopped struggling. He hadn't managed to shake off the blanket and sat still, holding the man's arm, listening keenly, wondering what the new swishing noise was. An iron bar swung through the air and made contact with his back, with his legs, his arms, his back again.

They took everything: the money, travelers' checks, what little jewelry there was, and Rachel's watch, pulled off her arm as she lay bleeding and crying. When it was all done they tied them up, Abraham black and blue under his blanket, his whimpering wife next to him. He lay under the blanket trying to remember things about the men. They were both Glaswegian, one called Jim or Jimmy, one called Pat; one was big and stocky, the other thin.

The men decided not to leave until the sun came up so as not to raise suspicion. Settling down in the living room, they drank the last of a bottle of fifteen-year-old Glenmorangie Abraham had been keeping for best.

Left alone in the bedroom, Abraham tried to free himself but couldn't.

"Don't." Rachel was struggling to stay awake. "Please. Stay still. They'll hit us."

So Abraham stayed still for his wife. He stayed still and listened to her dry breath rattle around the room they had shared for thirty years.

Eventually a watery white light began to seep through the blanket.

"Is it getting light?" he asked, but Rachel didn't answer.

The men were there again, in the room, walking over to them. Abraham flinched away, but they weren't there to hit him. They tied more ropes around them, tightening the ones already on the couple. They were standing up to leave when Rachel spoke again.

"Please," she said, her breath shallow, "send an ambulance for me. Please."

They didn't answer. They walked to the door.

She called again. "Please send an ambulance —"

"Shut up, shut up. We'll send an ambulance. All right?"

The door slammed behind them and they were gone.

III

Meehan and Griffiths were outside Kilmarnock on the deserted road to Glasgow, doing eighty and singing a dirty song about the different-colored hairs on a whore's cunt, both pleased that they hadn't taken the risk of robbing the office, when they passed a crying girl in a miniskirt and shiny white boots.

"Stop!" shouted Meehan. "Slow down."

Griffiths sat upright suddenly, looking around for cop cars.

"Did you see her?" Meehan thumbed behind them. "There was a girl crying back there."

Griffiths slowed the car and pulled over, squinting into his rearview mirror. He threw the car into reverse and careered backwards towards her.

Irene Burns didn't have the legs for a miniskirt. She had calves like a navvy but a big chest, and to Meehan's and Griffiths's eyes that balanced her out a bit. She had a drink in her but was only sixteen and wasn't used to it. She was sobbing so hard she could barely explain what had happened. She had been hitchhiking with her pal Isobel when two men offered them a lift home. They got into a white car, an Anglia, and one of the men got out a half bottle of whisky. They were driving along and Isobel started winching one man, but Irene didn't fancy hers, wouldn't let him touch her, so the men got annoyed, stopped at the side of the road, and put her out. Now Isobel was all alone in a car with two strange men, Irene was ten miles from home, drunk for the first time in her life, and she didn't know what she was going to tell Isobel's mother.

Meehan reached into the back of the Triumph and opened the passenger door. "You get in, pet," he said. "If anyone can catch that car it's this man."

Griffiths grinned out at her. He was missing quite a lot of teeth, and it made her smile a little. He gave her a salute and called "Hello there" in a silly voice, like Eccles from *The Goon Show*. Irene climbed in the back, feeling better already.

Before he became a thief Griffiths was a racer, and he was a talented driver. Within five minutes they saw the white Anglia in front of them on the road. It was going slow, doing about thirty, weaving back and forth across the road. Griffiths slowed and pulled up, keeping shoulder to shoulder. The other driver was a young country boy spruced up for a night out. In the back of the car a girl with a mashed-up beehive was necking another guy.

"Isobel!" squealed Irene. "That's her! That's her with him."

The driver looked at them and Meehan gestured to him to pull over to the side. He saw the country boy hesitate, his eyes flickering from the road in front of him to their car, trying to work out who they were and why he should comply. Irene wound down her window and shouted for her friend, but

Isobel ignored the call and carried on kissing ferociously, her new friend's hand lost in her candy-floss hair. The country boy slowed and pulled off to the side. Griffiths had barely stopped the Triumph in front of them when Irene pulled open the passenger door and ran out, heaving open the Anglia door and tugging her friend out of the backseat and into the road. Isobel shook her off with a single bat of her hand. She was a big girl who didn't look like she would ever need saving. Below her miniskirt her tights had made a suspension bridge between her knees.

In the Triumph, Meehan sighed. "What d'ye reckon? Maybe we should just leave them."

They watched for another minute. Isobel pulled up her tights by the waistband. Irene was howling again. She seemed to be having a drama of her own, as if she was in a completely separate movie.

"They're just wee girls, though," said Meehan, watching Isobel move in a way that made her big, fluid breasts tremble beneath her jersey.

Griffiths flashed him a cheeky smile. "Isobel's game, though, eh?"

Meehan's face broke into a wonky smile. He cleared his throat and smeared his hair down. Exaggerating his hard-man swagger, he walked over and put his hand in his jacket pocket as if he had a blade.

"These girls are too young to be out at this time. I'm taking them home."

The men in the car glanced at each other, dropping their shoulders.

Meehan leaned down, filling the open window. "Want to make something of it?"

The boys shook their heads.

Meehan gestured to the girls to get in the back of the Triumph. Isobel burped and pulled down her jersey as Irene, too drunk to realize that the danger was by, sobbed and dragged her towards the Triumph.

"Right, boys," said Meehan, enjoying himself, playing it like an off-duty policeman. "Back up and pull out." He slapped the roof of the car. "On your way."

Far from fulfilling her promise as a jailbait temptress, Isobel fell asleep as soon as she got into the car. She sat with her fat legs sprawled across the backseat, snoring vehemently. Irene sobbed with fright and drink all the way to Isobel's and then on to her own house. Whenever she managed to stop crying, she told Meehan and Griffiths that they were awful good, dead kind, and the thought would start her crying again.

She was irritating the life out of them.

The sun was halfway up in the sky and the milkmen were finishing their rounds by the time they arrived at a row of brown-and-white prefabs on the outskirts of Kilmarnock. The curtains were open in Irene's living room, the lights on inside.

"My ma'll be frantic," she said, rubbing her swollen, itchy eyes. "She'll be phoning the polis and everything."

They made her get out quickly at that. Griffiths sped all the way back to Glasgow. They'd missed the meat market and skipped breakfast, parting slightly sick of each other, knowing they'd be pals again after a sleep and a feed.

IV

Mr. and Mrs. Ross lay on the floor for two more nights and two more days. They heard children playing in the street outside and cars rolling past their house. The telephone rang in the hall. A couple of dog walkers met on the pavement outside their bedroom window and chatted for a while. They lay on the floor until Monday morning at ten o'clock, when their cleaner turned up for work as usual and used her own key to get in.

Rachel Ross sighed her last breath as the ambulance drew to a soft stop outside the hospital.

NINETEEN

HEATHER'S LUCKY BREAK

1981

I

Heather gathered the keys for her mother's car from the hall table and tiptoed out of the house. Heavy rain masked the noise of the closing door and Heather's feet crunching over the moat of gravel around the house. She swung her bag into the passenger seat, shut the door carefully, and started the red Golf GTI, leaving the lights off until she had cleared the drive.

The country roads were quiet all the way into town and stayed quiet as she approached the city center. It was just past midnight on a Friday night, but the rain had chased everyone off the streets. Every third car was a cab. Even the buses had stopped. Going at full speed, the windscreen wipers only managed to pull back the curtain of rain periodically, and sheets of water rippled down hills.

Waiting at a traffic light, Heather rummaged in her handbag on the seat next to her, feeling for her cigarettes. The lights changed before she could take one out of the packet, and she found herself on the green side of every light into town. It wasn't until she reached Cowcaddens that she managed to put one in her mouth and press the lighter on the dashboard. She inhaled, and the smoke made her lungs feel dirty and clogged. On the way out it did the same to her teeth. It felt good.

The Pancake Place was straight across the road from a shuttered and padlocked side entrance to Central station. A big van was parked right in front of the doors, so she parked a few spaces back and checked her makeup in the rearview mirror. Her lipstick was coming off in the middle where she had sucked her cigarette. She took the No. 17 Frosty Pink from her handbag and one last puff before touching up her lips. She opened the door, stepped out into the wet street, dropping the half-smoked cigarette to hiss to death into the wet, and ran into the café.

The Pancake Place menu was a testament to the versatility of the humble pancake: it was offered with everything, from a dollop of cheap jam to a pair of eggs and black pudding. Open until four a.m., the café had become a haven for late-night shift workers, students on their way home from the dancing, and tired street prostitutes giving their feet a rest. The overwhelming impression of the decor was dark brown. Plastic timbers had been grafted into a suspended ceiling and fake oak partitions built between the tables. To add a touch of olde worlde authenticity, laminated menus were propped up in darkwood stands.

It was quiet, and Heather immediately spotted the man sitting at the back table reading a copy of yesterday's *Scottish Daily News*, just as he had promised. He was younger than she had expected from his voice and looked too rough for the paper he was reading. He was dressed like a construction worker, in a heavy jacket and a black woollen hat pulled down over his ears.

"Hello," she said, trying to look unexcited and professional.

He seemed puzzled. He looked her up and down, taking in her expensive red overcoat and thick lipstick, and went back to reading his paper.

"You called me?" she said.

He looked up at her again, annoyed this time. "Do I know you?"

It was a different voice from the one on the phone, and Heather looked behind her to see if there was another man in a donkey jacket reading the *Daily News*. There wasn't. She checked her watch. It was one in the morning. She was right on time.

"I think . . ." She looked at the empty seat across from him. "May I?"

"May you what?"

"May I sit down?"

He folded his paper shut and cleared his throat. "Gonnae leave me alone?"

"Didn't you phone me and ask me to come here?"

"I never phoned ye."

"But someone phoned me."

"Well," he said, opening his paper again, "it wasn't me that phoned ye." He glanced at her and saw how disappointed she was. "I'm very sorry."

"I was to look for a man in a donkey jacket reading the *Daily News*."

"I think someone's playing a joke on ye. Sorry."

Heather suddenly understood. It was one of those bastards at the *Daily News*, one of the morning-shift boys having a laugh at her expense. They'd be watching her. They'd be in here or across the road, laughing at her.

"Okay," she said, her voice cracking on the second syllable as the disappointment choked her. "Thank you."

She backed off, glancing around the café, making sure there wasn't someone else in the room who met the description. Two tarty women in high heels and evening wear were huddled together near the back; a stoned mod girl was sitting with two boys in leather jackets, each red-eyed and slow moving; an old, old man hunched in an overcoat with tobacco-stained arthritic fingers. No one looked back at her.

She stood inside the door looking out at the shitting rain, blinking hard and trying not to cry. She lifted a paper napkin from under the cutlery on the nearest table and wiped the itchy lipstick off. There would be no London. She would never get a job up here either, because the union had taken against her and those bastards never forgot a grudge.

They were inside, she guessed; someone in the café was watching her. She fumbled a cigarette from her packet and lit it, taking a deep, bitter drag. She felt fat tears welling up, uncontrollable, because she was tired and it was late at night and she'd set such hopes on coming here.

She opened the door and stepped out into the rain, pulling the car keys from her pocket, only vaguely aware of the figure following her out. The street was empty of parked cars, but somehow the big van had backed up nearer to the Golf, so that she would have to reverse first to get out. Cursing it, herself, and every spiteful shit who worked at the *Daily News*, she turned sideways to slip between the van and the bonnet of the little red GTI.

The van door flew open, hitting her in the face, breaking her nose with a dull thunk. A large, rough hand fell over her face, covering it entirely, smearing what was left of her Frosty Pink lipstick over her chin. She heard him behind her, the man from the café. She heard him speak to the grabbing man, heard him object. Thinking him her savior, she tried to turn to him, but the hands in front of her grabbed her neck, lifting her by her throat into the back of the van.

Donkey Jacket hardly spoke above a whisper. "Wrong fucking bird, ya mug ye."

II

When Heather came to she knew she was in the van and felt it moving fast, along a motorway or a good flat road. She was lying on her side, on a flat surface, with a towel that smelled of sour milk hooked over her head. She was missing a shoe, and her hands were tied together with rope behind her back. Through the waves of shock and nausea she realized that her face was very swollen; the pain seemed to radiate out from the bridge of her nose, engulfing her eyes and cheeks and ears, almost meeting round the back of her head again. Her nose was blocked with blood. She tried to blow it clean, but it hurt too much. She could hear the faint sound of a radio coming from the front of the cab, a sound of voices, and poor, dead John Lennon's "Imagine" came on.

At first she thought again that it must be some of the morning boys playing a prank that had gone too far, but they were never sober enough to drive, especially not late at night, and they wouldn't have hurt her physically. She wondered for a moment if Paddy Meehan's family were exacting their revenge, but that couldn't be right either. She remembered the hand around her throat and realized, suddenly and clearly, that she didn't know these men and they didn't know her. They were going to kill her.

Moving carefully, rubbing a relatively pain-free part of her chin repeatedly against her shoulder, she tried and failed to get the smelly towel off. She began to panic, rubbing frantically, regardless of the pain. When the driver hurried or slowed she drifted a little over to the side.

She was struggling with the rope around her wrists and feet, getting nowhere, when the van pulled off the road, took a couple of sharp turns that slid her around the floor, and then came to a creeping stop in a very dark place. The driver got out and a bright overhead light came on. They were outside, somewhere dark. She could hear a river and feet crunching around to the side of the van.

Heather worked her hands up and down, her skin rubbing hard against the tight rope, trying to loosen the cord but embedding it instead in her raw skin. The van door opened, the hood was unhooked from her head, and the man in the donkey jacket looked in at her. He was holding a short-handled shovel. Heather tried to smile.

When Donkey Jacket saw her brutally

swollen face, eyes like oranges, chin and hair smeared with blood and snot, he looked perplexed. "That's not her."

From around the side of the van she heard another voice muttering, "Ye said ye'd follow her out and ye did."

An older face looked in at her, frightened, shaking his head. She couldn't be sure, seeing him upside down, she couldn't be altogether sure, but she thought his eyes were wet for her and sorry for what he had done. His sympathy made her think for a moment that they might let her go, and relief swept from her crown to her toes, a cold wash that unclenched her aching jaw and eased her throbbing shoulders.

Donkey Jacket lifted the spade from his side, holding it with both hands near the shovel end. "And ye said she was dead," he said.

The older man's cracked voice gave his emotion away. "She'd stopped breathing. I thought she was."

Donkey Jacket nudged him playfully and raised the shovel to chest height. "See? You teach me about things." His voice was rich and calm. "And now I can teach you things."

He swung his arm freely, bringing the metal shovel down fast and crushing Heather's skull against the van floor.

TWENTY

EVER SO LONELY

I

Paddy's weekend was as poor and friend-less as she could remember. She spent the whole of Saturday skulking around the big library in town, keeping out of the house, reading old newspapers about the Dempsie case that told her nothing she didn't already know.

She hadn't realized the degree of local animosity towards her until she passed Ina Harris, a vulgar woman she knew to be a friend of Mimi Ogilvy's, on her way home from the library. Ina turned quite deliberately and spat at Paddy's feet. She was hardly an arbiter of good manners herself: she often answered her door without her teeth in and was a famously light-fingered cleaner. She kept having to change her job all the time because the day and hour she started anywhere she'd look for the fiddle, steal what she could, and had to leave before she got found out. She got a job cleaning operating theaters once and came home with a bag full of scalpels and gauze. Everyone in Eastfield knew about her.

When Paddy opened her drowsy eyes on the Sunday and saw the two cups of hot tea on her side table, she thought for a moment it was a normal weekend. Con's only chore around the house was to make the Sunday-morning cuppas and deliver them to the bedrooms, easing everyone up and getting them ready for ten o'clock mass. Paddy blinked, feeling especially excited about seeing Sean at chapel. It was only when she recalled why seeing him meant so much to her that she remembered it wasn't a normal time.

She sat up in bed, sipping her tea, thinking about all the disapproving Ina Harrises she would have to face today. Sean would be there and would ignore her. Her family wouldn't speak to her, and everyone in town was watching her and whispering about her crime. Mary Ann would stand loyally by her, but she'd laugh an eloquent articulation of Paddy's shame and fright.

She listened as everyone in the house

took their turn of the bathroom. Mary Ann was rinsing her teeth when Trish called up the stairs to tell them it was half nine, mind now, they'd need to set off in ten minutes. Mary Ann came back into the bedroom and made an astonished face to see Paddy still in bed. Paddy made the face back and Mary Ann giggled, gave her one last open-mouthed gawp, and left.

Paddy lay in bed, still wearing her pajamas, reading *L'Etranger*, a book Dub had lent her, because she knew the French title would upset her father. She heard the scuffle and whispers at the bottom of the stairs, followed by Con's tread. He stopped outside, knocked, and opened the door, looking around the room expectantly. She wanted to sit up and challenge him, say something incendiary that would make him speak to her and have a fight for once in his pathetic life. But she didn't. She sat in bed with her eyes fixed on the page, slowly slipping under the covers, protecting her father's dignity at the expense of her own.

Con snorted angrily twice and left, shutting the door to the room tight to show how annoyed he was. He tramped downstairs again, she heard the front door shut, and like bubbles bursting, the family was gone.

A calm fell over the house. Paddy listened just to make sure no one had been left behind. They were really gone. She was alone in the house for perhaps the first time in ten years. Even if no one else was in the house, Trisha was usually in the kitchen or at least near it. Paddy threw back the covers and bolted downstairs to the phone.

Mimi Fucking Ogilvy answered in her best Sunday voice.

"Is Sean there?"

"Who may I say it is?"

"Can I speak to Sean, please?"

Paddy could feel Mimi's tiny mind grind out a thought before she hung up on her.

Paddy waited in the hall, sitting briefly on the stairs, knowing that Sean would have been in the house getting ready for mass and would have heard the phone ring. He'd know it was her: no one else he could possibly know would need to phone on a Sunday morning, because they were all on the way to the chapel and would see each other anyway. He wasn't going to call her back. She checked her watch. He would have left to get to mass now. He wasn't calling back.

Back upstairs she threw on some clothes and took off her engagement ring, leaving it sitting by her bed, knowing her mum would come in to make the bed while she was out and would see it there. She hoped it would worry her.

She ate a quick breakfast of cereal. She could have made six boiled eggs, but the grapefruit were all off, and the chemical reaction didn't work without them. Filling her canvas bag with biscuits, she set off for the town, hurrying to get the train past Rutherglen station before mass came out. She didn't want to run into half the congregation. Sitting on the train, Paddy looked at her chubby hands dispassionately. She liked them better without the poor ring.

In town she bought a ticket to an afternoon showing of *Raging Bull*, not because she wanted to see it, but so that she could tell Sean she had already seen it if he asked her later. She didn't want him thinking she would wait around for him all the time. She felt like a friendless idiot, handing her single ticket over to the usherette. Unprompted, Paddy told her that her friend who had been coming with her was prone to illness and wasn't well enough to come and that's why she was alone. The usherette was hungover and dressed like a bellhop, in a washed-out red-and-gray uniform. She let Paddy finish her excuse and then silently pointed the way upstairs with her ticket skewer.

Paddy sat near the back, calculating that fewer people would be able to see her there, and opened her handbag of biscuits. One hour into the film she realized that she had never enjoyed a movie as much in her life. She wasn't wondering what Sean thought about it or making jokes or checking that she got her share of the sweets, she was just enveloped by the music and the dark. She even forgot to eat.

II

She arrived back in Eastfield a full hour before anyone could reasonably expect their tea to be ready. It was too painful to go and sit in her bedroom before tea as well as after. The curtains were thick in the living room window, and the settee was too low to see anyway, but she could tell from the quality of the blueness of the light that the telly was on. A head stood up from an armchair — one of the brothers — and went into the kitchen. She had another whole night of internal exile ahead of her.

Sneaking past the front gate, she lifted the garage key from under a brick. If her dad saw the light on he'd think it was their neighbors, the Beatties, and stay well away. As she pulled it open, the garage side door concertinaed a thin black carpet of mulch.

The air inside was cold, a damp cloud hanging over everything, eating into her fingertips and ear lobes, carrying the cold into every corner. Paddy kept her coat on and sat down in a slightly moist brown armchair. She finished the biscuits in her handbag, eating them one after another as if it was a chore.

The Beatties had managed to pack a wild amount of stuff into the Meehans' garage. They had erected a set of precarious shelves from bricks and odd planks of wood against one wall and had stacked cardboard boxes full of bric-a-brac on them. Paddy stood up, picking her damp tights off the backs of her legs, and looked through the boxes, the soft cardboard coming apart in her hand when she tried to tug it.

The Beatties went on foreign holidays and got to keep toys from when they were younger. The Meehan children were made to give theirs away to charities just when they stopped playing with them but before they lost all proprietorial sense over them. In one box they had stored a Union Jack biscuit tin from the Silver Jubilee and a cheaply framed picture of the Queen as a young woman, holding on to the back of a chair. Black speckled mold grew across her long pink skirt.

Paddy sat in the cold armchair, looking around the room. If she had been a Beattie she could write an article about Thomas Dempsie and Baby Brian. She could say it was the anniversary of Thomas's death, explain the Barnhill connection clearly, and let readers draw their own conclusion. She could do it if she didn't care what her family thought. They were punishing her already, and she hadn't done anything. She was suffering their wrath anyway, she might as well do the Judas deed. But she felt bad enough for having upset her mother when she hadn't done anything. Heather Allen would do it, even if it were her family. She would grit her teeth and write the Dempsie article.

Forgetting for the moment that she had taken Sean's ring off, she touched her ring finger with her thumb and experienced a momentary horror when she found her finger bare. The impression of it was deep on her finger: the red mark had faded, but the skin remained smoother where the band had been. She definitely liked her hand better without it.

By the time she got into bed that night, she noticed that she had changed her habit of twisting her engagement ring to stroking its silky absence fondly.

TWENTY-ONE

SADLY

I

Paddy sat on the bench in the newsroom, watching the editors filter back in slowly after the privilege of lunch, their tempers sweetened by a midday pint and a hot meal. The journalists, who had to make do with ten stolen minutes in the canteen or a sandwich at their desks, watched them insolently, feet up on desks, fags dangling from mouths, the antagonism between the two groups palpable. They hated each other because editors gave the orders and chewed up the journalists' work, while the journalists produced and bitched about editors' cuts, even when their copy had been improved a hundredfold, perhaps especially then.

A clump of editors were standing in the middle of the newsroom, sharing a final joke, when a flurry in the corridor caught everyone's eye. William McGuigan, the paper's chairman, as rarely seen in the newsroom as empathy or encouragement, made a dramatic double-doored entrance from the lifts. His large port-wine lips had deflated with age and lost their edges so that they reminded Paddy of an overripe fruit. He was flanked by five men, two in police uniform and three in plainclothes. One of them, a white-haired man in a pristine gabardine jacket, stood authoritatively out in front of the others, eyeing the room, suspicious of everyone.

The newsroom fell silent. The presence of so much authority made everyone feel as if they were about to be arrested and summarily put to the wall. Stuck behind the crowd, Dub climbed up on the bench and Paddy stepped up next to him.

As the focal point of a crowd at silent attention, McGuigan looked around, savoring the moment. "Gentlemen, these are police officers." He flicked a hand at the uniformed officers and dropped his voice. "Something very sad has happened." He paused dramatically.

The white-haired policeman stepped impatiently in front of him. "Listen to me," he shouted, his delivery loud and functional, a lorry to McGuigan's sports car. "A body was found in the Clyde this morning. Sadly, we have good reason to believe it is that of Heather Allen."

Assuming a despairing suicide, a hundred guilty glances ricocheted around the room, many of them resting on Paddy, who was holding her breath. From the corner of her eye she saw Dub glare back at the accusers protectively.

"We believe that the young lady was murdered," bellowed the officer, drawing all eyes back to him. "Her car was found outside Central station, and we are asking for your help. If anyone has any information they think is relevant, please come to us. Do not wait for us to come to you."

Determined to carve a portion of the attention for himself, McGuigan stepped in front of the policeman. "I have assured the officers that you will cooperate, and let me say this: woe betide anyone who doesn't." Reading his audience's faces, he realized that threats were not appropriate. He tried to soften them with a laugh, but it died on his lips.

Several people crossed their arms. Someone muttered, "Fucking arse." The white-haired officer stepped in front of McGuigan again. They seemed to be very slowly working their way across the room.

"We have set up interview rooms downstairs. Rooms 211 and 212." The officer glanced at McGuigan for confirmation. "We'll be taking some of you down there for interview." He took a tiny black notepad out of his pocket and opened it. "Can we have Patricia Meehan and Peter McIltchie first."

Paddy stepped down from the bench, finding her knees wobbly with shock, and worked her way out to the front of the room, meeting Dr. Pete in front of the white-haired policeman. Around them the crowd of journalists and editors moved away, whispering about them and about Heather's terrible end.

Two newsmen darted up for a few words with the police officer and caused McGuigan to raise his hands and address the room again. "Oh, yes, *of course* we will be reporting on this, but we'll be doing it in cooperation with the police. We will, however, be withholding some information strategically, and all stories *will* go through the news editors to make sure that is done consistently." He smiled, stretching his baggy purple lips to their maximum, pleased to have had the last word. Everyone was listening to him, but no one was letting it show.

Paddy and Dr. Pete waited while the white-haired officer gave urgent orders to one of his underlings about doors or watching doors or something. McGuigan, keen to get back on a cheery footing with the senior officer, said something to him about getting his own back over a game of golf. The man didn't answer him.

Paddy couldn't take it in: Heather was dead. Someone had killed her. Dr. Pete was sweating, his top lip and forehead damp, and he seemed to be tensing his shoulder in an odd way, as if he had fallen over on it. One of the younger policemen, a squat-faced man with a thick neck, nodded hello to him. Pete tipped his head back to acknowledge the greeting but flinched at the sudden movement, holding his shoulder, nodding briskly when the man asked him if he was all right. He looked guilty of something terrible, and Paddy knew why. She wanted to run down to McGrade in the Press Bar and get him a drink, but didn't think the police would let her. He held his arm and shifted his weight, moving himself out of the group and nearer to Paddy.

"Why do they want to talk to you?" she said quietly. "I know why me, but why you?"

"I'm an easy press." He sounded breathless. "I know one of the officers. Drank with his father."

"Plus you always know what's going on."

She sounded like an arse-lick because she was avoiding stating the obvious: that Pete was the bully in chief, the head of the pack that had hounded Heather from her job. The police would ask him if the newsroom boys had gone any further than chasing her out of the office, if they had followed her home and killed her.

"You." The white-haired officer turned back and pointed at Paddy without any preliminaries. "You go with him. McIltchie, if you don't mind, you're with me. How are you?"

"Aye. Going on." Pete dabbed at the sweat on his top lip.

Pete and Paddy stayed close to each other as they were escorted out to the lifts they were never allowed to use. She guessed he was about three whiskies short of normal.

"Not be long," said Paddy as the doors slid open in front of them.

"Better not be. I'm melting."

Inside the lift the mirrored walls exaggerated the officers into a small, unfriendly brigade. Paddy was a full head shorter than everyone else. She was lost in a forest of torsos. One floor down, the lift doors opened and they spilled out into editorial.

The corridor through editorial ran along the outside wall of the building. The harsh daylight flooding through the window did nothing to flatter Dr. Pete's waxy complexion. Paddy glanced out into the street and noticed two cars outside, one parked at either end of the road, idling, neither of them taking advantage of the large, half-empty car park. They were police cars, watching the building to see who would try to leave now that the body had been found. The police were sure it was someone at the paper.

In the corridor the policemen at the front of the procession opened two doors next to each other and siphoned Paddy into one room, inviting Dr. Pete into the other.

II

The conference room held a large table with seating for fifteen. Paddy looked at her hands and realized she was trembling slightly. She was alone, frightened, and ten years younger than the two brawny men who were going to question her, outgunned anyway because they were asking the questions.

The squat-faced man who had tried to speak to Pete was in charge in their room. He picked out the places for them, pointing his companion into a seat, putting Paddy next to him, and taking the opposite side of the table for himself. She hadn't noticed before they sat down because he was so tall, but the policeman to her left was blond and square-jawed, with electric-blue eyes. Pete's friend was dark and fat and older. His face looked squashed, his nose flat, as if someone had sat on it while the clay was still wet.

The squat man looked her in the eye, establishing himself as the boss.

"I'm DS Patterson and this is DC McGovern."

She smiled at both, but neither of them caught her eye. It wasn't open hostility, but neither of them seemed particularly interested in making new friends. Patterson took out a notepad and flipped to the relevant page, asking her to confirm her name and position as a copyboy and to give her home address.

"You had a fight with Heather, didn't you? What was that about?"

Paddy looked around the table for a moment, wondering whether she had any reason not to tell the truth about Callum. "My fiancé's related to one of the boys in the Wilcox case."

"The what?"

"The Baby Brian case."

The policemen shot each other significant looks and glanced at their papers for a moment, changing expressions before looking up again. The squat one nodded at her to go on.

"When I found out, I confided in Heather, and she wrote the story up and syndicated it."

"Syndicated?"

"She sold the story to an agency, and they sell it on to lots of other papers, papers whose markets don't overlap." They didn't look any more enlightened. "The English papers. The story was everywhere. My family won't believe I didn't do it, and now they won't talk to me. I don't even know if I'm still engaged. I don't know if my fiancé'll have me back."

"So you were angry with her?"

She considered lying but didn't think she could carry it off. "I was."

"So you hit her?"

"No, we had an argument in the toilet."

She closed an eye and shifted in her seat.

"You seem uncomfortable."

"I didn't hit her."

"You did something."

"I held her head down the toilet and flushed it." It sounded so thuggish she tried to excuse herself. "I'm sorry I did it now."

"It must take quite a temper to actually hold someone's head down the toilet and flush it."

The beautiful policeman caught her eye and smiled encouragingly. "Have you got a temper?" She realized suddenly that he'd been brought in to question the wee fat bird deliberately. Resentful, she crossed her legs and turned to Patterson.

"Are you working on the Baby Brian case?"

They glanced at each other. "Our division is, yes."

"Have you ever heard of a wee boy that died called Thomas Dempsie?"

Patterson barked an indignant laugh. It was an odd reaction. Even McGovern seemed surprised.

"Does no one think there are similarities between the two?"

"No," said Patterson angrily. "If you knew anything about the cases, you'd know they were completely different."

"But Barnhill —"

"Meehan." He said it too loud, shouting over her. McGovern watched him, trying not to frown too openly. "We're here to ask you about Heather Allen, not to speculate about ancient cases."

"Thomas Dempsie was found in Barnhill. And it was his anniversary. Exact to the day."

"How would you even know about that?" He looked at her carefully. "Who have you been talking to?'

"I was just asking if you'd thought about it."

"Well, don't." He was getting very angry. "Don't ask. Answer."

Paddy suddenly remembered that the editorial toilets were two doors down the corridor, and she remembered Heather sitting on the sanitary bin. She wanted to cry.

"Are they really sure it was Heather?"

"They can't say for sure. She was in a bad state. We can't use dental records, but we're quite sure it's her. Whoever it is, it's wearing her coat. Her parents are going to identify the body now."

"Why can't you use dental records?"

He said it with a certain relish. "Her skull was smashed in."

It was the bareness of the statement that shocked Paddy, and suddenly she could see it, Heather's body lying on the floor of the toilets in editorial, a halo of jammy mess, her blond hair spread out like the rays of the sun and a shuffled confusion of skin and bone in the middle.

McGovern handed her a paper hankie. She struggled to speak.

"Is there a chance it might not be her?"

"We think it is." Patterson leaned in, watching her face. She couldn't help but feel he was punishing her for asking him questions. "We need you to be as honest as possible. You may know something important. Being honest might help us catch whoever did this."

Paddy blew her nose and nodded.

"Did Heather have a boyfriend?"

Paddy shook her head. "She doesn't have one."

"Are you sure? Couldn't she have had a secret boyfriend that she didn't tell you about?"

"I think she'd have told me. She got pretty jealous when I talked about my fiancé."

She looked up at McGovern and he smiled inappropriately.

"So you think she'd have told you if she was having an affair with anyone working here?"

Paddy snorted. "No way. She wouldn't go out with anyone here, she was too career conscious."

"What difference would that make?"

"She'd have been labeled a tart. She just wouldn't do it."

"What if it gave her an advantage at work?"

Paddy wavered. "Well, she was very ambitious."

"She was very good-looking," said McGovern. "It can't have been easy for you: two girls working in an office, one of them —" He caught Patterson's eye and broke off.

"When one of them's beautiful and I'm a right dog?"

"I didn't say that."

She could have slapped his perfect face into yesterday. "It's what you meant."

She talked fast and loud to hide her hurt pride. "To be honest, it's easier working here if you're not that good-looking. With Heather they were always making sexy jokes about her and then hating her for not fancying them back."

"Did it bother her?"

"It must have. She wanted to be a journalist, not a bunny girl. But she played on it. She'd have used anything to get ahead. Even her looks."

Paddy glanced at McGovern, leveling the accusation at him as well. He smiled enchantingly, oblivious to the implied insult. He really was gorgeous. It was a shame Heather wasn't here, she thought before she caught herself. She was sure they'd have fancied each other.

"Were you jealous of Heather?" Patterson asked carefully.

She didn't want to answer. It pained her to admit it and made her look small, but they had said it might help if she was honest. "Yes, I was."

Had Patterson had any manners he would have left it there, but he didn't. He kept asking for more details. What aspects of Heather's life was she jealous of? How jealous? Did she hate her, would she say that? Well, if not hate, then dislike? Was that why she attacked her in the toilet? Paddy tried to answer as honestly as possible, every time. She didn't know what was relevant but gradually came to realize that while the state of her friendship with Heather might be, asking her what she currently weighed wasn't. She resisted, and he insisted. Just answer the questions, Miss Meehan, he said seriously, we'll decide what's relevant. McGovern wasn't as fly. She saw him grinning a couple of times, leaning back in his chair so that she wouldn't see. Patterson was humiliating her deliberately, punishing her for having the cheek to suggest she knew something about Brian Wilcox.

By the end of the interview Paddy felt belittled and stupid, and suddenly knew things about herself that she wasn't nearly ready to face. She was fiercely competitive and had always wanted to go to university herself. She had catalogued and coveted every one of Heather's advantages, envied her clothes and figure, but believed that she was smarter — that's where she was the winner. Paddy had always hoped she was gracious in her limitations and could enjoy other girls being thin and good-looking, but she discovered in front of two strange policemen that she wasn't. She was a mean-spirited wee shite and she'd privately hoped some awful catastrophe would befall Heather.

Changing the subject, Patterson told her that Heather seemed to have taken her mother's car in the middle of the night and parked outside Central station. Why would she go into town alone on a Friday night? Did she have any contacts she'd meet regularly? Could she have been investigating anything? Had Heather ever taken her to the Pancake Place at night? Paddy shook her head. Heather wouldn't go to the Pancake Place at her own instigation. There were two all-night cafés in Glasgow: the Pancake Place was one, but the other one, Change at Jamaica, had a baby grand piano and a jazz set at weekends. It occurred to Paddy that if Heather had chosen a midnight venue, she would have gone there. She would have gone to the Pancake Place only if someone invited her there.

They finally let her go, holding open the door and telling her to come back and see them if she remembered anything or heard anything she thought was relevant. They still wouldn't catch her eye. She sloped off, feeling exposed and foolish.

She took the back stairs but hesitated on the first step. She couldn't face the newsroom yet. She headed downstairs to get a breath of air. One flight down she found Dr. Pete. He was damp and shivering with pain, clinging to the railing. He glanced at her feet.

"Don't tell anyone," he whispered.

"D'you want a hand to get down?"

He nodded, rolling his shoulder back stiffly. Paddy took his left elbow and led him down to the ground floor. He was shuffling like an old man, every muscle in his body taut and rigid. Every few steps a tiny inadvertent groan was carried on his breath. When they were facing the outside door he shook off her hand, took a deep breath, and straightened himself up, standing tall. He set his face to a blank sneer.

"Tell no one."

As Paddy watched him push the bar on the door and walk out into the street, she knew that he would never have let her see him that vulnerable if he thought her significant in any way.

III

Two hours later half of the newsroom had been questioned. They all went to the door when their names were called, walking out cocky and coming back sheepish. The men had been told more details of Heather's death than Paddy, and word burned its way around the newsroom: Heather's head had been beaten in with a block of concrete or a metal thing, and she'd been dead when she was dumped in the river. No one, not even the morning boys, had managed to come up with a joke about it yet. A two-hour joke lag was as reverent as a full day's silent mourning at the *News*. Half of them didn't believe it was her. The other half thought a boyfriend had done it.

The newsroom was so disrupted by Heather's death that Paddy still hadn't managed to go for lunch and there was only an hour and a half left on her shift. Keck sat next to her on the bench, touching its surface near her leg by way of symbolic physical contact. "It's been a shock. Why don't you skip your break and just go home?"

"No, I want to stay on. Everyone'll be working late tonight. I want to stay on." She needed to stay on. She didn't feel clean enough to go home.

Finally sent on her lunch break, Paddy left the building and found herself heading for the river. She hadn't eaten anything, so she stopped in a newsagent's and bought a packet of cheese-and-onion crisps for savory and a chocolate bar with nuts and raisins for sweet, together with a packet of ten Embassy Regal.

It was good hiding weather. A bitter, heavy drizzle fell from a gray sky, and she pulled up her duffel coat hood, wrapping the coarse material tight around her chest. She ate the crisps and chocolate as she walked, dodging the heavy-eyed lunch-hour drunks, marooned until the pubs opened again at five, who busied themselves by begging for loose change to piss away on drink. Paddy found a stretch of railing out of the way of pedestrians and turned her face to the water.

As she watched the rain needle the slow river, she smoked and had no trouble inhaling. She hadn't known how much she'd resented Heather or how ugly she'd felt next to her. With all her defenses down, Paddy could see that she wasn't a nice girl at all. Maybe Sean and her family were right: she was nasty and mean and fat and stupid. She was an arsehole.

She hung over the steel railings, smoking and watching the thick, gray water, self-pitying tears sliding down her face, and wished that Sean were there to hold her head against his chest and stop her seeing.

TWENTY-TWO

HEATHER'S LEAD

I

Paddy stood looking into the mouth of the postbox, the soft rain pattering on her hood as midmorning commuters brushed past her on their way to work. Her Valentine card to Sean had dropped like a lead weight into the black void, and now she didn't know if she had done the right thing. He'd get it before the actual day; she'd posted it too early. If only the card hadn't been quite as soppy. She was afraid the stench of desperation would stick to it and he'd guess how much she needed to see him. She wouldn't be able to take in what had happened to Heather until she told him, until he was there to hold her hand and make it okay.

She was still worrying about the card when she got into the office. Her back shift

327

started at ten, during the slump before the morning editorial meeting, and the newsroom wasn't busy. Keck waved her over to the bench and told her excitedly that the police were looking for her again. They had been pissing everyone around all morning, pulling staff down to the interview rooms for three-minute questionings, checking people's work times with the employment records. They interrupted someone on a difficult-to-get line from Poland, insisting that he come downstairs with them. Farquarson was livid about it. He was heard shouting down the phone to McGuigan, telling him he wanted the police put out of the building.

"I said I'd send you down right away," said Keck, watching her approach Farquarson's door. "You've to go right now."

Paddy nodded at him as she knocked on the glass. "In a minute."

Farquarson called out permission to come in.

"Can I talk to you for a minute?"

"Literally a minute?"

"Yeah."

"Okay." He put down the sheet of paper he was reading. "Start now."

She leaned on his desk, bending her

fingers back and rocking to and fro as she spoke. "I've got an idea that there's another story hiding inside the Baby Brian one because the case is very similar to another case that happened to another child who lived in Townhead, on the same estate actually, but it was eight years ago and I went to Steps on the train and it doesn't make sense for the boys to take a train past Barnhill to hide the baby when Barnhill's full of disused buildings and waste ground." She looked up. "What do you think?"

Farquarson was looking past her to the door.

"Liddel phoned Poland and he's giving his copy to the editor now. D'you want to give it tops?"

Terry Hewitt was standing behind her, taking all of Farquarson's attention. He smiled straight at Paddy, making her drop her eyes and turn briskly away.

"We'll see what he's got first," said Farquarson. "But, aye, bring it in before the meeting starts."

Hewitt withdrew, leaving Paddy standing, forgetting what she'd said and what she hadn't said.

Farquarson looked up at her. "I'm sick of this. Everyone's been in here with a different idea for a Baby Brian story." He picked his teeth and stared at the wall for a moment. "Okay. No one's mentioned this previous case. Find out more about it, write it up, and maybe we can run it for contrast or something during the trial."

It was all Paddy could do not to skip the two flights down to the police on editorial.

The corridor was overheated, the air thick with fibers and dust from the rarely used lush carpet. Paddy could hear low voices through the door. She waited in the corridor, looking out the window. The police cars were gone from the street. *Scottish Daily News* delivery vans were backed up nose to tail like a troop of elephants, waiting for bales of the final edition. The drivers were gathered in an empty van near the front, keeping out of the way of the rain, laughing and smoking together.

Remembering the look in Terry Hewitt's eye, she found herself salivating. She corrected herself: he wasn't better-looking than Sean. He might be more attractive, but he wasn't better-looking. She had chosen the wrong Valentine's card for Sean. It was padded blue silk and said "I love you" inside; bought it on a whim that morning. Open, bare-faced emotion was out of character, but it was how she really felt about him. He wasn't returning her calls as it was. She should have matched his coolness and kept her dignity. She hoped he didn't show it to Mimi.

Voices approached her through one of the closed doors, and she turned to see it open. A bald policeman was accompanying one of the women from personnel, crying behind her thick-lensed glasses, her faraway eyes pinpricks of red regret. The officer patted her elbow and muttered empty words of comfort.

"I don't want tae —" She broke off, kneading a cotton hankie into a flat plane and blowing her nose into it.

The impatient officer pushed the crying woman by the upper arm out into the corridor, swinging her around the corner towards the lifts. The woman turned and crossed the doorway, still sniffling and covering her mouth with her handkerchief as she made her way towards the back stairs. He watched her double back and looked puzzled.

"We're not allowed to use the lifts," explained Paddy.

He shook his head, looking at her for the first time. "Who are you?"

"Paddy Meehan." She felt as if she'd done something wrong but couldn't think what it might be. "You were asking for me upstairs? I just got in."

He didn't look pleased to see her and glanced back at someone sitting at the table. It was Patterson, the squat-faced bully from yesterday. Patterson looked a little flushed when he saw it was her.

"Got any more brilliant ideas for us?"

"I'll go away if you want."

The bald officer stepped aside to let her in, glancing behind her into the corridor to make sure there wasn't a queue forming.

The policemen had clearly been there all morning: four big white tea mugs from the canteen were drained and drip-stained, red-and-gold wrappers from caramel log biscuits were folded into interesting shapes on one side of the table, rolled up into tight little balls on the other.

Patterson stood up as Paddy approached, pulling out a seat for her, managing to make her feel that she had let everyone down by not already being in the chair. The sheet of paper in front of his seat had diagrams on it drawn in ballpoint, circles joined and overlapping with lines scored between them, retraced over and over. On a separate sheet, a long list of names was illegibly written in longhand, some with ticks, some with crosses next to them.

"So . . ." Patterson slid into his seat and looked her up and down as if he'd heard something about her. He left the moment hanging in the air between them.

"What did you want to see me for?" she asked flatly, determined to be more wily than she was yesterday.

"We want to ask you about the radio car and the night you and Heather were supposed to go out in it. What happened?"

"What do you mean?"

"Weren't you both supposed to be going?"

"She dropped out."

"Why?"

Paddy thought about it for a moment. They were after McVie. "Dunno. She couldn't be bothered. She didn't think there was a story in it."

Patterson nodded and hummed, tapping his rough diagram with his pen. "Right?" He rolled out his bottom lip and nodded softly, as if he was seriously considering the possibility. "See, I heard that Heather thought McVie had a thing about her."

Paddy tutted and shook her head. "D'you know how many men she thought had a thing about her? Every man in here, and she was mostly right. McVie's harmless; he didn't mean anything by it."

"Is he a letch?"

Paddy laughed alone for a moment. "How long have you been in this building? They're all letches. The print room's wall-papered in pornography. Most of them can't hold a conversation with a woman without staring at her chest. If letching was a concern you'd need to instigate a policy of internment for the entire paper."

The officers looked at her for a telling moment. Only someone from a Republican background would use a loaded word like "internment." She knew it was still rare for a Catholic to work in a middle-class pro-fession like the papers, or even the police. Paddy was a new generation and had never knowingly suffered anti-Catholic discrimi-nation, but she still enjoyed the status of political underdog. She squared her shoul-ders and looked Patterson straight in the eye, raising an eyebrow, embarrassing him into continuing.

"So you went out in the radio car," he said, four hundred years of bloodshed lying unacknowledged between them. "And what happened?"

She shrugged. "Nothing. We went on a couple of calls, a suicide and a gang fight in Govan. It was interesting."

"What day was it?"

"Monday, last week."

He made a note of it in one of his inter-connecting bubbles. "Now, think carefully: did Heather know anyone who lived in Townhead?"

"Townhead? I don't think so. She was posh."

"She never mentioned anyone to you? A friend, someone she might go up there to see?"

"No. Why?"

"Any idea why she would go up there last Thursday evening?"

It was the same night Paddy had been there after visiting Tracy Dempsie. She was glad she hadn't bumped into Heather; she didn't know what she would have said.

"I don't know why she was up there," she told Patterson. "It's bound to be some-thing to do with Baby Brian."

"Bound to be? You seem very sure about her motives."

He had that spark in his eye. He was going for her again, but this time she was ready.

"What's your problem with me?" she said angrily. "Why're you always picking on me?"

Patterson looked a little bit startled. "I'm simply asking a question."

"And I'm simply answering them." She

had frightened him, and she was pleased.

"Fine." Patterson stood up and pulled at the back of her chair. "That's all. Get out."

She stood up. "You are a rude wee bastard."

"Out, or I'll arrest you for breach."

Paddy looked at his bald colleague, who affirmed with an incline of his head that Patterson was mad enough to do it and she should go while she could.

Patterson pointed at the door. "We'll come for you again if we need you." He waved her out into the corridor and shut the door firmly in her face, giving it a little extra tug as if to stop her getting back in.

She called the door an arsehole, but it gave her no relief.

On the back stairs she picked up a new edition from the stack and locked herself in the toilets on editorial. For ten minutes she sat there staring blankly at the back of the door, sweating softly. Heather seemed very dead now. They could have met that night. Heather might even have been in Townhead at Thomas Dempsie's house, she could have found the clippings herself, she was brighter than she seemed sometimes. Paddy lit a cigarette and inhaled deep into her lungs to wake herself up. The nicotine hit her system, firing up her nerves and making the back of her skull throb.

She looked at the paper. The black-bordered photograph of Heather on the front page was a formal, posed picture. She was very pretty: she had a dainty little button nose and nice teeth, and her hair was as thick as possible without being coarse. Paddy remembered unraveling long, golden threads from her fingers outside the newsroom. It occurred to her that the editors must have been kicking themselves for using the proprietorial approach with Baby Brian when they could have used it almost justifiably with Heather. She had gone from being an outcast to the beloved daughter of the *Daily News* in less than a week.

On the inside pages Heather's mother spoke of her heartbreak, highlighting all that was best in Heather's life: her academic ability, her kindness, her sense of humor, and her three Duke of Edinburgh awards. She asked why anyone would want to snuff that out, as if the murderer had, God-like, given due weight to every deed Heather had ever done, judged her, and decided to kill her anyway. The mother was photographed outside the Allens' enormous Georgian house, looking exhausted and angry.

On the opposite page a kidney victim

(31) was trying to raise money for a dialysis machine by holding a sponsored tea party. The Evil Baby Brian Boys were still being investigated. Their old school was pictured, a photo of the empty playground in an eerie light with sweet wrappers and crisp packets floating around, the debris of a hundred packed lunches. It mentioned that the school was Roman Catholic twice in the text and once below the picture.

Paddy looked at the picture of Heather again. They had been kicking around Townhead on the same evening. If Paddy had met her she might still be alive. Maybe they would have had a fight and made up and Heather would have invited her along to the Pancake Place to meet a contact. But they wouldn't have made up and Heather would never have shared a contact or an advantage if she could help it.

Paddy dropped the cigarette between her legs and into the toilet bowl, folded her paper neatly, and went up to the clippings library.

II

Helen was off sick, they said, with a head cold, and Paddy was glad of it. The other

338

librarians were difficult and rude, but she knew they'd give her what she wanted. The woman serving her was Sandy, Helen's right hand in the library. Sandy was secretly a very pleasant, helpful woman, but it was a side of her personality she only got to show when Helen wasn't there to tut at it.

Paddy told her that the police had requested any gray slips filled out by Heather Allen in the last week and a half.

"Slips?"

"Yeah, what clippings she requested in the last week or so. They want me to take it down to them."

Sandy bit her lip. "God, isn't it awful sad?"

"It's her family I feel for," said Paddy.

"I know, I know." She opened a drawer beneath the counter and pulled out a foolscap file marked "A," searching through it with nimble fingers. "Nothing in the last week. But she'd a lot of stuff two weeks before that." She pulled out the sheets and flipped through them. "Yes, I remember those ones. All about Sheena Easton and Bellshill." She pulled them out of the file and sat them on the counter. "She was writing an article."

"But nothing in the last week?"

"Nothing for two weeks."

"Oh, and Farquarson wants any clippings on an old case." Paddy tried to look nonchalant. "Thomas Dempsie. It's an old murder. Some of them'll be under Alfred Dempsie."

The afternoon was busy, and Paddy didn't get the chance to read the clippings before she went home. She left them hidden in a drawer in the photographers' office, underneath the picture editor's portfolio, knowing they would be safe there.

On the train home she leaned her head against the window and imagined Heather up in Townhead on the same night as her, asking questions and banging on doors. She might have met Kevin McConnell as well, but Paddy didn't think so. He wouldn't have wasted time flirting with Paddy if Heather had been there.

The house was a husk. They had now been ignoring her for nearly a week, and Mary Ann couldn't say when it would end. The silence had hardened from a sorrowful quiet to a bitter sneer. Marty smirked straight at her when they passed each other on the stairs; Trisha no longer served her careful dinners but dished up carelessly overboiled potatoes and unsalted soup;

and her father and brothers stayed out as much as possible.

Things were getting worse, but Paddy had come to enjoy the solitude and silence of it. It left swathes of space in her head, and across these great prairies she stumbled from Thomas Dempsie to the layout of Townhead and the railway in Steps where Baby Brian had been found. The elements were there, she was sure, but her unpracticed mind couldn't tease sense from them.

She sat in her bedroom looking out the window at the garden, watching the steam from the washing machine curl up the outside wall. She imagined Sean sitting near her, just out of the scope of her vision. In her mind she reached back and touched him, comforting herself. He kissed her neck and floated off to another part of the house, leaving her warm and happy. She was getting used to being alone.

TWENTY-THREE

BRINGING IT
ALL BACK HOME
1968

I

It was a quiet Tuesday before Christmas and the department store was half empty. Meehan wiped the top of the glass cabinet with a yellow cloth, paying attention to his hands so that he didn't drift off. He could get the boxes out from under the counter and change the order around — that would keep him busy. He was thirty-three years old and only just learning the rudimentary goldbricking skills everyone else knew by their fifteenth birthday.

It was a parole job, to keep the board happy. It choked him, taking orders from wee Jonny, a fairy who wore hair spray and had twenty years on the shop floor, but Meehan's father was dying of cancer and he couldn't get revoked just now. He had never been much to the old man, but he was determined to be there for him now. The old man had never been much to him, right enough. He couldn't remember his father ever making him happy, or giving him time; mostly he was a figure feared in the house for random violence. He dreaded to think how his own kids would remember him.

Jonny minced up to the counter. "May I assist?"

"I am thinking of sending a pen as a gift to my friend in Germany."

Meehan hadn't heard that accent since Rolf handed him over to the British consulate. He turned and blurted, *"Sind sie Deutsch?"*

The woman looked up, surprised and delighted, and stepped immediately along the counter to him.

"Are you East German?" Meehan asked.

"Yes, I am," she said in crisp English. "I am from Dresden."

Meehan looked into her sea-green eyes as she spoke, but his attention was on the periphery. She was tall and blond, dressed in an elegant leopard skin coat with leather trim and matching belt, pulled tight to show off her slender waist. Her nails were painted beige, and she was holding a pair of beige kid gloves that matched her handbag. She drew the gloves softly through her free hand, over and again. She looked too good for Glasgow, too good for the Lewis's fountain pen counter, and it made him suspicious.

Meehan had come to expect them. After George Blake escaped and they discovered the two-way radio in his cell, the Secret Service had come back to him, drilling him for the information he'd freely given them in West Berlin after Rolf handed him over. They moved him into solitary for three months with meals through the door, his only human contact periodic visits from the Service, alternately angry and calm, coaxing and threatening. They were convinced he was holding out. He couldn't tell them that he had no loyalties, not to them and not to the East, where the guards didn't shake hands and Rolf could pretend to like him for a year and a half. Meehan's only loyalty was to his mates and his family, and he didn't even like most of them that much.

They released him on parole but followed him all the time. He often found well-dressed men watching the front of their house in the Gorbals high flats. A stranger had been seen using a key to get in and out of his mother's house on a day when everyone else was at work. The telephone clicked loudly after they picked it up. If Meehan made an arrangement by phone, an immaculate loner with a copper's haircut would be sitting in the pub or club or café when he arrived, always reading a paper but never turning the page.

The woman was a beauty, though. Not police. Definitely Secret Service.

"And how do you come to be in Glasgow?" he asked her.

"My husband is English, in the diplomatic service, and we are posted here." Her gaze slipped from his to the glass-topped counter, and she added quietly, "His work is very secret."

It was clumsy and unsophisticated, but she wasn't embarrassed — like Rolf when Meehan realized he despised him, not a flicker of shame. They all thought he was an idiot. He wanted to show her he knew, to say that he knew who she was and what she was there for, but she was gorgeous and there was just the faintest chance of touching her.

He pointed at the pen in front of her. "Would you like to see one of these?"

"No, thank you, I am simply looking with curiosity. Why is it the case that you speak German?"

Meehan shrugged. "I lived there for a while." He would have said it was in the East to give them more to talk about, but he didn't know where Rolf and his friends had kept him. "In Frankfurt."

"And yet your accent sounds from the East." She raised her perfect eyebrows.

Meehan tried not to smile: he hadn't said enough for her to hear his accent.

"I do not know many German speakers here." She touched her white blond hair gently, drawing his eye to the intricacies of the coloring. "I find myself quite lonely."

Jonny looked at Meehan, pursing his lips approvingly. He moved away to the far edge of the counter, leaving them alone. Meehan took out some pens from under the counter and let her look at them, lifting them and putting them down again, stroking the tortoiseshell casing on one, smiling at the extra-large inkwell on another. Their fingers touched once as he handed over a Cross with a calligraphic nib, his fingertip brushing her inner wrist. Her hand was as soft and warm as butter, and he would have given up the job just to touch it with his lips. He began to perspire.

346

She was a gorgeous twenty-five-year-old blonde, put together like a Miss World. Meehan knew what he looked like: he was five foot eight, acne-scarred, and out of shape. Done up he wasn't much of a prize, but wearing a cheap uniform blazer and standing behind a counter, he must look a mess.

"Well, it was very nice to meet you," she said, proffering a hand. "Perhaps I may come in again and talk with you in German?"

"Das wäre schön," he said, and took her hand, intending to shake it firmly but professionally. She put her pretty hand in his, her fingertips curling as she pulled away, stroking the full length of his palm and making his mouth water. She turned on her perfect heels and clip-clopped away.

Jonny was at his elbow in a moment. "Patrick, you're a hit with the ladies. I'd never have guessed. Is she coming back in? What was that ye said to her?"

"She said she'd come back in." Meehan caught his breath. "And I said that would be lovely."

"That coat must have cost what we earn in a month," said Jonny, catching a final glimpse of her heading for the stairs to the exit. "From Paris, by the look of it."

II

Meehan left the job two months later without ever telling Jonny his suspicions about her. The beautiful German appeared to him just once more, in the pub where he was meeting James Griffiths before their recce jaunt to Stranraer — the night he'd never be able to forget.

He and Griffiths had arranged to meet on the phone, and Griffiths had blurted out the name of the pub. He wasn't the brightest and he couldn't remember the code. Paddy was just pleased that he hadn't said "tax decal robbery" and "Stranraer" on the phone as well.

The woman was alone when he came in. She was drinking a small lemonade and standing at the bar. She chatted with Meehan, expressing surprise at their meeting again, having no trouble remembering where she had seen him before. Meehan didn't handle it well. He knew she was there because of Griffiths's mistake and was wary and afraid. He was a little rude to her. She was wearing the coat again but this time had higher shoes on, beige court shoes, and a pale blue scarf at her throat. When she left, the entire pub turned and watched, staring at the door as it shut and bounced open again, giving them one more flash of her perfect ankle.

Later, after Rachel Ross died, during his seven long years in solitary confinement, Meehan remembered the woman and the way she slipped her hand through his, the way her hips moved inside her coat, the touch of her lipstick-sticky lips against each other. He had never seen such a beautiful woman outside the movies. He wondered whether she might have been his in another life. If he'd had an education, been born three miles to the west or south of the Gorbals, maybe he could have been charming and rich, a sophisticated linguist, a poet or painter, good enough for a woman like her.

He made up a history for her: She was a spy, yes, but she had been forced into it after escaping from the East. The British had threatened to hand her back over if she didn't work for them. She had a husband, a handsome man with a job in science, but he had died young and left her alone. Meehan liked to think that although good-looking, the dead husband might have been a short man with bad skin, that Meehan might remind her of him in some way. She became a golden light in the dark years ahead. It was the one good thing about the aftermath of the East and Stranraer and the subsequent years of hell: being caught in the middle of it all meant that he had met her.

III

Seven years later Meehan was on exercise, walking around a concrete yard in a burst of black rain. Water smashed off the concrete, bouncing up his trouser legs, making his bare legs wet. He walked in a slow circle, his collar pulled up, while the guards watched him from the shelter of the doorway. He only got out once a fortnight. Apart from two months somewhere in the middle, he had always been kept in a solitary cell because he refused to work.

He wished he could draw. He'd do a picture of the yard and put it up on his wall and imagine himself out here whenever he wanted. He'd draw the Tapp Inn in the Gorbals, where all his cronies drank. Meehan had laughed louder and longer in the Tapp Inn than anywhere else. He'd draw it from outside, the colored glass windows and high white walls, and leave the door open so he could see the bar and fat Hannah Sweeny cleaning the glasses.

Over the years he had spent most of his time in Peterhead Prison on the gray, wind-lashed Aberdeen coast, and he had been in his present cell for eight months, but wherever they kept him the cells all looked the same. The walls were painted with thick paint, a gloss so that it could be washed clean whatever happened, even if a man had his throat cut and sprayed blood everywhere.

The thick paint meant that prisoners could scratch messages into the wall with the softest of implements: a sharpened spoon or a nail from a bed, sometimes even with a bit of flint found in the exercise yard. Paddy had read every single word on these walls. He had made up stories for the messages to pass the time. J. McC. TWO YEARS + FIVE DAYS was a street fighter from Edinburgh who robbed a post office. SHITEBALLS was a ned, a nonearning thug who beat his wife to death with a shoe. The stories had become so familiar that Paddy had fallen out with some of them. He was sure LICK MY CUNT had been written by a nonce, and the Rangers graffiti wound him up so he had stuck some of his pictures over them. The messages from one poof to another annoyed him. He felt implicated by their sexiness and tender words, so he stuck pictures over them too. The things he hung on his wall formed a senseless pattern, some up high, some down low — full stops to imaginary arguments.

Prisoners weren't usually allowed to put up pictures in solitary, but they let Meehan do it because he had been in for so long. He had seven things on his wall, one for every year he had served for Rachel Ross. He felt it was an important statement that he hadn't chosen to put up scuddy pictures of birds like guys who were waiting out their time. Instead, he had chosen to pin up important letters about his case, including a Crown Office letter stating that his application to sue the police for perjury had been received. He wasn't allowed to bring the case but was proud that he had tried; it was an obscure part of Scots law, and he had discovered it himself. The *Sunday Times* special investigation into his case was pinned to the wall as well, and nearby a *Scottish Daily News* front page: a confession to the murder of Rachel Ross by Ian Waddell. Waddell wouldn't name the second man, the only person in the world who could corroborate his story and release Paddy Meehan.

The only color picture on the wall was

the red-and-black script on the cover of the book Ludovic Kennedy had written about his conviction. Next to it a one-page point-by-point dismissal of the case, from the disputed traces of Rachel Ross's blood on Meehan's trousers to the paper scraps from Abraham's safe being found in Griffiths's pocket.

He was trying hard to keep his mind. He counted things over and over: the bars, the squares of the mesh covering the window, the bangs on the pipes as they heated up in the morning and cooled at night. He had tried to count every cut in the wall, every line scratch, but the distinctions became too technical, and he couldn't decide between continuous lines that changed direction and individual incisions. He talked to himself in a normal voice, without shame or embarrassment, quite unworried about who would hear him. He said the same things over and over. Bastards. Arseholes. Not me, pal, it wasn't me. *Das wäre schön. Das wäre schön, Lieben. Mein Lieben.*

She sauntered through his cell a hundred times a night, asking for pens and finding herself lonely, moving her snaky hips like a dancer. Sometimes she danced for him, tiny steps, raising a foot and then another, the belt on her leopard-skin coat swinging to and fro. A Mediterranean summer gleam shone around her. She rarely looked at him, keeping her grassy-green eyes on her feet as she danced and staring straight ahead when she walked. He didn't just see her when he wanted a tug either. He saw her when he felt low; when he saw himself in his filthy surroundings and read the messages from the men who had been in here before him; when he suspected that he was just like them, no better, no mistake. Then she would come and bring the light and speak to him in broken German. When his appeals were turned down and the home secretary decided against reopening the case, then she would come to him. Sometimes she would sit on his horsehair bed and hold his hand. Her skin was soft, like air. Other times he didn't see her but just knew she was out of his line of vision. He reached back to touch her sometimes, and she might touch his neck with her manicured fingertips before floating away, leaving him warm and happy.

He had to ration her company to keep it special. During the worst times he tried to keep her out of his thoughts altogether, afraid she would become tainted by the association.

Coming back from exercise, Meehan walked through the open door into his cell and stood dripping onto the floor, keeping his back to the door so the screw couldn't see him smiling. He loved the rain.

TWENTY-FOUR

IMPOSSIBLY SOPHISTICATED SOUP

1981

The waitress brought her over a mug of tea and two poached eggs on toast. It was a café no one from the *News* ever used because it was up a very steep hill, next to Rotten Row maternity hospital. The plates were chipped, the mugs were stained, but the place was clean in the corners and the pattern on the Formica worktops had been worn away with endless scrubbing and bleaching. Paddy liked the warm room, liked it that they used butter instead of margarine, and that the eggs were freshly made to order. The large window onto the street was always steamed over, reducing the outside world to passing ghosts. Paddy had chosen poached eggs on toast because it was a bit like the Mayo Clinic Diet: eggs was eggs after all.

She took the clippings envelope out of her pocket and slipped two fingers in, pulling out the folded, yellowing newspapers to read while she ate. The articles hadn't been opened for years and had dried around one another in a tidy little package. She flattened them carefully and flicked through, finding an interview with Tracy Dempsie from the time just after Thomas was found dead but before Alfred was accused. Tracy said that whoever did this to her boy should be hanged and it was a shame that they weren't hanging people anymore because that's what she'd like to see. Even in sanitized quotes she sounded a bit nuts.

Another story made it clear, through aspersion and innuendo, that Tracy had run away from her first husband to be with Alfred. They seemed to have met at the ballroom dancing, which was a fancy way of saying that despite being married, Tracy was hanging around a meat market looking for a man. The photographs showed her looking not a minute younger than she had when Paddy went to visit her. Her hair was pulled up in exactly the same style, but the skin on her face had less give. She was sitting in a living room strewn with toys and clutching a photograph of her young son. Thomas had big eyes and blond hair that curled at the tips. He grinned at the person holding the camera, squeezing tight every muscle on his tiny face.

As she reread the text of the long articles, she was struck by how beautifully written they were. The language was so crisp that wherever her eye landed it skidded effortlessly to the end of the paragraph. She looked for the byline and found that they were all written by Peter McIltchie. She was staggered: she had never known Dr. Pete to produce anything like usable copy. He wasn't even trusted to churn out holiday cover for the Honest Man column, a despised weekly opinion piece cynically shaped to chime with the readership's most ill-informed prejudices. Being saddled with the column was more than a sign that a journalist's star was sinking, it was the professional equivalent of a tolling bell.

Paddy carefully dried the grease off her fingers with a paper napkin before folding up the clippings along their well-established creases, setting them on top of one another in chronological order, and slipping them carefully back into the stiff brown envelope. She finished off her last bite of buttery toast and stood up to put on her coat.

Terry Hewitt was standing in front of her, wearing his black leather with the red shoulders. If Sean had been drawn with a ruler, Terry was a sketch, all crumpled shirt and uneven skin. His fingertips were balanced nervously on the back of a chair. He looked away and wrinkled his forehead, as if they were at the end of the conversation instead of the beginning, and twitched a one-second smile, more of an entreaty than a greeting.

"What are you doing here?"

"Having my lunch." She was about to extrapolate into a joke or a gibe about how fat she was but stopped herself, remembering his calling her a fat lassie in the Press Bar. She picked up her bag and pulled on her coat. "I'll leave you my table."

She turned to go, but Terry reached across and tugged at her sleeve. "Wait, Meehan." He blanched, embarrassed at the intimacy of using her name. "I want to talk to you."

Paddy bristled. "What about?"

He smiled at her, his lips retracting across his teeth again. She liked that. It made him look so hesitant. "Baby Brian. I heard you talking to Farquarson."

She stopped and crossed her arms. "You're not going to try and steal my story, are you? Because I've had enough of that for one week."

"If I was going to steal it from you I'd hardly be here, would I? I'm interested."

He raised his eyebrows and looked at her chair, inviting her to sit with him. She dropped her resentment for a moment and imagined that maybe her crush could be reciprocated, just a little. But boys like Terry Hewitt liked girls from houses, girls with slim necks and thick hair who went to uni to study theater.

Her temper flared up again. "I heard you asking Dr. Pete who I was."

He looked puzzled. "I don't remember that."

"In the Press Bar. I heard you ask who the fat lassie was."

He blushed deep into his shirt collar. "Oh," he said meekly. "I didn't mean you."

"Right? Was Hattie Jacques in the bar that day?"

He rolled his head away from her. "I just wanted to know who you were. I'm sorry." He cringed. "It was the morning-shift boys, you know? I couldn't very well —"

"It's no excuse for being fucking rude."

360

She sounded more angry than she meant to.

He raised an imploring hand. "If you wanted to know who I was, what would you ask them? Who's the handsome guy with the perfect figure?" He saw her waver. "If you give me ten minutes I can stretch to a Blue Riband."

It was as cheap as chocolate biscuits came. She smiled and upped the ante. "Plus a mug of tea."

He stroked his chin. "You're a hard woman, but okay."

Feigning reluctance, she let her duffel coat slip from her shoulders and took her seat again. Terry sat across from her, putting one palm flat on the tabletop as if he was going to reach forward and take her hand in his. The waitress took their order for two cups of tea, a bowl of soup, and a chocolate biscuit. Paddy thought he was having a three-course meal.

"I can't wait long."

"It's just a bowl of soup."

He was only having soup. She had never known anyone sit down to soup as a meal. Soup was a watery precursor to a meal, a poor man's filler to stop the children eating all the potatoes. She looked at Terry with renewed admiration. He seemed impossibly sophisticated.

He did the reticent smile again, and she realized that he was working her. She wondered if other women had weaknesses for bonny men. They never seemed to talk about it.

"Did I hear that you were related to someone in the case?"

Now would be a good time to mention her fiancé, but she wasn't sure if she still had one. "How would I know what you've heard? We've never spoken to each other before."

"I know, and it's a damn shame," he said, and made her smile.

The waitress came straight back over with two mugs of tangy brown tea and his soup. Terry used his spoon, scooping the soup away from himself, impeccably mannered.

"I wanted to ask if we could work together on the article about the previous case."

"It's my idea, why would I want you to work on it with me?"

"Well, I thought about that: I could help you write it up. If you want to move up from the bench you'd want Farquarson to use a substantial chunk of your unaltered copy. Otherwise they'll just think you're a researcher. It's harder than you think, and

I've got experience of writing long articles."

She knew he was exaggerating his experience a bit. She'd taken his copy to the print room once or twice and read it on the stairs. It was good, but it wasn't that good. Still, he would be able to organize the ideas at least, show her how to get from one paragraph to another and keep herself out of it. It was a chance to get her name on something.

"I could be Samantha, your lovely assistant." He patted his hair. "Add a bit of glamour to the act."

Paddy smiled despite herself. Terry was arrogant. She saw him allying himself with certain people in the newsroom, the smart guys who picked the right stories and knew what was going on. He was blatantly ambitious, eager to make a space for himself in the world. If he kissed a girl he wouldn't be prudish about it. He wouldn't do self-effacing voluntary work with the poor or refuse to have sex until his wedding night. He was the anti-Sean.

"I know where one of the boys lives. I've been to his house."

"So, he is a relative?"

Paddy didn't want to mention Sean to him. She wanted to keep them separate. "A distant relative."

"Is that why you're interested in the case?"

"No, I'm interested because the police are making a lot of jumps. The boys disappeared for hours. Then they took the baby past Barnhill, which is where they live. It's got acres of overgrown waste ground, but they took him miles away to Steps. Then, supposedly, they crossed over a live rail, did the deed, and got a train back into town, but they weren't seen on the train or in the swing park or walking back to Barnhill. They could have been helicoptered in for all anyone knows."

"They were seen, on the train. A witness came forward last Friday."

Her heart sank a little. "Witnesses can be wrong."

"This seems pretty solid. It's an old woman. She's not an attention seeker. The police must be pretty sure or they wouldn't be telling anyone about her."

"Aye, well." Paddy sipped her tea. "Just because they're sure . . ."

They watched the echoes of cars and buses blur past the steamed-up window. Paddy wanted to tell him about Abraham Ross, how the police made sure he picked Meehan out of a lineup. Mr. Ross was certain Meehan was the man. He fainted at the lineup he was so sure, but then he changed his mind before the trial. Witnesses could be swayed, they could change their minds. The woman might be an idiot.

"I've got a car," Terry said suddenly, hesitating because it sounded as if he was boasting.

They looked at each other and laughed.

"Good for you," said Paddy. "I can eat my own weight in boiled eggs."

She had meant it half as a reference to her miracle diet, half as a hollow boast. Terry didn't understand either but found it terribly funny, so funny he lost his tentative smile and opened wide, laughing loudly. For a first conversation with the object of a month-long crush, it was going incredibly well.

"No," he said. "I wasn't just boasting about the car. I meant, d'you want to come to Barnhill with me and have a look? I'm busy tomorrow, but we could go on Friday after work."

She hesitated. Valentine's Day fell on the Saturday, and she would want to stay in on Friday waiting for Sean's reconciliatory call.

"I could do with the protection," he continued. "It's a bit rough up there, and I'm a lover, not a fighter."

It was the first time Paddy had ever heard a Glaswegian man admit openly that he couldn't beat anyone in a fight at any time.

"You'll need protection. It's a bit grim up there. Could you make it Saturday afternoon instead?"

"*Excelente,*" Terry said, toasting her with his mug. "If we work well together, maybe we could do a couple of paragraphs about the hunger strikers' march as well." The march was due to take place on Saturday, and everyone in Glasgow knew there was going to be trouble. If they had been talking to each other, Trisha would have forbidden her to go. "You could bring your Papish eyes and tell me what you see."

"How do you know I'm a Pape?"

"Is Patricia Meehan your undercover name?"

"No, my undercover name's Patricia Elizabeth Mary Magdalene Meehan."

He grinned. "Mary Magdalene?"

"My confirmation name," she explained. "You get to choose a saint you like or want to emulate."

"You wanted to emulate a prostitute?"

She shook her head. "I didn't know what she did for a living. She was the only woman with a job."

They smiled at each other.

"Saturday's fine."

"During the day," she said, in case he thought she meant anything by it.

"Great," he said.

She made up an elaborate lie: she would meet him, but she had urgent business in town on Saturday and could only meet him at the far end of King Street, at a bus stop that was far enough away from the paper to ensure they wouldn't be seen together. Terry flashed his smile at the table as she made the arrangement, knowing why she was doing it. Even the suspicion of spending free time with a man from the paper would be tantamount to civil death.

Outside the café the harsh light was bright. The lunchtime buses rattled past, full of mums with young kids and students from the poly. Paddy looked up the quiet road and back at the café. It was in a siding to a main road, and it didn't have a hanging sign. It was well hidden from passersby. She only knew about it because of the time Caroline was in Rotten Row having Baby Con.

"How did you find me up here?" she asked.

"You come here a lot, don't you? I've seen you."

The words hung between them, as shocking as an inadvertent kiss on the lips, and Terry seemed suddenly flustered.

He punched her arm. "See you later, then," he said, and spun around, heading down the hill like an angry speed walker.

TWENTY-FIVE

DR. PETE'S CONDITION

I

The sun forgot to rise on Thursday. Outside the newsroom windows the city was stuck in perpetual twilight, the sky darkened by a bank of thick black cloud. Every light in the newsroom blazed bright. It was two in the afternoon, but it felt like a busy midnight shift, as if some great catastrophe had occurred in the dead of night, causing them all to be called back in to draw up a fresh edition.

Paddy was looking for Dr. Pete to ask him about Thomas Dempsie. She had been all over the building, buzzing about on errands, excelling herself by doing three canteen runs in fifteen minutes. Keck had warned her to slow down. Pete was nowhere, and the pack of early-shift workers were lawless without him, laughing at underlings and drinking at their desks in full view of Father Richards and the editors. It was bad form for them to make their indolence so blatant: it would make it harder for Richards to take their side when the inevitable fresh dispute came up.

She was loitering on the back stairs, reading a page proof about a house fire at a party in Deptford, when she ran into Dub.

"If you're still looking for Dr. Pete, I was down for Kevin Hatcher's medicine. He's sitting in the Press Bar alone. Called in sick, apparently."

"Called in sick but he's sitting in the bar?"

"Yup."

"That's a bit cheeky, isn't it?"

"Oh, yeah."

She found Keck hanging around the sports desk and asked if she could kick off early because she'd stayed late on Monday. He told her to go, pleased to get rid of her: she was working so hard she was showing himself and Dub in a bad light.

The Press Bar smelled like a hangover. The sound of McGrade cleaning up the glasses after lunch echoed mournfully around the empty room. Dr. Pete was sitting alone at the usual morning-boys table near the back with a crisp whisky and two half-pints of bitter lined up in front of him. A read newspaper sat on the seat next to him, thumbed into a messy pillow. On his table a paper mat tanned with beer had been torn into fibrous strips and rearranged into a rudimentary jigsaw. Paddy could tell by the depth of cigarette ends in his ashtray that he had been there for some time.

He saw Paddy coming towards the table and sat up, dropping his eyes to the jigsaw, expecting her to give him a message. You're on a warning, maybe, or Never darken the newsroom door again.

Paddy stood at the side of the table, taking cover behind a chair. "Hello."

Pete looked up and frowned, dropping his bushy eyebrows to shade his eyes. "What do you want?"

"Um, I wanted to ask you about something."

"Spit it out and then piss off."

It was not going to be a Love Is . . . moment, she just knew it. "I wanted to ask you about the Thomas Dempsie murder case. I read some clippings of the articles you wrote about it."

Pete looked up at her, and something, possibly a warm thing, flashed at the back of his misery-scarred eyes. He turned the whisky glass in front of him with a slow

371

hand and lifted it, throwing the whisky to the back of his throat and swallowing. He didn't even give the customary little gasp afterwards; he might have been drinking tea. Running a gray tongue along the front of his teeth, he put down the glass.

"Sit, then."

Paddy did as she was told but kept her chair away from the dirty table, pulling the edges of her duffel coat around her lap. Still spinning the empty glass, Pete smiled to himself, his eyes surprisingly warm.

"Hide your distaste, woman. You'll have to sit at dirty tables with drunk old men if you want to work in papers."

"I'm scared."

Pete reeled his head in surprise. "Why?"

She wasn't sure how to say it. "You're a bit brutal sometimes."

"Only with an audience." He looked at her for a moment and went back to spinning his glass. "I'm a show-off. My audience is suspicious of kindness."

"Yeah, that's the trouble with working here. Everyone's a cynic."

His eyes softened. "We're all heart-broken idealists. That's what no one gets about journalists: only true romantics get jaded. What do you want to know about Dempsie?"

She bent over her knees towards him. "Do you remember the case?"

Pete nodded slowly.

"Baby Brian was taken on Thomas Dempsie's anniversary. Whoever killed Thomas would be thinking about him then." She let it linger for a moment.

"I know that," said Pete quietly.

It wasn't the reaction she was expecting. "The boys were about the same age. Plus Thomas was found in Barnhill, half a mile from where the arrested boys live."

Pete sighed heavily and sat back in his chair. "Look," he said seriously, "I'm not sitting here with you ten feet away and not even a drink in your hand. What will you have?"

"I don't really drink."

Pete looked skeptical. He raised a finger at McGrade, dropping the tip to point at Paddy. McGrade brought over a half-pint of sweet Heineken, a beer mat to sit it on, and a stale cloth to wipe the table with. She had to shift her chair around the table to get away from the smell, coincidentally moving closer to Pete. He nodded approvingly and gestured to her drink. She took a sip and found it tasted nicer than she expected, like ginger beer but more refreshing. Pete looked at how much she had taken and nodded approvingly when he saw it was a quarter gone.

Paddy leaned across the table. "Doesn't that seem strange to you that there are so many similarities between Baby Brian and Dempsie?"

He shrugged carelessly. "You see everything at least twice if you stay in this game long enough. It all comes around again. Same things again and again. It doesn't mean they're related to each other."

"It's too much of a coincidence."

Pete picked at a string of tobacco that had stuck to his lip. "Every year, usually just before Christmas, a woman in Glasgow is stabbed to death by her man."

"That's not that unusual," said Paddy.

"With a bit of broken window. They fight, a window gets broken, and he stabs her with a bit of the glass. Every single year it happens in the same way. It doesn't make sense that it happens then, but it does. Every year. It's a cycle. It's inevitable. You see patterns when you work for long enough. In the end, nothing's new."

"I'd like to know what happened back then."

Pete moved the empty whisky glass to the side, pulling the first beer glass to him. "Dempsie was a big story. The coverage was huge. The Moors Murders were relatively fresh in people's minds, and the child was so very young, sweet — good pictures, ye know?"

"How come you got all the interviews with Tracy Dempsie? Were you assigned them?"

"No, I doorstepped her. I found out the address and waited outside, in the rain, for three hours until she let me in." He raised an eyebrow. "I really cared in those days. That surprises you, doesn't it?"

It didn't, but Paddy nodded to be polite. "Was Alfred there when you interviewed her?"

"Yeah, he was there. I saw him with his other kid, the older one."

"His stepson?"

"Yeah. He didn't like that boy, it was obvious, but he loved his son, the wee one. He was torn apart."

"Is there a chance he did it?"

"Oh, Dempsie was innocent."

Pete's chin hardened a little. He lifted his glass of beer, raising his eyes to the door as someone came in. She turned back to see Father Richards standing at the door, looking over at him, furious. Dr. Pete stared back, daring Richards to come over and make him care, but Richards ordered a drink and sat down at the far end of the bar.

"No one really believed Dempsie'd done it, but it had been four months and no conviction. They needed someone. He didn't have an alibi, and these things have a life of their own. The only person who half believed he was the killer was Tracy. She tried to sell her story after he was convicted, but no one would buy. That was then, of course. They'd buy it now."

"I heard the Yorkshire Ripper's wife got ten grand."

"I heard twenty." He drank the half-pint of beer in one tip of the glass, put the empty on the table, and looked suddenly younger. He licked his lips, managing a playful eye roll. "Different days. Back then there were about three crime reporters working the city. We could go for a pint together and just decide to leave things alone if we wanted. It's a different game now. It's all circulation wars and young bucks. They'd cut the arse off their own mother for a byline. It was about finding the truth and checks and balances when I was starting out."

"Woodward and Bernstein and Ludovic Kennedy?"

He winked at her. "Exactly, wee hen. Exactly. We were a proud people back then. Not like now." He gestured around the room. "A troop of whores."

Paddy smiled. She was enjoying herself, surprised that he was such good company. He had hardly even sworn at her and was going to the trouble of making her feel as if they were in the same business, instead of being a big brainy journalist and a daft wee copyboy.

"The woman," said Paddy. "Tracy. What did you make of her?"

"Ah, Tracy. Walking wounded, one of life's casualties. She was loyal to Alfred until he was taken in for questioning, and then she wanted to drop the dime on him. I don't know what she was like before the baby died, but when I met her she was all over the place, mad with grief. She'd have said anything the police wanted her to say, they only had to ask. She gave them an excuse to arrest him. Told them he wasn't really home when he said he was, cut an hour out here and there."

"How do you know that? Did the police tell you?"

"Aye, well, we were all on the case together. They became good friends, those coppers, we grew up together." He smiled at his drink. "It wasn't a good thing, though. Makes it harder to question a conviction if your pals won it. It takes an outsider to do that."

"Tracy can't have been that soft. She left her previous man."

"I think Alfred Dempsie came and got her, which is different to leaving. Then Dempsie killed himself." He raised his beer glass. "Large ones all round." He looked at Paddy's glass and twitched the corners of his mouth down. "You're not drinking. The news trade works on alcohol. You'd better learn if you're as ambitious as you seem."

She wasn't halfway through her first drink yet but accepted another to please him, and McGrade brought it over. She took a slurp and Pete checked the level in the glass again.

"Not so good this time."

She tried again.

"Better," he said, lifting the fresh whisky nearer to his hand.

"But if you all knew it was wrong, why was Dempsie in prison for five years before he killed himself? Why didn't anyone question the conviction?"

"Weight of evidence. Heavy-handed policing. They'd planted everything on him to get the conviction. You can overturn one bit of evidence, but not three or four. Then it hints at police corruption, and the courts don't want to get into that." He nodded at her. "See, there was only one bit of evidence planted in the Meehan case."

"I know."

"The paper from the Rosses' safe found in Griffiths's pocket after he was shot. You interested in Paddy Meehan?"

"A bit."

"I know him, by the way, if you want to meet him."

It was a bit sudden; Paddy didn't have her defenses up. "Oh," she said. "No. No, not really."

"He's a tricky bastard. Always annoyed. Not unreasonably, I suppose."

"I heard that."

Pete bellowed in a rich baritone: "Are you going to talk to me?"

Startled, Paddy sat up before she realized that he was talking to someone behind her. Richards was walking towards them, his face thunderous.

"You're wasting your time, Richards. I don't give a monkey's anymore."

"You phoned in sick." Richards sneered. "And then coming in here? What's wrong with you?"

"Liver cancer." Pete drank down his beer and set the empty glass to the side. "I've got cancer."

A horrible hush descended on the room. Paddy could see Richards processing the information, thinking it over, wondering whether Dr. Pete would dare lie about something like that.

"Balls."

"I got the word yesterday, and this bar is where I want to be."

Richards paused momentarily and then backed off, walking slowly back to his seat at the bar, checking Pete over his shoulder to see if he was joking. Everyone in the bar pretended they hadn't heard him and turned the pages in their papers or placed their glasses back on tables, muffling the silence.

When they were left alone, Paddy thought she should say something. "That must have been a blow."

"It's one way to get the word out, eh?" Pete looked at his drink and nodded dreamily. "This bar," he said slowly, "I like this bar."

McGrade scurried over with a fresh round of drinks from Richards, who stayed far away and nodded to them both. Paddy looked at her new half-pint. She had three glasses in front of her and hadn't finished the first one yet.

"Those Baby Brian Boys," said Pete, trying to get back to the conversation they were having before the bomb. "The police'll get a conviction. They'll have to."

"Could they have planted evidence on the Brian Boys?"

Pete curled his lip. "I'd put money on the evidence being good. If you know how to watch for the pattern, planted evidence only comes out weeks later, when they're getting frustrated. They don't start off with a plant in a big case. They might put corroborating evidence down, though. It goes on more than you think."

The bar was starting to fill up. Behind Pete a man passed on his way to the toilet, undoing his fly before reaching the door. She didn't belong here and wanted to leave. She lifted her sleeve and carefully checked her watch as a preliminary move.

Pete spoke quietly. "Please don't go."

"But I need —"

"If you go, Richards'll come over here. It's been a long day, and it's hard work being pitied."

So they sat together, a man facing the end of his life and a young girl struggling to kick-start hers. They drank together, and then Paddy started smoking with him. Cigarettes and drink complemented each other perfectly, she discovered, like white bread and peanut butter. She drank an all-time personal best of four half-pints.

They talked about anything that came to mind, their thoughts swimming sympathetically, barely connecting. Paddy told him about the Beatties' stuff in the garage, about how she'd always hated it when she saw the Queen's picture up in offices, because of what she represented. She always saw her smiling and handing out OBEs to the soldiers who shot into the crowd on Bloody Sunday, but she'd looked at the Beatties' portrait of her and thought she might actually be quite a nice woman, doing her best. She talked about her Auntie Ann, who raised money for the IRA with raffle tickets and then went on antiabortion marches.

Dr. Pete talked about a wife who had left for England years before and how she would cook a leg of lamb for special occasions. She stuck the meat with rosemary she grew in their garden and sat potatoes under it to roast in the lamb fat. The meat was as sweet as tablet, as moist as beer; it lingered on the tongue like a prayer. Before he met her he had never eaten food that made him feel as if he had just woken up to the world. The way she cooked that lamb was beautiful. She had black hair and was so slight he could lift her up and swing her over a puddle with one arm around her waist. He hadn't talked about her in a long time.

The doors were busy with men finishing their shift. Another couple of journalists drifted towards the table, looking for a seat and a joke, but Pete blanked them and they moved off elsewhere.

More uninhibited than she had ever been, Paddy confided in Dr. Pete that she loved his writing in the Dempsie articles and asked him why he didn't write anymore.

His jaundiced eyes slid across the floor of the pub and he blinked slowly. "I'm writing a book. I've been writing a book about John MacLean and Red Clydeside. They keep you back . . . My wife left . . ."

Even through the haze of alcohol, Paddy knew he was making excuses. Everyone at the *News* was writing a book; she was writing a book about Meehan in her head. Pete had just given up and joined the other lazy cynics. She couldn't imagine him fit enough to lift a woman over a puddle with one hand. She wanted to say something nice but couldn't think of a pleasantry appropriate to a man who'd pissed his life away.

Both doors opened simultaneously, letting a blast of bitterly cold air swirl into the bar. A number of men clattered noisily towards the table. It was the morning boys, coming in team-handed to visit their leader. Unbidden, they pulled over seats and settled around the table. Paddy stood up, staggering to the side a little, surprised by how drunk she was. She and Dr. Pete nodded to each other. Their time was over.

"Let that be a lesson to you," said Pete, and he broke eye contact with her, looking back at his drink. Paddy took her half-pint with her as she pulled away into the crowd.

By now the Press Bar was heaving. The air was treacle thick with smoke and the sweet smell of spilled drink. Farquarson was standing by the door, disagreeing with a short man in front of him. A sharp, attention-grabbing, acid undertone was coming from the near corner: a sports boy had snuck in a vinegar-soused fish supper and was surreptitiously eating it off his knees. Apart from Paddy there were only three other women in the room: one, a redhead in a purple sequined top, was flirting with a table of men and being bought drinks; the other two were sitting together, one of them the beady-eyed woman who'd cried as the squat-faced policeman showed her out of the interview room. Both women stared blankly ahead as they nursed small red drinks in round glasses. Keck was hanging around a table of sports guys, laughing and leaning over while they ignored him, forcing himself on the reluctant company.

Paddy decided to go home. She tried to slip behind Farquarson, but he turned to let her squeeze through and the moment for pretending not to have seen each other was past. He tried to incorporate her into the conversation he was having about football with the small man, but she didn't know anything about it.

"Ah ha," he said. "More of a rugby woman, are you?"

"I don't really watch sport."

"Right." Farquarson took another sip. "Ah, Margaret Mary McGuire." He grabbed the arm of the redhead, who was sidling past. "How the devil are you?" Margaret Mary didn't seem very pleased to see Farquarson, but he persevered. "Have you met our own Patricia Meehan? She's something else, something else." He

385

swung away abruptly, leaving the two women stuck with each other.

Margaret Mary, who was too old to be wearing a sparkly top and too ginger to be wearing a purple anything, looked Paddy up and down. Her face soured. "What age are you?"

"Eighteen," said Paddy, bold with drink. "Why, what age are you?"

"Get stuffed," said Margaret Mary, and recommenced her sashay to the toilets.

"Hiya."

Keck was pressing just a little closer to Paddy than the crowd warranted. It hurt her neck and eyes to look up at him.

"Right, Keck?"

"Come on over and I'll introduce you to the guys." He motioned towards the sports journalists, who hadn't even noticed he'd gone.

"I'm all right, Keck. I'm finishing my drink and going in a minute."

"You should come over, it's a brilliant laugh." His eyes swiveled paranoiacally around the noisy room. "Women don't like sport, eh? What do women like, anyway?" He looked at Margaret Mary's back. "What do they want from men? Big cars? You're chiselers, eh?"

"Yeah," she said, itching to get away. "If

you keep coming out with crap like that the only women who'll keep you company'll be self-loathing nut-jobs. There are lots of nice women in the world."

He smiled like a hostage trying not to alert the police. "I'm always frightened to talk to you in case you think, 'What's that dirty wee bastard been thinking about me?' " His glassy eyes were fixed on her neck. She could tell he was thinking about her tits but didn't have the courage just to stare at them. "I'm an animal in bed, you know."

Paddy drained her glass and feigned bewilderment. "How does that work? Have you got a magic mattress or something?"

At the door she turned for a last fond look round the bar and found Pete staring after her in silent entreaty, asking her to get him out of there. Paddy waved goodbye, pretending she had misread his eyes, and left him to be enveloped in a crowd of his own kind.

II

She sobered up on the train home, sucking her way through a packet of mints to cover the smell of drink and fags. She looked out

the window at the passing lights of Rutherglen town hall and thought about the witness who had seen the boys on the train.
The witness might not be credible. McVie
knew all the policemen in Glasgow; he'd be
able to find out something about it for her.

The house was dead. Trisha sat stiffly in
the front room as Paddy ate in the kitchen,
watching Adam and the Ants on *Top of the
Pops*. They both knew she only had it on
for the noise, so they wouldn't be left alone
together in the crushing silence. Paddy finished her dinner, watching the back of her
mum's head, enjoying the detached numbness afforded by the alcohol. She filled her
pockets with custard creams and went upstairs to her bed.

She lay on top of the covers, staring at
the ceiling and eating mechanically
through the biscuits, letting the crumbs
spill into her hair and ears. Valentine's was
on Saturday — just one more lonely day to
go. He might not phone tomorrow night,
but she knew she'd see him on Saturday. It
would be frosty at first, but they'd kiss and
touch and sort it out. Sometimes, when
she thought about Sean, his handsome face
melted into Terry Hewitt's, with his pretty
manners and hesitant smile.

There were definite noises downstairs:

someone coming in and getting their tea, and then another couple of people in the living room, everyone talking quietly and abruptly to one another. Muffled footsteps came up the stairs, and someone stopped off to use the toilet. The bedroom door opened and Mary Ann came in, looking serious. She shut the door carefully, climbed across her own bed to Paddy's, and sat down, poking Paddy in the ribs.

"It's finishing on Saturday," she whispered. "We're having a tea for you, and that'll be it over." She kissed Paddy's forehead, excited as a child at Christmas. "You smell like a brewery."

Mary Ann went out to change into her nightclothes in the bathroom and left Paddy alone. She took another biscuit from her pocket and chewed it meditatively. To hell with them. She wasn't going to be in on Saturday. She was going out with Terry during the day, and in the evening she'd be out at the pictures with Sean.

TWENTY-SIX

FAT BUT FUNNY

I

Paddy shucked off her coat by the door and walked across to the bench. A balding sub-editor with a small horn of hair on his forehead caught her eye and muttered hello. It made her feel suspicious and worried. She didn't answer back. Ten minutes later, a different journalist patted her arm and said he was sorry when she brought him a box of staples.

She was on the bench, wondering whether she'd done something in the pub that she didn't remember, when Dub came back from the print room. She told him what had happened and said she was worried they were being friendly for a bad reason.

Dub stretched his skinny legs out in front of him. "Name a bad reason for being friendly."

"Dunno. I was in the Press Bar for a few hours yesterday afternoon. I just hope they don't think I'm fast or something."

Dub snorted. "No one thinks that."

She looked nervously around the room for clues. She didn't know if it was the after-effects of the drink the day before, but she was as tense as a trip wire this morning.

"Keck confided that he's worried in case I guess all the dirty things he's been thinking about me."

Dub laughed and told her that Keck was a crippled-dick-wank-donkey-fucker and he had the photos to prove it. Paddy liked the word and laughed along with him, enjoying the camaraderie of having a mutual enemy.

They stayed on the bench, letting Keck take the calls, chatting for a while. Dub told her the police had been chucked out of the building. Farquarson and McGuigan had had a set-to because they were disrupting the running of the paper, pulling people out of meetings and making all the women cry. They'd missed a big story on Poland because of them, lost a phone line when the police yanked Liddel off the newsroom floor.

It wasn't until after the editorial meeting that she finally heard why everyone was being nice to her; it was one of those morsels of city gossip that could never be used in the paper, like the children's names or the details of how Brian had died. Callum Ogilvy had attempted suicide the night before and been rushed to hospital. He'd used a knife and done it under a table in the refectory with everyone there. He almost cut his hand off. It was so bad they had to operate. Only because he was almost a relative Paddy suddenly thought she should go and visit him. The thought stayed with her; Sean could probably go and visit Callum. If she went with him she could interview the boy for the paper. Her family would never talk to her again if she did that. She'd have to think of something else.

She approached the subeditor on the news desk, the horned man who had shot her a sympathetic glance earlier, and asked him for McVie's contact details. He got the phone number from someone on features.

"I heard you were related to that Ogilvy boy."

Paddy was copying out the telephone number from a Rolodex card and didn't answer.

"You can't choose your family, can you?"

"Or your colleagues," said Paddy, picking up a phone receiver without even asking for permission.

"McVie won't want you to call him."

"He'll be fine." She dialed the number. "I know him. Honestly, he won't mind. He gave me his number before but I lost it."

McVie sounded groggy. "What in the name of pissing hell are you doing phoning me at home, you fat cow?"

"Fine, yeah." Paddy looked at the sub and pressed her lips together, nodding to show the call was welcome.

"Where the hell did you get my number from?"

"Oh, so I suppose, aye." She spun away from the table and scratched her nose, covering her mouth. "Listen, I need a favor."

"It's ten o'clock in the fucking morning. Ye can shove your favors up your arse."

"The police asked me about Heather and you." She dropped her voice. "They wanted to know about the calls car and why you invited her out."

He hesitated. "What did you tell them?"

"What should I have told them? Nothing happened. You're a good guy."

He sighed and lowered his hackles. "What's the favor, then?" She drew breath to speak, but he interrupted. "It better not be big or involve me leaving the house in the next hour."

"I want the name of the witness who saw the Baby Brian Boys on the train."

"Why?"

"I don't believe they were on the train at all."

"What's the difference how it went down? They did it, there was blood all over them. She picked them out of a lineup fair and square."

She didn't want to tell McVie her suspicions, much less reiterate them in the newsroom, where anyone could be listening. "It makes a difference to me."

"Because you're a relative?"

It was easier just to agree. "Yeah."

"Well, it'll take a lot of string pulling. Witnesses are special cases. If anything comes out of this I want my name on it."

"Come on, McVie." She smiled weakly and looked around the room. "You know I'm an idiot. Nothing's going to come out of it."

He was suddenly wide awake and interested. "You're really onto something, aren't you?"

Paddy bit her lip. "Yeah," she said, trying to sound enthused. "I really think

I've got a big story here. I promise your name'll go on it, right next to mine."

"Ah." He thought about it for a moment. "Well, now I don't know what to think."

"I was talking to JT about the witness. He said women always come forward and it's usually for attention."

"Balls, that's just like the man. It's much more complicated than that. People want to see things. Some think they see things. Some wish they could see things. People who say it's for attention are arseholes."

"For Godsake, everyone in the world can't be an arsehole except you and me."

"I never said you weren't an arsehole."

She almost laughed out loud. "You know, McVie, you're a real character."

She could hear the smirk in his voice. "Funny," he said. "Fat, but funny."

II

Farquarson had noticed that half the staff were using little pens stolen from bookies' shops and thought it looked unprofessional. As Paddy went around the tables giving out fresh Biros to everyone, she thought about Paddy Meehan and the lineup, when Abraham Ross, fresh from his dead wife's bedside, picked him out and then fainted in front of him.

Meehan had talked about the injustice of it afterwards, but no local journalist would listen. Every convicted man in Barlinnie Prison claimed he had been set up, and Meehan was a well-known old con, neither liked nor respected and hardly known for his principled core. It wasn't until Ludovic Kennedy began researching his book about the case that the details of the day were documented.

Meehan had gone into the police station feeling confident. Griffiths was dead and the paper from the Rosses' safe had been found in his pocket, but it was a plant and really strong evidence was starting to go his way. The Kilmarnock girls had been found and were coming to identify him, and he had been told that the two robbers had referred to each other as Pat and Jim throughout the job. The police would know that no professional criminal would ever call another by his real name. Plus the police were looking for two guys from Glasgow, and Griffiths had a deep Lancastrian accent. Everyone who ever met him commented on it.

He thought it odd that the defense and prosecution witnesses were coming to the same identity parade: usually the prosecution had one and then, often later, the defense had a different one. But he had never been done for murder and decided that the crime was so heinous that even the police were eager to get to the truth of it. It was only days before the start of the trial when he saw the girls' names on the list of witnesses and saw that they were listed for the prosecution. The police would claim that Meehan and Griffiths had picked up the girls to give themselves alibis. The young girls, hazy in their memory and intimidated by the court, would slide the times and places back and forth to fit the case.

As soon as it began, the identity parade seemed strange. Meehan had participated in enough lineups to know that it wasn't being held in the lineup room. Instead they were gathered in the CID muster room, the place where the officers assembled before a shift. It was a big square room with windows on the far wall and two doors, one on the left, one on the right, both leading into separate changing rooms. Four other men of Meehan's age and build milled around, glancing at their neighbor's shoes, each wondering if he did really look like that. They were only there for the couple of bob — good money for half an hour's work.

Meehan felt calm. The lassies would pick him out, he knew they would. He'd got out of the car and they'd each seen him straight on. For once in his life he was glad of the acne scarring on his cheeks, knowing that it made him distinctive enough to remember, even through a haze of drink and in a bad light.

They heard people gathering behind one of the doors, and the two attendant police officers shuffled the ID men into a line, letting Meehan take whichever place he wanted. He stood closest to the door so that they would come to him first. When they had all settled into place the officer knocked on the door and opened it.

Irene Burns came into the room accompanied by a copper and a lawyer in a cheap suit. The moment her eyes fell on Meehan it was obvious she remembered. She didn't even look at the others in the line, just raised her finger, hardly five feet away, pointing directly at his nose. What small vestige of religious feeling Meehan had left in his heart prompted him to thank someone somewhere. The officers led her off to the far changing room, and Meehan noticed that she had a thick ladder up the back of her calf and had scuffed her heel. She was still a child herself.

Isobel came next, looking very young and rather prim. Her hair was a neat little dome, and she had a hairband in it with a bow at the side. Again, she recognized him immediately, hardly glancing at the others. She hung around nervously by the far wall as if she wanted to run back into the changing room.

Meehan spoke to her. "It's all right, pet, don't worry about it. Go ahead."

Isobel gave a little sigh of relief and pointed at him. "It's him," she said.

Meehan smiled at her and got a smile back. Isobel patted her hair coyly, as if he'd complimented her. He found himself smiling after her, watching her generous arse as she disappeared off into the far changing room.

Three other witnesses came through. He would learn later that each of them had seen the men leaving the Ross house in the morning. Not one of them picked Meehan out. One of them was certain it was number four; another couldn't say; the other felt it might be number three.

The men in the lineup knew that the final witness was the big one, the victim himself, and they watched the door next to Meehan expectantly, anticipating the end of the chore and the two bob they had been promised. It was the far door that opened, the door all the other witnesses had left by. The lineup men snickered at the obvious ploy: the girls could easily have told Mr. Ross where the mark was standing, but Meehan felt quite confident. The girls had picked him out. He had his alibi.

Rheumy-eyed Mr. Ross, frail as a baby bird, had a big black bruise covering one side of his face and a brawny female nurse supporting his arm. The detective sergeant led the old man along the line, straight to Meehan. He ordered Meehan to read a line written on a scrap of paper.

Meehan was puzzled. He should have been told beforehand if he was to say anything. They were breaching protocol to eliminate him, he felt sure. He repeated the line flatly.

"Shut up, shut up. We'll send an ambulance. All right?"

The old man's knees buckled. "My God, my God," shouted Mr. Ross, falling back into the arms of his nurse. "That's the voice. I know it, I know it."

III

The temperature had dipped again and Paddy could hardly feel the tip of her nose.

400

She rubbed it with her gloved hand, trying to encourage the blood back into it, and turned the corner to the given address. She sighed up at the red sandstone. It was a neat front-door flat in a three-up tenement on the Southside, in a more than decent neighborhood. A passing soft rain had darkened the stone to patches of black, every window was clean, every sill in good order. The close passage through to the back was tiled in green and cream. Across the tidy square of front garden Mrs. Simnel's front door screamed good order. Pale yellow storm doors were folded back, revealing a perfectly polished brass letter box and matching knocker sitting over a pristine doormat. Paddy had been hoping for somewhere a bit less respectable and solid.

As she approached the door she could hear a distant radio through the etched glass, tuned to an easy-listening station. The doorbell rang out in two complementary tones and a woman's shape shimmered into view. Paddy huddled in her duffel coat and watched as the shadow woman patted her hair and pulled a pair of rubber gloves off her hands before opening the door.

A small puff of domestic perfection

wafted out at Paddy standing on the cold doorstep. A saccharine version of "Fly Me to the Moon" was playing in the kitchen. The hall smelled of crumbled biscuits and warm tea.

Mrs. Simnel wore flat brown shoes and a cream skirt and blouse. Her hair was pulled gently up into a graying French roll. Paddy explained that she was researching a story about the Baby Brian Boys and had been given her name by one of the officers at the station. Mrs. Simnel looked surprised and smiled kindly.

"But what age are you, for goodness' sake? Are you at college?"

Paddy supposed that she was, yes, studying for A levels too, if that was what Mrs. Simnel wanted.

"Good for you," said Mrs. Simnel. "It's so important to get an education."

"It is." Her accent was softening the way it sometimes did when she spoke to Farquarson. "Terribly, terribly important."

"And here you are out on a cold night, working away."

Paddy smiled bravely, touching her cold nose again, hunching her shoulders. She could tell that Mrs. Simnel still wasn't quite sure of her: she held firmly on to the door handle, creating a barrier between her warm house and Paddy on the outside.

"Did you have far to come?"

"Not really." Paddy leaned in confidingly. "Actually, my daddy dropped me off on the corner."

"I see." Mrs. Simnel's eyes widened, delighted. "I see. Well, come in and warm yourself up. Let's get you a cup of tea."

With the door shut behind her Paddy breathed in the warmth and comfort of the generous hall. The ceiling was high, with delicate plaster leaves trailing around the cornice. Mrs. Simnel took her duffel and hung it by the label on a coatrack behind the door. On the floor beneath the coats sat two pairs of well-worn Wellingtons and a shooting stick, as if the green fields of Perthshire were just beyond the front door instead of the Southside streets of Scotland's largest city. Paddy wanted to live here, to be from here, to be surrounded by helping hands who would encourage her ambitions instead of being afraid of them.

"Now, let's have a cup of tea and see what we can do for your college project."

It was the biggest kitchen Paddy had ever been in. Her entire family could have gathered by the sink and still have left room for a car.

Mrs. Simnel had been polishing a strap

of ornamental horse brasses when Paddy knocked on the door, and now she picked up the newspaper with the blackened cloth and ornaments and simply moved it out of the way of the tea and biscuits. Fading sunlight filtered in through the window, absorbed by thriving plants on the sill, glinting off the ceramic tiles on the floor. Mrs. Simnel served up tea and biscuits on genteel flowery crockery. She didn't use mugs either, but cups and matching saucers. The china cup was so light that even full of tea it could be lifted with a gentle pinch of thumb and forefinger.

Mrs. Simnel told the story of the Baby Brian Boys well, recalling the information as she did, sliding her eyes to the side and wondering about things, bringing up details after thinking about them for a moment. She was a widow and had eight sons, all of whom lived nearby, all of whom had children of their own. She had been a primary-school teacher in her younger day and could recognize children very well, because they're all different, aren't they? All individuals. Paddy resigned herself to the truth of it: Mrs. Simnel had been on the train at exactly the time she said and had seen three kids.

She had been on her way to visit her

sister who lived in Cumbernauld and, knowing she would be coming back in the dark and not being a confident driver, decided to leave the car and take the train. Sarah — her sister was called Sarah — was expecting her at eight o'clock so she took the seven twenty-five, which was due in at five to eight. It took her five minutes to walk around to the house from the station.

Paddy nibbled the biscuit off a fig roll and sipped her tea. She wanted to live like this when she had a house of her own. She didn't want to use mugs or eat biscuits out of the packet anymore.

Relaxing into her company, Mrs. Simnel gestured towards the ornamental brasses and asked if Paddy would mind her carrying on. No; Paddy even offered to help, but there wasn't a spare set of rubber gloves under the sink, so she just had to sit there, nibbling biscuits and watching as the woman dabbed Brasso onto the metal and conjured blackness out of nothing.

Mrs. Simnel had never been a witness to anything else before and was a little uncomfortable at coming forward. She was surprised how well mannered the police were. She'd expected them to be rather more thuggish, frankly, the officers lower down the ranks at least. As she made the snobbish observation her eyes fell on Paddy's cheap black crewneck. She blinked, forgiving herself the offense, and shifted the emphasis. They made her a cup of tea before they went in to see the line of boys and gave it to her in a china cup, with a biscuit, an iced ring, of all things. Wasn't that dainty? A pink iced ring. Not what you'd expect from big burly men at all.

She was the perfect witness, recalling details and colors and times exactly, as though she had been rehearsing all her life for this one moment. And she didn't for an instant seem like a woman who was short of attention.

"Those boys who did this," she said sadly. "Those boys are only ten years old. It makes me shiver to think about it."

"Yes, their backgrounds are very deprived," said Paddy, hoping to temper her attitude to them if nothing else.

"I know. They told me that the dark-haired one had never been to a dentist. Not once in his entire life." She put down her cloth for a moment. "It must hurt, to have those teeth. And the diet you'd need to make them so . . . I couldn't finish my biscuit."

It hit Paddy like a cold wash. "You couldn't finish the iced ring?"

"No," said Mrs. Simnel. "I just put it down on the saucer. I mean, it must hurt to have such bad teeth. Even if the parents can't take the child to the dentist, why don't the schools do something?"

Paddy pretended that her father was picking her up at the bus stop on Clarkston Road. Mrs. Simnel waved her off, wishing her good luck with the project and her exams. As Paddy walked to the end of the street she heard the woman closing the storm doors firmly behind her. She should hurry home or she'd miss Sean if he phoned about their Valentine's date tomorrow, but she didn't know where the buses ran to from here and she was numbed by Mrs. Simnel.

She walked past the bus terminus and under a railway bridge, following the road over the high crescent of Prospecthill. It was a leafy bump of land, one of two neighboring hillocks overlooking the broad valley plain. At the crest of the hill she paused, hands in her pockets, looking out over the lights of the Friday-night city. She mapped her way around the distant streets using the red neon sign on the *Daily Record* building as a starting point.

This time last week Heather Allen was

alive and had parked her car in Union Street over there. Paddy had walked down to Queen Street station that night; she could just see its illuminated fan of glass. She had taken the train to Steps and stood by the tracks. This time last week Mrs. Simnel had gone to the police about the boys she saw on the train. They gave her tea and biscuits before she went in to pick them out of a lineup, casually mentioning Callum Ogilvy's bad teeth to her and the fact that he'd never been to a dentist. She must have known Callum the moment she saw him. They'd primed her just as carefully as Abraham Ross had been primed. The police were determined to put the boys alone on the train, and Paddy couldn't understand why.

TWENTY-SEVEN

RED-HOT SPITE DATE

I

Sean didn't call, and now there was no card. Paddy stared so hard at the bare doormat that she could see small grains of mud and dirt between the brown bristles. Her hot feet began to stick to the plastic floor protector. She cursed her stupid fucking soppy bastard card. It became bigger and bluer and more italicized the more she remembered it. Ashamed of hoping and afraid of being seen, she ran back upstairs to her bedroom.

II

It was quiet in the town. The streets emptied under a heavy sky, shoppers hurrying home before the hunger strikers' march began or the heavy rain came on again. She watched down the road, facing into cold rain, resisting the urge to pull up her hood because it made her look so young and unsophisticated. Thoughts of Sean made her throat ache. She couldn't stand it if he abandoned her altogether. She was frightened of herself without him.

A filthy white Volkswagen Beetle peeled off from the thin traffic and pulled into the bus stop. The whitewall tires were caked in gray dirt and the front fender was rusted and painted over with a watery white treatment. Terry leaned an elbow on the passenger seat and smiled up at her. She pulled open the door and climbed in.

"I thought you might not be there for a minute."

She struggled to shut the creaky door behind her. "Why?"

" 'Cause of the rain." He pointed to the gray sky.

He was nervous too, and she liked it.

She looked up through the windscreen. "Is that where rain comes from?" she said, trying to tease him but sounding sarcastic.

Terry restarted the car. The engine was old and tired, one of the wheels was making an oddly intense ticking noise, and the gears crunched like a mouth full of gravel, but still Paddy marveled at someone near her age having the money to buy a car.

"This is the coolest motor I've ever been in," she said, pleasing him and making up for sounding like a bitch.

They looked away from each other, each smiling out the window. Paddy hoped she was seen out on her spite date, that someone would tell Sean and he'd feel as upset and frightened and jealous as she did at the moment. She had considered and rejected the possibility that Sean was seeing someone else: it wasn't his style, he was too self-righteous.

Terry slowed for a red light at George Square, and they saw steel barriers cordoning off the central space in preparation for the postmarch rally. They weren't the usual barriers, keeping marchers on the central concourse and safe from traffic; they were corridors for funneling marchers through, keeping them on the roads and away from sidewalks. Angry vandals had already managed to spray-paint slogans on nearby buildings. A bank straight in front of them had UP THE PROVOS across a window; another hand had added MUST DIE in red. The rival slogans made the square look like the venue for a battle of the bands more than the site of a political rally.

Terry drew a wary breath in through his teeth. "It's going to be mental. They're busing Ulster Defense militants in from Larkhall."

He said it as if he knew the area. Paddy smiled at the dashboard of his car and his expensive leather jacket.

"Are you from Larkhall, Terry?"

He glanced at her. "No."

"Whereabouts are ye from?"

He hesitated. "Newton Mearns."

"Fancy," she said, hoping she didn't sound bitchy again, because she meant it.

Newton Mearns was intimidating nice. It was a prosperous, middle-class area on the far south side of the city, with nice houses in big grounds and a lot of cared-for gardens. Even the roads were full of vegetation. Paddy and Sean had been out for a day there once, looking for a nice pub Sean had heard about from some workmates. They couldn't find the pub and were back at the bus stop on the opposite side of the road within twenty minutes. Paddy kept her hood up while Sean smoked a fag and threw stones at cows. They were relieved when the bus arrived to take them back to the city. They never went there again.

Terry's eyes slid towards her. "Newton Mearns isn't all posh," he said, as if he knew what she was thinking. "Some parts of it are quite rough, you know."

"Is that right? You from the rough part, are ye?"

He didn't answer. It wasn't going very well. She was trying to be jokey, but she was tense and kept sounding like a snidey know-all.

"I'd like to nip home first." He glanced at her. "Is that okay?"

"The Mearns is miles away."

"No, I've got my own place. I'm just around the corner."

Paddy was so impressed she covered her mouth to stop herself from gasping a sarcastic comment. He had a car and his own flat. His parents must be millionaires.

The old car rattled up through the town to Sauchiehall Street, home to drunken students, cinemas, and curry houses, and parked outside a newsagent's. Terry pulled the keys out of the ignition with a flourish and turned to face her.

"Want to come up?" He saw her reluctance and added, "Just be for a minute. I've been working all morning. I want to change my top."

She tried not to say the first thing on her

413

tongue, which was piss off. Eastfield girls would be wary of entering a boy's house if his parents were out. Terry didn't seem embarrassed to be asking her, though. Maybe in Newton Mearns girls went in and out of boys' houses all the time and were just good friends. They probably played tennis together and spent time in conservatories, eating fresh fruit. His breath brushed two hairs from her forehead.

"Okay," she said. "Let's see your gaff."

It was a dingy close with a worn wooden balustrade and a filthy concrete floor. Dirt gathered along the base of the walls. The front doors to the flats became increasingly grotty from landing to landing, and by the third floor they were either chipped and battered or blank pine replacements for those that had been kicked in during drunken arguments. An overhead roof window flooded the filthy stairwell with bright daylight so that every dirty corner was crisp and visible, every brown smear on the walls so vivid she could almost taste it. She kept close to Terry, who was bounding up the stairs ahead of her.

"Why do you need a car," she asked, finding herself breathless halfway through the steep climb, "when you live so near work?"

"I only use the car to impress women."

Surprised and flattered at being called a woman, and the subject of anyone's attempt to impress, she laughed and lashed out, punching him on the thigh.

Six up, on the top-floor landing, two big doors faced each other across a jumble of bicycle parts and a brown corduroy armchair. Terry took a stern bunch of keys to a cardboard front door that would have blown open in a stiff breeze.

The hallway didn't have any lights in it. More bikes were parked behind the door, and every available surface was covered in posters of rock bands: the Floyd, the Quo, Thin Lizzie.

"God," said Paddy quietly. "Wake up to the eighties."

Terry led her to a door at the back, undid the padlock on it, and used a long key for the mortise lock below the handle. As the door to his room opened she was struck by a beguiling smell, a mixture of musky sebum and lemon — concentrated scent of big, dirty men.

If Terry was a millionaire he wasn't making a show of it. His bedroom was long and narrow. A single window at the far end stared straight into the top-floor windows of the mean little tenement opposite. Between his unmade single bed and the sink, a paper suitcase did for a table. Terry kept some tins of beans and corned beef on it, sitting next to an open waxed-paper packet of white bread and a tub of cheap margarine. The bedsheets were orange, the blankets a grubby cream. He had no hanging space for clothes, so he had carefully balanced ironed shirts on hangers from the picture rail around the room. A spindly spider plant on the bookshelf seemed to be slowly lowering its young to the ground, eager for them to escape.

Stepping deep into the room so that Paddy had to follow him, Terry opened a drawer and took out a clean white T-shirt, folded with the front flat as if it was shop-new. He let his leather jacket slide down his arms to the floor, untucked his white work shirt, and undid the top three buttons. He put his hand to the fourth and wavered.

"For Godsake," she said. "I've got two brothers. I've seen men without their shirts on before."

Terry raised an eyebrow. "But my nipples are unusually beautiful, Patricia, and you're only flesh and blood."

Paddy giggled and looked away, watching him in her peripheral vision as he yanked the shirt over his head without unbuttoning it. He stepped towards her quickly, a sudden outrage on his face, and shouted, "Don't look at me!"

His arms were too thin, but his chest was covered in tufts of soft, black, curly hair, arranged in a handsome T shape, the tail of it disappearing into the waistband of his trousers. His nipples were deep pink, the hair radiating away from them like eyelashes, making his chest into a startled face. She grinned and watched him pull on his fresh T-shirt. She wished Sean could see them.

"Didn't your parents mind you moving out?"

"Ah," said Terry, lifting his jacket from the floor. "They died. In a car accident."

"I'm sorry."

"No, I'm . . ." He shook his head. "Stupid. I shouldn't have told you that."

"Why not?"

Embarrassed, he screwed an eye shut and shrugged. "People don't really want to know about stuff like that. It makes them uncomfortable."

"The fusty man-smell in here makes me more uncomfortable."

He smiled weakly at her and glanced away.

"I am sorry about your folks. It must have been a bit crap."

He nodded at the floor. "That's exactly what it was. It is. A bit crap. Why have you stopped wearing your engagement ring?"

As they locked up the room and walked slowly down the stairs, Paddy told him about the shunning, about Sean shutting the door on her, and her midnight games with Mary Ann. By the time they'd reached the car, Terry knew more about what was going on in her family than Paddy's own mum.

He opened the passenger door for her. "He didn't phone back?"

"Not once." She climbed into the seat and waited until Terry was in the driver's side. "Wouldn't even come to the phone when I called him. Nothing."

"He sounds like a spineless wee shite." He started the engine. "But I would say that, wouldn't I?"

For the first time in her life, Paddy felt like a full-grown woman.

III

Barnhill was a brutal landscape. The barren little hill of low-slung houses sat

418

tight against the windy hill, cowering from swooping gangs of black crows. It was hemmed in to the east and west by high-rise flats soaring thirty stories up into a big gray sky. The high flats were built with asbestos, tissue, and spit; victims of running damp, they were popular with no one but shit-machine pigeons. To the south, between Barnhill and the city, sat the sprawling St. Rollox engineering works, which had supplied train carriages to half the Empire. The two institutions went into decline hand in hand, and gradually the surrounding land was abandoned, left littered with chemical residues and bits of scrap, contaminated and useless.

Barnhill itself was little more than a circuit of five or six long streets of identical houses, a squat row of shops with a turret at the corner, a post office, and a school. The recent recession showed in the area. The shopping bags the women carried were all from discount shops, and men, white faces crumpled against the brazen rain, gathered outside the bookies and the pub, too broke to go in.

"This place is a shithole," Paddy said.

"It's not that bad," said Terry, who would never have to countenance living there.

He pulled the car out onto the bleak Red Road. The road dipped between two soot-blackened walls and suddenly they were around the corner from the house. Paddy slid down in her seat, imagining that Sean and all the Ogilvys would be standing around in groups on the curb as they had been on the day of Callum's father's funeral, dressed in sombre blacks and grays, saying good-bye to Callum Ogilvy's mother, making hollow promises to see her again soon.

The Ogilvy house was on a sharp hillside. Crumbling concrete steps led up to it, and the grass in the steep front garden was knee-deep. Paddy wasn't certain that she would be able to remember which house it was, but someone had helpfully aerosoled FILTH OUT on the wall at the bottom of the garden.

The living room window was boarded over. The house might have been abandoned, but the front door was opened a little and bits of plastic toys were scattered across the front garden, while a stuffed pink thing with balding patches lay on a cushion of lush green grass, soaking up the rain. As they cruised slowly past the house Paddy saw a small leg in brown flares sticking backwards out of the front door, swaying on the toe as if a coy child had turned back into the house to ask a question.

Paddy sat back deep in her seat, watching the sad house pass. Quite suddenly the weight of her family and Sean's disapproval seemed justified. If women didn't conform, this is what happened. She would end up in a rundown council house with a hundred starving children and no extended family to help out during the hard times. It took her a tearful moment to remember that she hadn't done anything wrong.

She turned and looked at Terry, desperate to think about something else. He was looking ahead, unaware of her for the moment, thoughtlessly slacking saliva around with his tongue. The sound made her stomach warm.

"What are you smiling at?" he asked.

"Nothing."

They were driving down a short connection between two long roads when they saw what they were sure was the other Baby Brian Boy's house. It was on the ground floor of a four-in-a-block cottage, and below the window, starting from the ground, a sooty trail sprang up the brickwork where someone had tried to set a fire.

Fresh putty was still unpainted where the window had been replaced, light still catching a linseed-oil glisten. Even before the vandalism, Paddy could see, it wasn't a wealthy home. The curtains were faded and dusty, the patchy grass was overgrown in the front garden, and the drive up to the door was so potholed that it couldn't have been used by a car in a long time.

Terry gunned the engine. "Let's go to Townhead and see the layout there."

The rain came on as they drove down the broad dual carriageway through Sighthill. The high flats there were monolithic walls of homes, standing sentry on the summit of a small hill. The only other feature in the area was a large cemetery, not high Victorian but a poor person's cemetery of small gravestones marshaled into neat rows. The wind pushed the rain sideways, into the faces of the pedestrians, catching the legs of people cowering in bus shelters. It took eight minutes in the car to cover the distance between the Baby Brian Boys' houses and the Wilcox home. By the time they arrived in Townhead the rain had stopped, leaving the streets dark and glistening.

Even with the car windows up and the noisy engine running they could hear the hunger strikers' march three blocks away. Hundreds of male voices shouted in unison, chanting through the silent city. Paddy had been on nuclear disarmament marches, where the noise was less aggressive, the chanting mellowed by women's voices, but this sounded different: they sounded like a wild army. Every so often a call would go out and be answered by the mob. Whichever way they turned, the sound seemed to be getting closer.

Following Paddy's directions they found the Wilcox house and pulled up by the sidewalk. A few small bunches of posies had been added to the display of drooping yellow ribbons on the railings. Apart from that the house looked the same as it had when she'd come with McVie, but the streets were deserted. Even though it was Saturday the children on the scheme had been forbidden to play in the street because of the trouble there would be in town. A wave of sound rolled up the hill from the march.

"I like this," said Terry. "I like cruising around with you, playing at journalists."

She nodded. "So do I. I'll be Bob Woodward."

"I'll go Bernstein, just this once." He smiled. "D'you ever wonder how those guys felt as they fell asleep at night? They didn't just report miscarriages of justice, they corrected them. How cool is that? That's what I want to do."

"Me too," said Paddy, breathless and startled at how perfectly he had articulated her lifelong ambition. "That's all I've ever wanted to do."

They looked at each other, for once nothing between them, eye to eye. She couldn't look away, didn't want to in case he was going to say something, and he stared back. They sat there for a moment, stuck like dogs, panic rising in Paddy's throat, until they tore their eyes away, cleared their throats, and caught their breath. She thought she heard him mutter an exclamation, but was too embarrassed to ask what it was.

"Look." Her sudden voice filled the car, and she pointed ahead to Gina's house. "There's the alley to the swing park."

"Is it? Yeah? Is that it? Did they come down here?"

"No one saw them, but the police still think so." She turned to look at him but lost her nerve and stared at his ear.

They heard it before they saw it, high-pitched and carried on the cold air, less a tune than a collection of notes. The ice-cream van was coming. From front doors and gardens small children began to appear on the pavements. Paddy turned in her seat, watching back down the road to where they were gathering in the car park. Something about it bothered her.

The queue was small for a Saturday afternoon. A young mum with a baby on her hip and a dirty-faced toddler, chaperoned by an older sister, watched the road expectantly, the young excited at the proximity of sugar, the older ones drawing together, glancing around, defensive and careful because of what had happened to poor Brian Wilcox.

Terry sighed. "Shall we go?"

It was then that Paddy realized what was wrong with the scene. Gina's house was up the road. The children were all waiting in completely the wrong place. The grocery-van man had told her that the ice-cream van stopped in front of Gina's house.

The music got louder as the van turned the corner, the tinny tune bouncing off the flats and rolling up the street towards them.

"Eh?"

She looked at Terry. He was waiting for an answer.

"Eh, what?" she said abruptly.

"Eh, shall we go?"

She looked back down the road. The ice-cream van might have moved its stop position. It might have been thought insensitive to keep stopping outside the Wilcox house. Maybe they didn't want the association and moved down the street.

"Hang on a minute."

She opened her door and stepped out into the street, shutting the car door behind her, looking for someone to ask. A small blond boy in a blue anorak was running towards her on his way to the small crowd at the van.

"Son," she said.

He ignored her and continued to head past her to the van and the quickly dissipating queue.

"Son." She stood in his way. "Wee man, I'll give ye tenpence."

The boy glanced at her and slowed. He was skinny, and the lip up to his nose was chapped raw.

Paddy took the big coin from her pocket. "Does the ice-cream van always stop down there?"

"Aye." He held out his hand.

"Did it always, or just recently?"

"Aye, always." He licked at his raw top lip with a dexterous tongue.

"Did it not used to stop up there?" She pointed back at Gina Wilcox's.

The boy put his hands on his hips and huffed up at her. "Missus, I'm not missing that van," he said definitely.

Paddy gave him his coin and he belted off down the road. Terry was watching her, frowning from inside the car. She held up a finger and walked down towards the ice-cream van. By the time she was halfway there the engine had started up and the van was moving off, leaving the satisfied children eating happily. Paddy watched the van pass Terry's car and the Wilcox house, drive up out of sight, and reappear again on the cross, heading over to Maryhill. The music wasn't sounding, and it wasn't stopping again anytime soon.

She turned back to the kids. The boy in the anorak was clutching a quiver of Curly Wurlys, pointing at Paddy and explaining his wealth to another child.

"Did that ice-cream van ever used to stop there?" She pointed back towards the Wilcox place.

"Nut," said the parka boy, and the wee girls around him confirmed what he said.

"It stops here," said a plump girl in glasses.

"It always stops here," said a bigger girl.

Paddy nodded. "What time does your grocery van come on a Saturday?"

The children looked blankly at one another. It was a ridiculous question. Most of them were far too young to tell the time, never mind predict patterns in retail provision.

"Is it in the afternoon? Is it soon?"

"Aye, soon, but his sweets are mostly rubbish," said the parka boy, misunderstanding the purpose of her interest.

Paddy thanked them and walked back to the car, opened the door, and held on to the roof, hanging in. "Terry, listen, I'm going to go into town from here. I need to get home, really. Is that okay?"

He frowned and nodded at the window. "Sure, fine. Get in and I'll drive you down to the station."

She patted the roof twice and glanced up the road. "Aren't you going back to the office to finish up?"

"Finish up what?"

"Finish up what you were doing earlier."

"Oh." He smiled, shaking his head a little too adamantly. "Yeah, I could, yeah. I'll do that, yeah."

He had a pleading little look in his eye. Paddy couldn't stop herself. She knelt on the dimpled plastic seat, leaned over, gave him a perfectly soft kiss on his cheek, and pulled back before he could do anything with it.

"I'll see you later, Terry."

She slammed the door as he answered and never heard what he said in return. She walked off down the road, cutting across a bit of lawn, heading into the heart of the housing scheme.

TWENTY-EIGHT

BY A HAIR

I

Paddy waited for almost forty minutes in the dark mouth of the lane beside the Wilcox house. It was a balding sliver of ground left between the two houses, worn into a single track by scuffling feet. Sometimes it seemed to Paddy that the whole of the built-up city was nothing more than a series of interludes between patches of abandoned waste ground and wartime bomb sites. Grass on either side of the path glistened, black diamonds trembling on the razor-sharp tips. The far end of the dark path blossomed into a brightly lit street, and across the road she could see the low picket fence around the swing park, empty now but lit by orange streetlights, dark shadows pooling under the swing seats and slides.

She smoked a cigarette to pass the time, thinking of poor Heather sitting on the bin and being annoyed in the editorial toilets. Paddy'd give anything to be back there again. She dropped the cigarette and stepped on it, watching her toe rub it into the soft mud, bursting the paper and spreading speckled tobacco shreds over the grass.

A movement at the far end of the lane caught her eye. The black outline of a woman, holding the hand of a small girl, was looking down into the lane, hesitant when she saw Paddy's dark profile, androgynous and threatening.

"I'm waiting for the grocery van," Paddy called reassuringly.

Still the woman waited, her hand tightening around the balled fist of the small girl. Paddy stepped back out into the light in front of the Wilcox house, and the woman moved towards her, muttering something to the child.

"Sorry," said Paddy as she approached. "I didn't mean to scare ye."

Close up, the woman was younger than her beige mac and headscarf implied. She shot Paddy a disgusted look and yanked the child across her path, away from Paddy. She was right in a way: Paddy

431

shouldn't be hanging around in dark lanes frightening women and children going about their business.

"Is the fella Naismith's van due soon?"

The woman didn't look at her, but muttered aye, ten minutes. Might not be Naismith but. Sometimes his son drove it for him.

Paddy took the two unrequested sentences as forgiveness and watched the retreating back of the woman moving down the street. At most she was two years older than Paddy, already a mother and already pinched and angry.

She could see Sean at home, sitting in his mum's hall, on the black plastic seat attached to the telephone table, holding the moss-green receiver to his ear, listening to the phone ring on the telephone table in her mum's hall. Trisha would tell him Paddy wasn't in, and then he'd be worried. He might not be bothered about contacting her, he might have decided to ignore her for another month beyond the family shunning. She didn't feel she could predict him anymore, and it made her like him less but want him more. She looked up to find a black velvet stain racing across the sky.

The rainstorm came without warning, so

heavy and abrupt that although she ran the hundred yards to a block of flats, the water running down the street was soon deep enough to reach over the sole of her boots and sneak in through the stitching. She stood in the doorway, holding up her hood with both hands, watching as the sky dropped cold slits of silver, obliterating the ambient noise from the motorway and the chanting of the protest marchers. The road surface was a rippling black sheet. The rain gathered at the bottom of the hill, bubbling around drains. Her feet were wet, her black woollen tights soaking up the water like blotting paper, distributing it evenly around her ankles.

She saw the headlights hitting raindrops first. Creeping along behind the twin beams, Naismith's van felt its way along the road, meekly speeding up at the base of the hill to get clean through a deep puddle and stopping on the hill incline. The back door opened and Naismith himself peered out, getting a faceful of rain before ducking back in. From a nearby house a woman came running as fast as she could, head down, holding the neck of her overcoat tightly shut. Paddy waited in the doorway for a bit, until the customer might be finished and about to step down from the van.

She didn't want to wait outside in the rain.

She kept her head down, holding her hood shut over her mouth, and jogged across the road. Cold water squelched between her toes. She'd have wet feet for the rest of the day and would have to pack the boots with toilet paper when she got home and leave them by the fire.

Naismith must have been quick off the mark. The back door to the van was locked by the time she reached it, and the chassis juddered as the engine rumbled into life. She ran around to the driver's window and banged on it, afraid she might have waited in vain and ruined her monkey boots for nothing.

From inside the cab Naismith smiled down at her, his quiff a little askew from being caught in the rain. He wound down the window a little, pumping hard with his elbow, and shouted into the street, "Refreshers?"

Paddy smiled up into the rain, letting go of her hood so that it slipped back a little, the rain running down her face. "I saw the ice-cream van," she shouted.

He looked puzzled.

"The van," she shouted again, pointing to the lane. "It doesn't stop there. I wanted to ask ye about it."

He frowned down at her.

"He doesn't stop there," she repeated.

He shook his head and pointed to the passenger door, holding his mouth up to the open window. "Cannae hear ye. Come in a minute."

Paddy nodded and ran in front of the van, the white headlights giving detail and texture to the black river coming down the hill. She opened the passenger door, stuck one foot onto a chrome-trimmed step built into the side of the van, and pulled herself up into the cab.

It was warm in the cab and still smelled of fresh morning rolls. The seats were thick, cream-colored leather with brown piping trim.

"Oh no, my duffel coat's drenched." She pulled the wet material away from under her. "I don't want to wet your seats."

"Good leather doesn't mind wet so much. It's the cheap stuff that hates the wet."

He reached across her chest to the door, his elbow coming just too close to her tits to make her feel comfortable, and pulled the door shut behind her. He saw her stiffen away from him and retracted his arm quickly back towards the wheel, upset that he had frightened her.

"I'm not . . . I didn't mean that," he said, suddenly embarrassed. "I was just shutting the door."

"Oh, aye," said Paddy, feeling she had wrongly accused the nice man. He looked so crestfallen and ashamed that she felt she should offer him a squeeze of her tits just to show she didn't suspect him of trying to cop a feel.

"Well." He tried to smile, but looked miserable and nervous. "Anyway, what can I do ye for?"

"Yeah, listen, I waited for the ice-cream van, and it doesn't stop there." She pointed up the road again.

He looked blank, and she suddenly realized that he hardly remembered her.

"I was asking ye about the Baby Brian Boys the other evening, I don't know if you remember." He shook his head a little. "I said they had no reason to pass the Wilcox house, and you said the ice-cream van stopped there and they'd've come down to buy penny chews. D'ye remember?"

"I remember ye bought a packet of Refreshers."

She shook her head. "Sorry, you must talk to a hundred people a day. I watched, and it turns out that the van doesn't stop there at all. But I wanted to ask ye if it used to, ye know? Like, maybe the ice-cream guy — Hughie, you said his name was?"

She looked at him and he paused for a beat before nodding.

"Yeah, did Hughie used to stop there? Did he change his routine because the wee boy died and he felt bad or something?"

A fat drop of rain fell from Paddy's hair, racing down her face and dripping off her chin.

Naismith looked startled, as if he was seeing her for the very first time. "Good God in Govan, you are absolute soaked. Here." He flicked on the cab light and looked for something on the floor.

The inside of the cab was a work of art. The covers of 45 records had been taped around the inside of the windscreen: Jerry Lee Lewis, Frankie Vaughan, Gene Vincent and the Blue Caps, colorized pictures of young men, their teeth laughably white, their lips a camp pink. The pictures were held to the window by a mesh of Sellotape, yellow and crusty after years in the sun. At the right hand of the windscreen, just where the driver's eye would fall most often, was a pastel drawing of a blond Jesus in a blue dress, smiling kindly at the circle of small children gazing up at him.

"This is a wee palace," said Paddy, enjoying the big leather chair molding around her body, watching him feel under his seat.

He sat up and smiled. "It is, aye." He handed her a brown, stale-smelling towel, sewn double along one seam, like a pocket.

Paddy dabbed at her hair politely, avoiding her mouth and nose, and pointed at the religious picture. "I didn't have you down for a Holy Roller."

He nodded, looking straight ahead, watching the rain fall onto the windscreen. His eyes flickered down the street, checking each door for customers. "Born again," he said quietly. "I'd led a worthless life before and maybe will again, but through the grace of God I have known peace."

It sounded like a load of Protestant codswallop to her, but he seemed sincere enough, if a little melancholy. Born-agains were usually a bit more upbeat about the experience. She imagined she saw him blink away a tear before he spoke again.

"Hughie may have changed his routine. I don't really know." He lifted a hand and ran his pinkie nail between his two front teeth. "I don't really know."

Paddy smiled, and looked at the towel in

438

her lap. "I wondered because, see, if the van stopped further down there when the baby went missing, then the boys'd probably go around the back and not even pass the Wilcox house."

She played with it, rolling it around her finger, a long, golden strand of hair so thick it was almost coarse, retaining its gentle wave despite being pulled tight. She was enjoying the familiar texture before she realized what it was. She'd know it anywhere. It was one of Heather Allen's hairs.

Still staring forwards, eyes zigzagging from door to door, Naismith raised his hand above his head, moving slowly, trying not to startle her. He found the switch without looking and turned off the cabin light. Softly his arm dropped, his fingers alighting on the steering wheel. They sat still together, Paddy's eyes fixed on his face. Orange streetlights filtered through the molten rain on the windscreen. His features looked as if they were melting.

"So maybe he changed his route," he said softly.

Her face was frozen. "Maybe."

He turned to look at her, and she could see that he was sad. They looked clear into each other's eyes for the smallest moment, Paddy's eyes pleading with him not to

439

touch her, Naismith regretful but resolved to do what he had to do.

"You'll catch your death walking home in this weather," he said stiffly. "Let me drop ye off somewhere."

He started the engine before she could speak, releasing the hand brake and engaging the clutch. The van slid forwards a foot into the black future, but Paddy's suddenly scrambling fingers felt along the door behind her, jerking the handle down. She threw her weight against it and dropped backwards out of the cab into a wet void. As she fell, turning her head to see where she would land, she felt Naismith's hot fingertips brush her ear.

She made contact with the ground two feet before she expected to, landing heavily on the side of her leg, twisting it and dropping the towel. She was winded, lying in a flowing inch of rainwater, conscious of the ominous numbness in her knee, when behind her she heard the hand brake crunch on and the driver's door fly open. A scalding burst of adrenaline brought her to her feet, but her knee wouldn't straighten and she fell. She rose again on all fours, springing forwards, hands slapping on the wet ground, through soft mud on the grassy verge, out to the main road, and over to the deserted bus station without remembering to check for traffic.

She had never run so fast in her life, never been more completely in her body. Her wet feet squelched in her boots, toes pushing her forwards against the wet ground, heading down into the town. When the feeling came back into her knee there was a burn and a sharp, shooting pain that ran up to her hip. When she felt tired or her lungs began to sting, she felt the rain hitting her ear. She imagined it was Naismith's fingers and ran on, heading towards the only human sound she could hear: the chanting in George Square.

She bolted past the side entrance to Queen Street station and down, turning the corner and finding herself behind a line of policemen forming a cordon against protesters on George Square. Their black woollen tunics had soaked up the rain, and they glistened like beetles' shells. The marchers had just arrived in the square, a mixture of angry militant Republicans and frightened civil rights marchers, flowing along the metal barriers like cattle at market, hemmed in by a black fence of policemen linking arms. At the far end of the square she could see a line of mounted policemen cutting off an exit road, their rain cloaks tented over the horses' bodies. She ran over to the line of policemen and touched the back of one of them.

"Please, help me."

He turned and looked at her, letting go of his neighbor and grabbing her elbow, tugging her in front of the line. His eyes were open a little too wide. He seemed frightened and excited in equal measure.

"I've been attacked."

He leaned into her and shouted in her face, "Get in front of the barrier."

She was in front of him and moving in the direction he had asked her to go when he quite unnecessarily shook her, making her topple to the side on her bad knee. He was smiling. Paddy backed off towards the frightened mob, skirting the metal barriers and heading away from the front line. She was right to get away. By the time she reached the corner of the square and looked back, it was a riot. A section of the march had burst its banks, and everyone was running from something. Hooves clattered on the tarmac, and Paddy saw waves of people, terrified and hanging on to one another, dragging friends away by their jackets and coats, holding arms over their heads for protection. Policemen billowed around the corner, batons raised at the people running away, hitting and dragging them backwards into the panic. She backed off, limping up the road, heading towards the office. She could phone home from there at least, tell her mum she had been attacked, and ask her to come and get her. She could call the police as well and get some of the old geezers to sit with her until someone came to help her.

The rain had slowed to drizzle as she circled back towards the office, coming at it from the unlit back of the car park. Ahead of her she could see that the canteen was dark and the newsroom lights were only on at one side of the room. The brightest of the beacon lights were outside the Press Bar. A guy in a sports jacket and slacks came out the door and paused to look up at the unfriendly sky. He could have been any one of the ugly, ridiculous men, but she'd never been more pleased to see anyone. He wrinkled his nose at the threatening sky, carefully checked the change in his pocket, and turned back, going inside for just one more, until the cold rain went off a little more.

Paddy limped after him, smiling as she stepped onto the dirt edge of the car park. Her knee was burning, not just the skin now but the bones. She stopped. She was suddenly cold, subconsciously aware of a blackness, a shape in a space that was rarely filled. The grocery van was parked in the dark far corner of the car park, all its lights off.

She backed off into shadow and looked. He was sitting back in the cab, his face in shadow, his arms crossed, watching the front of the building. He knew where she worked.

II

Paddy saw the white Volkswagen parked outside and knew Terry was in his flat. The knowledge that she was about to see a friendly face made her cry as she limped hurriedly past the third floor. When Terry opened the door her dignity crumpled and she stood, hands limp by her side, sobbing with fright.

He gave her a warm sweater to put on and a dry towel for her hair. He pulled off her boots and tights, cleaned the dirt out of her cut knee with a warm flannel, and made her a cup of black tea. It had to be tea because his flatmates had taken to locking their coffee away in their rooms and he'd forgotten to steal any from work.

He packed her boots with newspaper to soak up the worst of the rain, sat down close to her on the side of the bed, then put on both bars of the electric fire to heat her up. He gave her some dry bread to eat from his suitcase table. The bread filled a hole but, through some forgotten accident of proximity, tasted faintly of fish.

Instead of braving a city-center police station on this evening of evenings, they decided to phone and tell them about Naismith, but the pay phone in the hall wasn't working, and the public box six floors down was broken too. They decided to go and see Tracy Dempsie, to ask if the grocery van had been anywhere near her house when Thomas had disappeared, but they didn't do anything about that either. They decided to write a long article about Thomas Dempsie, but stayed sitting on the side of Terry's bed, sipping black tea, Paddy's damp thigh pressed against his.

Terry put the black-and-white portable on, and they watched the news. A red-faced presenter announced the headlines, and the march only made the fifth item. A hundred and fifty protesters had been arrested after trouble broke out in Glasgow during a pro-IRA march; police suspected the involvement of organized groups.

There was no mention of the hunger strikes, no mention of the mounted policemen hemming the crowd in. Even the local news brushed over it, showing footage of a very drunk man crumpled in a doorway while a pair of police horses walked calmly past the camera, the officers smiling down at the public they were there to serve.

"Truth's a rare commodity these days," said Terry, his knee pressing sharply against her thigh.

"It's justice that's rare," said Paddy. "Truth's relative."

They were sitting, pretending to look at a scar on his hand, when Terry suggested lying down. Paddy had guessed what he was going to say and got nervous, interrupting him to point to a pile of car magazines and say something sarcastic about them. She had to wait for another ten minutes of irrelevant small talk before he suggested it again.

They lay on their sides facing each other because the bed was too small to do otherwise. Paddy gathered her hands in front of her chest defensively, and Terry lay with his head propped on one arm, the other resting along the line of his body.

"Hello, Mary Magdalene," he said softly.

She cringed at the cheesiness of his approach and raised her hand, waving as if to someone twenty feet away. "Hiya!" she shouted. "Hiya, how're ye?"

She saw a flash of annoyance on his face, and his hand shot forward, holding the waving hand by the wrist, pulling it down to the bed. She suddenly saw herself, lying on a stranger's grubby bed without her ring. She rolled forward and kissed Terry on the lips, not unguarded and provoking like she would have been with Sean, but explorative, a careful taste of him. He held her wrist tight as he returned the kiss, his mouth pressing hard, graceless somehow, grazing his lip along the sharp edge of her teeth. He let go of her arm and his hand hovered above her. It landed softly on her hip, too low to be innocent. The heat from his palm swept through her, warming her chest and neck and gut. She kissed him again, touching him, putting her hand under his T-shirt, feeling skin and hair and smelling him around her in a cloud.

He was tugging her sweater over her head when she thought of Sean sitting on the back step to her mother's kitchen. She thought of him looking down their garden to the lonely, windswept tree. She saw his hand land gently on hers. The skin on his knuckles was perfectly smooth, that's how young he was.

Terry's damp fingers scumbled across the skin on her bare stomach. Her rolls of fat seemed to multiply under his hand. He asked her what she liked, and she said everything was great, lovely, just there, yeah, but she felt nothing but the facts of their movement, the scratching blanket, the fingers hooked inside her. He lay on top of her, leaving a trail of cooling saliva on her neck, and she sighed as she supposed she should, breathing faster when he did, acting and knowing she was acting, wondering if he knew. The blanket slid off them, and her legs and feet were cold. She blankly bided her time until it was over. Terry tensed, suddenly covered in a thin film of sweat, which cooled instantly into a cold wash. She didn't want to touch him.

"That was great," panted Terry, slithering out of her.

"Yeah." She breathed heavily, as if she had been carried away too.

He lay next to her, catching his breath. She tried not to touch him and stared at the ceiling. There was nothing to it. She was relieved. Her virginity was no longer a giant, weighty gift. She didn't have to find someone to bestow it on. It was gone. Sean was gone.

"Terry?" She nudged him, needing some company. "Hey, Terry, what time is it now?"

But Terry was asleep. Paddy slipped a finger between her legs and looked at it. She didn't see any blood. Terry didn't even need to know what had happened.

III

Two deep, vibrant orange bars glowed across the dark room. The electric fire sported little empty ash zeros where they had lit cigarettes against the bars. The curtains didn't shut properly, and even lying in the bed Paddy could see into the flats opposite, watching as a man readied himself for a Saturday night on the town and a woman made dinner for a thin man.

Terry slept for twenty minutes like a dead man, and when he woke up he told her a lot of gossip about the people at work. Kevin Hatcher, the drunken pictures editor, was only twenty-eight and had once won an international photography award for a photo essay about nomadic tribes of the Gobi Desert. Richards had stood for election as a Communist Party member. Tony Benn spoke on a platform with him and everything. Paddy was amazed. Then they had a long, pleasant argument about the relative value of *Tiswas* and *Swap Shop*, killing time before they had to be grown up again. He stroked her shoulder, looking at it with half-shut eyes, then leaned down to let his lips rest against the skin.

"I'm very fat at the moment," she said softly, as if the weight was an occasional condition that afflicted her.

"You're gorgeous. Womanly." He touched her breast and she blushed.

"I got a real fright today," she said quickly, "with that guy."

"We'll go to the police tomorrow, when things are calmer. They'll have let most of the marchers out by noon, it'll be quiet. There's good material in this, you know. There's at least one article in it."

She'd never told anyone before, and her worries spilled across her lips before she could stop them. "I don't think I can write. I don't know why, but I can't think straight when I sit down at a desk. I can see bits of it but I can't fit them together."

"That's just craft," he said. "No one

knows that stuff straightaway. You need to learn all that stuff."

"Really?"

"You'll learn. Don't worry." He stroked his hand up and down her soft belly. "It's just practice."

She could feel him pressing his cock against her leg and knew he was ready to go again.

"Shall we have another smoke?"

"Okay." Terry helped himself to one of her Embassy Regal cigarettes and climbed out of the bed, shamelessly walking naked across the room to the heater, crouching down to light it on the bars. "Heather Allen used to smoke these."

"God rest poor Heather." Paddy imagined her lying on the floor of the grocery van, among the bread dust. "What was she doing up in Townhead that night?"

"It turns out she wasn't in Townhead at all. When they checked it out, she was at an uncle's house having dinner with her parents. The witness who came forward must have confused her with someone else. Weird that they got her name right, though."

A sudden drop of pressure made one of Paddy's ears pop. There was only one of them in the Townhead scheme that night.

She'd called herself Heather Allen when she spoke to the shy man in the navy overcoat, and it wasn't the first time. She'd introduced herself as Heather Allen to Naismith when she first met him, the day the syndicated article was published in the paper. That's how he knew where she worked.

He'd killed the wrong girl.

TWENTY-NINE

LIFE IN A SCOTCH
SITTING ROOM

I

Terry dropped her on the main road and tried to kiss her, but she ducked out of the car quickly. It would be bad enough that she was seen getting out of a man's car, much less kissing him. She leaned back.

"I'll see you tomorrow, then?"

He mugged hurt at her. "You'll shag me but not kiss me? That's a bit Mary Magdalene."

"Shut up."

She smiled and slammed the door shut, watching as he drove away. When he turned the distant corner her grin dissolved. She pulled the neck of her coat up around her and headed into the Star. Every house was full tonight; every front

453

room was filled with the blue-and-white shifting flash of the Saturday night television. Paddy's feet were cold and wet inside her boots. Her bare toes curled against the paper sole, peeling the top layer off, gathering it between her toes. She walked straight past her house, past the Beatties', taking an overgrown lane out of the scheme and into the next door field. She climbed up to a wild bit of cliff overlooking an industrial valley that stretched for two miles over to the East End. The brae was considered a wild, slightly dangerous place, but Paddy needed to be alone.

It was dark and wet underfoot. She took the less-worn parallel path a couple of feet uphill from the muddy main track, trying to keep out of the mud and puddles. Within twenty feet she had cleared the bushes and trees and was on the bare hillside. The sounds of buses and cars and a lone whining motorbike wafted up the hill. She followed the hill around until she was no longer facing the city. White stars shone from the inky sky.

She looked out over the dying industrial valley. There was an ironworks down there that had given off the sulfurous smell of bad eggs night and day for as long as she had been alive, but now the lights were dark and all the men had been laid off. Smaller factories around it in the valley were closing down, farther down the river the shipyards were laying off, and every morning brought news of brand-new endings. The proud city was dying. Paddy lit her fifth cigarette of the day and blinked back tears as she thought of Sean and Naismith and what might have happened had he managed to grab her.

She was responsible for Heather's death. She'd wished her harm when she gave her name to Naismith. And what was a wish but a vulgar prayer to whoever else happened to be listening.

II

It was half past ten when Paddy slipped her key in the front door. As she opened it the first thing she noticed was the television was off and the living room was empty. An ominous light spilled into the hall from the kitchen. She didn't have time to hang up her coat before she heard her father's voice calling her through, trying to sound calm.

She saw a snapshot as she passed the serving hatch to the living room. Her family were gathered around the kitchen table, her mother and father grim-faced, the boys and Mary Ann huddled close together in a little row. Mary Ann was smirking at the tabletop, pressing her lips first to one side and then the other, trying not to scream with laughter. The boys stared at the table, dying with discomfort at the confrontation, the very men their father had made them. She noted sadly that Sean wasn't there and the only unoccupied place at the table was untouched, a clean glass sitting by it, clearly intended for her.

The kitchen table was scattered with the remains of a stillborn party: triangular sandwiches curling into sarcastic grins, a jug of weak orange squash, and an unopened bottle of sweet, viscous Liebfraumilch. As a centerpiece to the table sat a small white cake. The decorative silver balls on Marty's side of the table had been pulled out, leaving bullet holes in the icing.

Paddy held her coat over her arm, standing in the kitchen doorway like a visitor who didn't plan to stay long. She saw herself through their eyes: in at ten thirty without her engagement ring on, with mud on her shoes and tear-swollen eyes.

Con was so tense that he had to turn his entire body to look at her, twitching his little moustache side to side like a comedy humbug.

"It's late, I know," she said.

Her dad couldn't cope. It was enough that a child had defied him, but for her not to be penitent and for it to be his youngest daughter was too much.

"How dare you," he spluttered, the whites of his eyes turning red. "I will not be spoken to . . . I will not be spoken to —"

Trisha pressed her hand over Con's. "Where have you been all day?"

"I was at a friend's house."

"Which friend? We've phoned everyone."

"It's someone you don't know."

The boys glanced nervously at each other. Mary Ann took a deep, shuddering breath and bit her hand. The family knew everyone; they were everyone.

Her mother choked back a sob. "Patricia, where are your tights?"

Paddy looked down at her bare legs. One of her fat knees was capped with a large scarlet scab. She could imagine what her mother thought: that she had been chased by a gang of men in some sort of bizarre Protestant sex ceremony. It was kind of true.

She bristled. "I didn't want to come home. I can't stand the atmosphere here."

457

"Well, who made the atmosphere here what it is?" Con shouted, standing up and leaning over the table. "You did. You bloody made it."

Trish pulled him by the sleeve down into his seat. "Quiet, Con, stay calm."

"Look," Paddy shouted, "I was at the hunger strikers' march. I fell and hurt my knee and I had to take off the tights to clean the dirt out of the cut."

She shifted her heavy coat to the other arm and lifted her knee for them to see. It looked very dramatic in the bright light. The cut was scabbing up brown at the edge but still wet and yellow on the inside. They stared, but no one said anything. Marty looked suspiciously at Paddy, as if she had done it deliberately for sympathy.

Her mother stood up. "A hundred and fifty people were arrested in the town today. We've been phoning every police station in the city."

"I wasn't arrested, I just got knocked over."

"Well, thank God for that, anyway," said her father loudly.

"I'm very tired," said Paddy. "I'm very, very tired." She didn't know what else to say, so she backed out of the kitchen.

Gerald responded instinctively. "G'night, God bless."

Paddy heard her mother muttering angrily to him as she hung up her coat and climbed the stairs.

She lay down fully dressed and stared at the ceiling, thinking about Heather Allen's shuffled teeth and the stray hairs stuck in the stinking towel. Paddy had ruined herself and killed a girl. She had done terrible, terrible things.

III

The bed was shaking. She opened her sticky eyes and found Trisha sitting on the side, crying, a hand pressed tight against her mouth, worried and frightened and small.

Paddy had never seen her mother look so helpless. They reached for each other, hands knocking against faces, head against head, as Trisha folded up her baby in a watery mist of coos and sighs.

"I'm so worried for you," she said when she finally had her breath.

Paddy sniffed hard. "You don't have to worry for me."

"But last Sunday ye missed mass, and

now yesterday . . . I'm frightened for you."

"Don't worry, Mum."

Trisha smiled anxiously and stroked Paddy's hair back off her face. "Will you come to mass for me?"

"Mum . . ."

"Please, do it — for me?"

Paddy had been hoping last week would set a precedent. She hadn't planned to go to mass. She didn't believe in it and never had. The whole parish hated her. She'd had sex with a man she wasn't married to. She'd told a lie that killed a woman. The last thing she wanted to do was pause an hour and consider her conscience.

"Please?"

So Paddy went to mass for her mother, who went for her father, who went to set a good example for his children.

IV

Parishioners greeted friends and chatted in the chapel yard. The Meehans felt themselves being watched by the rest of the congregation as they walked around the corner and entered the low-walled yard. Gerald and Marty pretended not to care. Every thirty seconds or so Mary Ann gave out alarmed little yipping barks, laughs delivered too quickly to have any breath behind them. Paddy stared straight ahead, looking at no one. She felt a hand on her arm. Her father was there, his hand on her elbow, showing a united face for other people's benefit.

The Meehans didn't linger on the steps but went straight in and sat along a pew two-thirds of the way up the chapel, where they always sat, near to the ostentatiously religious families but not with them.

Father Bowen began the service, accompanied by the squalling of small children stationed at the back, their parents ready for a quick exit if the babies got too noisy. Paddy didn't dare look at the benches where the Ogilvys sat, but guessed from the shape of the shadows in the right-hand corner of her eye that Sean was sitting with his mother and two older brothers, their wives, and an assortment of fidgeting nephews and nieces.

She stood and sat as required, her mind obsessively circling Heather Allen. Someone had killed her because they thought she was Paddy, but she couldn't imagine why anyone would want to kill her in the first place. It was to do with Townhead, to do with the man in the grocery van, maybe even something to do with Thomas Dempsie.

Five young girls from Trinity school made the offertory procession, and stilted bidding prayers were read out by boys from the same year. Prayers were offered up for the repose of Granny Annie's soul. Communion was run like a military operation: the deacons stood at the side of the pews, letting out and holding back the communicants, only ever allowing four or five to queue in the aisle. Those who didn't have souls clean enough to receive the Eucharist had to stay behind alone on the bench. Paddy sat alone on the bench, feeling watched by the people behind, imagining Ina Harris spitting at her up the aisle.

At the end of the service, when they were all going in peace to love and serve the Lord, Paddy found Sean waiting by her pew. He genuflected with her, and they fell into step for the silent walk down the aisle, shuffling through the main doors and shaking hands with Father Bowen. Paddy looked back to the congregation flooding out and saw the pink relief on her father's face because Sean Ogilvy was back onside. They tripped down the stairs to the yard.

"So." Sean dug at the edge of a concrete

slab with the toe of his shoe. "Do you want to come to the pictures tonight? We never got to see that film."

"I didn't do it."

Sean glanced at the people next to him. "I don't want to talk about that here."

"Well, I do."

"Paddy, you brought it on yourself —"

"Shut up, Sean." She moved around so her father and mother couldn't see her face. "Listen, your cousin is being set up. Those children were driven there to kill that child, and no one cares but me. No one gives a shit, and if he was from a better family everyone would want to know what went wrong." He looked angrily down at her, and she dipped her head. "I meant his immediate family."

He was quiet for so long she had no alternative but to look up.

"Where's your ring?" he said.

"I took it off. When I didn't hear from you I didn't know if I was still engaged."

"We're engaged until I tell you otherwise."

She almost laughed at him. "Piss off."

"You made a promise," he said, "for better or worse."

"No, I didn't. I haven't promised those things yet, remember?"

"I'm not having an argument with you here," he said firmly.

Paddy shifted her weight from one leg to the other, rubbing the raw, soft tissue in her pants to remind herself about the night before. She smiled at him. Across the yard her father was smiling and talking to her mother.

"Okay, Sean, you want to go to the pictures with me? Let's go to the pictures."

"Tonight?" he said accusingly.

"You're on."

"I'll pick you up at seven." He walked away, brushing past her and knocking her with his shoulder. "And put your ring on."

V

Walking Paddy to the train station from the chapel, Mary Ann waited until they were behind the Castle Bar before asking if she had seen Stephen Tolpy's trousers from the back. Paddy hadn't, and Mary Ann was laughing too hard to explain why the trousers were funny. Paddy watched her pink face, her twitching nostrils, and joined in for no good reason. The girls laughed all the way down the stairs to the platform, both wondering how anything could be this funny and laughing again at the fact that it was.

The platform was a strip of unsheltered concrete sitting in a large tract of overgrown land. To the north, beyond some low-level buildings, was a view of the city, right to the cathedral and the Drygate high flats. Behind the peaks and spires of the city they could see the clean, snowcapped hills. The wind hurtled across the flat land, coming from the town, making those waiting turn their backs and look away. Together the sisters turned into the wind, narrowing their eyes tightly, catching the dust and grit on their eyelashes, and walked the length of the platform, arms linked and still laughing.

Mary Ann squeezed Paddy's arm. "I'm glad that fight's over."

Paddy knew it wasn't. "I didn't do it, you know."

She squeezed again, harder this time. "I don't care if ye did. I sometimes wish someone would do something and just —" But she stopped herself.

The train arrived, and Mary Ann waited until it was pulling out of the station, waving to Paddy and laughing, acting as though she was going away for a long time. Paddy waved back and giggled until Mary

Ann was out of sight. She knew the fight would never be finished. She'd never belong in the heart of them as she had before.

VI

As Paddy sat on the shuddering train into town, she remembered Meehan and his family and the unbridgeable distance between them.

After seven years protesting in jail, two books about the case, and a television documentary, Meehan had been offered parole papers.

"Sign them," the officer said. "Put your name there and you'll be out by the end of the week."

"Do I have to say I'm guilty?"

"You know you do."

Meehan had been in solitary for seven years, had got to walk in the yard for only twenty minutes once a fortnight. They wanted an excuse to release him, but it had to be on their terms. Meehan took a chance and said no. They wanted him out. Ludovic Kennedy's book about the flaws in the case had raised his profile so much that keeping him in was bringing the justice system into disrepute.

Five days later he was standing in his wife Betty's front room, holding a whisky tumbler in one hand and his royal pardon in the other, raising a glass with his family of strangers. It hurt his eyes to look at them. The colors they wore were so bright and their faces closed to him. His daughter was thin and gray, left weak by the treatment she had received for her nervous breakdown. His eldest son's jaw was clenched even when he drank, a rope of muscle cutting across his face. And there was his big stupid cousin Alec and his ugly wife, neither of whom had ever liked Meehan much. They didn't care whether he was guilty or innocent. They were only there because he'd been on telly.

Meehan knew he looked bad. He had the dry, gray skin long-term prisoners always had, and he had lost three stone over the years. He was a skinny old man now. Out of all of them only Betty looked good. She had dyed her hair blond, and it softened her. She was dressed in a white cotton pantsuit and red sandals, and she had been using a sunlamp: she had a faint white stripe across the bridge of her nose from the goggles. Before he went in Betty dressed dowdy; she used to be afraid of color. Now he watched her over the rim of his glass as he drank and saw a cheerful spark in her eye. Someone had put it there, and he knew it wasn't him. He didn't even have the heart to feel jealous. He had depended on Betty his entire adult life — he half despised her for being so dependable — but now she was moving away he felt nothing but admiration. He wished her well, he really did. He felt that she had got out too.

This was Betty's front room, not theirs. This little square room with a window that looked over the river, it rightfully belonged to her. She had made it clear that he was welcome and would be sleeping on the settee. He would get digs as soon as possible and give her peace.

Cousin Alec and his wife left, and the kids went down to the shops for half an hour to leave them alone. Betty and Meehan sat in silence side by side on the settee, drinking tea and slowly eating biscuits.

THIRTY

THE MR. PATTERSONS

I

Terry was waiting in his car, his arm slung over the back of his seat, mock casual, watching the station door for her. She was twenty minutes late, and he looked as if he'd been there for a while. He had washed his hair and shaved, taking the shadow from his chin, making him look boyish and eager. Paddy felt her skin bristle excitedly at the sight of him. She looked away and took a deep breath as she crossed the road. He leaned across the passenger seat and opened the door for her. She slid in next to him.

"Hiya."

"Hiya."

They looked at each other for a hard moment, their eyes locked.

"How's the knee today?"

"Fine."

They sat in silence. Terry's hand moved forward, invisible under the dashboard, covering hers. "I had an amazing time last night."

"Me too."

His hand pressed on hers. "Actually, I had four amazing times last night."

"You don't need to boast to me, Terry. I was there."

"I know." He bared his teeth. "But it's a personal best, and I can't tell anyone else. Shall we go?"

Paddy nodded, dreading his taking away his hand, savoring the heat from the heart of his palm. He turned to face the road, put both hands on the steering wheel, and sighed contentedly.

Neither of them knew which police station to go to, nor could they recall which division had done the questioning. They drove up to the Press Bar, which was open on Sundays, a fact that Paddy had never noticed before. It opened in the afternoon, Terry explained, for the staff who were getting Monday's edition together, and he was sure that someone there would know which station had been handling it. He drove down Albion Street slowly, with Paddy sitting low on the seat, checking for the grocery van.

A smattering of cars were arranged near the front of the car park, and the *News* delivery vans were parked along Albion Street, locked up and waiting for the next edition. Still concerned for her safety, Terry stopped at the door to the bar and let her climb out through the passenger door and run in while he went off and parked. She arrived breathless with nerves, an agitated face in a room of drink-softened men.

Richards was sitting alone at the bar, boring McGrade with second-hand jokes and commonplace observations. A team of three printers were sitting at a table together, relaxed, chatting just enough to keep the beer company. Dr. Pete was alone at a table near the back. In the three days since she had seen him his skin seemed to have aged a decade. He sucked in his cheeks as he drank, and the withered skin around his mouth puckered into radial lines. It was warm in the bar, but he had his overcoat pulled tight around him.

Paddy walked over. She had meant to work her way around to inquiring after his health, but it was so obviously wrong for the man to be sitting in a pub in his condition that she blurted it out.

"You look fucked."

He smiled up at her and blinked slowly.

"Fucked, is it?" he drawled, hands in pockets, pulling the tails of his coat around his thighs. "I'll tell you fucked. Thomas Dempsie, murdered in 1973, found at Barnhill by the train station. Father Alfred Dempsie, found guilty, hanged himself, sad case, blah, blah, blah." He smiled at her again and gave a jaunty little salute. "See, yeah? I remember you, remember what you were asking about. I remember it all."

"Have you been here since Thursday?"

"Was it Thursday?" He seemed quite surprised and lit a fag to mark the moment.

"You'll kill yourself in a month like this."

"Balls to the lot of them," he said quietly.

"Listen, was there ever mention of a grocery van being seen in the area when Thomas Dempsie went missing?"

Dr. Pete thought for a moment, blinking at his glass of beer before lifting it to his mouth and draining it. "Nut."

"Are you sure?"

The door to the bar opened behind her and she felt a stiff breeze on her neck. The feet moved towards her and she knew it was Terry.

"Certain."

472

"What about a guy called Henry Naismith, ever heard of him?"

Terry arrived at the edge of the table and Pete looked up at him.

"How are you, Pete, all right?"

Pete nodded, smiling vaguely at the wall.

"Can I get you a drink?"

Pete nodded again and Terry pointed questioningly at Paddy. She asked for lemonade and held her ground when they insisted she have something else. Her stomach couldn't take it, she said; once a week was more than enough for her.

Terry moved off to the bar, and Pete smirked knowingly and chewed the inside of his cheek for a moment. "You should watch out. A woman can't afford to get a reputation in this business."

"Am I not allowed friends my own age?"

"It shows. The way a man holds a woman's eye like that — steadily, as if the whole world was just a secret between them." It was the way he used to write — she could hear the unique tone — but instead of going on for ten paragraphs he stopped dead and looked at his glass.

Terry arrived back at the table with a packet of ten Embassy Regal and the drinks: a lemonade for Paddy, a half-pint for himself, and a half-and-half for Dr.

Pete. He put down the cigarettes in front of Paddy. "That's for last night," he said, making her flinch in front of Pete. "What are ye talking about?"

"Whether there is a connection between Naismith and Tracy Dempsie," said Paddy, carefully changing the subject.

Dr. Pete's eyes were wide and wet, three degrees removed from the table. He picked up his whisky glass and threw the contents into the back of his throat, his lip curling in either disgust or pain, Paddy couldn't quite tell. Then he lifted the half-pint of beer to see if a sip of that would help. It didn't.

"D'you know what I'd like now?" Pete looked at Paddy and only at her. "I'd like a plate of lamb." He dropped his head and wept into his beer.

Terry had to tap him on the elbow and repeat his name a couple of times to get his attention, and asked him for the name of the police station that was dealing with Heather's murder. Pete told them it was Anderston station, and be sure to ask for Davie Patterson — Pete knew his father. Paddy smiled a thank-you but had no intention of asking for the squat-faced policeman. He couldn't possibly be the only man on the investigation team.

When she looked up she found Pete watching her again.

"Henry Naismith," he said, "was Tracy Dempsie's first husband."

"Her husband? The one she left for Alfred Dempsie?"

He slumped and nodded sadly at his beer. "Aye."

II

The lobby walls were paneled in a cheap, dark veneer, which clashed with yellowing turquoise linoleum on the floor. Anderston station had twice as many chairs as the police station she had been in with McVie, three rows of five screwed to the floor.

The desk sergeant's post was on a rostrum so high that Paddy peered over the lip like a child in a chip shop. A tired young officer in full uniform was sitting in a creaking wooden chair that protested loudly when he moved more than half an inch in either direction. It was Sunday, he informed them, no one was in today. They could talk to someone if they were prepared to wait, but he didn't know when anyone would be available. It might be better if they phoned tomorrow.

"We've got some pretty important information about Heather Allen's murder. We think we should tell someone right away," said Terry, raised with the expectation that important people would listen to him.

The desk sergeant looked suspicious. "Heather Allen, is it?"

It was clear to Paddy that he didn't know who they were talking about.

"Yes, Heather Allen," said Terry. "The girl who was found in the river last weekend with her head caved in. We know something about it and we need to tell someone."

The sergeant nodded. His chair let out a furious creak as he pointed them towards the far wall. "Go and wait over there. Someone'll be out in a minute."

They walked across the floor to the first set of chairs and sat down in time to see the sergeant disappear through a doorway to his right.

Two minutes later he returned, his eyebrows drawn tight with surprise, and flicked his finger at them to come over. "They're coming straight out," he said.

They waited for ten minutes, smoking a cigarette between them. Terry was putting it out on the floor when a door opened behind the desk sergeant. Patterson and

476

McGovern stumbled through it looking playful and mischievous, as though they had just been having a good laugh. All roads in the Heather Allen case seemed to go through Patterson. Paddy was dismayed, and he wasn't pleased to see her either. He balked, put out a hand to stop McGovern going to the trouble of leaving the rostrum, and called over to her.

"Ah, yeah. What do you want?"

Paddy stood up. She didn't want to go over to him, she wanted him to come to her.

"Pete McIltchie sent me," she said, trying to make it clear that she didn't want to see him either. "I need to tell someone something about Heather."

He didn't move towards her but stood up straight, picking at a mark on the desk in front of him.

"McIltchie?"

"He told me to come and see you."

He nodded up at her. "Is it new information?"

"Yes." And still he stayed ten yards away, making her talk to him over the heads of Terry and the desk sergeant. She decided just to shout: "I was picked up by someone in Townhead and I found one of Heather's hairs on a towel. The guy tried to attack me."

Patterson nodded at the desk and glanced back at McGovern. Paddy was sure that if they had been alone, if McGovern and the desk sergeant and Terry hadn't been there, he would have told her to piss off.

"Okay," he muttered. "Come through to an interview room."

McGovern followed Patterson out from behind the desk, stepping down so that they were on her level, and showed her to a double doorway at the side. Patterson pinched her upper arm firmly, as if she needed coaxing. Terry tried to follow, but McGovern put a firm hand on his chest.

"We're not going to be long."

Terry looked at Paddy protectively. "I'd like to stay with her."

Patterson pursed his lips. "No," he said firmly.

McGovern's eyes shone triumphantly, pleased at the petty point, and Paddy took it as a bad sign.

Beyond the doors the broad corridor was paneled in the same dark wood veneer as the waiting room. The turquoise floor was stained with a yellow streak down the center. Paddy could smell tea and toast from not far away. The Sunday shift seemed like a mellow call, but it wasn't translating into any benign feeling towards her. As they walked along the corridor in front of her, the two burly policemen's shoulders were almost touching. Neither of them wanted to look at her.

Twenty yards down the corridor Patterson knocked briskly on a door, paused, and opened it, peering in to see if the room was empty. He flicked a finger at her. "In."

Paddy stepped into the room, not at all certain they weren't going to shut the door and walk away. She heard a voice in the corridor calling Patterson, a low voice asking something.

"I've just got someone in, sir." Patterson's voice sounded higher than when he spoke to her. "About Heather Allen."

The white-haired man who had vied with McGuigan for the attention of the newsroom looked in through the door. He was wearing weekend clothes, navy slacks and a gray sweater, as stiff and formal as a uniform.

"Hello," she said.

He looked at her duffel coat suspiciously and addressed Patterson. "Don't take too long. I've got work for you."

Patterson nodded, enjoying the implied slight to Paddy. He followed her into the room and took a seat at the table without offering her one. She sat down anyway.

McGovern sat down opposite her and lit a cigarette.

"Tell me," he said, suppressing a smile, "why do you call yourself Paddy Meehan?"

Patterson smirked next to him.

"It's my name."

"No, it isn't," said McGovern. "Your name's Patricia Meehan. You chose to call yourself Paddy Meehan."

She had always known her name would excite comment, that it gave her away as a Pape and marked her out at work, but she hadn't anticipated it being regarded as a reproach by the police. The two men looked at her, enjoying her discomfort.

"I've always been called that. Is that why you don't like me? Because my name's Paddy Meehan?"

It was a mistake. She'd left herself wide open; they could fill in any number of insults now: We don't like you because you're fat, we don't like you because you're ugly. McGovern and Patterson didn't even bother filling in the caption. They sniggered at her mistake, McGovern turning it into a laugh as he thought of a quip, Patterson losing interest, taking a deep breath, and scratching at the corner of his mouth with his fingernail.

"I've come here to tell you something important," she said quietly.

Patterson nodded at the table. "Fire away, Scoop."

McGovern tittered.

She didn't know where to start, so she took it chronologically. She told them about the grocery van and the ice-cream van's stops and about the smelly towel on the floor of the van and Heather's hair and the man trying to grab her ear and sitting outside her work. She listened to herself talk and realized that it all sounded meaningless and circumstantial. McGovern asked her if the towel was still in the van, and she had to admit that she had held on to it and then lost it in the street somewhere. He picked up his cigarettes from the table, slipped the lighter into the packet, and put them in his pocket, getting ready to leave. She began to speak faster, leaving out the fact that she had given Heather's name to several people. It was when she said the name Henry Naismith that she saw a flicker of something approaching interest.

Patterson looked at her. "Naismith?"

"He's the man who runs the grocery van. He was Tracy Dempsie's first husband. He could have killed Thomas and then Baby Brian."

"He didn't kill Baby Brian. Your cousin killed him."

"He's not my cousin."

"Naismith didn't kill Thomas Dempsie," said Patterson certainly.

"How can you know that for sure?"

"He had an alibi. He was in the cells when that boy was killed."

He caught Paddy's eye, and a hot flush was just discernible on his cheeks. He had the details of the case to hand in the same way that she had old Paddy Meehan's.

"And how would you know that?" she said quietly.

McGovern piped up to defend his friend, adding it as a throwaway fact, thinking nothing of it. "Turns out his old man worked that case."

"The Thomas Dempsie case?"

McGovern nodded innocently. "That's how he knows Pete McIltchie. His dad knew him from back then."

Patterson colored a little and nodded at the table, pressing his lips tight together and raising his eyebrows. "Naismith was in the cells the night the boy was killed."

"He'd been arrested?"

"It was just an affray. He was a senior in a gang back then, caused a lot of damage. He was broken up when that kid died. He got religion just after it, went through a big conversion."

"He's got a history of violence?"

"He was a street fighter at the tail end of the sixties, but he's a nice old guy now, he wouldn't hurt anyone."

"Well, he tried to hurt me."

Patterson shook his head. "Look, we know Naismith didn't kill anyone."

"But Alfred Dempsie did?"

It was only an implied slight, but when she saw the reaction she wouldn't have wanted to slag off Patterson's dad overtly. He narrowed his mean little eyes and the red flush on his face deepened.

"You don't know anything about that," he said.

"I know enough."

McGovern was watching them, a small, vacant smile on his beautiful face, not quite knowing what was going on. Patterson slid his hands back off the table, slapped it once, and clicked his tongue on the roof of his mouth.

"So, you think Heather Allen was in the van, but you took the evidence out and lost it in the road. And now you're sure it's got something to do with Thomas Dempsie? What are you going to do about it?"

He looked at her intently, his eyes

flicking angrily across her face. He thought she was going to write an article exposing his dad for setting up Alfred Dempsie. He must have pored over the details of the case over the years and known his dad had set Dempsie up. She could see the shame burning bright behind his eyes. She was flattered and pleased that he didn't know she was just a copyboy.

"I don't know what I'm going to do yet."

Suddenly Patterson was on his feet. He jerked the door open as he pulled her coat off the back of the chair and shoved it into her arms.

"Look," she said, trying one last time. "I could have imagined the hair and him going for me, I know that, but he was waiting outside my work when I went back there last night. How would he know where I worked?"

Patterson pulled her into the corridor by the arm. "Unfortunately we can't arrest people for parking outside your work. This thing with you and Naismith's just a misunderstanding. Maybe you left something in his cab and he wants to return it to you or something."

"Yeah. That's bound to be why he's got Heather Allen's hair in his van, isn't it?"

Leaving McGovern behind, Patterson

led Paddy through the door to the waiting room, acting as if she had hurt his feelings. Still holding on to her arm, he pulled her across the floor, depositing her arm into the tender care of Terry.

"Don't worry," he told Terry. "The man in question is known to us. We'll be having a word, telling him to lay off and stay away from her and the paper."

"Hey! Talk to me, not him."

Patterson turned, his face a mask of disgust. "You shouldn't be getting into vans with men you don't know. Old guys like Naismith are prone to get the wrong idea, and you'd have no one to blame but yourself if he did."

He turned and walked away. The desk sergeant raised an amused eyebrow.

Terry looked at her. "I'm guessing it didn't go that well."

"You'd be guessing right."

Outside the station they climbed into the car and sat staring out the windscreen for a moment, Paddy stunned, Terry patient.

"The red-faced guy there?" she said finally. "His dad investigated Thomas Dempsie. There's no way the police will ever open that case again."

"What if we approach Farquarson —"

"Terry," she said, turning to him.

"Listen to me. We're nothing. McGuigan and Farquarson won't print an article denouncing the Strathclyde police force on our say-so."

"They won't publish, will they?"

"They won't publish a speculative story. We'd need definite proof. And in the meantime no one's the slightest bit interested in searching Naismith's van. Those wee boys are going to get the blame."

"We can't let this happen."

"I know." She looked out the window, following the path of a crisp packet across the windy road. "I know."

III

It was always quiet on the editorial floor, but the absence of doors opening or movement through the corridors lent the air a peculiar weight. Paddy kept close to the wall, staying away from the windows as she crept along to the last door before the back stairs. Her fingers were touching the door handle before it occurred to her that the toilets might even be locked over the weekend.

The handle turned, she felt a gentle click, and the door to the ladies' opened.

With a last glance into the corridor, she stepped in. Whether she was smelling or remembering it she couldn't quite tell, but the tang of Heather's Anaïs Anaïs perfume caught her throat, and she had to press her eyes shut and take a deep breath before making herself move on.

The cleaners had been. The sink had been wiped down, the used towels emptied from the wire-mesh bin, and the sanitary towel bin, its top still crumpled from Heather's weight, had been moved back into the corner of the far cubicle. Paddy bent down and ran her finger over the hollow. Naismith was going to walk, and Callum Ogilvy and the other child would lose their lives because the cleaners had been. She turned to go, catching sight of herself in the full-length mirror by the door. Her chin sloped straight into her chest. She was putting on weight. She spun away from the mirror, and her gaze landed on the floor at the back of the toilet, a stray glint causing her to stop dead. She smiled. That cleaner was a lazy cow. She had mopped the floor without sweeping it first, pushing the debris against the wall under the low cistern, convinced no one would look there between one shift and the next.

Paddy bent down a little and smiled. She

could see the threads, dulled with dust particles clinging to them, but they were there: a little golden bundle of Heather Allen's hair.

IV

Terry sat on his bed, head bent over the phone book, running his finger down the list of names while Paddy leaned against the wall and watched him. The bedsheets were creased in the middle from the night before. She didn't want to sit down next to him, didn't want to approach the bed or touch the sheets. With the overhead light on she could see that a fuzzy gray oval had formed in the middle where Terry slept. She could hardly believe that she had lain there the night before, her bare skin touching the grubby linen, her hands moving slowly over him, faking pleasure. She searched her soul for the crippling shame she had been warned about but couldn't find it. She wasn't a virgin anymore, and no one knew but her. She crossed her arms, hugging herself, and tried not to smile.

"There's a few in Baillieston," he said. "Three in Cumbernauld."

"Must be a family."

"Must be." His eyes followed his fingers to the bottom corner of the list, and then he turned the page. "Here, H. Naismith."

Paddy stepped quickly towards him. "Is there one there?"

"Yeah, H. Naismith, Dykemuir Street."

She remembered the address from the mass card they had sent after Callum Ogilvy's father died.

"That's Callum Ogilvy's street," she said. "Naismith lives in bloody Barnhill."

V

Of all the houses in the street it was the most unremarkable. Naismith's house was modest and tidy, the curtains hung neatly. The short front garden had been paved over with red slabs that had sunk irregularly into the sand beneath, their edges sticking up and down. An empty hanging plant basket at the side of the front door swung with a mild metronomic regularity in the evening wind. The grocery van was parked proudly outside.

Twenty yards away across the road, in the incline of the hill, sat the Ogilvy house. Looking out the passenger window as they passed, Paddy could see where weeds and weather were eating through the brick in the garden wall, chewing into the FILTH OUT slogan, the weight of soil from the garden forcing the bricks to buckle out onto the pavement.

Barnhill was not the preferred residence of motorists. Terry had parked near the Ogilvys', but his white Volkswagen was still the only car in the dark street apart from Naismith's grocery van. They were acutely conspicuous.

"Shit. We might as well have phoned ahead to tell him we were coming."

"I know," said Terry, peering through the windscreen into the deserted street. He started the engine again and pulled the car out into the road, pulling off quickly as though they were going somewhere.

"What about here?" said Paddy as they passed an empty pub car park two streets away.

Terry shook his head. "That's not safer. There're more witnesses here."

They passed by, and Paddy saw in the window the backs of a man and a woman sitting close in the warm amber light, their heads inclined together. They drove on, following a broad road out towards the Springburn bypass. A stretch of waste ground next to the road was dark with nothing nearby but an abandoned, boarded-up tenement building and a pavement running outside it. Terry slowed the car a little and glanced at her inquiringly.

"No, too obvious."

He sped up, heading farther away again.

"But Terry, the farther we go from the van the farther we've got to walk back to it. We're more likely to be seen."

"Ah, you're right." He slowed over to the side of the road and swung the car through a sharp circle. "Let's just do it."

He drove down Callum Ogilvy's road, parked the car twenty feet behind the van, and turned off the engine. He zipped up his leather jacket, tugging the toggle at the end twice, making sure it was up properly. Paddy watched him. Terry was sweating with nerves. They had agreed beforehand that this would be his job, knowing that if Naismith saw Paddy he'd go for her, but Terry was very jittery. She didn't know if he would be able to pull it off.

"Are we sure about this?" he said, talking quickly, as if he was afraid to breathe out.

"I am. Are you?"

He nodded, looking anxiously out the window. "He was in the cells when Thomas Dempsie was killed, though."

491

"He could easily have taken him earlier and hidden him. Tracy Dempsie would hardly be the most reliable person to get times from. Dr. Pete said she changed the times back and forth when they interviewed her."

"Right." He nodded out the window again. "You're sure, then?"

"Terry, look where he lives: he knows Callum Ogilvy, Thomas Dempsie was his ex-wife's wean by her new man, and his rounds are in Townhead. He must have passed Baby Brian every day. He fits in with all of it perfectly."

"Yes," he said, still frowning at the street.

"We're only making them check his van. If they don't find any other evidence, he'll walk."

"He'll walk." Terry nodded. "He'll walk."

"But they will find evidence. I'm sure they will. They'll find evidence of the Wilcox baby and Heather as well, I'm sure they will."

"You're sure they will." His nervous nodding grew faster and he began to rock forward slightly on his seat. "Sure they will."

He threw open the door and stepped out

into the street in one seamless move, striding towards the van with his head down. He stayed in the road, keeping the van between himself and Naismith's front door, stepped up on the chrome-trimmed step on the driver's side, keeping his balance by resting his belly against the door, flattening himself against the body of the cab.

Paddy was staring straight at the van, but if she hadn't known Terry was there she wouldn't have seen him. His elbow rose, and she saw a flash of light from the screwdriver as he pulled it from his pocket. He jacked the window down, working with the winding mechanism, emptied the contents of the green hand towel in through the window, and stepped away from the cab. Then he walked back towards her, his shoulders still up around his ears, his eyes on the ground in front of him. Paddy watched his face and saw that he was grinning.

VI

She pressed the rim of the receiver tight against her ear, wondering. Terry was watching her from the car. She was certain they were doing the right thing when she was with him, but as soon as she was alone in the call box, dialing the number for Anderston police station, she wondered if the whole idea seemed sensible only because she wanted to show off to him, acting confident of the facts the way she had acted about sex in his bed the night before. Her pulse throbbed in her throat as she blurted out the story to the officer on the other end: She had seen Heather Allen on that Friday night getting into a grocery van outside the Pancake Place in Union Street; she didn't know whose van it was, but it was purple and old and she'd seen it doing rounds in Townhead. She hung up when he asked for her name and address.

Striding back to the car, she hoped she looked as confident as Terry had when walking away from Naismith's van.

"Is that it?"

"Done," she said, catching her breath. "Done and done."

Terry drove her all the way to the first leg of the Star, and she didn't care if she was seen with him. Around the Star, front room lights were on as families settled around the telly after *Songs of Praise*. Terry smiled at the little houses and said he liked it.

"All the houses are facing each other,

though. Don't the neighbors all watch each other?"

"Oh, yeah," said Paddy. "Everyone knows everything. Even the Prods know who's skipping mass. Cheers for running me home."

They looked at each other, a bold, bald stare, and she was dismayed to see a tiny ambivalent twitch on his chin.

"We did a good thing today, Terry."

"I hope we did."

They would be forever bound together by what they had done, and they both knew it.

She climbed out of the low car, regretting the fact that her fat arse was the last thing to leave his line of sight, and bent down to look at him once more. She saw him sitting in the sagging seat, his little pot belly straining through his T-shirt, saw herself lingering too long to talk, reluctant to leave his company. If Pete could see what there was between them, then other people could too. Sean would be hurt to his core.

"We'll hear in the morning, anyway. I'll see you then." She withdrew and slammed the car door behind her.

She could see his face as he took the rickety car around the roundabout. He

looked scared but bared his teeth in a
smile as he came past. She waved back,
watching the rusting backside of the car
until Terry was gone.

THIRTY-ONE

GOOD-BYE

They were still treating her like a walking sack of pitiful contagion. Marty wouldn't speak or look at her when they were alone together, Con pressed his lips tightly together when they passed on the stairs, as if she were a stranger he had heard unpleasant things about. She had seen them do it to Marty and had happily participated in it herself, but she wasn't going to let them wear her down.

She sat alone on her bed, looking at the engagement ring on her finger. The ring felt tight and cut into the skin — she had put on weight in the last week or so — but she kept it on. Sean might not help her otherwise. She could hear Marty listening to the radio in the next-door room, John Peel's droning monotone interspersed with bursts of synth music and thrashing punk vocals.

She jumped up when she heard the

doorbell downstairs. She heard her mother greeting Sean in the hall with a loud, cheerful whoop followed by a hundred tittering questions about his week, talking as if he had been away at sea for two years. The voices drew closer, and she heard their soft tread on the carpeted stairs.

They were almost up the stairs when Paddy suddenly fumbled the ring off her finger. She grabbed the little velvet box from the dresser and tried to fit the band back into the foam slit, but her hands were too jittery. She dropped the ring inside the box and snapped the lid shut just before the bedroom door opened.

Sean looked in at her. He was wearing formal clothes, his new shiny bomber jacket over a crisp orange Airtex shirt, troublingly close in tone to Terry Hewitt's bedsheets. Trisha was standing behind him. "Here's Sean to see you." Her voice was manically cheerful.

"Hiya."

Paddy stood up. "Let's go, then."

"Well, we're a bit early," said Sean, angling to come into the room for a snog.

"But the buses . . ."

Paddy looked vaguely at her mother, willing her to move out of the way. She didn't want to talk to him here, not with her mother creeping past on the landing, downstairs praying to JC for a Catholic outcome, and smiling hopefully every time they came down for a cup of tea.

"Let's go," she said, keeping her eyes down stubbornly.

Down in the hall, Trisha helped them on with their coats. She patted Paddy on the arm, signaling a motherly message about compromise and keeping a man: Don't let him go, perhaps; or, Agree to anything.

Outside in the crisp air Paddy looked back through the mottled glass and saw the outline of her mother standing still with her head bowed in prayer. She wanted to kick the fucking door in.

"Which cinema do you want to go to?" asked Sean, pulling up his collar.

"Can we go up the brae?"

Sean raised a suggestive eyebrow. There was never any evidence of it, but rumors abounded of sexy goings-on up the brae, just because it was dark and out of sight. Paddy didn't giggle or respond the way he expected.

"I need to talk to you," she said seriously.

His face tensed. For the first time since he shut his front door on her, Paddy felt that he was on the back foot, not her.

"Okay," he said. "Let's go up the brae."

They walked to the end of the street in silence, to the raw mud path leading up the hill. It was a long corridor, with bushes on either side. Sean took out his cigarettes to have something to do, and Paddy tapped him on the back.

"Give us a fag, eh?"

He looked surprised: he had never known her to smoke. He held out the packet and she took one, holding it between her lips and tipping her head to the side to take the light from the match in his cupped hand. She didn't really like smoking. It made her teeth feel dirty and her blood pressure rise, but she liked the idea of being a narrow-eyed, knowing smoker.

"We're never getting to the pictures, are we?"

Paddy exhaled, looking down the dark path.

"Is it because it's a boxing flick? We don't need to go and see that one; we could go and see a romance if you like."

"No, no, I liked that film."

"Ye saw it already?"

"Yeah." He looked suspicious. "I went on my own. It's been a lonely week."

She scratched her nose and saw his eye fall on her naked ring finger.

"Come on," she said, pushing him forwards, following him along the wild path until the bushes cleared.

They found their way along the steep hillside until the lights from the Eastfield Star were eclipsed by the bushes and trees behind them. Paddy found a flat shelf of rock and sat down on it, crossing her legs and clearing her coat next to her to leave room for Sean. Less elegantly, he lowered himself beside her, stiff from a hard day's carrying.

"Since when do you smoke?"

Paddy shrugged, staring out at the flat valley below them. She started to speak and stopped, taking a smoky draw before starting again. She felt in her pocket and found the engagement ring box. She held it out to him, afraid to look in his eyes and see the hurt there.

"I need to give you this back, Sean. I'm not getting married."

He laughed at the abruptness of it and looked at her, hoping for a moment that she'd laugh back and it would be all right. She didn't. She stared ahead, squinting at the road below them, tucking her hands into her sleeves.

"It's not you, you're wonderful. If I wanted to get married to anyone, it would be you, but I don't. I'm too young."

"We're only engaged," he pleaded.

"Sean, I don't want to get married."

"You feel that way now —"

"I might never want to get married."

He stopped, grasping for the first time the enormity of the change in her. "Have you turned lesbian or something?"

Paddy looked at the man she might have spent her life with. He didn't mean to be unkind. He was handsome and noble and decent, but, God help him, just not very bright.

"I want a career and I don't think I can get married and have one, so I'm choosing the career."

He shot her a warning look. "Why do you need to try and be a man? What's wrong with just being a woman?"

"That's stupid, Sean."

"It's good enough for every other girl in the family."

"Shut up."

"Your mum's gonnae —"

"Don't! Don't bring my family into this, Seanie. This is about you and me and everything we've meant to each other." Her eyes ran despite her, filling her nose and making her breathless. "I can't talk to you without thousands of relatives invading the pitch. Never mind my mum and dad and the Pope and all our future children, we need to talk about you and me. Just you and me."

"I only bring them in because we're getting married, Paddy. I only do that because I'm serious about ye."

She was crying openly now, her face wet, crying not just for the loss of Sean, but for the fright she'd had, and for Dr. Pete and Thomas Dempsie, crying for the loss of certainty. Sean fumbled for her hand, pulling it out of the sleeve of her duffel coat and holding it in both of his. Her fingers were cold, and as he rubbed them to warm her, he felt the smooth skin where her ring should have been and began to cry himself.

"I didn't do anything wrong," he said.

"It's not what I want."

"I got punched at work because of you."

"It's not what I want."

"But I love you."

They held hands and wept, unaccustomed to sharp emotion, looking away from each other into the dark.

When the tears had stopped, her hand was swollen red with all the rubbing. Sean took out his cigarettes again and lit one without offering, dropping the packet back in his jacket pocket.

"Why did you agree to marry me, then,

if you didn't want to?" he said bitterly.

Paddy leaned over and took out the cigarette packet, helping herself to one, making him smile. She put it in her mouth and pointed it at him.

"Give us a light."

Sean leaned into her, touching the red tip of his cigarette to hers. She inhaled, sucking in her cheeks, drawing fire from him.

"I want you to get me in to see Callum Ogilvy." She exhaled and waited for him to shout at her.

"I can't get you in," he said softly.

"Yes you can. You're his family. You could get to see him now he's in hospital."

Sean wrapped his arms around his knees, pulling them into his chest, touching a knee to his forehead. "I can't believe you're asking me for help with your career."

"It will help my career." She nodded guiltily. "It will, I can't deny that. On the other hand, it'll make a big difference to Callum. Eventually he'll be interviewed, and if it's by anyone else they'll make him out to be an evil child and he'll be stuck with it for the rest of his life. At least this way we can control how he's portrayed."

"And you get a big exclusive?"

"We could fight about it," she said,

taking the cigarette out of her mouth and blowing on the tip to encourage it, "or we can accept that's how it is and stay pals."

"You're choosing your career over me?"

"Sean, I'm not what you want." She felt energetic suddenly, excited that she was out of the yoke of her engagement. "I'd have been a rotten wife. I'd make your life a misery. I'd have been the worst Catholic wife in history."

He nudged her with his elbow. "You'd be a good mum."

"Not a Catholic mother, not me."

He touched her ankle, stroking the back of his fingers down her tights, testing to see if it was okay to touch. "Aye, ye would."

She rocked towards his ear. "I don't even believe in Jesus."

He looked incredulous. "Get tae hell."

"Honestly."

"But you were in the Sacred Heart prayer group for a year."

"I only went because you were there."

He slapped her arm, exaggerating his surprise to have an excuse to touch her. "But you always bless yourself when you go in or out of a house."

"My mum likes it. I've never had a drop of faith. I knew I was lying when I made my first communion." She grinned, relieved that someone finally knew. "I've never told a soul that. You're the only one who knows. Now you know why I'm trying to get away from the family all the time."

"Bloody hell."

"I know." She raised her hands skyward. "I've spent half my life on my knees thinking it was rubbish."

They smiled at each other. The wind blew Sean's hair the wrong way, and a train passed in the valley below. Paddy raised her shoulders and snuggled inside her coat. It felt different with Terry: she felt close to Sean, but there was no fire.

"One thing, though, and I know I don't have any right to ask ye favors right now, but about the engagement: gonnae not tell my mum?"

He looked at her for a moment and his eyes softened. "That's no bother, wee pal."

She reached up and touched his cheek with her chilly fingertips. "Look at ye. You're so handsome, Sean. I'm not even good-looking enough to go out with you."

Sean took a draw on his cigarette. "You know what, Paddy. I always let you say things like that 'cause I liked it that you're modest. But you're a good-looking girl. You've got a small waist and big lips. People say it all the time."

It felt like a warm bubble bursting in her head. She searched her memory for corroborating evidence that she was attractive but couldn't find any. The boys at school weren't mad for her. Men didn't approach her on the street. She didn't ever remember being complimented before.

She laughed awkwardly and hit his arm. "Piss off."

"You are." He looked away, uncomfortable that she was making him elaborate. "You're beautiful to me."

"Only to you, though?"

"Eh?"

"Am I only beautiful to you?"

Sean nudged her gently.

"No. You're beautiful, Paddy. Just beautiful."

They sat together quietly, smoking cigarettes and looking out over the valley. Every time she thought about what he'd said, Paddy felt dizzy. It could change everything if it was true. She had always hated her face. She hated her looks so much she was embarrassed to leave the house some mornings. They sat, and during a couple of quiet pauses she felt a burst of gratitude so overwhelming that she almost asked him to marry her.

THIRTY-TWO

DON'T LIKE MONDAYS

I

She woke up more aware of the day ahead than the weekend that had passed. Terry was going in early to get out all the Dempsie clippings and stop anyone else's using them. He was going to phone around the police stations and then try to speak to McVie and Billy, who was probably a less self-interested source of information, to find out if anything had happened overnight to Naismith. Then he was going to approach Farquarson and ask if they could write the story themselves. She hoped Terry would be enough of a draw. She certainly wasn't on her own.

The family didn't notice a difference in her as they ate breakfast. Trisha boiled her three eggs as an act of reconciliation, and Gerald passed her the milk for her coffee before she asked for it. She sat and ate among them, watching the toast rack pass from person to person and Trisha dishing out the porridge. She acted normally, her mind back in the weekend, thinking her way through Naismith's van, the riot, and Terry Hewitt's bed.

The frost gave everything in the world a sharp edge, and the weak sun couldn't burn the morning off the land. Even Paddy's breath was a cloud of sharp crystals as she hurried carefully across slippery pavements to the station.

She found a seat on the train and sat down heavily, wincing at the tenderness of the flesh between her legs. It gave her more of a thrill than the sex itself had. She thought of herself sitting in Terry's passenger seat, watching him walk back from Naismith's van, of the cold, damp rock on the windy brae. Sean could go out with other girls now if he wanted. He could hold their hands and kiss them and promise them a cozy future. In time she would just be someone he used to know.

When she saw Terry Hewitt standing outside the door of the *Daily News* building with his hands in his pockets, one leg bent and resting on the wall behind him, she knew somehow that he was

509

hoping he looked like James Dean. He looked like a plump guy leaning on a wall.

She was still a long way away and, abandoning his pose, he glanced down the road to look for her, knowing she would be coming from the train station. When he spotted her outline in the distance, a duffel coat and ankle boots, scurrying towards him, he did a double take and self-consciously resumed his stance. She was standing just feet away before he looked up again. He looked angry.

"You're wanted in the Beast Master's office. Right away."

Paddy glanced at her watch. "But the editorial meeting's about to start."

"Right away."

He turned away, ready to lead her upstairs, but she caught the tail of his leather.

"Shit, Terry, what happened?"

He didn't stop or even look back. He flapped his hand for her to follow, leading the way through the black marble lobby. The echo of Terry's metal-capped shoes ricocheted off the cold ceiling and walls. The Two Alisons simultaneously turned their heads and watched them cross the floor. Paddy knew it was serious. Not only had Terry been sent to intercept her and take her straight to Farquarson, he was escorting her through the formal entrance, the entrance for strangers who didn't belong to the paper.

He jogged up the stairs in front of her, and Paddy hit his leg. "Stop," she pleaded, but he didn't. He marched on, and she had no option but to follow him. "Terry, please?" He sped up as if he were trying to get away from her.

She was losing her breath as they arrived on the newsroom floor. She was about to start a fresh plea, but he crossed the landing in two steps and threw open the doors to the newsroom. Not a single face looked at them, not one head rose nor idle eye fell upon them as Terry led her across the hundred-foot stretch of carpet to Farquarson's office. Even Keck kept his eyes lowered as she passed the bench, pretending not to hear her mumble a needy little "hiya." Only Dub looked at her, a little sadly, and she had the distinct feeling that he was saying good-bye.

The black venetian blinds were drawn, the door shut. Terry rapped twice, rattling the loose glass, and pushed open the door, stepping back to let her in ahead of him. Paddy crossed the threshold.

Farquarson was alone, bent over his desk, alternately moving two cutout lead paragraphs back and forth over a page proof. He sat back, glancing blankly at Hewitt, completely ignoring Paddy. She still had her coat on and was suddenly very warm.

"Boss?"

She dabbed her forehead with her sleeve. She felt every eye in the newsroom watching her back, seeing the sweat pop on her neck, noting how fat she was.

"Thomas Dempsie." Farquarson left it hanging in the air as if it was an order.

She was almost afraid to move. "How do you mean?"

"You were right. There was a tie-in with Brian Wilcox after all."

Paddy looked back at Terry, grinning behind her. A news editor sitting at a typewriter looked her straight in the eye. Keck was sitting on the bench, his back to them, listening, and she could tell by the angle of his head that he was depressed.

"So, here's the plan," continued Farquarson. "You'll write up the Dempsie case as a history, straightforward, shouldn't be too hard. If it isn't complete shite we'll use it as an insert next week."

"Next week? Won't we have to wait until the trial?"

Terry smiled triumphantly and kicked

her gently on the ankle. "That's the good news. There isn't going to be a trial. Naismith confessed."

"To what?"

"Everything. He confessed to murdering Thomas Dempsie, to taking Brian Wilcox and forcing the boys to kill him, to kidnapping Heather Allen and killing her — everything."

She frowned. "Why would he confess to everything?"

"Well," said Farquarson, "they found evidence in his van linking him to Heather and blood that matches Brian Wilcox's."

Paddy looked around at Terry, still grinning by the door. "But why suddenly confess, and why admit to Thomas Dempsie all these years later? Especially when he had an alibi. He'd be clearing the name of the guy who stole his wife."

Farquarson shrugged. "Maybe he felt bad?"

Terry nodded encouragingly. "He had Jesus stickers all over his van. Maybe he wanted to come clean."

"The Jesus stickers should make him stop killing people, not come clean after he was caught." She wanted to believe it, but she just didn't. "He was going to kill me to protect himself the other day, but suddenly he feels the need to unburden himself?"

Farquarson had little time for rumination on the dark interior of men's souls. "Balls to that. The charges against the boys have been reduced to conspiracy to commit murder. They'll fare much better, so it's good news."

She nodded, trying to convince herself that he was right: it was good news.

"We've arranged it with the relatives when we can finally get access to them, after Naismith's convicted."

"How does he know the boys?"

"They didn't say." Farquarson looked at Terry. "I think they live in the same area as him."

Terry nodded. "They used to hang around the van, the neighbors told the police. James O'Connor, that's the other boy, both his parents are absent. He lives with his grandparents."

"Absent?"

"Drunks."

"Yeah, great," said Farquarson, drawing them back to the moment. "So JT will interview the boys. Meehan, you can liaise with him, give him any tips about the background, that kind of thing."

"I want Callum," she said loudly. "I want the Ogilvy interview myself."

Farquarson looked stunned. "No way. It's too big."

"If JT interviews him he'll be brutal. He'll make Callum look like an evil wee shite, and he isn't. I can get to meet the boy before anyone else, and Terry'll help me write it up."

They argued back and forth for twenty minutes. Farquarson wouldn't be able to edit the piece forever, she'd have to submit something worth publishing. The real problem was getting the interview while anyone still cared about it. Paddy lied and said she'd already arranged to get in and see him this week. If Sean went in a huff, she'd be stuffed.

Finally, Farquarson asked her to submit eight hundred words on Dempsie before Friday and give him the interview material as and when. "On a personal note," he added, sitting back in his chair and scratching his balls happily, "let me say I hate precocious little bastards like you two and I hope you burn out in your twenties. Get out."

When the door was shut behind them Terry punched her arm and told her well done in full view of everyone in the news-room. Embarrassed but grateful, Paddy glanced around and a features sub caught her eye, a little accepting smile tugging at the corner of his mouth, as if he had never noticed her before but was now interested in things she might have to say. Kat Beesley raised a congratulatory eyebrow. Paddy looked for Dr. Pete, hoping he would have heard about her good work, but couldn't see him.

She felt silly taking her seat on the bench again. Dub said he was pleased but moved away from her, catching any calls that came up and avoiding her eye. Keck smiled at her, but they could both feel that she didn't belong there anymore. She traced the give of the wood with her thumbnail and found it hard to believe that all this good was coming to her after the many small betrayals she had committed in the past week.

II

Paddy could feel it: she was halfway off the bench already. Editors were looking straight at her when they asked for teas, journalists were talking to her, passing comments, acknowledging her existence. Keck was acting sucky. It felt like a repeat of the time in school when she gave a rousing talk about the Paddy Meehan case to her English

516

class, implying that Meehan had been victimized because he was Catholic. The suggestion had had a particular attraction for the students at Trinity, and the talk had shifted her status from a fat nothing to a someone regarded as a profound thinker and defender of their future freedoms. As she matured she thought the reason they had set him up was because he was a committed socialist; later still she realized that they chose him because he had a record and no alibi. However false the premise for her social success at school, she had still enjoyed it, and she did so now. Neither thoughts of Heather Allen nor Sean's new freedom could dampen the warming shiver of ambition. She could see herself walking past the bench at night, looking at the grooves from her nails, on her way to somewhere amazing. She saw herself in the morning, spotting them as she came into work from her own flat in the city, from a lover's bed, from an important story.

At lunchtime, instead of skulking around the town she made straight for the canteen and found Terry Hewitt sitting at a busy table by the window. He waved her over.

"I saved you a place," he said, excited to see her.

"How did you know I'd be going on lunch now?"

"Keck said you'd be going about one."

Asking Keck when she was going on lunch seemed a bit clingy and subservient, but Paddy tried not to frown or say anything snide. It was the culture of the place to use any advantage to bully one another, but she'd promised herself she wouldn't be like that.

"Can I get ye a tea?" she said.

Terry cocked his head, not understanding. "Aye. A tea'd be nice."

She waited in the queue like everyone else, cooling her hot hands on the cold metal railing in front of the food display cabinets. A journalist she had brought tea a hundred times turned around when he saw her standing behind him.

"Oh, it's you."

Paddy nodded modestly.

"I always thought you were a daft bint."

She knew he meant it as a compliment. She looked around to see who else was admiring her and found Dub standing behind her.

"Hiya," she said. "I never saw you there."

Dub lifted his chin as a greeting.

"What's been happening with you

518

today?" she added, hoping to prompt him into asking her back.

"Nothing," said Dub, looking over her head to the lamb bridies drying out on a tray.

"Terry and me are at a table by the window — why don't you sit with us?"

It was an invitation to the big table, and they both knew it.

"Nah, I'm all right. Got stuff to do in town."

"Oh." She was disappointed.

"Well done, anyway. I heard."

"Cheers, Dub. I'm celebrating, that's why I wanted you to sit with us."

Dub shrugged, still reluctant.

She didn't want him to stop being her friend just because she'd had a bit of luck. She pointed to the vat of hot custard. "I'm only having a pudding today."

Dub mock-snarled at her. "What am I, your biographer? Shut up about yourself."

They laughed together at his cheek, and Scary Mary hit her tray with the soup ladle because it was Paddy's turn and she wasn't paying attention. While she ordered two teas and a sponge in custard, Dub skipped ahead of her in the queue. She turned to speak to him again, but he was gone.

Terry was sitting against the window, on

the inside of a long table, jealously guarding the seat opposite him. She gave him his tea and a warning look when she caught him glancing at her body.

"Sorry," said Terry, the excitement catching in his throat. "So, what's our plan now?"

"Well, we need to go back to Tracy Dempsie and get a photo of Naismith."

"We could go after work today."

"I can't. I've promised to do something."

He made big, sad eyes at her. "But we've got to plan the interview, work out a schedule of questions."

"I can't. I'm sorry. I promised to be somewhere. I'm on a late tomorrow, we could go in the morning."

"Why can't you do it today?"

"I just can't."

"It's to do with that ned builder, isn't it?"

She could see he regretted the comment as soon as it was out of his mouth.

"You don't know Sean," she snapped. "He's not a ned. He's a lovely person."

Terry held up his hands in surrender. "Okay."

"He's a good man," she repeated.

He nodded. "Right."

But his eyes were smiling, and she knew

she had betrayed Sean. It was as if the sex were a matter between him and Terry and she was just a little fat prop.

The newsmen at the table smiled fractiously as they left, sliding into the spare seats.

"By the way," he said on their way downstairs, "did you hear about Pete?"

She hadn't thought about Pete once since this morning's excitement and felt a guilty pang as she realized she had him to thank for it all.

"What about him?"

"He's in the Royal." Terry frowned. "An ambulance was called to the Press Bar last night after hours."

THIRTY-THREE

CALLUM

I

Paddy could feel the wind gathering on the platform, a small gust of excited air. The feeling increased as she climbed the stairs, and the other commuters pulled their coats around them, knowing it was coming. She turned the corner and struggled into the push. Five feet beyond the corner it was calm again, the wind gone as suddenly as an imagined symptom.

The underground exit was between two high tenements, in a dingy alleyway where shopkeepers dumped foul-smelling rubbish and men relieved themselves on the way home from the pub. At the end of the alley she could see Sean waiting for her in a shaft of light, looking very far away. A hopeful little smile tickled his lips when he saw her coming. He had defied his mum to contact Callum, and Paddy knew how hard it would have been for him to do that.

He swung his brown roll bag into his left hand, reflexively reaching out for her coming towards him, remembering too late that he wasn't allowed to touch her. He patted her shoulder awkwardly. She remembered Terry Hewitt's nipples suddenly and smiled, squeezing her eyes tight to hide tiny tears.

"Hiya," she said, mirroring Sean's awkward gesture by patting his shoulder back. "Thanks for this, Seanie."

"No bother," he said.

They fell into step, walking close but feeling a hundred miles distant because they couldn't hold hands. Sean bumped shoulders with her as they waited at the lights.

"To be honest, I'm glad you asked me to come and see him," he shouted over the noise of the traffic. "They said he's asked not to see his mum anymore and no one else has been in touch from the family. I'm not allowed to take food in to him because they're worried someone'll try to kill him."

She rubbed his back, caving in to a compulsion to feel the warmth of his skin and let her hand linger for a moment between his shoulder blades. Sean arched away from the touch. The traffic in front of them stopped and they crossed over, saved from a scene by the green man.

The modern hospital was set on a small, sharp hill, back from the busy road. It was a recent build, all straight lines and pragmatic compromises, erected and then almost instantly meshed over to stop incontinent pigeons turning it into a biohazard.

The entrance was round the back. Thirty feet behind the new hospital was the abandoned old gothic building it had replaced, a turreted baronial flurry, now empty, the windows and doors on the ground floor boarded up. They entered the new building through a small door at the back and took the lift up to the fifth floor, sweating at the unexpected high temperature. Sean held out his hand.

"You need to put this on." It was the engagement ring box. "They'll only let you in if they think you're my fiancée."

Paddy apologized with her eyes and took the familiar ring out of the box. It was uncomfortably tight; she could feel the top of her finger swell under the pressure. The doors opened at five to a cluck of student nurses smiling polite audience grins as two middle-aged doctors chatted.

Sean and Paddy followed the signs around three corridors to a nurses' station in a corridor. The table was layered in pink and green forms. They were met by a pretty little blond nurse with a crimped wedge haircut and blue eyeliner. Her figure was so slight she looked prepubescent. When Sean and the nurse smiled at each other Paddy wanted to slap her.

"I've been told to ask for Sergeant Hamilton," said Sean quietly.

The nurse's smile deflated. "I'll get Matron."

She disappeared into an office behind the desk. Matron, a snippy woman in her forties, fiddled with the watch pinned to her chest and asked them again if they were looking for a sergeant. What was his name? Was he expecting them? The questions were a pointless rehash of Sean's basic statement, but Paddy could tell that the woman was thrilled they were there, that she was thinking about the story she would have to tell one day, when she could talk about it. She looked Sean up and down, noting his dusty work boots and cheap slacks. He had changed out of his work clothes and looked clean but was still noticeably poor. Mimi bought his shoes in the Barras market and picked up second-hand shirts for him in Murphy's at the Bridgate. Paddy was used to being the poorest-looking person in the newsroom. She kept her engagement finger on view to show that they were decent.

The matron picked up the phone on the desk, running her tongue along the front of her teeth as she dialed a four-digit number. She turned away and whispered into the receiver, nodding and repeating "uh huh" when the other person spoke. She hung up, raised her eyebrows at the phone and pinched her lips.

"He'll be here in a moment," she said, as if it were against her express advice.

The sergeant was in the corridor before the matron had time to make them feel any worse. He was solid and broad-shouldered, with graying hair and a kind face. He came towards them, shaking his head as he dabbed the sweat from his brow.

"Oof," he said to the matron, "too hot in here." He turned his attention to Sean, giving him a look-over. "Right, now, can I have some sort of identification from the both of yees."

It was an order, not a question. Sean had brought his post office savings book and a union ticket, Paddy had her library card.

"Okay, pal, coat off."

Paddy gladly took off her duffel coat and handed it to the policeman, who checked the pockets and lining. Sean handed over his Harrier jacket.

"Can't be too careful," said the sergeant, smiling as he searched the coats, trying to keep it light. "Care is the watchword here." He patted Sean down but balked at doing the same to Paddy, who was wearing a pencil skirt and a plain sweater. He checked the contents of Sean's roll bag, flicking through things with a cautious finger, frowning when he saw a Celtic poster.

"All the stuff in there's for him. Is that okay?" Sean sounded timid and young.

"Aye." His eyes flickered over all the different bits in it. "Aye, this is all okay."

Handing the bag back, he gestured for them to follow him.

It was disconcertingly hot in the hospital. They each began to sweat as they made their way around corners and down gray corridors, taking a small spur off the main passage. Beyond another corner they could see two policemen outside a door, one sitting, the other standing, both drinking out of cups and saucers, a well-thumbed tabloid sitting on the floor underneath the chair. They stiffened when the sergeant approached, hiding the cups of tea and pulling their uniforms straight. Paddy guessed that their boss wasn't so sweet all the time.

"These young people are here to visit . . ." He hesitated, unsure what to call him. "The wee fella." And he gestured to them to open the door.

They all turned to the door, looked at it expectantly, and the sergeant took a step forwards.

"I'll sit in with ye for a bit, just to make sure it's okay."

He stepped back, they all took a breath, and the policeman nearest the door turned the handle.

The private room had a narrow entrance and a bathroom off to the left on the way in. It was dark and thick with the sharp scent of bleach and pine. The first thing Paddy noticed was the old gothic hospital looming in at the window, the skyline jagged with castellations and blank black windows. Tucked in around the corner was a metal-framed bed with a clipboard attached to the foot. Sitting in the bed, backlit by a harsh reading light, was Callum Ogilvy.

He looked tiny. He didn't seem to have gained any weight since they saw him a year ago, but it might have been the position he was sitting in. The covers were over his knees and he was reading a battered and torn comic, frozen in the position he had been in when they opened the door, his finger pointing at a part of the page, his mouth open to form a word. At first she thought it might have been handcuffs, but then she realized that it was a thick bandage around his wrist where he had cut it. He looked frightening and skinny, like a shriveled, ancient, evil genius.

"All right, wee man?"

Callum raised his eyes and gawped silently. Sean sat down on the side of his bed.

"D'ye 'member me?"

He nodded slowly, his eyes flickering across Sean's face. "You're my big cousin."

"What's this?" Sean pointed to his wrist. "You been having a bit of trouble?"

Paddy didn't see the tears immediately because of the sharp light behind him, but she heard Callum gasp a breath, his face still immobile. A fat tear dropped off his face onto the bed. Sean moved up the bed, put his arms around the boy, and held him firmly. The boy sat stiff as a doll, his face bare to the room, his mouth a black oval, and cried.

It took twenty minutes for him to stop. The policeman left after five. Paddy moved over to the window and turned her back; otherwise her eye naturally fell on the boy's face, and that was too hard to look at. She could see into the darkened wards across the way. One floor down she could see old bedsteads stacked against a wall. As the darkness gathered behind the window the reflection of the pool of light on Callum's bed became sharper and sharper. She could see that his eyes were swollen shut.

"Son?" It was Sean's voice, but he was whispering. "Is that better?"

Callum nodded. Sean patted the boy's back to signal an end to the embrace and shifted around so he was sitting next to him.

"D'ye remember Paddy, my fiancée?"

Callum looked over at her. Even in the fuzzy reflection she could see he didn't like her.

"Celtic," he said, exhausted, and turning his attention back to Sean. "You support Celtic."

"Don't you support Celtic?"

Callum looked at Paddy's back again.

"It's a shame if you don't," said Sean, "because I've brought ye a poster for your wall." He picked up the roll bag and zipped it open, taking out a small poster and unrolling it on the bed. It was battered around the edges, but Callum liked it. He put his hand on it and looked at Sean, claiming ownership. His eyes moved to the bag on the bed and Sean laughed. "You're an Ogilvy all right. Will we see what else is in there?"

Callum smiled, creasing his puffy face. Sean pulled out a jigsaw of the first team, a *Beano* comic and a *Dandy*, and a plastic pencil case that looked like it was made of denim. He sat them on top of the poster, each bit of rubbish adding to the last, making a compound gift mountain.

Callum grinned avariciously at the pile of crap on his bed.

"D'ye like that?"

He nodded.

"I was going to bring you a load of sweets, like Crunchies and Starbars but I wasn't allowed because of these." Sean touched the bandages on Callum's wrist. "If ye don't do that again they'll let me."

"I'm not gonnae do that." Callum's tiny voice was raw. "You're my big cousin."

"That's right, wee man." Sean sat back on the bed with him so they were both facing out into the room. "I am, wee man.

Paddy, put the big lights on, eh?"

When she moved over to the door and flicked the switch, the whole room changed character. Callum was just a wee skinny boy in a bed. He even looked a bit like Sean. They could have been brothers.

"D'ye like the *Dandy*?"

Callum nodded, so Sean pulled it out of the pile and started running his finger down a story and doing the voices, the way Paddy had seen him do with his nieces and nephews. Callum settled back against his chest, watching the finger move along the page, only half listening to what he was saying. Paddy watched them in the reflection on the window. Sean'd make a great father, and she was sorry that it wouldn't be with her.

The boys read through a Desperate Dan story together, Callum giving a token laugh at the punch line. Then Sean put his hand flat on the page.

"Callum, listen. Paddy wants to ask you something."

Callum looked up at her, resenting both her presence and her claim over Sean.

Paddy's mouth was suddenly dry. She sat down at the far end of the bed, the high metal bedstead digging into the fat on her hip.

"Hiya, Callum. D'ye remember me?"

He nodded at the comic and lifted Sean's hand, turning the page and dropping the hand back onto it.

"How do you know James O'Connor? Is he at your school?"

Callum looked inquiringly at Sean, who nodded. "Aye," he said curtly.

"Are you two pals?"

Callum kept his eyes on the page. "Not anymore."

"Why not anymore?"

It was just the right question. Callum became animated. "He told them I did it, and I never. It was him, he did it." Sean frowned at the back of the boy's head.

"Tell me this about when the baby died, Callum: did you go there in a train?"

The boy's body tensed up tight, his shoulders rising slowly to his ears.

"Did ye?" asked Sean.

He kept his eyes on the comic. "Police said we did."

"What do you say, though?" asked Paddy.

Callum gave a forced laugh at the last drawing on the page and started at the top of the next page. He was determined to ignore Paddy, so Sean repeated the question.

"How do you say you got there, son?"

Callum looked at Sean's mouth and let

his own hang open for a moment. He shut it and shook his head.

"How did you get there, then?" asked Paddy.

He started picking at the edge of the page anxiously, worrying his nail through the paper. Sean repeated the question for her again. Callum shook his head violently and stopped abruptly, his eyes wide and bright and wet with fright. Sean rubbed his hair loudly.

"Are ye gonnae tell us?"

"We got there in a motor."

Sean glanced at Paddy, knowing what she wanted to ask. "What kind of motor, Callum?"

His face was a bitter little fist. "Van. Grocer's van."

Paddy treated herself to a lopsided smile. She had been right after all.

"We never went on the train. He gave us the tickets so's it would look like we did." He looked back at the comic, wishing they were still doing that instead of this.

"Did you tell the police this?"

"Never asked," he said definitely. "Women are dirty cunts."

Shocked, Sean stared at Paddy.

"They stink. I've seen pictures of them getting banged."

Paddy blinked back, tacitly agreeing to ignore it.

"Who was driving the van?" asked Sean.

"James's pal."

"Mr. Naismith?" asked Paddy.

Callum forgot to ignore her. "Aye, Mr. Naismith. With the earring."

"He doesn't have an earring, does he?"

"Aye."

"I've met him, and I didn't see an earring."

Callum shrugged. "Maybe he hasn't got one, then. He's James's pal."

If the overhead light had not been on, Paddy might have missed the sideways flicker in his eyes, sliding over to another thought somewhere out of sight.

"He'll rip my arsehole with his cock if I tell on him, but he's not a fucking poof, right?"

Both Sean and Paddy shuddered. Sean dragged his eyes across the page of the comic. Paddy saw her reflection in the window. She was disguising her disgust with a grotesquely cheerful smile, but it didn't reach her eyes. The tiny child in the window was watching her.

"He'd wipe his cunt with you anyway," he whispered.

She turned back and reached out to pat

his knee under the blanket, but Callum whipped his leg away, repulsed. She let her hand land on the bed near him and patted that instead.

"Thanks, son. It can't be nice being asked about that."

Callum casually turned a page on his comic and murmured, "Stinky cunts."

II

The way Sean stood in the lift made Paddy think of an old, sad man: he hung from his bones. She leaned against the opposite wall, wishing she hadn't asked Callum about any of it. Naismith didn't have an earring. A Teddy boy would never have an ear pierced. If Callum was telling the truth, she'd set Naismith up for something he didn't do. Terry Hewitt's career would be ruined. Frightened, she reached over to slip her hand into Sean's, but he shook her gently off.

Outside in the bitter evening air Sean took out his cigarettes and gave her one. They lit up in the shadow of the dead hospital. He dipped at the knee and took her hand again, squeezing kindly, but still unable to look at her.

Sean thanked her dutifully for making him go to see Callum. He was going back, he said, he was going back and, God help that boy, Sean knew he was innocent. The wee soul hadn't done anything wrong.

"But they found his fingerprints on the baby and everything."

"They could have been planted. I know he didn't do it."

"How can you know?"

"I know he didn't do it. He just said, 'I never did it.' I'm going to start a campaign for him."

It was more of a loyalty test than a matter of abstract truth.

"I don't think he is innocent."

"Did you just meet the same child as me?"

"Sean, there's a difference between a hunch and a wish," she said sharply, pre-occupied with her own catastrophe.

Sean kept hold of her hand but slack-ened his grip. Each alone, they walked down to Partick, keeping to the back roads and the dark places.

Down at the train station they showed their travel passes and took the escalator up to the high platform. There no-where to sit in the waiting room at the top of the stairs. It was full of commuters, and the air was uncomfortably moist and warm from their breath. It was dark outside on the platform. From the high vantage point they could see the big sky over the river and the silhouette of short-headed ship-yard cranes, once busy but now still, dinosaur skeletons against the orange sky. She wanted to tell Sean what she'd done, confess the arrogance that had led her to set Naismith up, but the words caught in her throat, making her heart race.

The warm train arrived and they took seats near the front, sitting close together, silent and tired, their thighs pressing against each other, their hands touching sometimes when they shared a cigarette. When Sean handed over the cigarette and his lean fingertips touched hers, she wanted to grab him with the other hand and tell him she had done an unforgivable thing to a man, she'd told an awful, world-ending lie. But Naismith had confessed to everything: he had tried to attack her and had followed her to her work. She began to wonder if he did reach for her after all, if they were Heather's hairs she had seen on the brown towel.

She made him get off at Rutherglen and leave her on the train, but she stood up on the quiet carriageway and saw him to the door, as if it were her home.

"I'll phone you tomorrow," he said.

"Gonnae?"

He leaned down for a hug, holding his pelvis a foot away from her and bending in, as if she would attack him if he touched her. He sighed a pleasured groan into her ear, for an embrace as warm as a poke with a sharp twig.

She stayed on her feet as the train moved, and watched him walk down the cold platform, his hands in his jacket pockets, his head hanging heavy on his shoulders. As the moving train passed him Paddy felt he was sliding into her glorious yellow past; ahead was nothing but the lonely gray devastation she had created. But she still had a glimmer of hope. Maybe, somehow, she was still justified. Callum could be wrong.

THIRTY-FOUR

MR. NAISMITH

I

It was ten o'clock in the morning and the frost still lingered in the shadow of the high-rise blocks. A sniping wind was gathering strength, sweeping down the sides of the buildings, flicking hair and hems as Paddy and Terry picked their way carefully down the long flight of steps, avoiding the icy edges. The housing scheme they were walking through was a low-level offshoot of the Drygate high flats, built for pensioners and sickly people, no children allowed. The modest lawns between blocks were interspersed with giant yellow sandstone, left over from a monumental time.

"That's all that's left of Duke Street Prison. See over there?" Terry pointed to the bottom of a bit of yellow wall. "That's where the condemned cell was. They used to hang them on that patch of grass."

Paddy looked and nodded, pretending to listen.

"You're quiet today."

She hummed an answer. She was afraid to speak. Panic was swelling the back of her throat, gagging her. If she spoke she might just denounce herself.

"And you look knackered."

"Piss off."

But she knew he was right. She'd hardly slept the night before. Wide-eyed, she'd lain on her back, tracing patterns in the ceiling plaster, thinking about Callum and what he had said. She'd lain awake looking at it every way she could, willfully misinterpreting what he had said and trying to make it sit comfortably. It was three thirty before she finally admitted to herself that Callum was telling her Naismith was innocent.

"So," said Terry cheerfully, "Tracy Dempsie: is there anything else you want to warn me about?"

"The carpet in the hall — it's horrendous."

He nodded seriously. "Thanks for that. I'd hate to be caught unawares."

Paddy smiled at the unexpected return. Terry was always slightly sharper than she expected him to be. She glanced over and saw his little belly jiggling under his shirt as his foot hit the step.

"I see ye," he muttered.

She looked up to find him watching the ground in front of him.

"You see me what?"

"You, giving me the glad eye."

She smiled and found her eyes filling suddenly. It would be easier to bear if he weren't so sweet.

Blinking back a tide of guilt, Paddy led him across the crumbling floor of the car park and into the Drygate lobby. Both lifts were out of order: a small, handwritten notice in jagged capitals was pinned to the lift doors.

They trudged up the grim stairwell, kicking through glue tins and plastic bags on one landing and the loose pages of a pornographic magazine on another. Paddy let Terry lead so that he wouldn't be staring at her fat behind.

Up on Tracy's landing the suction weight of wind pulled the landing door so tightly closed that it took both of them to lever it open. The deafening wind flattened her hair and tugged at her heavy coat. Terry clutched the neck of his heavy leather jacket as they crept along the inside wall of the balcony. Paddy knocked heavily on Tracy Dempsie's door.

She had raised her hand to knock again when Tracy opened it, wearing yesterday's makeup in all the wrong places. She had taken an extra pill or two, and her housecoat was buttoned one step out. She blinked slowly when she saw Paddy and raised her cigarette to her mouth. The hot ash tip flew into her hair, singeing it.

"You're not Heather Allen."

Paddy hoped Terry hadn't heard.

"I saw her picture in the paper. You're not her. She's dead."

Terry looked curious. Paddy could feel his eyes on her face.

"Tracy, I heard Henry Naismith was arrested."

At the mention of her ex-man the fight went out of Tracy. Her head dropped forward on her neck and she turned and walked away down the hall. A swirling gust of wind jerked the door open. Paddy wiped her feet before stepping in. Shutting the door carefully behind him, dulling the noise, Terry looked from the busy carpet to Paddy and let off a silent scream.

Following the trail of smoke through the hall and into the living room, they found Tracy slumped on the settee, staring blankly at her knees. The angry wind hissed outside the window.

"Henry," she said quietly. "They said he confessed to killing Thomas as well. He couldn't have. He wouldn't have."

Paddy sat down on the edge of the settee next to her, their knees almost touching. She desperately wanted to say something kind and helpful, but there was nothing to say. As if she could see it in her eyes, Tracy reached out and took Paddy's hand, holding it by the thumb, absentmindedly lifting and dropping it as she took a draw from her fag.

"He was a hard man, though, wasn't he?"

Tracy sucked smoke through clenched teeth and tipped her head back. "Henry's a good man. He was in the gangs when he was younger, aye, but the gangs just fight each other. And anyway, he's a born-again Christian now, he's not going to attack a wean."

"But he confessed, Tracy."

"So what?" She looked up at them, pleading, as if they had any authority in the matter. "They could just be saying that."

Paddy had almost forgotten Terry was standing behind her until he hovered into her line of vision. He cleared his throat carefully before he spoke.

"Mrs. Dempsie, why would he confess if he didn't do it?"

Tracy shook her head at the carpet and looked bewildered. "They'd mibbe make him?" Her medically dulled eyes slowly traced the dervish pattern on the carpet as she thought back. She blinked slowly at the floor and then blinked again, her eyebrows forming a plaintive little triangle. "Henry won't kill hisself like Alfred did. He's got religion."

Paddy watched Tracy bring the cigarette to her mouth and knew in a sudden, chilling moment that she was staring at carnage she had created. She was the policeman who had planted paper in James Griffiths's pocket. She had never in her life wanted to go to confession, but she did now.

She squeezed Tracy's hand hard. "I'm so sorry for all your troubles."

Bewildered but touched, Tracy squeezed back, shaking Paddy's hand awkwardly by the thumb. "Thanks."

"I mean it." She clasped Tracy's hand tightly in both of hers as shame overwhelmed her. "I'm really so sorry. Honestly."

Tracy Dempsie was on long-term medication and had treated herself to a little extra dose today, but even she was finding Paddy's behavior odd. She smiled uncomfortably and wriggled her hand free.

Terry stepped forward.

"Mrs. Dempsie, I wonder if you would have a photograph of Henry? We don't want to use the police photo, we want a nice one for the paper."

It was a smart lie. The police hadn't released a photo of Naismith, and they weren't likely to either, but Terry had guessed that Tracy didn't know that and would want Henry to look his best in the paper. His professionalism was a reproach to Paddy, who sniffed and dabbed the damp tip of her nose with the back of her hand.

"Aye." Tracy bumped her bum to the edge of the settee and stood up awkwardly, tottering a step to the side before shuffling out into the hall.

Terry waited until Tracy was out of earshot. "Fucking hell," he murmured. "What is going on with you?"

She tried to breathe in but her chin crumpled. Terry kicked the underside of her foot and growled at her. "Go to the toilet and sort yourself out."

She stood up. "Don't you be cheeky to me."

"Don't act like a silly cow, then."

She kicked him hard on the ankle bone, leaving him panting and cursing her under his breath.

Out in the dark hallway she could hear Tracy raking noisily through papers behind one of the doors. The bathroom had a little ceramic sign on the door, a picture of a toilet with a wreath of roses around it. The room had been decorated in the same era as the hallway. Orange wallpaper was blistered at the edges, pleading to be pulled off. The fixtures were a clashing pink, the bath stained rusty brown where the cold tap had dripped and corroded the plug hole. An orange bar of soap was welded between the sink taps, and the pale lemon carpet smelled of dust and bleach.

Paddy locked the door and pulled down the toilet lid, sitting down and curling over her knees. She tried to think of something Terry had done wrong to mitigate her offense to him. She thought through her night in his bed, this morning, his behavior at work, but couldn't think of anything. She knew she had to phone the police and take the blame for the ball of hair in the van. She could feel it as a vibration, but every fiber of her being balked at the prospect of owning up. She'd lose everything, but it was right that she should: she'd killed Heather and framed Naismith.

She made herself sit up straight. In the dock at the high court Paddy Meehan had given a dignified speech after his conviction. He must have felt more beleaguered than she was now. She stood up and looked at herself in the cloudy mirror. "You have made a terrible mistake," she whispered quietly. "I am innocent of this crime and so is Jim Griffiths." She sniffed hard and straightened her duffel coat, ruffling her black hair to make it stand up again. She looked herself in the eye and saw nothing but guilt and fear and fat. "You have made a terrible mistake." She had integrity. She wouldn't sacrifice a man's life for her career. She might contemplate it, and she knew that was terrible, but she wouldn't do it.

Flushing the toilet for effect, she drew a deep breath, unlocked the door, and stepped across the hall to the living room.

Terry had taken her place on the settee next to Tracy and was smiling dutifully at an open photo album. It was bound in red plastic with gold trim around the edges. She had stored it under something heavy, and some of the cellophane sheets had been flattened the wrong way and were hanging out.

Tracy had a new fag lit and was pointing at a picture. "Me on holiday. Isle of Wight. Good legs, eh?"

"Yeah," Terry said, looking up at Paddy as she came in and giving her a conciliatory smile. "Look," he said. "Tracy in a swimming costume."

Paddy walked over to Tracy's arm of the settee and looked over her shoulder. The Tracy in the picture was younger and quite pretty, posing carefully on a bank-holiday-busy beach, one foot propped in front of the other like a fifties model. Paddy nodded. "Great."

On the opposite page Henry Naismith was dressed in drainpipe trousers and a powder blue drape coat. Hanging on his arm was young Tracy in bobby socks and a pink shift dress, her hair in a high ponytail, her eyes accidentally closed at the moment the shutter blinked.

Terry caught Paddy's eye but she broke off quickly. He touched the face of the photograph.

"Did Henry ever hit the kids when you were together?"

"Me and Henry only had Garry. Alfred was Thomas's daddy."

Terry carried on as if he'd known that all along. "And did Henry hit Garry?"

"No. He mostly ignored us until I went with Alfred, and then he went mental, kicking in doors and that, going to Alfred's work and waiting for him." She seemed flattered at the memory. Her mouth twitched in an uncertain smile. "Alfred just went out the back way. Course, just after Thomas died Henry got religion. He was so sad about Thomas you'd have thought it was his own wean that died. He tried to make up for how he'd been, tried to be a good dad to Garry. Devoted all his time to him."

She turned the album page to a photo of herself in a maxicoat and knee-high boots with a baby perched on her hip. The child stared at the camera with an odd intensity.

"What a beautiful baby," said Terry. "He's lovely looking. Is he yours?"

"That's my Garry." Tracy covered the child's face with her fingertips. "My wee boy."

Paddy hardly dared to ask. "Have ye got any more of him?"

Tracy did have other photos of Garry. She flicked through his first Christmas, a neighbor's wedding scramble, a granny's birthday, and the boy grew up in front of Paddy's eyes. She had assumed that Naismith and Tracy's child was still young, that he had been only a few years older than Thomas Dempsie when he died. In fact he would have been about twelve when Thomas died. Old enough to take the child himself. Tracy turned a page and suddenly Garry was grown up, standing by his dad's grocery van in summer, sunlight glinting off a gold stud in his ear. Paddy recognized him perfectly. He was the handsome boy she had met in Townhead the night before Heather was murdered, the boy who called himself Kevin McConnell.

Paddy couldn't hear the wind or what Terry was saying about the pictures. All she could hear was her own heartbeat, and all she could feel was the cold sweat on her spine. The shady sexual threat in Callum Ogilvy's words came back to her as imminent and personal. The night they met, Garry must have followed her from Tracy's to Townhead. He must have heard from Tracy that a journalist called Heather Allen had been in the house and traced her footsteps, waiting patiently before approaching so that she wouldn't connect him with his mother. Garry wasn't just vicious, he was careful. He might be in this flat right now. She mapped the fastest route to the front door. If he came at her she could hit him, use something to hit him. She could defend herself.

"Does Garry live here?" she asked quickly.

"Naw." Tracy scratched her thigh through her housecoat. "He stays up in Barnhill with his dad. They're as close as brothers, those two. Do everything together. Garry does whatever his dad says. This picture" — she pulled back the crackling cellophane cover and peeled the Teddy boy photograph off the glue striations — "this is the nicest one."

"How about this one?" Terry turned the page back to one of Naismith standing in the garden in Townhead.

Paddy could feel her pulse on her throat. She felt sure that Tracy would be able to see the throb in her jugular if she looked up.

"He'd do anything for our boy. He's training him to take over the van. He'd never hurt a child —"

Paddy cut across her. "We'd better go."

Terry's mouth dropped open a little.

"We should," she said insistently. "I need to go."

"We'll just get the picture," said Terry carefully, taking the photo album from Tracy before she had time to object and lifting out the picture he wanted.

Paddy was starting to sweat. "I'm off."

He looked at her defiantly. "We need to thank Tracy for all her help."

But Paddy was already at the door of the living room. "Good-bye."

She hurried across the hall and opened the door to the howling vortex, narrowing her eyes against the stray dust, racing along the balcony to the stairs. She pulled at the door, using her weight when she felt that it wouldn't give. For a terrifying moment she thought Garry was behind it, smiling calmly and holding it closed effortlessly. Terry leaned over her shoulder and pushed open the door with one hand. She tumbled into the echoing stairwell, into the acrid stench of solvent and piss.

"Are you nuts? What the hell was all that about?"

She spun to face him, grabbed his neck with both hands, and shook, mistaking Terry for the real threat, making him lose his footing until his flailing hand fell on the metal banister and he managed to steady himself.

They stood still, Paddy holding his neck, Terry bent curiously towards and away from her, averting his eyes in submission. The muffled vibration of their struggle throbbed through the thick concrete. Horrified, she opened her fingers and Terry stood up slowly. He straightened his jacket without looking at her. They walked down together, Paddy panting until she got her breath back, Terry saying nothing. Downstairs, they crossed the lobby, walked out into the day, and parted without speaking.

II

Dr. Pete was propped up on marshmallow pillows, looking out the window at a high statue of the Protestant Reformationist John Knox. She was quite sure they weren't his own pajamas. They had the stiffness of institutionally laundered clothes. Boil-washing had faded them to a sun-bleached blue that clashed horribly with his yellow skin. The crisp white sheet in his lap was folded neatly down, and sometimes, while he was talking, he would stroke it thoughtfully.

"Ludicrous. Knox was an anti-iconoclast. He wouldn't have approved of a statue." He smiled distantly. "If they weren't Calvinists you'd suspect the memorial committee of having a sense of humor."

Paddy didn't know anything about the various Protestant splinters, but she smiled to please him.

It was a modern extension to the old hospital, with copper-tinted windows facing onto the necropolis, a jagged Victorian mini-Manhattan of exuberant architecture, erected when celebrating death wasn't yet taboo. The three other beds in Dr. Pete's room had a large floor space around each for all the equipment they might need. The patient in the bed across the way was unconscious, an unpromising strip of skin under a paper-pristine sheet. Expensive equipment was conferenced around his bed: a heart monitor, a hissing pump, a drip, and a blinking television screen. Next to him his ruddy-cheeked wife sat reading the *Sun*, squinting as if it required concentration.

It was an unhappy accident that the cancer ward overlooked the graveyard, but one which Dr. Pete, full of medication and clear of pain for the first time in months, was enjoying. Sober, pepped-up, and without his habitual pained slouch, he was suddenly a very different man. It no longer seemed infeasible that he had swung women over puddles or written beautifully. He had been talking about John Knox's statue at the top of the hill for ten minutes, picking his words carefully as he related the history of its construction and why it had been built in the middle of what became a huge graveyard.

"But by then no one cared where he was. Why did you come?" Pete's steady eyes seared into hers.

"Just wondered how you were," she lied. "I wanted to see how ye were."

Pete watched his fingertips running over the stiff hem of the sheet. "Well, I'm dying, as you can see."

She smiled politely again. She had come here to hide for half an hour. The visit was supposed to be a lighthearted stopover to break up a very bad day, but it wasn't working out at all. She decided to hand over her token gift and get out. The cellophane wrapper crackled loudly as she pulled a bottle of garish orange energy drink out of her bag.

"Lucozade."

He sat up, genuinely pleased, and patted the top of his bedside locker. "Put it up there." She opened the door to the cabinet, but he stopped her. "No, no, put it on top."

He glanced around the room, and she followed his eye to the other patients' lockers. Every one of them had bottles and bags of sweets and flowers and cards stacked on them, but Pete's was completely bare.

"I was rushed in this time. When I came in before, I brought my own. I won't be pitied by bloody nurses."

He wouldn't have said it if he hadn't been on morphine, and she was shocked to hear that he was so alone. Whenever she'd been to visit relatives in hospital she'd had to queue in the corridor, waiting for a batch of family to leave before she could get in. She felt ashamed for him and changed the subject.

"I've always wondered," she said, "why do they call you Dr. Pete?"

"I am a doctor. I've got a doctorate in divinity."

She waited for him to laugh at her credulity and admit it was a joke, but he didn't.

"Why did you do that?"

"I wanted to be a minister. I'm a son of the manse."

"Your dad was a minister?"

"And his father before him."

"You're less like a minister than anyone I've ever met."

"I was a disappointment. I liked what you said to Richards, about substituting the basic text. My family couldn't conceive of a life outside the kirk. I'm just getting there myself."

"I lost my faith early, before I made my first communion. I still can't tell my family."

He reached across, a beatific light in his eye, and patted her hand. "Lie to them. Let them not worry. I hurt my father. It was needless. I didn't change his mind and he didn't change mine. We argued on the day he died."

Paddy shook her head. "I can't fight with my father. He's very meek."

"Ah, the meek. Playing the long game. Sneaky bastards."

The man across the room let out a soft groan. His wife reached out and patted the bed without taking her eyes off the paper.

"That man'll be dead in the morning," said Pete. "If he's lucky."

Paddy glanced over at the man and felt her face flush suddenly. She hadn't come here to have her nose rubbed in the inevitability of death. Pete saw her eyes redden and looked alarmed.

"No, it's not about you," she blurted, realizing too late that it would be wrong to say she didn't care that he was going to die. "Oh God almighty, Pete, I've done an awful thing. I planted evidence on Henry Naismith and now he's confessed to killing Brian Wilcox. I was sure it was him."

"What did you plant?"

"Hair." She rubbed her eyes hard. "Heather Allen's hair. And he confessed to killing her and Thomas Dempsie as well."

"Naismith didn't kill Thomas Dempsie. He was in the cells that night."

"I know. So if he's confessing to that as well, how genuine can the confession to Baby Brian be?"

Pete's eyes widened calmly. "Why would he make a false confession?"

"It was his son. He's protecting his boy."

Pete frowned for a moment. "Garry Naismith."

"That's right. Garry killed Thomas and let Alfred take the blame."

"Did Alfred Dempsie know that's what happened?"

"Maybe. I think Naismith found out about Garry and blamed himself. I think he's been covering up for his son ever since."

"Makes sense. Henry saw the light after Thomas died. Changed his life." Pete could have been discussing biscuits. "Naismith's giving up his life to save his boy. Greater love hath no man."

She nodded at the familiar phrase heard out of context. "You did do divinity, didn't you?"

The curtain on the far side of the bed swept back suddenly, and a neat nurse looked at them accusingly.

"What are you doing here?" She addressed Paddy, pulling her lips back in a smile that wouldn't have fooled anyone. Her eyes were set wide and prominent.

"Visiting," said Paddy.

The nurse's mouth spasmed wide, and she busied herself tidying the folds in the curtain. "Family are allowed to visit outside visiting hours, but I'm afraid everyone else has to come between three and eight." She turned to face Paddy square on. "You'll have to leave."

Confused and embarrassed, Paddy reached for her bag.

"Iona, Iona." Pete pushed himself up on the pillow, coming alive at the possibility of a fight. "Get your thumb out of your arse. She's my daughter."

Nurse Iona glanced at his ring finger.

"That's right, she's a bastard. A love child. I wouldn't marry her pregnant mother because she was ugly and below marriageable age." He lifted his bandaged hand. "In Texas. Give me more?"

The nurse was staring unkindly at Paddy, taking in her cheap black sweater. It was bobbled under the arms and stretched at the bottom from being self-consciously tugged down to hide her body whenever she stood up off the bench.

"It's not time for more, Mr. McIltchie, as well you know." She looked from Paddy to Pete but couldn't find any echo of his face in hers. "If she is your daughter, why isn't she down as your next of kin?"

"She's untrustworthy. A dipsomaniac." Pete's face was bright with innocent enjoyment. "When I die she'll be in here pulling rings from my fingers before you can say 'cock and balls.'"

Iona thanked him not to use that language and pissed about a bit, taking his pulse and looking at her watch, before leaving them alone again. Pete sighed contentedly and stroked the sheet.

"There, you have to come back and visit me now."

"She's a bit scary."

Pete pulled himself up and leaned across the bed confidentially. His breath smelled foul. "She's a fucking cow. I watch her going around this room bullying them all. I try to frighten her back. She scratches when she washes me. Every time." He leaned back against the pillow and looked at the door. "I don't want to die in here. Have to keep fighting." He frowned briefly at the sheet, banishing whatever thought was interfering with his medication. "Sad." He shook his head. "As if we're not scared enough in here. I'd hate to recant at this stage."

Paddy didn't know what to say, so she apologized again. He didn't notice. "I'm dying," he told the sheet, sounding surprised to hear it himself. "And I don't believe in God. I hope I don't get scared at the last minute."

"I've got to go, Pete."

"Where?"

"I need to get the bus to Anderston and tell that wee bastard Patterson what I've done. There's nothing else for it." She half hoped he'd think of something.

"Right enough."

She saw into her future, and the best she could hope for was a job in a shop or a factory. She wouldn't marry; she knew that she'd only marry someone if she panicked now and didn't have a career. The disappointment was so bitter it made her bones ache.

"I'll never be a journalist now."

"That's right."

She looked at him. He was staring up at John Knox. She wasn't at all sure he was really listening. He had other things on his mind, she supposed.

"It would be a shame to recant at this stage," she said quietly.

He became animated suddenly. "Wouldn't it? Fear. 'S fear. There are ministers and lay preachers and hairy beasts patrolling the corridors of this hospital, waiting. They can smell moments of weakness. I don't want to weaken. I'd die sad. This, here" — he pointed at the cannula on the back of his hand — "this is my last defense against them. I'd like to go out on a big burst of that."

It took her the rest of the visit to work out that he was talking about his four-hourly doses of morphine.

THIRTY-FIVE

A LEAVING DO

I

Paddy stood with the other passengers in a neat row, all watching down the road for the bus, their faces pinched against the biting, dusty wind. The bus stop was a shelterless pole on the edge of a Hiroshima desert landscape. The area around the hospital had been razed of its tenements and not yet redeveloped. Ghost blocks were linked by a network of pointless sidewalks and crazed roads leading nowhere. The air smelled dry and dead. Here and there developers had erected fences around their own precious plot, but the wind still had a good, clear run across the land. Tiny dunes of gray dust gathered at the curb.

Paddy promised herself a binge reward. After she had been to the police station and spoken to Patterson she would eat two

Marathon bars one after the other. It didn't matter how fat she got now, because Sean was lost and she would never face the harsh light of the newsroom again. She wasn't going back. She bowed her head and felt the loss of her future as a drop of pressure. She'd have to work in a shop or something, wear a uniform and take shit from a manageress. She'd probably panic and marry someone unsuitable, just because they asked her, and end up living next to her ma, wondering what the hell happened for the rest of her life.

The passenger at the front of the queue stepped forward, a reflex response to the sight of the bus turning a faraway corner, and the others followed, reaching into pockets and bags for bus passes and loose change for the fare.

Two Marathons and a cheese-and-onion pastry from Greggs the baker's. And a fudge doughnut. As the bus pulled up alongside, she was planning how she would get all the food up to her room and manage to be alone.

The conductor was all nose. He stood thoughtlessly scratching his balls through his pocket lining as Paddy stepped onto the open platform and asked, "D'ye go past Anderston?"

"Other way. You want the 164. They're every twenty minutes."

She stepped off backwards onto the pavement and backed away, digging her hands deep into her pockets, watching the tail of the bus pull away from the curb. She became aware that the sharpness of the wind had changed on the back of her neck.

"Right?" He swung around in front of her, his eyes a brilliant, burnished green. He was wearing a black woolly hat. The stud in his left earlobe glinted brightly against the gray landscape.

"You're not Heather Allen."

His pink tongue left a wet trail as it slid across his bottom lip. When Paddy looked into his eyes, her delusions about being able to defend herself evaporated. Cold fear seized her joints, making her stand stiff in front of him while her legs told her to run. She had been able to bully Heather and Terry, but she knew it would be pointless with Garry Naismith. He would go further faster, and it wasn't because he had more to lose. He wanted to. He liked it.

"I need to see you."

Her family thought she was at work. She wouldn't be missed for hours, and the police had their man; they weren't looking for anyone else. She ducked behind him in panic and saw the back of the bus retreat down the dusty road. His hand was on her elbow, a polite request for her time.

"You know my old man."

"I need to go," she said, but stayed where she was. "I need to get somewhere."

It was a subtle shift of position: his hand dropped an inch, his thumb and forefinger coming together around the tendon on her elbow. Her stomach heaved at the pain, flooding her mouth with saliva, and she arched backwards, trying to release his grip. Garry Naismith loomed, smiling gently at her lips, leaning over as if he might kiss her.

"I see women like you all the time." He squeezed again. "But ye won't refuse me this time."

His free hand rose at his side. Beyond the veil of pain radiating from her elbow, she was aware of his fingers curved comfortably around a dull, matte egg. She didn't realize it was a rock until the cold stone weight of it hit the back of her head and the night came down.

She wasn't dead. It was daylight, and she was bent over from the waist, moving forwards across a gray pavement, black woolly tights wrinkled around her ankles, unsteady feet tripping over each other. An arm was hooked under her armpit, supporting her weight, guiding her by the elbow. Her scalp was hot and damp, and she had to concentrate hard to work out that the itching on her hairline was caused by the woolly hat he had pulled onto her head.

Another pair of feet coming towards them. A lady's shoes: brown, sensible, and a blue shopping bag. The woman spoke, and the supporting arm spoke back, making a joke of it. Paddy slumped forwards and was yanked upright. They moved on.

It was darker. She was sitting on something soft, slumped to the side at an angle that made her side and back hurt. The floor beneath her feet rumbled. She was in a taxi and he was at her side, still holding her elbow, his nimble fingers ready to pinch if she did anything. Imagining the future felt like wading through hot sand, but she tried: they were traveling, on their way to somewhere she would never leave. Her mind yearned to slip back into the warm water, but she fought hard to stay conscious. Slowly she dropped forwards, her chin gently pressed against her knee, and she saw on the floor the squashed end of a cigarette. Meehan never gave up. He spent seven years in solitary confinement, was despised and vilified, and still he never gave up. Using the muscles on her back, she pulled her head up a little.

"Heb," she shouted, but her voice was weak and toneless.

His fingers twitched and a spasm of white-hot pain convulsed her body.

"Aye, pal," he said loudly, talking to the driver. "Dead drunk, daft cow."

"Heb."

Garry Naismith laughed loud and long, covering the sound of her whimpering until she slid forwards and gave in.

The searing pain at the back of her head seemed to have lifted a little. She was looking down at a sidewalk from a great height, falling forwards face-first, and then a sudden stop into his strong and steady arms. Behind her the taxi door slammed hard, and she lifted her eyes to see an empty hanging plant basket by a familiar front door. She stood taller and saw a long, empty road, steep front gardens opposite, and a crumbling garden wall across the street with graffiti on it. FILTH OUT. They were at Naismith's house in Barnhill, but the grocery van was gone from the pavement. The police must have it.

The police. The thought made her come alive, but the police weren't here. The police had been here and weren't coming back. They had their man and the case was closed.

He opened the gate and quickly pulled her across the paved-over ground. The red slabs had settled unevenly and there was a curb to be negotiated at every step. He lifted her by her armpits to the front door, pulling out his key as he approached and opening it in one swift movement. By the time she thought to call for help the door was shut behind her. Garry Naismith grabbed the crown of the hat and yanked it off. A warm dribble of blood tickled as it ran down the back of Paddy's neck.

The hallway carpet was pink, the walls a cold gray, and Paddy knew it was the last time she would see it if she didn't do something. She threw her head back.

"Callum Ogilvy!" she shouted, so loud it startled them both.

Garry stopped still.

"He's my cousin," she said, conflating their relationship. "You raped him and made him kill that boy."

Naismith slapped her across the back of

the head, sending an electric pain down her spine. She fell onto her side and he put his foot on the side of her face. When she spoke she found that her voice was a breathy whisper.

"You raped him, didn't ye?"

"Those weans came to *me*." She heard him thump his chest with his fist and was glad she couldn't look up to see his face. "They came looking for *me*. They needed *me*. No one else gave a fuck about him, and let me tell you, that dirty wee bastard James needed no convincing. He wanted things I'd never thought of. Even brought his pal with him."

She could imagine poor, fatherless Callum doing anything he could to impress Garry — Garry with a job, Garry with a cool earring, Garry with a clean house and a van full of sweets outside the door. It must have been a safe place to go, the Naismiths', a relatively clean place. If she were Callum she'd have come here with his friend. Boys that age craved heroes.

"Wasn't Callum's idea to take the baby, though, was it? That was you. Was it Thomas's anniversary that made you think of him?"

He didn't speak. She felt the weighty seconds drag by and imagined him raising his hand above her, raising a baseball bat, raising a knife. His foot came off her face, and she glanced up to see his tortured smile.

"Do you think of Thomas on his anniversary?"

"I think about Thomas all the time."

"Why did you kill him?"

"Never said I did."

"I'm not asking for a confession. I just want to know why."

He shrugged. "It was an accident. When we were playing."

"And Henry helped you cover up?"

"He wanted to be a good dad. A better dad. Better than Dempsie."

"And he did that by throwing your wee brother's body onto the railway line to be cut in half? He was willing to kill me to protect you, and now he's confessed to everything? Why would he feel that guilty about you?"

"You" — he had his eyes shut, and his booming voice managed to drown her out — "don't understand how it is between men. Women don't understand. There's no point in explaining."

"He did it to you, and you did it to them? Is that how it is between men? Did you get them to kill Brian so they'd be like you? So you'd have something over them, the way Henry held Thomas's death over you?"

He stood up suddenly, flaring backwards, and took her forearm with both his hands, dragging her backwards up the stairs, bumping her awkwardly like a big cardboard box. Paddy knew that upstairs was not going to be good for her. She scrabbled her feet, trying to grab hold of something, looking for a banister to jam her feet in, but it was a sheer wall.

Garry yanked her up, almost pulling her arm out of its socket, bumping her heavily on her hip and buttocks. She couldn't catch her breath enough to speak until they got to the top of the stairs.

"What about Heather Allen? She hadn't done anything to you."

"We made a mistake." Garry let go of her and lifted a sunshine-yellow lamp off the hall table. He was sweating. "Got the right girl this time, though, eh?"

He brought the lamp down heavily onto her head, and she passed out.

II

The pain behind her eyes was excruciating. She peeled them open and found herself on the floor in the bedroom, sitting on a red acrylic carpet at the side of a double bed, jammed between the divan and a cold wall. Above her the curtains were drawn on a small window, but she could see thin daylight glowing behind the cheap red material. Her wrists were tied behind her back, a rough hemp rope cutting into the skin. Her feet were out in front of her on the floor, her ankles bound in an incomprehensible series of knots.

The door to the room was open slightly. He wasn't afraid of anyone's coming home. They were completely alone. A white plastic fitted wall unit covered the facing wall, and a large Bible sat open in the dressing table insert, gold edging to the pages. She saw a small crucifix on the wall above the bed and knew she was in Henry Naismith's bedroom. There was no help to be had.

She bent forward, managing to get her hands between the base of the bed and the mattress, and pushed herself up to her feet. She looked up, staggering backwards and falling onto her bruised backside when she saw a blood-splattered woman across the room, peering tentatively from behind the wall unit. She sat straight up, pulling at the bedding, tucked her legs under her, and looked for the terrifying woman, trying to be ready for her. It was a mirror. A black lump of blood-matted hair was clumped above one of her ears. Scarlet lines ran horizontally across her cheek to her mouth where she had been lying on her side. Her face was swollen and bruised.

If Ludovic Kennedy were writing this story, she would just have to wait to be saved. Her tenacity and willingness to confess would be her salvation. But it wasn't a story, and she realized suddenly, to her horror, that she was going to die and no one would do anything about it. They might not even find her body. There was no justice.

Outside the room soft steps crept across the landing. The only advantage she had over him was that he didn't know she was conscious. She curled up on her side. He was going to kill her, and all she could think about was the front page of the *Daily News* carrying the story of her death. Just the facts and not the details. Not the detail that the room smelled of a man's greasy hair; not that the carpet hadn't been hoovered and she was looking at a layer of dust under the bed; not that the door was opening behind her and the feet were coming into the room.

He kicked her hard in the back. "Get up."

She twitched at the blow but kept her eyes shut. He leaned down, crouching over her. She could smell soap on his skin. He felt her blood-encrusted hair, touched the cut on her scalp with a fingertip; she could hear the wet sound. He pressed to provoke a response, but Paddy kept her face slack. The skin was numb anyway.

"It's about time," he told her softly, "that you learned who's in charge here."

Fitting his hands under her arms, he lifted Paddy, yanking the dead weight of her half onto the mattress before walking around to the other side and pulling her on properly.

He was going to pull off all her clothes under the harsh light and look at her and touch her. He was going to kill her, and she hadn't done anything yet, had never been out of Scotland or got thin or lived alone or made any kind of mark on the world. She couldn't stop herself crying. Her face contorted and she sobbed aloud, keeping her eyes shut because she was too afraid to open them.

"That's good," he said, climbing onto the bed, tucking himself in behind her so he was lying along the length of her, not touching. "Keep it up, make it loud. I like it."

He leaned his face over her from behind and, as he whispered, his soft lips brushed her earlobe, his hot breath tickled the tiny hairs in her ear canal, making her raise her shoulder defensively. He saw girls like her all the time. All the time. He knew she wanted it — is that what she was crying for? Because she wanted it so much. She had to take what she could get because she was fat.

As Paddy heard him say that, a hot flush ran up her spine. It was too much, to be called fat at her last moment on earth. She kept her eyes shut and swung her face around to meet his, opening her mouth as wide as she could, and bit down hard. She squealed a furious wet gurgle and locked her teeth on a loose piece of flesh. The metallic tang of blood flooded her mouth. She opened her eyes. She was biting his lower lip. Garry yelped and pulled away far enough for the side of his face to be in focus. One green eye was wide open, the white showing all around, like the eye of a frightened horse. He was hitting her again, and she knew from the wet heat on her face that she was bleeding, but she was too afraid to open her mouth and let go. She would have to eventually, but when she did he would kill her. Before then she would mark him, such a deep mark that they couldn't fail to find him.

Garry's hand came down again and again, thumping her on the side of the head, but she held on, shaking her head to deepen the cut, breathing out and spluttering his blood into his eye. She felt the tips of her front teeth touching through the last membrane of skin. The chunk of lip was coming away.

A deafening crack shook the far wall as the door exploded inwards, crashing off the wall and snapping one of the hinges. A thousand hands landed on her legs and arms, pulling her by the arm, the wrist, the rope binding her ankles. As they tore at her she felt the tips of her incisors touch and tear. Garry Naismith was kneeling on the bed, an arm around his neck and a policeman on either arm, a torrent of blood falling onto his father's bed. His bottom lip was hanging off, baring his lower teeth.

The policemen helped her up and undid the ropes around her wrists and ankles, all of them shouting and calling to one another, a mess of nerve-jangling noise after the silence. Paddy vomited a stomachful of blood and saliva onto her boots.

When she stood back up she found Patterson watching her, his arms crossed, his face taut with disgust.

She glanced over her shoulder and saw herself in the dressing-table mirror, blood trailing across her face like the fingers of a hand, wet blood running from her mouth, her chin cupped in scarlet. For the rest of her life, every time she looked over her shoulder and accidentally saw her face in a mirror, that would be the image she was expecting to see.

"Mother of God," she panted, watery blood flecking from her mouth. "Mother of *fucking* God."

III

She was afraid to ask anything for fear that she'd give them more material against her than they already had. They sat her downstairs in the sparse living room. The pink carpet followed through from the hall, and the walls were still gray. A big stone-clad fire surround overstated the case for a small two-bar fire. It was a cold room. There was no settee, and the two armchairs were far apart, both facing the television. The ornaments on the fire surround were tokens of hominess: a mouse climbing out of a brandy glass, a small china house. Nailed to the wall was a series of school photos of Garry, as a child in a mustard sweater, in a uniform, with and without his front teeth.

A fat constable had to pull a chair all the way across the room to talk to her. Someone had phoned the *News* repeatedly, asking for her and reporting her missing, until Dub alerted the police. They retraced her steps to the Royal and found her yellow canvas bag on the pavement. She listened and nodded, wondering how they could possibly have known she'd been at the Royal. She'd stormed away from Terry and hadn't told him where she was going. The constable told her that they now knew someone had falsely reported seeing Heather get into Naismith's van, so they thought it was possible someone else was responsible for the murders. She hardly dared ask how they knew but slumped in the chair, touching the cuts on her head to cover her face.

A younger constable had been watching her from the door and stepped across, touching her gently on the shoulder.

"We should get you to the hospital, miss."

"I'm fine, really." She tried to look up, but her head ached too much.

"Let me wash some of the blood off and we can see what's under there."

Paddy kept her head down and followed him meekly down the busy hall and into the kitchen, where he boiled a kettle on the cooker for some warm water and, bending her over the sink, gently sponged the bloody clots from her hair. He had to wash slowly to get the most from the frugal amount of warm water, scooping it onto the back of her neck and softly shoving it over her scalp, avoiding contact with the open wound just behind her left ear. Her knees were a little wobbly with shock, so he rested his hand on her back to keep her standing steady. She thought it the most intimate moment she had ever experienced with a man.

"There now." He patted her shoulder, signaling for her to stand, and handed her a towel to dab her hair with. "I've done a first-aid course and I know this much: we need to get you to hospital and get that checked out."

"Okay," she said, feeling that she wouldn't mind being arrested if he was there. "Will ye let me go home afterwards?"

"No, the doctors'll want to keep you in if you lost consciousness," he said, misunderstanding the question. "Did you pass out?"

"No," she lied. "Not for a minute."

The constable stopped someone in the hall to tell them where they were going and asked the fat constable to come with him. He led her through the open front door into the street. Four police cars were lined up outside, one with its headlights still on, the flasher blinking lazily on the roof. The wind chilled her wet hair, contracting her scalp, making it sting, and almost bringing feeling back to the cut behind her ear. Paddy stood upright and breathed in the afternoon air. She could handle it. If they arrested her and ended her career at the *News* and Sean wouldn't talk to her, she would manage.

She caught his eye and smiled before she realized it was him. She had been blinded by the flasher, but between red waves she saw Dr. Pete sitting in the back of the police car, looking calmly at her through the window. He was wearing a beige raincoat over his blue pajamas. She waved at him, and he raised his hand balletically, motioning her down the path towards him and miming the fact that he couldn't get the door open from the inside or wind the window down. The first-aider opened the front door and let her speak to him across the back of the seat.

"I told them that I planted the hair in the van and made the false call." Pete held on to the headrest with a hand that still had the tube taped to it. The same soft drawl in his voice was more pronounced than before. "The operator said I sounded like a woman when I phoned. Do I sound like a woman to you?"

They looked each other in the eye for a moment, until the policeman took her elbow. "We need to get you checked out," he said.

"Pete, I'm awed by ye. I don't know what to say."

"Buy me a drink sometime."

The policeman pulled her away. Paddy touched Pete's yellowed fingertips. They were warm and as dry as dust.

IV

Paddy could feel the atmosphere as she approached on the street. It wasn't a loudness so much as a manic trill carried on the cold air. Every one of the frosted windows in the Press Bar had a mess of bodies behind it.

Paddy touched the bandage with her fingertips, checking to see if the wound was as sensitive as she'd remembered. The doctor had given her a few stitches on her head, and the nurses had put a gauze over it, taping it onto her ear and hair like a jaunty hat. The young policeman had taken a statement while they waited and, after asking over his car radio, said she could go home if she went straight to Anderston police station in the morning. He offered to drop her home, but she refused. This was where she wanted to be.

She opened the door, sucking a cloud of warm, smoky smog out into the street. It was a bacchanalian scene. There were women in the bar tonight, quite a lot of women, and the mood of the crowd was wildly happy. The sports boys were singing a song so tuneless it might have been a series of different songs. Richards was at the bar, laughing loudly, his head tipped back like a supervillain, making the man next to him very angry indeed. Purple-topped Margaret Mary was standing side on to Farquarson, laughing and banging her tits off his arm. The news desk boys were conducting a relay whisky-drinking competition, and there, in the middle of them, was Dr. Pete, his eyes as bright as morning stars, his skin a deep and resonant yellow under the harsh lights.

She raised her hand to wave, but he didn't see her. Instead of demanding his attention she went to the bar and bought him a double of the best malt McGrade stocked. She watched McGrade carry the drink over and put it down on the table in front of him, whispering what it was and who it was from. Pete didn't look up to thank her but sipped the drink reverently instead of throwing it to the back of his throat, and smiled at it as he turned the glass with his thumb and forefinger.

She walked around the entire room looking for Terry and noticed that the men were ignoring her to a pronounced degree. It was a mark of respect. Terry wasn't among the men playing the whisky-drinking game by the toilets, and he wasn't propped up anywhere along the length of the bar. Dub was sitting on a bench behind the door with a crowd of printmen, arguing about German bands and whether "O Superman" qualified as music.

"Hiya." She slid onto the seat next to him, and Dub grinned and moved up to make room for her.

"That," he said, pointing at her bandage, "is a new look for you, isn't it?"

"Yeah, I thought I'd experiment with some brain-surgery themed outfits."

"Suits ye. Makes you look like someone with interesting things to say."

" 'Ouch'?"

"Yeah, and 'argh.' "

Paddy gestured at the scene in front of them. "Is it me or is this madder than usual?"

"Settle back," Dub answered, handing her someone else's half-pint off the busy table, "and I'll tell you a story."

The way Dub told the story, the evening had started off with Dr. Pete arriving at the newsroom door, released on police bail and still wearing his hospital pajamas. He announced that he was fucked if he was going to take a minute more of this shite. He was leaving to write his book about MacLean; it would make anyone sick the way the fucking staff were treated in this place, and all because of McGuigan. A more reflective analyst would have noted that McGuigan was in no way responsible for Dr. Pete's complaints, but the newsroom loved a ruckus. He swept down to editorial, and they followed behind him like a crowd of angry villagers. Even Farquarson went with them, half laughing while ordering them to return to their desks at once, protesting as effectively as a jolly octogenarian being tickled by his favorite grandchildren.

Pete burst into McGuigan's office and shouted a lot of rubbish, pulling him around by a lapel at one point and telling him he had a mouth like an arse. He resigned and said he'd never be back.

Pete's reckless excitement had spread and multiplied — emotional loaves and fishes — and the atmosphere in the Press Bar felt less like a damp Tuesday in February and more like a lonely sailor's millennial Hogmanay shore leave.

Paddy laughed at the story, enjoying herself, occasionally touching her hand to her sore head to see if the feeling had come back to the skin. She lifted the drink to sip a couple of times but couldn't get past the image of a sweaty man slavering over the lip of the glass.

The door opened next to them and Terry Hewitt stepped in, looking around the room. Paddy cringed and leaned over, tugging on the hem of his leather jacket to get his attention. He nodded when he saw it was her, acting as if they had arranged to meet there, and came to sit by her, forcing Dub to slide up the bench even further so that he was jammed uncomfortably into the corner. He stood up, offering to get a round in but failing to ask Terry what he wanted.

"Wild night," said Terry softly.

"I'm so sorry."

" 'S okay. I've just finished a draft for to-morrow with Garry in."

"No, I'm so sorry I convinced you it was Henry, I had no business —"

"You realized it was Garry when we were at Tracy's, didn't you?"

"Yeah."

"You should have said something to me."

She'd been ashamed of being wrong, but tried to dress it up. "I wanted to protect you," she explained, her voice trailing off weakly at the obvious lie.

Terry nodded and muttered "Fair enough" under his breath, letting her off with it.

"Will I get credited for the story?"

Terry looked a little reproachful. "I gave you first credit in the morning edition."

"I did nearly die for the story." She sounded defensive.

"I know."

"I am entitled."

"I know."

Across the room, Dub scowled over at them from the bar.

"Is Dub gay, do you think?"

Terry watched her face curiously.

"You know, I really don't think he is."

Paddy looked up at the bar. Dub frowned at Terry again and took an angry draw on a cigarette. Beyond him, Pete was standing behind a wall of whisky drinkers, swaying slightly, his eyes shut. Dub glared over at them again. Paddy gave him a cheery little wave. He tipped his chin at her and flared his nostrils. Next to her, Terry cleared his throat loudly. It was getting a bit intense. Perplexed at what was going on, Paddy suddenly craved the calm of home. She patted her knees decisively.

"Well, I'm going to say good night to Pete."

" 'Kay." Terry pressed his knee against hers and whispered, "Will I see you in tomorrow, wee Paddy Meehan?"

Embarrassed at the intimacy, Paddy smiled into her half-pint. "Mibbe's aye," she said, "and mibbe's naw." She stood up and walked away, wearing a soft smile to match Terry's.

Halfway through the fog of men she bumped into McVie. Even he, the most mean-spirited man at the *News*, was drinking and enjoying the carnival atmosphere. He cornered her by the fag machine and tried to think of advice to give her, having enjoyed his moment in the chair when they were out in the calls car. He had not one morsel left and was rather drunk, so he gave her some slurred second-hand wisdom, passing it off as his own. Don't take shit from anyone. Don't buy things on hire purchase. Never back a horse called Lucky. Don't go on holiday to Blackpool, it's fucking horrible there.

By the time she got away from McVie, Pete was slumped in the corner, his eyes shut and his face slack. She had to fight her way through the whisky drinkers to get to him.

"Careful!" shouted one as she pushed past him, tipping his drink and making him spill a little whisky on the floor. He saw her going for Pete. "Don't try to wake him up. He's been in hospital, he needs his sleep."

Paddy sat down next to Pete and slipped her fingers around his wrist. His pulse was still.

"He's not asleep," she said quietly.

"Yeah," shouted one of the guys at the table. "He's the king, man, he's the fucking king. He's had us in here since five o'clock."

"He's not asleep," she whispered, taking Pete's cold, lonely hand in hers and bringing it to her lips.

THIRTY-SIX

HOME

Paddy stood in the cold, pressing her hands into her pockets. Her warm, white sigh flowered and lingered in front of her.

Over the fence and through the window she could see the tops of their heads in the living room. Sean was sitting in one armchair, Con in the other, and they were watching the television news together. The light was on in Marty's bedroom, and she could just discern the faint hum of a radio. Mary Ann would be having a bath. Trisha would be in the kitchen tending the food, warming plates ready for her return from work.

She told her feet to take her to the door, but she stayed, watching over the hedge, unwilling. Sean said something and Con nodded. Her parents didn't know that they had split up. She wasn't sure Sean had taken it in yet either, but it was nice that he was there. He wasn't angry at her, anyway.

They'd go mad when they saw the bandage on her head, and now her eyes were raw from crying. She couldn't tell them that her friend had died in a pub. She certainly couldn't tell them about Garry Naismith.

She tried to think of a plausible lie that wouldn't make her mum forbid her from going to work. She'd been mugged. No, that suggested danger in the town. There was a fight on the train — everyone took trains. A fight on the train, and she, cautious and careful, got up to get off and was hit on the head by a stray bottle. The train staff took her to hospital, but she was fine. The fighting men were arrested. One of them was fat. That sort of detail made it plausible. He had a Rangers football top on. They'd want to believe that.

The cold night nibbled at her face. Paddy saw a jagged frost forming on the leaves of the hedge. Custard-cream crumbs taking refuge in the seams of her pocket had worked their way under her fingernails. She felt Pete's hands in hers again and promised herself that she'd never forget him or what he had done for her.

It was getting late. She dawdled reluctantly through the garden gate and stopped by the pile of bricks. She knelt down, her fingers feeling the mulchy ground for the key to the Beatties' garage.

She'd have a smoke with the Queen and remember her friend Pete for a while before she went in.

AUTHOR'S NOTE

The Patrick "Paddy" Meehan portions of this novel are drawn from a real case. Paddy Meehan was a career safecracker who was found guilty of the high-profile murder of an elderly woman during a housebreaking. The case was a notorious miscarriage of justice in Scotland. Even after the real culprits had sold their story to a Sunday newspaper, it took a book by Ludovic Kennedy to prompt the reopening of the case and the royal pardon. The story told here is based largely on Meehan's accounts in interviews and books and on those of his solicitor, Joseph Beltrami. Some facts have been conflated to make them read more clearly — for example, Griffiths hijacked a number of cars during his shooting spree. Only the emotional content is substantially fictionalized.

In the late eighties I interviewed Paddy Meehan. Neither of us wanted to be there.

We were both trying to please my mum, Edith.

During a summer in the late eighties Edith was working as a manicurist in the Argyle Market, a ramshackle series of booths in a first-floor corridor off a main shopping thoroughfare in central Glasgow. At the same time, Paddy Meehan was selling his vanity-published book, *Framed by MI5*, at the bottom of the stairs that led up to the market. Edith's nail booth was very classy: she wore a white uniform, had a desk and a sofa, and even had a working telephone installed. Meehan approached her and asked if he could receive important calls there because the Secret Service had bugged the public pay phone. Being a lady, she graciously agreed, but asked if he would return the favor by telling his story to her daughter. She would be interested, Edith said, because she was a law student. I actually wasn't interested, I didn't know anything about him or the case, and I had exams coming up, but my mum said I had to buy him a cup of tea.

The market canteen was deserted in the half hour before closing time. We were the only customers, and Meehan sat facing the door, watching over my shoulder. I was young and arrogant and in a hurry, and I only half listened to his story. He had told it so often that at times I think even he wasn't listening, but he told it well and still got angry when he remembered prison and being mobbed in Ayr.

Afterwards I asked him to go over part of it again. He said he had been recruited into the communist underworld network by a shadowy figure named Hector who had first appeared when he worked in the shipyards. He bumped into him unexpectedly in London outside the embassy and now thought he was an *agent provocateur* from MI5, the UK Security Service. Although it appeared from his prison records that he had remained in Leicester Prison for a five-stretch, he actually escaped and ran away to the USSR. There he gave the Soviets information about prison layouts which they used to spring George Blake, a former officer for the Secret Intelligence Service (MI6) who had been caught spying for the Soviets. More incendiary than that, he claimed that he had warned MI5 about the method Blake used to escape. Either they failed to heed his warnings, he said, or they deliberately let Blake get away.

It sounded ridiculous to me. I told him I didn't believe that MI5 would try to ensure his silence by framing him for a high-profile murder. He insisted, became agitated and flushed, and at one point almost tearful. I suddenly saw myself, an arrogant law student sitting in a dirty café correcting a red-faced old bloke about the narrative arc of his life.

Meehan insisted that his life made sense. He wasn't prepared to accept that his life, like most eventful lives, was nothing but a series of comic mishaps and tragedies strung together in a meaningless pattern. Someone knew what was going on and had directed it all. In looking for a shadowy instigator, it seemed as though he was insisting that God existed.

We finished our tea and cigarettes and parted on a sour note. He blanked me for the rest of the summer. Every time I passed him at the foot of the stairs on my way up to visit my mum, he'd busy himself tidying the piles of books or look into the distance with narrowed eyes, pretending to spot an imaginary friend. I always said hello just to let him snub me.

As I've grown older I've come to realize that nothing silences an awkward truth more effectively than ridicule. His story was implausible enough to be true.

Meehan kept on telling his story. He told it to anyone he met.

He died of throat cancer in 1994.

ACKNOWLEDGMENTS

This book just couldn't have happened without the efforts and insights of Selina Walker, and I cannot thank her enough for her patience and sharp eye. Katrina Whone, Rachel Calder, and Reagan Arthur also gave me great direction nearer the end.

Many people have helped with my research. Thanks and lunches are due to Stephen McGinty, Linda Watson-Brown, and Val McDermid, who gave me invaluable insights into the workings of a busy newsroom in the early eighties. Also to Kester Aspden for materials kindly given for no return.

Inspiration for the story was provided by the brilliant Dr. Clare McDermid's work into the social construction of child offenders, most of which had to be cut out but will doubtless appear in another project at a later date.

Thanks also to Gerry Considine, who did his usual and gave me legal advice. Or did he this time? I can't remember. Maybe it was Philip Considine or John Considine who gave me legal advice. If so, it'll all be wrong because they're not lawyers. Maybe it was Auntie Betty Considine. Is there a new European convention concerning wee cups of tea and fruit loaf?

Most of all, my undying gratitude to Steve, Monica, and Edith for their support during the scariest of wonderful times.

ABOUT THE AUTHOR

Denise Mina is the author of *Garnethill*, which won the John Creasey Memorial Prize for best first crime novel, *Exile*, *Resolution*, and *Deception*. She lives in Glasgow.